LT

Praise for the Mackenzies series

"Big, arrogant, sexy highlanders—Jennifer Ashley writes the kind of heroes I crave."

—Elizabeth Hoyt, *New York Times* bestselling author

"I adore this novel: It's heartrending, funny, honest, and true. I want to know the hero—no, I want to *marry* the hero!"

—Eloisa James, *New York Times* bestselling author

"Skillfully nuanced characterization and an abundance of steamy sensuality give Ashley's latest impeccably crafted historical its irresistible literary flavor." —*Chicago Tribune*

"A sexy, passion-filled romance that will keep you reading until dawn."

—Julianne MacLean, *USA Today* bestselling author

"Ashley creates marvelous, unforgettable, and heart-stopping stories with unique heroes. She touches on a multitude of human emotions while never losing sight of the love story. With lush prose and memorable scenes, readers learn how wounded characters can be healed by the power of love. Memorable, remarkable, tender, and touching, here is a book to cherish, reread, and sigh over time and again."

—*RT Book Reviews* (Top Pick)

"RITA Award–winning Ashley excels at creating multilayered, realistically complex characters . . . She also delivers abundant sensual passion." —*Booklist*

"A sensual, gorgeous story."

—*Joyfully Reviewed* (Recommended Read)

"Passionate, well-drawn characters, breathless romance, and a memorable love story." —Library Journal

continued . . .

“Jennifer Ashley writes very sensual, sexy books . . . If you haven’t tried these, I definitely recommend.”

—*Smexy Books*

“A heartfelt, emotional historical romance with danger and intrigue around every corner . . . A great read!”

—*Fresh Fiction*

Titles by Jennifer Ashley

The Mackenzies

THE MADNESS OF LORD IAN MACKENZIE
LADY ISABELLA'S SCANDALOUS MARRIAGE
THE MANY SINS OF LORD CAMERON
THE DUKE'S PERFECT WIFE
A MACKENZIE FAMILY CHRISTMAS
THE SEDUCTION OF ELLIOT MCBRIDE
THE UNTAMED MACKENZIE
(An InterMix eBook)
THE WICKED DEEDS OF DANIEL MACKENZIE
SCANDAL AND THE DUCHESS
(An InterMix eBook)
RULES FOR A PROPER GOVERNESS
THE SCANDALOUS MACKENZIES
(Anthology)
THE STOLEN MACKENZIE BRIDE

Shifters Unbound

PRIDE MATES
PRIMAL BONDS
BODYGUARD
WILD CAT
HARD MATED
MATE CLAIMED
LONE WOLF
(An InterMix eBook)
TIGER MAGIC
FERAL HEAT
(An InterMix eBook)
WILD WOLF
SHIFTER MATES
(Anthology)
MATE BOND

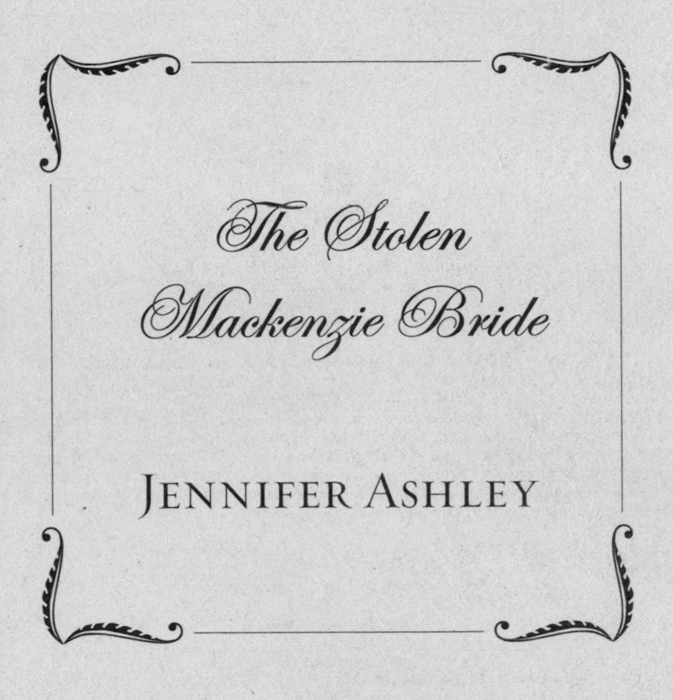

The Stolen Mackenzie Bride

JENNIFER ASHLEY

BERKLEY SENSATION, NEW YORK

An imprint of Penguin Random House LLC
375 Hudson Street, New York, New York 10014

THE STOLEN MACKENZIE BRIDE

A Berkley Sensation Book / published by arrangement with the author

For more information, visit penguin.com.

ISBN: 978-0-425-26602-1

PUBLISHING HISTORY
Berkley Sensation mass-market paperback edition / October 2015

PRINTED IN THE UNITED STATES OF AMERICA

10 9 8 7 6 5 4 3 2 1

Cover art by Gregg Gulbronson.
Cover design by George Long.
Interior text design by Laura K. Corless.

Thanks go to the many readers of the Mackenzies series who love these wild Highland brothers as much as I do. Your comments and ongoing support have been wonderful. Thank you! Thanks also go to my editor and all the people who work behind the scenes to publish a book and get it out into the world, a difficult task at the best of times.

And, of course, to my husband, who is ready to discuss anything from the uniforms of Cumberland's army to how to clean a black powder pistol. He listens, soothes, and makes sure I always have a good stock of iced tea.

This was a very special book for me, allowing me to delve into the sad events of the Jacobite uprising and put my Mackenzies right in the middle of it. I hope readers enjoy meeting Ian Mackenzie's ancestor Malcolm and his unruly Highland family.

Chapter 1

EDINBURGH, 1745

"Mm, what sweet morsel is *that*?"

Mal Mackenzie, youngest of five brothers, called at various times in his life *Young Malcolm*, *the Devil Mackenzie*, and *would ye get out of it, ye pain in my arse*—the last mostly by his father and oldest brother—voiced the words as the tedious gathering suddenly grew more interesting.

The morsel was a young woman. What else would it be, with Mal?

"Oh, aye," his brother Alec muttered as he leaned against the wall, in a foul temper. "Of course ye'd notice the prettiest lass in the room. The most untouchable as well."

The lady in question glided through the drawing room on the arm of a man who must be her father. She wore a gown of rich material much like those of other young women here, but she stood out among them like a fiery bloom among weeds.

They were paraded, these ladies, laced into bodices and tight stomachers that showed a soft enticement of bosom, skirts swaying as they moved. They walked with eyes downcast to indicate what demure creatures they were—suitable wives for the bachelors, young and old, who'd come to view them.

Malcolm's lady, in contrast, had her head up, smiling at all, though the smile was somewhat strained. Her thoughts were elsewhere.

She had red-gold hair that caught the candlelight as she passed beneath the chandeliers. Mal couldn't see the color of her eyes from where he stood, but he was certain they'd be clearest blue. Or green. Or gray.

She noted Malcolm staring at her and paused for the briefest moment, the smile fading. Mal, who'd been leaning next to Alec, pushed from the cold stone wall to stand up straight, fires weaving through his nerves.

The young woman took him in—a tall, rawboned Scotsman in a fine coat, dressed like an Englishman except for the plaid that covered his legs to his knees. Malcolm prided himself in not looking entirely like these English whelps—he'd pulled his thick brown-red hair into a queue instead of stuffing it under a powdered cocoon-like wig, and had tied his neckcloth in a loose knot.

The young woman's gaze met his, and the answering sparkle in her eyes woke every sense in Mal's body.

Then she turned her head, looking past him as she scanned the crowd for someone else.

The moment, as fleeting as it had been, reached out and wrapped itself around him. The tendrils of something inevitable entangled the being that was Malcolm Mackenzie, changing everything.

Malcolm all but shoved an elbow into Alec, who was pretending to be interested in the interaction of the English and Scottish elite. "Who is she?" Mal demanded.

Alec moodily studied the crowd. "The blond lass, you mean?"

"Her hair's not blond." Mal tilted his head as though that could help him look under her modest lace cap. "'Tis the color of sunshine, tinged with the fire of sunset."

"If you say so." Alec, two years older and one of a pair of twins, gave Mal a warning look. "She's not for you, runt."

Runt was another name for Malcolm, who'd begun life very small, but now topped most of his brothers and his father by at least an inch.

The words *not for you* never deterred Mal. "Why shouldn't she be?"

"Shall I run a list for ye?" Alec asked in irritation. "She is Lady Mary Lennox, daughter of the Earl of Wilfort. Wilfort has an estate as big as this city, more money than God, and power and influence in the cabinet. The family is one of the oldest in England—I think his ancestor fought alongside Henry the Fifth, or some such. All of which makes his daughter out of reach of the youngest son of a Scotsman with what the English claim is a trumped-up title. Not only that, she's engaged to another English lordship, so keep your large paws to yourself."

"Huh," Malcolm said, not worried in the least. "Poor little morsel."

Mal followed Lady Mary's progress through the room, noting the polite way she greeted her father's friends and the mothers of the other daughters. Correct, well trained—like a pedigreed horse brought in to demonstrate what a sweet-tempered creature it could be.

Malcolm saw more than that—the restless twitch of her eyes as she searched the room while pretending not to, the trembling of a ribbon on the red-gold curls at the back of her neck.

She was vibrancy contained, a creature of light and vigor straining at the tethers that held her. At any moment, the shell of her respectability would crack, and her incandescence would spill out.

Did no one but Mal see? Those around her smiled and spoke comfortably to her, as though they liked her, but their reactions were subdued, as were hers to them.

This was not her stage, not where she would shine. She needed to be free of this place, these enclosing walls. Out on the open heather maybe, in the Highlands of Mal's home, Kilmorgan, in the north. Her vibrancy wouldn't be swallowed there, but allowed to glow.

And she'd be with him, the layers of her clothing coming off in his hands, the warmth of her body rising to him. This woman belonged in Mal Mackenzie's bed, and he intended to take her there.

It would be a grand challenge. Lady Mary was surrounded, protected. Her father and the matrons circled her like guard dogs, to keep wolves like Mal at bay.

Mal made a noise in his throat like a growl. If they considered him a wolf, so be it.

"What are you grumbling over?" Alec answered, not happy. He did not want to be here; he hated Englishmen, and only duty to their father kept him calm in the corner instead of racing around picking fights.

"At last, something interesting in this place, and you have no use for it," Malcolm said. Alec was his favorite brother—well, the one who drove him the least mad—but Alec had his own tribulations.

"Let her be, Malcolm," Alec said sternly. "I'm supposed to be watching after you. You go near her, and you'll stir up a world of trouble. I'll not be facing Da's fists because I could nae keep you out of it."

"I could put you in the way of Da's fists, and maybe have your neck broken, with a few words, and you know it," Malcolm reminded him. "But I don't, do I? Why? Because you're me best mate, and I don't want you dead. The least ye could do is help me meet yon beautiful lass."

"And I'm calling to mind the last time I did ye such a favor. I remember pulling your naked self out of a burning house, and taking shot in my upper arm, which still hurts of a rainy morning. All because ye had to go after what wasn't yours."

Malcolm flushed at the memory. "Aye, any husband should be angry to find a strapping lad like me in his place next to his bonny wife, but he had no cause to set the bed on fire. Nearly killed the poor woman. Not surprised she left him behind and went to the colonies with her mum."

"He's still looking for ye, Mal, so stay clear of him."

"Nah, Da put the fear of God in him, and it was three years ago. And *that* lass isn't married." He waved a hand in the direction of the delectable Lady Mary.

"No," Alec said. "It'll be her father's pistol ye'll have to dodge instead."

"So, you'll not help me?"

"Not a bit of it."

Malcolm fell silent. He would never betray Alec's secret to their father—to anyone in the family—and Alec knew it. No leverage there.

"Ah, well." Malcolm's slow smile spread across his face. "I'll have to solve this conundrum on me own."

"That's what I'm afraid of," Alec said darkly.

The innocence of it, Mary was to reflect later, should be astonishing. That moment in time—she at Lady Bancroft's soiree in Edinburgh, her only worry her role of go-between in the forbidden liaison of her sister.

The simplicity of it; the nothingness . . . If Mary had left that night for home, if they'd reached Lincolnshire without her ever having seen the broad-shouldered Scotsman who gazed at her with such intensity, Mary would have lived the rest of her life in peace, moved out of the way like a chess piece, sheltered from the rest of the board.

That night, she stepped into the wrong square at the wrong time. A storm had kept them in Edinburgh, and her father and aunt had decided they might as well accept the invitation to Lady Bancroft's fashionable gathering.

Malcolm would not have been there either, if his father hadn't sent his brother Alec to spy for him. Alec had brought Malcolm along for camouflage, and also because Alec didn't trust Mal alone on the streets of Edinburgh—for very good reason.

Mary's life would have been so very different . . .

For the moment, Lady Mary Lennox existed in a bubble of safety, sure in her betrothal to Lord Halsey, and more worried about her shy little sister than herself.

Tonight's gathering was a decidedly political one. Lady Bancroft had invited prominent Scotsmen to her soiree to reassure those in Edinburgh that rumblings of the Jacobite rising were just that—rumblings. Never mind that Charles Stuart had landed somewhere in the west, never mind he was trying to raise an army. He'd never succeed, and they all knew it.

Highlanders were harmless, Lady Bancroft was implying, thoroughly adapted to civilized living—enlightened men of science. They blended effortlessly with the English aristocracy, did they not?

In that case, Lady Bancroft ought not to have invited the two young Scotsmen warming themselves near the great fireplace at the end of the hall. Mary saw them as she scanned the room for the Honorable Jeremy Drake, the note from Audrey to him burning inside her stomacher.

The Scotsmen looked much alike, brothers obviously. But civilized, they were not.

They'd dressed in waist-length frock coats with many buttons, linen shirts, neat stockings, and leather shoes. Instead of breeches, they wore kilts, loose plaid garments wrapped about their waists.

Other Scotsmen here, in knee breeches and wigs, were indistinguishable from their English counterparts, and moved quietly among the company. These two, on the other hand, looked as though they'd risen from the heather, rubbed the blue paint from their faces, put on coats, and stormed down to Edinburgh.

They wore their dark red hair pulled back into loose queues—no wigs—and lounged with a restlessness that spoke of hunting in long, cold winters, bonfires on the hills, and the wild ruthlessness of their Pictish and Norse ancestors.

Though the two stood calmly, their stances relaxed, they watched. Eyes that missed nothing picked out every person in the room. Wolves, invited to stand among the sheep.

When Mary's scanning gaze passed that of the younger one, his eyes sparked, and she paused.

In that moment, Mary smelled the sweetness of heather under sharp wind, felt the heat of sun in a broad sky. She'd been to the northern Highlands once, and she'd never forgotten the raw beauty of it, the terrifying emptiness and incredible wonder.

This Scotsman embodied all of that, sweeping her to the place and time, under the never-setting sun, when she'd felt afraid and free in the same breath.

The moment passed, and Mary turned away . . .

To find her life completely changed. One *tick* of the clock ago, she'd been serene about the path she'd agreed to, ready to fulfill her duty to her father and her betrothed. At the next *tick*, she felt herself plunging into a long, dark pit, and she'd consented to step off the edge.

Mary shook off the sensation with effort. She had a mission to fulfill, no time for idle thoughts.

She drew a deep breath and said vehemently, "Frogs and toadstools!"

A few ladies jumped, but her aunt Danae, used to Mary's epithets, turned to her calmly. "What is it, my dear?"

"My fan," Mary said, making a show of patting the folds of her skirts. "I've left the aggravating thing in the withdrawing room."

Aunt Danae, a plump partridge in a too-tight gown, put a soothing hand on Mary's. "Never mind, dear. Call for Whitman, and have her fetch it for you."

Their hostess, Lady Bancroft, who stood near, began to signal for one of her many footmen. Mary, who'd hidden the fan for the express purpose of going after it, said, "No need. Won't be a moment," and ran off before anyone could object.

Mary's fan was safely in a pocket under her skirt, so she quickly passed the withdrawing room and made for the stairs that led to the upper reaches of the house. Lady Bancroft was not spendthrift enough to waste candles lighting staircases, and Mary groped her way upward in the dark, only the moonlight through undraped windows to light her way.

Jeremy hadn't been in the vast drawing room below, nor had he been in any of the anterooms, so he must be waiting in his chambers above. Likely languishing there, distraught that Lord Wilfort had forbidden the match between him and Audrey. No matter, Mary would soon cheer him with Audrey's letter.

She made it to the upper landing, out of breath, and turned the corner for the wing that would take her to Jeremy.

A tall man stepped out of the shadows and into her path. Moonlight fell on a light-colored frock coat that topped a kilt of blue plaid.

He was one of the Highlanders from below, the younger one, who'd caught and held her with the heat in his eyes.

Primal fear brushed her. To be confronted by this man, a Highlander, in the dark, in this deserted part of the house was . . . exhilarating.

Mary also was touched with curiosity, wonder that such a being existed and was standing less than a foot from her. A warmth began in Mary's breastbone, spreading downward to her fingertips, and up into her face.

The man did not move. He was a hunter, motionless in the dark, sizing up his prey. At the moment, that prey was Mary.

Fanciful nonsense, Mary tried to tell herself. Likely he was staying in the house, perhaps on his way to his bedchamber.

Where he'd pull off his coat, unlace his shirt, lie back before the fire in casual undress . . .

Mary's throat went dry. She'd been listening too hard to Aunt Danae's tales of her conquests when she'd been a young woman. Aunt Danae had lived on passion and desire, but Mary was far too practical to want such things for herself. *Wasn't she?*

"I beg your pardon, sir," she said, trying to keep her voice steady. "My destination lies beyond you."

She spoke with the right note of haughtiness—after all, the Scots were a lesser people, drawn into civilization by the English. Or so her father claimed. Not that Mary truly believed in the natural superiority of Englishmen; she'd met too many Englishmen who were decidedly *in*ferior.

The man said nothing, only stood in place, caught by moonlight.

The touch of fear began to rise. Mary was alone and unprotected, and he was a creature of the uncivilized Highlands. The clansmen raided one another's lands, it was said, stealing cattle, women . . .

"No matter," Mary said when he did not speak. "I will simply go 'round the other way." The house was built in four wings that surrounded a courtyard below. "Good evening, sir."

She swung away but had taken only a step before the Scotsman pushed past her and stood in front of her once more.

Her heart beating rapidly now, Mary swung around again, ready to make a dash for Jeremy's chamber. Jeremy was not a small man—he could clout this Highlander about the head for frightening the woman he hoped would become his sister-in-law.

Mary stumbled and nearly fell as the Scotsman put himself in front of her *again*. A large hand on her shoulder pushed her back onto her feet.

"Steady, lass." His voice was a deep rumble, starting from somewhere in his belly and emerging as a warm vibration.

The hand on Mary's shoulder remained. No gentleman should touch a lady thus. He could grip her hand, but only when meeting her, dancing with her, or assisting her. The Highlander had stopped her from falling, yes, but he should withdraw now that she was upright again. Instead, he kept his hand on her, the appendage so large she was surprised his gloves fit him.

He stood close enough that Mary got a good look into his

eyes. They were unusual, to say the least. Not blue or green as a red-haired man's might be—they were tawny, like a lion's. The sensible side of her told her they must be hazel, but the gleam of gold held her in place as securely as the hand on her shoulder.

"Please let me pass, sir," Mary said, trying to sound severe, but she sounded about as severe as a kitten. In his opinion as well, because he smiled.

The smile transformed him. From a forbidding, terrifying giant, the Highlander became nearly human. The warmth in the smile reached all the way to his eyes, crinkling them at the corners.

"I will," he said in a voice that wrapped her in heat. "As soon as ye tell me where you're going, and who ye intend to meet."

Chapter 2

"Bolts and bodkins," Mary muttered.

"What?" the Scotsman asked, eyes widening in amusement. "What the devil does that mean?"

"Nothing," Mary said quickly. "My business here is hardly a concern of yours, sir. May I ask what *you* are doing up here?"

"Aye, well ye might." His fingers moved on her shoulder, the faint caress pouring fire into her bones. "You're up here alone, away from your chaperone. I saw you slip away, lass—it was cleverly done. You can nae be up to any good. So, I followed ye."

Naturally. Mary *wasn't* up to any good, as a matter of fact. She didn't truly believe this man would rush to her father and tell of Mary carrying a letter from Audrey to Jeremy, but he might tell *someone*, and the tale would circulate.

"I have an errand." Why Mary answered at all, she did not know. She should turn, retreat down the stairs, wait for a better moment. This was no business of a Scotsman's, no matter how tall, how heart-melting his touch.

"Errand, eh? Whatever it is, it has ye blushing rosy red. A yellow rose, I thought you when I first saw ye. Now I'd say you were pink."

It was not an easy task to meet his gaze, but Mary made

herself do it. "If you will not let me pass, then I will return to the drawing room. Good evening once again." She attempted a curtsy, but her knees were shaking so hard she could only dip the barest inch.

The chuckle that left his mouth was hotter than his touch. "I dinnae believe you're all stiffness and cold, lass. Ye have fine eyes, do ye know? The sea near Castle Kilmorgan is just that blue. 'Tis a beautiful sight."

Mary had a flash of it—blue-gray sea stretching from below sheer cliffs, a crumbling castle perched on a hill. The pair of them standing side by side while the Scottish wind blew cold around them and pressed them together. His arm would come around her, holding her, protecting . . .

Mary cleared her throat. "You have obviously rehearsed how to be flattering, sir. But not courteous."

Another chuckle, which vibrated through his fingers into her. "I'll let you by, lass. For a price."

The dark note in his voice made her shiver. "Of course," she said tightly. "Not because you are a gentleman with honor, courtesy, or discretion, but to gain something for yourself."

"Ah, ye try to be so frosty, lass, but you're nae good at it. One smile from your mouth, one flash of those eyes, and I wager men are puddles at your feet."

Mary had never noticed any gentlemen in puddles. They paid very little attention to her at all, but then, most were stopped by her formidable father before they could even speak to her.

"You are very forward, sir. But perhaps you cannot help it, being raised a Highlander."

The Scotsman laughed a sudden, true laugh, the sound filling the hall. Mary wanted to laugh with him, to throw off her troubles and sink against him, feeling his laughter with her entire body. The power of it loosened things inside her, opening what she never knew had been closed.

The Scotsman wiped his eyes. "You're nae good at insults either, my girl. Of course I've been raised a Highlander, which means I'm forward, stubborn, and know what I want when I see it. Ye have the same stubbornness, lass."

His laughter died as he leaned to her, fixing her with his amber-colored gaze, his hard warrior's face an inch from hers. "Run away with me, love, and marry me."

The things opening inside Mary gave a sudden wrench. Run away—from the tightness of her life, the path of duty before her, the walls of stone closing in on her. Leave with this beautiful barbarian for the open spaces of the Highlands, to the crags of mountains that marched to the sea, and the sky that stretched to forever.

Absolute nonsense, of course. This man did not want to marry her. He was flirting, teasing, delighted he'd found a young English miss wandering the house in the dark.

"I can hardly marry a man I've just met on an upstairs landing," Mary said. "I know nothing of you—not your name, your family, and most importantly, your character. Besides, I am betrothed."

"So I have heard. Who is this fortunate gentleman? Is it he you're rushing to meet for a bit of pre-wedding tryst?"

Now Mary wanted to laugh. "Certainly not." She couldn't imagine George Markham, Lord Halsey, doing anything so rash as having a pre-wedding tryst. Halsey was not a man who did anything rash, and he definitely was not moved by passion. "I am betrothed to the Earl of Halsey."

The Scotsman straightened with an abruptness that unnerved her. His hand left her shoulder, taking all the beautiful warmth with it.

"Dear God, ye can't, lass. You're a vibrant and beautiful woman. Don't throw it away on that whey-faced English bastard."

Mary blinked. She was no stranger to strong language—her father's cronies could burn the air when they'd had plenty to drink—but rarely were the words directed at her. "Goodness, what is there to object to about Lord Halsey? He is well respected, a gentleman, honorable, well spoken . . ."

". . . has a perpetual drip at the end of his nose." The Scotsman flipped his finger under the tip of his own appendage.

"He does not . . ." Mary trailed off. It was true that Halsey spent many conversations dabbing his nose with a handkerchief. "That is neither here nor there."

"Not something t' face on your wedding night." The Scotsman moved a step closer, his voice going soft. "Your wedding night, lass, should be a thing of beauty."

Mary had never thought about it. She knew exactly how a woman went about providing her husband an heir—Aunt

Danae had gone through every detail from start to finish, very thoroughly.

Some men, Aunt Danae said, made the experience quite enjoyable, while others were oafish pigs. Unfortunately, a lady never knew which her husband would turn out to be until she was climbing into the marriage bed with him.

Aunt Danae spoke from the experience of having three husbands as well as a number of lovers. In any case, the gentleman always believed *his* pleasure of tantamount importance, no matter what the woman thought.

Mary couldn't help wondering what this Scotsman would be like. He had big hands, wide shoulders, a strong body. His arms would hold his lady, the large hands would caress her, and he'd speak intimacies to her in his deep rumbling voice.

He took another step toward her. "A bride should be properly handled," he said. "Her husband gentle with her, guiding her every moment."

Mary moved back, but falteringly, worried she'd find the open stairwell behind her. Her Highlander caught her, gliding her around until her back was to a wall. Safe.

But not safe from him.

"If ye were my bride, Mary, I'd be so very tender with ye." One thumb brushed the skin of her shoulder, bared by the bodice's neckline. "Taking care with you, as though you were delicate porcelain."

His heat, the largeness of him, made her breath stop. And yet, where he touched her, the tiniest contact, was gentle, as though this brutish man truly could cradle and protect a fragile object.

"I'm not porcelain," Mary said, her voice strangled.

"Aye, that you are. Porcelain is breakable but strong at the same time. And beautiful."

His finger moved on her neckline, sliding slowly downward, the barest brush, to her bosom.

Mary had no business standing here letting this Highlander touch her. She was betrothed to a very important gentleman, a close friend of her father's, both fiancé and father in high favor at court and in government.

Mary would cement the friendship between the two, and her sons would be the culmination of the bargain. Mary was to provide the heirs and raise them to be as powerful and important as their father and grandfather, to take the two families into the next generation of greatness.

Nowhere in this grand scheme was Mary to stand in the upper reaches of a house and enjoy the caress of a mad Highlander, one of those Jacobites whose treachery simmered beneath the surface year after year.

She was not to oblige any gentleman until she had an heir and a spare in the nursery. Then, Aunt Danae had instructed, Mary might enjoy herself, but discreetly, and certainly not with a man who posed any danger whatsoever to her husband or father.

Careful planning and thought crumpled to nothing under the gloved fingertips at her breast, the heat that spread from his hand to consume the rest of her body.

This man was life, while Mary's path was existence. He was warmth, vivacity, freedom, while she was duty, obligation, sacrifice.

He drew his fingers along her bosom, a river of fire trailing to her heart. He dipped two fingers inside her bodice, and Mary closed her eyes.

She jerked them open a second later when his questing fingers found and withdrew Audrey's letter.

"Ah, now, what's this?"

Mary snatched at it. "Give me that."

The Highlander grinned with boyish mischief and swung away, holding the paper out of her reach. Mary chased him, but he evaded her, unfolding the letter and reading as he sidestepped away.

"*Billet doux*," he said. "Of the secret kind. The best." He skimmed the text quickly. "Oh, but this is beautiful."

Mary had been told that Highlanders lived most of their lives tending farm animals and couldn't read a word, but apparently this was not true. The letter was in French, which Audrey and Jeremy considered the language of the heart, and the savage Highlander was reading every word.

"She's very much in love, this lady," he said. "With a man with beautiful blue eyes. I wager not your Lord Halsey of the runny nose."

"I didn't write it," Mary said quickly. Why she cared whether this man believed she'd penned the letter or not, she couldn't fathom.

"I know you didn't. Unless your name is *Audrey*."

"Good heavens, she *signed* it?" Mary made to snatch the paper again, which he lifted out of her reach.

"She did indeed. Not the most discreet lady, is she? She should have written, *your best beloved*, or *your adoring lover*, or signed as some lady of Greek myth, as instructed in the manuals of love-letter writing."

"There are no manuals of—" Mary broke off and waved her hands. "You are a rogue, sir, and a tease. Give me back the letter. It has nothing to do with you."

"Now, that is not necessarily true." The Highlander folded the paper. "I had a wager with me brother, ye see, when I saw you evade your elders and run off alone. I wagered I would pry a kiss out of you. I can nae go back and tell him I failed, now, can I? So, English Rose, ye give me one small kiss, and I return t' ye this sad and indiscreet letter."

"One small kiss . . ." Mary said. The lips that would perform the kiss were stiff, barely to move. "Is that all?"

She wanted to bite out her tongue as the Highlander gave a shout of laughter. "Oh, no, Mary, I want more. So much more. I'm being kind t' ye, lass."

"And you should not use my given name. It's forward. Intimate, even." Mary's chest was tight, her words breathless.

"Aye, that's why I do it."

"Besides, I don't even know *your* name." Again, not what she meant to say.

He stopped laughing and put one hand on his chest. "Malcolm Daniel Mackenzie, at your service, lass. Youngest son of that tricky bloody bastard, the Duke of Kilmorgan. But me friends call me Mal."

Chapter 3

Mal. Mary liked it. Simple, yet filled the mouth with its very shape. The word, in both Latin and French, meant *badness.*

"One kiss, Mary." Malcolm was next to her again, the warmth of him enclosing her. "One, and your sister's letter is back safe with you."

Mary frowned at him. "How do you know she is my sister?"

"Because I asked me brother Alec, that font of knowledge, all about you."

"Then why did you ask who I was betrothed to? It is no secret."

Malcolm shrugged, the coat moving on his large shoulders. "I wanted to see how you'd tell me. With great pride? Embarrassment? Admiration? Your eyes glowing with love? Do you know what, Mary? You did none of that. You were as stiff as a clockwork automaton. Ye give me hope."

Mary curled her fingers. "Hope for what?"

"Hope for meself. Can I win the beautiful Mary and take her off to my cold Highland castle? I need a wife t' keep the winter nights warm."

"Wife?" Her voice cracked. "Thunder and rainstorms, now you *are* talking nonsense. I thought Highlanders raided each other's clans for wives, not English society soirees."

Another laugh, so deep and warm she wanted to embrace it. How wonderful to have laughter like that surround her every day, and on into the night.

"True, lass, in the bad old days, clans fought clans to the bloody death, stealing women, cattle, lands, and anything else we could lay our hands on. Now we insult each other in the halls of universities. 'Tis a bit of a disappointment for ye, I know."

Malcolm's smile was so wide, so infectious, that Mary couldn't help smiling too. She fought it—better to let this man think her austere—but she lost. Her mouth curved, and her face softened.

Mal ceased laughing. "Lass, ye are so very beautiful. I think you've just broken my heart."

He leaned down, cupping her face, turning it up to his. He was going to kiss her. Touch his smooth lips to hers, burn her with the heat of his mouth.

Mary hastily stepped back. "No, really, sir, you cannot."

Or she'd melt to him. She'd fall bonelessly to the floor, promise him anything, disgrace herself and her family, and run with him to his stone castle in the wild north. There she'd live, wrapped in plaids, surrounded by Highland children and a husband with laughter like sunshine.

"No?" Malcolm straightened. "Ye surely know how to plague a man, love. But I won't give up. I'll have your kiss. And you." His voice darkened. "I will, ye know. When my mind's set on a thing, I have it in the end. I promise ye."

Mary shivered, but not with cold. "Nonsense, you'll forget all about me when I'm gone. I leave for England as soon as the weather breaks."

"Then I'll pray for more bad weather. But for now, if I can't have the kiss, I'll settle for a lock of your lovely hair. To show my brother and not entirely lose the wager. Alec's the very devil when he wins. Never lets me hear the end of it. As the youngest brother, I must labor against them all to survive."

"I very much doubt that," Mary said with conviction. "I imagine you charm them all senseless. Very well, if a small lock will suffice, you may have it."

She regretted her compliance in the next instant, because his look of triumph nearly wiped her off her feet.

"Ah, Mary, you're a fine woman. I knew it the instant I looked at ye."

The way Mal spoke her name made Mary want to believe everything he said. "I have no scissors with me, so perhaps it is a moot point."

She jumped in alarm as a knife flashed in the darkness, a blade wide as two fingers. Good heavens, a knife like that could kill in the work of a moment.

Mal lifted a curl that hung below her shoulder, tightening it between his fingers. One practiced flick of the knife had it severed from the rest of her hair, the lock now resting in his hand. The knife disappeared back into its sheath just as rapidly.

All gentlemen in Mary's life wore swords and knew how to use them; indeed, many had been soldiers in the endless wars on the Continent and had fought duels of honor. But they never drew blades around her, and never moved with such quick, deadly efficiency.

This man was a killer, a warrior trained to answer the call of his clan chief and rush into battle for him. Anything elegant and civilized, he was not.

And yet, the knife had never touched her. Mary had not been in danger for a single second.

Mal lifted the lock to his lips. "I'll carry it next to me heart," he said, then reached out and touched her chin. "My English Rose."

Mary couldn't breathe. Malcolm touched the curl to his lips again, a sensual move.

She had been right not to let him kiss her. She'd be over his shoulder by now, as he carried her off with him to the place of heather and lochs under vast skies.

"*Mary?*" Aunt Danae's voice thundered up the stairs. "Drat the girl, where has she got to?"

Mary's breath poured back into her lungs. Her real life slammed into her, the cozy interlude with the dangerous Highlander fading like a dream.

She could be ruined if she were found up here alone with him. No unmarried young lady could be in the presence of a gentleman, especially one like this Highlander, without a chaperone, without tarnishing her character. She'd shame her father, Lord Halsey, her entire family. There were those who believed Danae no fit chaperone for the Lennox girls, with all her *affaires d'amour*. There would be talk, gossip, disapproval, knowing laughter. And Malcolm still had Audrey's blasted letter.

Malcolm's teasing look vanished, as though he understood her danger. "Best go on, lass. I'll deliver the letter for ye. Which is the lad's chamber?"

"No—good heavens, give it back to me. I'll take it to him later."

"Don't be daft, woman. This is your best chance—your auntie will be climbing up here any second. Be found with me, and you'll perish."

"*Mary!* Where are you, girl?"

"Ye see? Go," Mal urged. "The letter's safe with me." His smile returned, lighting those intriguing eyes. "Do ye trust me?"

"Not a jot," Mary said, but gave in. She didn't have much choice—she'd never wrest the letter back from him by force. "It's the last door on the right. Do not let *anyone* see you."

"No one ever does, sweet lady."

Mary looked him over one last time—likely she'd never see him again. Mal stood like a sentry in the darkness, his plaid unmoving.

These Highlanders were mad fighters, it was said, silent in the night until they struck with all their fury. Malcolm was like the dirk he kept sheathed beneath his coat, quiet for now, but potentially deadly.

"Go on," Mal said as she lingered. "I'll not betray ye, my English Rose."

The words were spoken with promise. Mary shook herself, turned, and headed for the staircase, holding her swaying skirts. She went down them as rapidly as her high heels would let her, her heart thumping hard.

"Mary," came a dark whisper behind her.

Mary paused on the landing and looked back. Malcolm leaned over the banister, his tail of hair falling beside his square, hard face. Even in the dark, his eyes burned her.

"Good night, lass," he said softly. He kissed his fingers, and blew across his fingertips in her direction. Mary swore the kiss landed on her lips.

Without a word, she turned away, but felt his gaze burn her all the way down the stairs.

Mal watched Mary hurry to meet her aunt, her skirts rippling like water. She was beauty itself, and Mal wanted her.

Not simply in bed—though he definitely would have that—he wanted her nearness, her warmth, that silken voice that tried to be haughty, the sudden flash of her smile. Mal's body tightened, goading him to pursue her and do all the good things he longed to.

He would. He'd see her again; he'd make certain of it.

Mal reflected as he moved down the passage on his errand that he'd already learned much about Lady Mary Lennox. She was passionate and romantic, beguilingly so, but tried to hide that nature under proper behavior. She'd wanted Malcolm to kiss her—he'd seen it in her heartrendingly blue eyes. Mary had stopped herself only at the last moment, and reluctantly.

She also had compassion, helping her sister communicate with a forbidden lover. If Mary *truly* believed in propriety, she'd never have condoned her sister writing such a heartfelt letter.

She also risked censure for being the go-between. This showed that Mary was fond enough of her sister to take risks for her. Brave then, as well.

Courage, passion, beauty, compassion, and something inside her that longed to be wicked—*what a woman*. One night in bed with her would be worth every step he took to get her there. Whatever errands Mal had to run for her, whatever *billet doux* he needed to carry, or drippy-nosed suitors to run through with his sword, he would do it all for his reward at the end.

Mary. Even her name was a joy to say. Mal spoke it out loud in the silence of the empty hall. He'd teach her to call him *Mal*, and she'd say it in her smooth voice when she was deep in passion.

She'd be reluctant at first, but Mal would coax her, like a bird to his hand, teaching her to trust, never breaking her. And then Mary would be his. *Not* having her now that Malcolm had seen her, spoken to her, breathed the air she did, was unthinkable.

The *how* of it, Mal thought he might know. The letter in his hand held the key. It was addressed to the Honorable Jeremy Drake, youngest of three brothers, a man who had little importance in the world. He wasn't likely to inherit the Bancroft peerage, and he'd be living off whatever allowance was given to him by his family. Very likely Mary's father, Wilfort, opposed the match on these grounds.

Malcolm was no stranger to life as a younger son. In England, if the son had no interest in politics, the military, or the church, he had very little to look forward to. Mal thanked the deity he was Scots, from a land with different inheritance rules.

Mal had turned his brains and the money from his deceased mother to build up a business, one that was doing very well. He had plenty now to support a wife like Mary, a woman who'd be used to the good things in life.

Mal reached the door at the end of the hall and rapped on the wood panels. He waited, hearing nothing from within.

Mal knocked again, again with the same response, but he'd not give up. Alec was probably looking for him, wanting to grow nice and drunk with him in a public house, leaving these cold English to their equally cold manor.

But Mal had to stay, at least until this task was finished. He was certain he'd found the way to Mary's heart, and it was through this door to the young Englishman on the other side.

He rattled the door handle, discovered it moved easily, and he went inside.

A young man was stretched out on the carpet in front of the fireplace. He lay face-up, unmoving, at an awkward angle. Mal's heart constricted, blackness dancing before his eyes.

There had been a sixth Mackenzie brother, Magnus, between the twins and the second oldest, Will. Magnus had never been a well lad, and they'd all striven to take care of him. Magnus been prone to illness, never failing to spend half the year in bed or wrapped in blankets in the great hall before the roaring fire.

One evening, Mal had entered Magnus's chamber and found him thus, stretched out on the hearthrug, unmoving. Magnus had fallen, and his heart, weakened even more from that year's illnesses, had given out.

Magnus had been all of eighteen, Mal fourteen.

Years fell away as Mal stared down at the young Englishman. Mal was a boy again, trying to rouse his gentle older brother, his heart shattering with grief when he couldn't. Magnus, with his compassion and kindness, had been worth all the rest of them put together.

Mal drew a sharp breath, and the darkness cleared. By the light of the dancing candles, Mal saw that this young man was clearly not Magnus. He was Mal's age, and robust, his face a good color, his limbs strong. He'd simply fallen asleep.

Malcolm leaned down and rocked his shoulder. "Wake up, man."

The Honorable Jeremy Drake blinked open his eyes. He stared at Mal in astonishment for a few heartbeats, then seized Mal's reaching arm, rolled to a stand, and swept his boot behind Mal's legs, knocking him off his feet.

Chapter 4

Malcolm had been a fighter all his life. Had to be, with four brawny brothers and a large father always trying to catch him and pound him with their fists. He managed to avoid falling, but he staggered, fighting to keep upright.

He was regaining his balance, his hand automatically moving for the other man's throat, when he found himself facing a drawn dagger.

"Who the devil are you?" Jeremy demanded. "Have the Jacobites marched on us already?"

Mal raised his hands. "Not a Jacobite, lad. Not me." Charles Edward Stuart could remain pontificating to his followers in the western Highlands forever, as far as Malcolm cared. "And if they do march, are you going to defend your entire house with a little stabber like that?"

For answer, Jeremy came at him. Mal caught his arm, bending it behind the young man's back and twisting the knife from his hand.

Jeremy was good, Mal had to admit. It was a struggle to hold him, and at last Mal had to release the twisting devil. Malcolm had the knife now, and brought it up between them.

Jeremy breathed hard, a dangerous light in his eyes. He had

black hair pulled into a loose queue, a strong body filling out a finely tailored coat and breeches, blue eyes, and a fiery look. He might be a youngest son, but Mal had the feeling that if he were ever allowed any power . . . *watch out.*

"Answer me," Jeremy said in a hard voice. "Who *are* you?"

"Lord Mal Mackenzie." Mal dipped his free hand into his pocket and pulled out the letter. "Sent to deliver your post."

Jeremy eyed it suspiciously. "What is that?"

"A love letter, ye ignorant Sassenach." Mal waved the folded paper in front of Jeremy's face. "From your paramour, young Audrey."

"What?" Jeremy snatched the letter. "What are you doing with it?"

"Sent here by Lady Mary herself. Commanded in the name of love."

Jeremy didn't soften, not believing a word of it. He jerked open the letter and read the first few lines before he looked up again. "Yes, all right."

Mal kept his grip on the knife but lowered his hand to his side. "I read the whole of it. She says some fine things about you."

Jeremy went scarlet. "You *read* it?"

"By accident. She's a skilled one with a pen, is Lady Audrey. Are ye very much in love with her?"

Jeremy kept his angry look in place a moment longer, then he groaned and dropped all pretense. "Good God, man. I adore her. But her father is determined to marry her to an old man to curry favor. The earl's daughters are nothing but bargaining pieces to him. Cattle for breeding."

"As it is with so many Englishmen."

Jeremy's glitter of anger returned. "*M*y father is different. Well, slightly different—he cares bugger-all about what woman I marry as long as I don't disgrace the family. Although one with bags full of money wouldn't come amiss."

"Aye, me father's much the same. *Leave off with your whores, Malcolm, and find a woman who'll bear me strong grandsons.*" Mal shrugged. "Only so he'll have more lads t' help with the work."

Jeremy studied Malcolm with more interest. "Are you such a man for the ladies?"

"Oh, aye. I'm all the time swayed by the flash of an ankle, the soft flesh of a shoulder. One wink of an eye, and I'm off." Although now that Mal had seen Mary, those days were at an end. "Me da says I've got unbalanced humors, which I inherited from me mum's side, he claims, wild men all. Me da, on the other hand, is dour. When men speak of dour Scotsmen, they mean my father, Daniel William Mackenzie, Duke of Kilmorgan. The dourest of them all."

Jeremy's eyes widened. "Good Lord, you're *that* Mackenzie? His son, I mean."

Malcolm bowed. "I have that misfortune."

"He's a slippery fish, so they say. Begging your pardon. My father and the Earl of Wilfort are watching him closely, you ought to know. No offense?"

The young man so ready to stab Malcolm a few moments ago was now apologizing for telling the truth about Malcolm's own father. Strange the effect that women and love had on crazed fighting men.

"Me da *is* slippery and can be a nasty bugger. You're not offending me there. And he's aware of Englishmen watching him—he's watching back. If you want to know what the devil he's up to, do not ask me. I don't know. I pay no attention. I sleep easier that way."

Jeremy sighed, looking miserable again. "Well, none of it matters. I love Audrey, she loves me, and her father has forbidden us to see each other. Here we are, lovers in a farce, unable to break free."

"You might just," Mal said.

"Hmm?" Jeremy shot him a puzzled look. "Why? What do you mean?"

Mal paused a dramatic moment before he spoke . . . which gave him time to think of what to say.

Mal had discovered how to win Mary. All he had to do was find a way for Jeremy and Audrey to marry, to ensure it happened without impediment, and to keep their families from tearing them apart. Once he did all this, Mary would smile upon him in gratitude. Mal had friends and connections to get Jeremy and Audrey to France, where the lovebirds could remain in safety while their families became used to the situation. Mary would kiss him for it.

Jeremy was a bright lad, of good family, not a charlatan

from the gutter. Once Audrey and he were bound in marriage, and no man could put them asunder, the families would likely come around to forgiving them.

Even if Lord Wilfort never forgave them, Mary would be happy, and that was all that mattered to Mal.

Mary would be much more inclined to throw off the chains of obligation and run away with Malcolm if he did her this favor. They'd go to France, marry, and enjoy themselves. And when Mal returned to Kilmorgan with the beautiful Mary and several strong and squalling bairns, the Duke of Dourness would come 'round and at least be civil. What could go wrong?

Mal set Jeremy's dagger on the table with a click. "Are ye willing to be guided by me? And by Mary, of course."

"You can help us?" Jeremy regarded Mal with evident doubt. "How?"

"Well, ye have to be willing to be brave. *And* to keep your mouth shut. How much money do you have?"

Jeremy went from hopeful to morose so quickly it was comical. "There's the rub. Not much. I'd have absconded with the girl months ago if I'd had the blunt."

"And that's the difference between Englishmen and Highlanders. We don't beggar our sons—well, all right, some do. But my father never did. Me mum left us all a wagonload of money, and I've made me own. Ye marry your lass, settle down to a profession, and pay me back when ye have a mind to."

"A profession." Jeremy gave Malcolm a glum look. "I haven't trained for much. I might tutor other gentlemen's sons, but I don't have the good conscience for the clergy, or the money for the army."

Malcolm hid his impatience. He was already liking Jeremy for his restless energy and determination, but the lad was giving up on life before he'd even started it.

"I have a going concern ye can be a part of. Help me sell my fine whisky to Englishmen such as yourself, and you'll be swimming in riches in no time. You'll keep young Audrey in satin slippers and lacy caps for the rest of her life."

Jeremy looked bewildered. "Why would you promise to do so much for me? You've only just met me. Is this some sort of Scottish trick?"

"Only a trick to get Mary Lennox to smile at me."

"Oh." Jeremy blinked. "Mary, eh?"

"Yes, Mary, the most beautiful creature who graces the earth," Malcolm said forcibly.

Jeremy looked doubtful again. "Mary? She's all right. A grand girl to help us. You say you're in love with her?"

"As much as you are with your Audrey."

"Ah." Jeremy's face cleared. "Now I understand. Then we are a hopeless pair of smitten gentlemen." He clapped Malcolm on the shoulder. "How about we leave this tower of despair and go get brutally drunk?"

Malcolm returned his grin, and agreed. But he made sure Jeremy left his dagger behind as they went down the back stairs, as silent as smoke, and out into the night.

Edinburgh was a city of contrasts. It was a place of learning, of thinkers, poets, and scientists, of ancient streets and spires, elegant and strong. It was also a city of narrow rookeries, jammed with buildings falling into one another, and people doing much the same.

The dark face of Edinburgh, in the old city, was where Mal and Jeremy headed now. It was late, gloomy, and cold, and the only people who noticed the tall Scotsman and equally tall Englishman at his side were those who scuttled off into warmth and kept out of their way.

The tavern Mal made for was squashed between two other shops, its upper stories sagging downward. Mal ducked under the door's solid lintel ahead of Jeremy, assessing the lay of the land.

Jeremy couldn't be mistaken for anything but upper-class English. In this place, it would generally not be a problem, but Mal knew there were a few patrons here so hotly Jacobite they'd find any excuse to cut anyone who didn't speak broad Scots. Mal advised Jeremy to stay near, keep his mouth closed, and smile a lot.

Mal's brother Alec lifted his tankard and sang out from the corner. Most of the clientele knew the Mackenzie brothers, and slurred greetings met Mal as he crossed the room.

"Didn't take ye long," Mal said, dropping onto the bench beside his brother.

Alec shrugged, one large, raw-boned hand on his tankard. "Ye went missing, and I soon had enough of posturing English shite." He threw a glance at Jeremy. "Ah, no offense, Drake."

"None taken," Jeremy answered, keeping his voice quiet as Mal had advised. "My father postures with the best of them. I'm not much for politics."

"The world is politics these days, lad," Alec said. "Who you talk to, where you drink, what you drink, the clothes you wear—all say something."

He looked Jeremy up and down, as though trying to interpret what a black frock coat with silver buttons and a lawn shirt meant.

Means he's young, Mal wanted to say. *And in love, and doesn't care about the machinations of the world.* Jeremy had already won a great deal of Mal's sympathy.

Jeremy glanced pointedly at Alec's tankard. "What does drinking ale say about *you*?"

Alec gave him a stony Scots look, worthy of their hard-faced father. No one could give a more brutal stare than the Duke of Kilmorgan, except for his sons.

In the next instant, Alec burst into raucous laughter. He thumped the table with his heavy hand, his head going back until he bumped the stone wall. "Your expression, lad. Too damn serious. Drink—if you're a friend of Mal's, you're a friend of mine."

Mal laughed out loud as well—Alec was as changeable as the wind, and Mal found it best to laugh and roll his eyes instead of taking him seriously.

A woman with thick blond hair trickling from a cap set down tankards in front of Mal and Jeremy. She looked into Jeremy's face then sent a glance at Mal and Alec. Mal nodded at her, vouching for him. The barmaid then beamed Mal a smile, sending the message that she served more than ale.

Mal had taken her offer a time or two, and those of her comelier friends upstairs, but that had been before he'd fallen in love. The next lady he'd be with would be Mary, and he'd not want another woman after her.

"Out with it," Alec said to Mal when the barmaid had retreated. "Did ye make your conquest?"

Jeremy looked interested. "Conquest?"

"Lady Mary," Mal told him.

"Oh yes. Mary." The young man could not seem to understand what a goddess Mary was. "She is betrothed, you know."

"Aye. But one obstacle at a time, lad." Mal drew his handkerchief from his pocket and opened it enough to show Alec the single lock of Mary's red-touched blond hair. Just the sight of it made Mal's body squeeze, and he quickly tucked the lock out of sight.

Alec had ceased laughing, and now watched Mal from his tawny eyes. Alec's hair and that of his twin, Angus, were the darkest of the brothers, containing only a hint of red. Their oldest brother, Duncan—his name was Daniel Duncannon Mackenzie, but everyone called him Duncan to distinguish him from their father—had hair of flame red. Duncan took the most after their mother—in looks, not temperament. Allison Mackenzie had been lively and laughing, a contrast to her stony husband, before she'd passed, scarred by smallpox.

Duncan took life far too seriously and could rage and storm even better than their father. Duncan was a staunch Jacobite and, given the chance, would singlehandedly dispatch King Geordie from the throne and throw James onto it. Never mind he'd kill himself in the doing of it. To Duncan, the sacrifice would be worth it.

God save us from fanatics. The Mackenzie men could grow obsessed at the drop of a hanky, but Duncan had made an art of it.

Alec was watching Mal now as though thinking Mal as mad as Duncan. Mal gazed stubbornly back at him.

When *Alec* wanted a woman, he went through fire to get her, didn't matter whether she was married and guarded by a burly husband and five equally burly brothers. Alec had barely escaped with his life during *that* incident, and only because Mal and Will had hauled him away in the dead of night.

Alec hadn't let obstacles stop him the last time he'd wanted a woman either. The consequences of that were yet to be felt.

"Here's to beautiful women," Mal said, lifting his tankard.

"Aye," Alec said fervently. "May they warm our beds for many years to come."

"Aye," Jeremy echoed, sounding wistful.

"And here's to getting them *into* those beds." Mal lifted his tankard again. "You and me, Master Jeremy, have our work cut out for us."

"That we do," Jeremy said. He tried to sound Scots and failed miserably. Mal and Alec collapsed into laughter, and Jeremy joined them after a moment. Then they proceeded to become heartily drunk.

"My lords." The barmaid was before them again. Some time had passed—Mal had no idea how much, but a few hours at least.

Jeremy was slumped against the wall, snoring softly. Alec was staring at the empty tankard in his hands, singing to it under his breath. He had somewhere gotten his hands on a charcoal stick, and he'd drawn pictures all over the table with it, as he liked to do. Alec was skilled at drawing, but the tavern keepers weren't always happy with him.

"Aye?" Mal looked up at the woman, who wore a harassed expression.

"It's your brother, my lords," she said, urgent. "I just heard. He's sure to be arrested. You must go quickly."

Chapter 5

The cold dampness of Edinburgh woke Mal out of his stupor as they moved down the narrow street to another equally narrow passage.

A discreet bawdy house was tucked here. Its proprietor had sent a boy running to the tavern in search of Will Mackenzie's brothers.

Mal understood why when they reached the place, Jeremy in tow. Shouting came from the upper reaches of the house, the rooms accessed by a rickety staircase that led to a leaning wooden gallery.

A deep voice was carrying on in Highland Scots, admonishing, demanding, then lapsing into cajoling, laughter, and singing. The songs were the same as Alec's but much, much louder.

The proprietress of the house, a thin woman with an angular face, was from Glasgow. Mal could usually understand only about two words in six she said, but tonight she was very clear.

"Get him out." She glared at Mal and Alec. "He'll bring the constables down on us if he does no' shut up and go away."

"Easy, love," Mal said. "We'll take him. Alec, pay the good lady for her trouble."

Alec shot an annoyed look at Mal, but his pouch of coins came out and silver found its way into the proprietress's hand.

The woman looked less unhappy but remained planted by the foot of the staircase, as though ready to shove them out at a moment's notice.

Mal tipped her a wink as he followed Alec up the stairs, Jeremy trailing behind. The tall lad looked around with much interest, indicating louder than words that he'd never been in a whorehouse before. The English whelp was too innocent to be believed.

"*She were a fiiiiine lassie,*" came the booming baritone. "*With a bosom so sweet, and bum so large, and between her legs a . . . laaaaaad.*"

"Is that a song?" Jeremy asked, his face red but his eyes sparkling with humor.

"He makes up his own," Mal said. "Young Master Jeremy, meet my brother, the rakehell himself, William Ferdinand Mackenzie."

Alec had crashed through the bolted door at the top of the stairs to reveal Will, clad in nothing but a plaid wrapped around his hips, standing on strong feet, serenading two tired-looking women who lounged on the bed. It was evident that they'd had enough of him.

Will turned blearily as they burst in. "Mal!" he shouted. "How fine to see ye, runt!" He spread his muscled arms and rushed at Mal, crushing him into a hug.

Will was the tallest of the Mackenzies, the biggest and broadest, a giant of a man with dark red hair. Being embraced by him was like being squashed by a bear. Will was as warm as a bear too, and about as hairy and smelly in his unkempt state. He must have been there for days.

Will lifted his head and looked past Mal at Alec. "Angus!" He shouted. "Won't hug you. You're a bastard. I only love the runt."

"I'm Alec," Alec said, sounding less drunk. "Angus is at home."

"Good!" Will pounded Mal on the back then released him. "He's not here to spoil our fun. Who is that?" Will scrubbed both massive hands through his unruly hair, which made it stand straight up, and pinned Jeremy with a tawny stare. "Are you a Mackenzie, lad?"

"'Fraid not," Jeremy returned. He only looked slightly

alarmed, which meant the boy had mettle. Will Mackenzie undressed and roaring drunk was not an easy thing to take.

"The Honorable Jeremy Drake, sir," Jeremy said. He executed a practiced though wobbly bow.

"He's a bloody Englishman!" Will rubbed his eyes and stared at him again. "What are ye doing with a bloody Sassenach, Mal? Did he arrest you?"

"He's a friend," Mal said. "*My* friend. Dress yourself, man. We're going."

"So soon?" Will looked confused. "But I've only just started the singing."

Alec took a comfortable seat on the bed, giving the ladies there a smile and also a few coins for putting up with his brother. "And you're in good voice," Alec said, soothing him. "We'll be off, and you can sing to us."

Will gave him a doubtful look. "Well, all right, but you're nae so pretty."

"I'm glad of it," Alec said. "Mal, get him decently clad . . . Och, man, I did nae need to see *that*!"

Will had stripped off the plaid and let it fall, revealing his hard-muscled thighs and the large thing dangling between his legs.

Alec covered his face and moaned. Mal ignored him while he fished up Will's clothes from all over the room and helped the big man put them on. Jeremy watched, still flushed with drink, but enjoying the comedy.

Will got stuck inside his shirt, his arms flailing, unable to find the holes. Mal helped him, got the shirt settled and the plaid wrapped about his waist again. Waistcoat, stockings, boots, frock coat—all went on—then Will had to spend at least fifteen minutes looking for his hat.

They discovered that the proprietress had it. When Mal and Alec finally shoved Will out of the bedroom and to the staircase, Jeremy trailing, the proprietress held up a battered Scots bonnet. Will had to be helped down the stairs—his legs kept bending every which way.

Will reached the bottom at last and grabbed the hat from the woman's thin hand. "Thank you very much," he slurred. "Ye have a fine establishment. Until next time."

He tried to bow and fell into Mal's arms. Mal pushed him

to his feet, hearing the clink of more coins as Alec placated the woman once again. Jeremy grabbed Will's other arm and assisted Mal in squeezing his brother through the narrow door and out into the cold cobbles.

Will threw off their holds as chill night air poured over them. "I'm fine. I can walk meself."

He couldn't, very well. The four of them stumbled down the passage and to a larger street.

"Where are we going?" Will asked at his usual bellow. "Another nice house?"

"Home," Alec said sternly. He looked at Jeremy. "Best you nip off to your own digs, lad. If Will gets us arrested, ye don't want to be with us."

Jeremy glanced at Mal, and Mal gave a reluctant nod. He liked Jeremy, but it was time to part ways for the night.

"Aye, go on." He locked his fingers around Jeremy's sleeve and pulled him aside. "I can call on you tomorrow, eh? So we can begin. I'll help you win the hand of young Audrey, and in return, you slip me in to see Mary. Right?"

"Yes." Jeremy's eyes warmed with his smile. He clasped Mal's hand with a firm grip of his own. "You're a gentleman, Mackenzie, even if you're a Highlander."

"Aye, don't I know it." Mal clapped him on the shoulder and shoved him away.

Jeremy tipped his hat to Alec and Will, and turned and walked away into the darkness. His footsteps were uneven, his gait slightly swaying, but he'd be all right.

"Now, then, Mal, help me." Alec scowled and bent to the task of getting Will indoors.

By the time they reached the house the Mackenzies lived in during their excursions to Edinburgh, Will was walking better on his own. A footman opened the front door of the house and assisted them inside; a second footman scurried down the back stairs to alert the rest of the staff that the Mackenzie brothers were home.

Will had lost most of his drunkenness by the time they reached his large bedchamber upstairs. Will let the rail-thin, red-haired valet who'd appeared—Naughton, who looked after them all when they were in the city—pull off his boots, then Will collapsed full-length onto the bed.

Naughton took the soiled boots away, as well as the frock coat Will had thrown off, frowning in disapproval at the mud on both. As soon as the door closed, Will sat up, the disoriented light leaving his eyes.

"Well, lads," he said.

Mal found a stool by the fire and stretched his feet to it. He hated being cold.

Only a few candles were lit in the chamber, and the dim and wavering light cast weird shadows. Alec's straggling hair was thrown into huge silhouette against the fireplace.

"Well?" Alec prompted.

"I heard quite a lot to tell Father," Will said. He looked pleased with himself. "A few of Cope's men were in that house." Sir John Cope was the English general unlucky enough to command the British troops in Scotland. He was expected to deal with Charles Stuart—Teàrlach Stiùbhart—and his Highlanders if they made their way toward Edinburgh. "They tried to ply me with questions, find out who was with Teàrlach and who wasn't, but alas for them, I could barely think, let alone speak, eh? Won't be able to go back there if it's full of loyalists, though, I'm thinking. Pity. It was a good house."

"You mean the ladies there would put up with ye," Alec said with good humor. "As long as ye paid them well."

"Enough from you, whelp. What have *you* got to say?"

"Plenty," Alec said. "But not about the Jacobites. Mal thinks he's smitten with an English lass. Daughter of Wilfort, no less."

Will pinned Mal with a fierce gaze. "Are ye mad, runt? Wilfort is at King Geordie's elbow."

"Not his daughter's fault," Mal said. "Mary's a lovely lass, and better company than you lot."

"Watch it, lad." Will sat all the way up, his laughter gone. "I've seen what happens to you when you want a woman. When ye want anything, actually. You pursue it beyond reason."

"Only when it's worth it." Mal folded his arms, looking back into the fire. Mary's hair was the color of the hottest part of flame.

Alec's shadow moved as he and Will exchanged a glance.

"This time 'tis dangerous," Alec said quietly. "What with Duncan hot to drag Charles Stuart to the throne and Da denying that with every breath, this is nae a good time to be near anything English. Ye deflower the daughter of the Earl of Wilfort, he'll come after ye with half the army and have your head on a spit. Leave her be, Mal."

The part of Mal that was his common sense told him his brothers were right. Mary wasn't a barmaid or a young Scottish lass he could woo without compunction.

Mary's father had power, wealth, and influence—he could destroy Mal and all the Mackenzies with him. Mal had no doubt that his own father, to keep his standing as Duke of Kilmorgan, would happily throw Mal to the wolves in order to placate the English bastards.

The other part of Mal—the part of him that let nothing stand in the way of what he wanted—knew he couldn't let Mary go.

Something had happened when he'd seen her, like a sudden completion of himself. As though he'd been walking alone most his life, and all at once knew he'd never be alone again.

This knowledge had intensified when Malcolm had touched her, had closed his fingers over the warm lock of her hair. Two parts of a single whole had met, briefly contacted, and had been pulled apart again.

Mal would spend the rest of his life if necessary to put those two halves together again.

He realized his brothers were watching him, waiting for him to reassure them. He couldn't. Mal could only look at them, willing them to understand.

Will and Alec exchanged glances again, this time resigned. They knew exactly what happened when Mal took something into his head.

It warmed Mal that they ceased trying to stop him. They were making a silent pact to watch over him, and keep their little brother as safe as they possibly could, no matter what.

~

Mary knew exactly when Malcolm Mackenzie walked into the salon. She had her back to the door, her fingers plucking out an even tune on the harpsichord, but she knew.

The very air seemed to vibrate, to warm. The sound of his low voice confirmed his presence and sent a shiver down her spine.

Mary's hands faltered. She missed a few notes, then more notes, which made Aunt Danae glance at her in concern.

Mary never made mistakes at the harpsichord. She learned every piece perfectly, note for note. Her music master despaired that she put absolutely no passion into the music, but Aunt Danae said that didn't matter—most of the people Mary would play for had no emotional response to music anyway and would only hear her technique.

But now Aunt Danae blinked as Mary skipped an entire page and stumbled the piece to the end. Her audience applauded dutifully, then put their heads together to criticize her in whispers. The need of people to constantly critique others puzzled her, but it was part of her world.

Mary left the stool, saying she needed air.

Aunt Danae caught her elbow. "All you all right, my dear? I knew this crush was a mistake. Lady Bancroft always overdoes. Ah, here is Master Jeremy, come to make it all bearable. And his . . . friend?"

The last was directed at Malcolm, who was dressed as he'd been last night, in formal frock coat over kilt, his smile wide, his tawny eyes sparkling.

Jeremy was with him, as though they were old acquaintances. Jeremy introduced Malcolm, and Mal held out his gloved hand toward Mary.

Chapter 6

Mary did not, absolutely did not, want to take Mal's hand, but everyone was looking. She touched her fingertips to his large palm, her knees automatically bending in a trained curtsy.

Mal closed his hand over hers, and everything sensible in her vanished. The immense strength of him came through his grip, leaving her breathless.

She ought to jerk away, chide him for being forward with his too-firm grasp. Though it wasn't done for ladies to scold gentlemen in public, they *could* admonish them for taking liberties.

Malcolm had only clasped her hand. Why should this make her shake?

Ah, but the *way* he did it, with that sinful gleam in his eye, the knowing tilt of his lips, shot heat up her arm to her heart.

"May I present Lord Malcolm Mackenzie?" Jeremy was saying. "Lady Dutton . . ." He indicated Aunt Danae. "And her niece Lady Mary Lennox."

"It's me pleasure," Malcolm said. He finally released Mary's hand and bowed over Aunt Danae's. He should have taken Aunt Danae's first, since she was the older of the pair, but Mal had already proved he played by no rules but his own. "Meeting such beauty in the crowded city makes the journey through the wilds t' get here worth it."

His accent had deepened, becoming more broadly Scots. Mary slanted him a narrow glance, and Malcolm returned the look blandly. A naughty spark rested deep in his eyes, making Mary want to burst into laughter.

She almost missed Jeremy's question as Malcolm stepped back.

"Lady Audrey does not attend today?"

Poor Jeremy. He tried to ask the question offhand, but his voice was choked, and Aunt Danae shot him a curious glance. Jeremy also didn't look very good—his skin was pale, his eyes red-rimmed.

Suffering for love? Mary peered more closely and spied bloodshot lines in his eyes, noted the dryness of his lips. Mal had the same symptoms, though Mal hid his discomfort behind a ready smile.

Suffering from drink, more like. And why were Malcolm and the Honorable Jeremy Drake so chummy on a sudden?

"My sister had headache," Mary said. Lord Wilfort, of course, had forbidden Audrey to go to the Bancroft house, where she might encounter Jeremy. "She sends her apologies but wished to remain quietly at home."

Mal pressed a hand to his heart. "We are devastated. Th' loss of another lovely lady to a gathering is pure distress. Give th' lassie our very best wishes."

Aunt Danae warmed to Mal's eloquence, as overdone as it was. He was playing gallant gentleman for reasons of his own.

"I will," Aunt Danae said. A handsome man could always soften her. "You are most kind, sir."

Kind, my foot. Malcolm was a duplicitous knave. Though *why* he was being duplicitous, and what he was up to, Mary had no idea.

"We're happy to see you," Aunt Danae went on to Jeremy. "The rest of the gathering is crashing tiresome. The same tunes pounded out on the harpsichord, the same lines recited, weak tea all around. Not a scrap of interesting gossip, though the world outside is full of it."

"Aye, all are speculating that Charles Stuart is on his way," Mal said easily. "I don't set any store by it, meself."

Aunt Danae gave him a startled glance, gaze falling to his kilt. As Mary had observed the previous night, Mal did not at all blend in with the English aristocracy and Scottish upper crust. He was a fighting man, and would never look like anything else.

"But you'd take up his banner, wouldn't you?" Aunt Danae said with her usual frankness. "And murder us all in our beds?"

"Nae, not me." Mal shook his head. "No one's starving and unhappy at Kilmorgan. We've no need for a crusade. Teàrlach Stiùbhart can take his white rose and his banner and go back to France. We're doing fine without him."

He spoke with conviction, and Aunt Danae relaxed, but something in Mal's eyes told Mary another story. His declaration that his family was doing well without backing Charles rang true. Not all Highlanders were for him. But the flicker of uneasiness Mary spied told her Mal's situation was more complex.

She was well aware of shifting loyalties of the Highland clans—her father spoke about them all the time. They'd declare for King George then turn around and hold secret meetings on how to support the Jacobites, or persuade the leaders of France and Spain to send arms against England.

"Crafty devils, the lot of them," Lord Wilfort had said. Thinking over Malcolm's behavior of the night before, Mary was beginning to agree with him.

Malcolm at the moment said nothing untoward, did nothing to embarrass Mary, didn't so much as give her a wink or a smile. But even his neutral expression made her remember the touch of his hand, the whisper of the knife as he cut her lock of hair.

His lips had softened as he'd kissed it. Mary's breath caught, remembering that.

As Aunt Danae and Jeremy continued the conversation, Malcolm very quietly put his fingers over his left breastbone and caught Mary's gaze. His coat would have a pocket there, on the inside. She knew her lock of hair was resting in it.

Mary flushed hotter. Would Malcolm show it to anyone? And what if he did? Mary hadn't bound it in a ribbon embroidered with her name. Who would rush about the room holding up the lock to find out whose head it matched?

Malcolm's lips tilted upward at the corners. *He* might.

No, no. She could not worry. Malcolm was a rake—she understood this. She'd met others like him, though they'd never dared try to seduce her. No, perhaps they'd not been *quite* like Malcolm.

Even so, Mal would finish enjoying himself here, then move on to the next woman he'd set afire with his smiles, his touch . . .

"Ah, Lady Dutton, Lady Mary." The voice was thin, though deep and male. Mary closed her eyes briefly as her intended, George Markham, Lord Halsey, joined the little huddle.

Mary smiled politely. Halsey stopped before her, and she curtsied to him. "My lord."

Never had her knees felt stiffer, the *my lord* so reluctant to come from her throat. All because Malcolm Mackenzie stood behind Halsey, the amusement in his eyes vast.

Halsey stepped to Mary's side. She tried to look everywhere but at him or Malcolm, lest either man see what was in her eyes.

"I came to rescue you," Halsey said. "Far too many Highlanders about for my taste, wouldn't you say, Mackenzie?"

So Halsey knew who Malcolm was. Of course he did—he had his eye on everyone in Scotland, very sure of who was loyal and who was not. In his own way, Lord Halsey was a dangerous man.

"For mine too," Malcolm answered. "Too many Scots in a room, and the place begins to smell. I have to start opening windows."

Halsey looked startled, then chuckled. Malcolm gave him a little smile in response, which only reminded Mary that Mal carried a thick-bladed dagger inside his coat and wielded it with dexterity.

Lord Halsey was not unattractive. His face was somewhat narrow, but his nose was thin and well formed, his square chin keeping his features from running to the effeminate. He had brown eyes, not too large, not too small, his brows dark. He wore a wig with one tail held by a black ribbon. Nothing ostentatious, just quietly elegant.

Halsey always appeared like this—subdued in dress and ornamentation, a man not prone to showing off. He held a lot of power, but didn't need to flaunt it. Everyone simply knew.

Halsey and Mary's father hadn't so much been invited to Viscount Bancroft's home, as they'd instigated the visit. Bancroft—Jeremy's father—who held a high social position in Edinburgh, had felt the need to obey.

That was the sort of game Halsey played, and the ones Mary had to smile at and endorse.

Malcolm watched Halsey. He didn't appear to, but he watched. He'd already known who Halsey was when Mary had announced he was her betrothed. Mary wondered how much Malcolm knew about him, and whether it would be worth it to find out.

Then again, Mary had no wish to dive into those waters. What her father and Halsey got up to, she mostly did not want to know. They had power, and she was there to make certain Halsey looked well while he manipulated and ruined others. Something sour bit her stomach.

Halsey had continued speaking in his smooth way with Jeremy—a bit patronizing to the lad, but polite. In the middle of his speech, he gave a sniff, calmly pulled out a handkerchief, and delicately dabbed the end of his nose.

Malcolm, behind his back, pointed to him, brows raised. *Ye see?* he mouthed.

Mary wanted to laugh. She strove to check herself, her lips twitching dangerously. Malcolm's slow smile spread across his face, and Mary couldn't hold it in.

She clamped her hand to her stomacher as a sound between a cough and a screech popped from her mouth.

"Are you sure you are all right, my dear?" Aunt Danae asked. "Perhaps you ought to lie down. I'm sure Lady Bancroft could find a comfortable chamber—"

"No," Mary said, her voice a croak. "Something made me cough, is all."

"Are you certain?" Aunt Danae peered at her. "You've been peaky since last night. I think this northern weather doesn't suit you."

"Aye, the weather this far south can be a bit hard to take," Malcolm said. "Edinburgh's air is liquid most of the time."

Halsey dabbed his nose again, but the look he shot Malcolm over his handkerchief was speculative. "You do not come to the city often, Mackenzie?"

Mal shook his head. "I like the open, me. Where I can stride from crag to crag and sleep among the sheep dung."

As Malcolm spoke, he tipped a wink to Aunt Danae, who tittered. "Now, then, young Highlander," she said. "I believe you're having fun with us ignorant Sassenach."

"Och, aye," Malcolm answered, straight-faced. "I admit t' teasing you a wee bit. Highland humor."

Aunt Danae tapped his arm with her fan. "Well, if they are all as personable as you, young man, we will have nothing to fear."

Halsey remained unmoved. He paid absolutely no attention to Mary, although her fingers rested on his arm. His focus was on Malcolm, as though he wondered how to arrest him, imprison him, and put him to the question on the spot.

Malcolm seemed in no way worried about this. He continued to converse with Aunt Danae as she asked him questions about life in the remote Highlands.

No one paid Mary much mind, in fact, which was a mercy. If any gazes had turned to her, they'd find her hot, flushed, and ready to bolt.

Malcolm's rumbling voice was a cushion of velvet, while Halsey spoke in his thin tone, a whisper of air. Mary knew that Halsey truly *could* have Malcolm arrested on any pretense, locked away while a confession—to anything—was beaten out of him. Not strictly legal, but the law did not look kindly upon perceived traitors.

Mal wasn't a traitor. He'd already made his views clear, hadn't he?

But he wore his kilt proudly and exaggerated his Highland lilt. Malcolm was far more intelligent than he was letting himself appear to be, a sign of a very dangerous man. He played with his audience, assessing them while keeping them from understanding him.

Mary stood rigidly, barely able to focus on the conversation. Finally, Halsey tugged her arm.

"Come, Mary, Lady Templeton wishes to speak to you. You will see much of her after we are married. Will you excuse us, Lady Dutton? I must steal your niece away."

Aunt Danae was not happy about this, but she gave Halsey a gracious nod. The young men were not consulted at all.

Jeremy made an elegant bow to Mary, leg extended, perfectly executed.

Malcolm observed him with amusement, then he bowed deeply from the waist, his legs straight. The sweep of his torso down and back up was breathtaking—a large man moving with flexible grace.

Mary's body warmed as Mal caught her eye, his hair disheveled from his swift bow. Mary had always thought of herself as cool and devoid of longing, but perhaps she'd simply never found anything that made her feel desire before.

She certainly felt it now, watching Mal casually brush back his hair, unworried that he wasn't as pristine as the Englishmen around him. Why did she have to feel her first true longing for a handsome Highlander with a wicked light in his eye, while she was betrothed to another?

Mary turned away, her thoughts in jangling confusion, as Halsey led her onward.

She could not stop herself from glancing behind her as she went. Jeremy and Aunt Danae had continued their conversation, comfortable with each other.

Malcolm watched Mary. His twinkling amusement, his teasing, had gone. His gaze was quiet but powerful, determination in every line of him. Again she likened him to the hidden blade he carried, quiet and resting for the moment, but at any time, he could cut with deadly force.

Mal caught and held Mary's gaze, his straight mouth telling her more than words that he was ready for battle. And he intended to win.

"Jeremy, lad, arrange for me to see Mary in private."

Jeremy gave Malcolm a startled look. They were alone again, Aunt Danae moving off to speak to those in her circle, the two young men left to their own devices.

"In private?" Jeremy raised his brows. "You want to ruin the girl?"

"How else am I to pass on messages from you to young Audrey? Think, lad. You want to marry Audrey, don't you?"

"Of course." Jeremy flushed. "I adore her. I want to make her the happiest woman in the world . . ."

"Yes, yes," Malcolm said. "Don't tell *me* all that. Tell Lady Audrey. Write that in a flowery letter—a short one, please—and give it to me. And for God's sake, don't put any names on it."

"No. I mean . . . yes. Let me find . . . Come on."

Jeremy led Malcolm out of the drawing room and up a flight of stairs to a private study. There Jeremy sat down at a desk, pulled out paper and pen, ink, and sander, and started painstakingly writing words. He scratched out most of them.

"For heaven's sake, man," Mal said impatiently. "She's the lady ye want to spend your life with. Tell her this—"

He snatched up a clean sheet of paper and thrust it under Jeremy's hand. Jeremy sighed, rubbed his eyes, and dipped the pen in ink once more.

"*I can't sleep o' nights, thinking of you,*" Malcolm dictated. "*Your hair, your eyes, your soft lips fill my mind and my heart. Your kisses bring me joy. I long for the softness of your bosom under my hand*—aye, go on and write that—ye spell it *b-o-s-o-m.* If she were a different sort of woman, ye could be more blunt."

Jeremy raised his head, his cheekbones pink. "Is this the kind of thing you want to write to Mary?"

"No, with Mary, I'd be a bit more direct, because she's seen something of the world already. I imagine your Audrey is kept fairly cloistered."

"Yes, damn it all."

"Then this letter should be so eloquent that Lady Audrey will break her chains and run into your arms. Now, to continue. *I crave a token, one small thing only—a ribbon, a lock of your hair, a handkerchief that I might wear about my person.*"

Jeremy nodded as he wrote. "Cheeky."

"Ye have to be bold, lad. We're told that ladies want cringing politeness from a gentleman, but what they really want is a bit of forwardness, even carnality. It's exciting for them."

"You know much about young Englishwomen, do you?" Jeremy paused to dip his pen again. "You who live in the Highlands with four brothers?"

"Women are much the same everywhere. Scottish, English, French. They like a rake, no matter how prudishly they say they do not. Keep writing. *I would treasure such a token from you, care for it, kiss it, my heart breaking because I would rather it be you in my arms, against my heart.*"

"Heady stuff." Jeremy's pen scratched. ". . . *against my heart*. Anything else?"

"*Send it quickly, my love, with my messenger, to ease my aching sorrow. Signed, your devoted servant in love.* If she has a pet name for ye that no one else knows, use that."

Jeremy flushed and grinned, the pen moving. He finished, shook sand over the sheet, tapped off the excess, and waved the paper until the ink dried.

Then Jeremy frowned. "Hang on. If I can contrive to pull Mary aside, why don't I give *her* the letter for Audrey instead of arranging a secret meeting for the two of you?"

Malcolm clenched his fists on the desk. "Because it gives me an excuse to be alone with her, damn it. You'll be helping me woo a lady at the same time I'm helping you. I'm madly in love with the woman."

"*Mad* is the word for it." Jeremy folded the letter and handed it to Malcolm, who tucked it into his pocket. "Mary will never give up Halsey. She's very dutiful, is Mary. If you think to make her your mistress after she's wed, I don't imagine that will work either. Mary is also very loyal. And proper."

"And unhappy," Malcolm said. "I see the way she looks at th' man. She'd rather marry a rotting fish, but someone's talked her into doing it."

"Families." Jeremy shook his head. "They make your life hell."

"Don't I know it." Malcolm shuddered. Families could be the very devil. Especially when they were Mackenzies.

"Jeremy, where are we going? You're being blasted mysterious."

Mary hurried along behind Jeremy, her hands full of her skirts, her feet moving quickly in her high heels.

Jeremy didn't answer, being too busy striding along the corridors of his family home. Mary assumed it had something to do with Audrey, and strove to keep up.

She was out of breath by the time Jeremy paused near a door in an obscure corner of the second floor, opened it, and stood back to let her enter ahead of him. As soon as Mary crossed the threshold, Jeremy turned away, slammed the door, and retreated, shutting her in with Malcolm Mackenzie.

Chapter 7

She was alone with him. The door closed. Even the inadequate chaperonage of Jeremy gone.

"Don't run away yet," Malcolm said. He came to her where she stood next to the door and placed his hand on the door frame. "Don't worry, Mary. Ye won't have to put up with me for long. Me dad's sent for me and m' brothers. We're off home to Kilmorgan."

Mary's protests died on her lips. "Oh." Her spirits, which had risen considerably upon seeing him, deflated. "Because of the uprising?"

"Aye. Me dad doesn't want his sons anywhere near Prince Teàrlach if he tries to march this way. Afraid we'll go mad and join him."

Mary's heart beat faster. Not so much for the thought of Charles Stuart heading for Edinburgh, but from Malcolm declaring he was leaving. The encounter finished almost before it had begun.

"When are you going?" she asked, voice faltering.

"Tomorrow."

"Oh," she repeated.

A strange emptiness filled her. But Mary should want Mal

gone, shouldn't she? Out of her life where he wouldn't plague her? She'd return with her father to Lincolnshire, Malcolm would remove to the north of Scotland, and their paths would not cross again.

This was wrong somehow. Their flirtation couldn't be over this soon. Their encounter was like a sonnet whose first lines had been written, but the last couplet left unfinished. Mary would be forever waiting for the rhyme at the end of the line.

"In light o' that, we have much work to do," Malcolm was saying. He didn't move from his stance over her, his strong hand resting near her cheek. "If ye want young Audrey off with Jeremy, we must move quick."

Mary blinked. "How do *you* know I'm trying to persuade Jeremy to elope with her?"

"Because I've made friends with Jeremy, and it's clear to anyone with eyes that he won't be happy unless he's wed to your sister. So we must get them married and away. I have friends in France they can stay with while things are settled. Are ye prepared to help me or no?"

"I . . ." Mary forced her thoughts in order. "Yes—I do want her gone. My father will be taking us back to Lincolnshire in the next week, so it must be soon."

"Good." Malcolm reached into his pocket for a folded paper. He leaned close to Mary and touched it to her nose. "This will tell Audrey Jeremy's feelings for her. I have a few more things to put into place, and then the pair of young lovers can be together without restraint."

Mary stared at him in surprise. "This is madness. Why should you help us?"

Mal shrugged. "Why shouldn't I? I see unhappiness, I want to fix it. I'm a youngest son, buffeted around by the wills of older brothers and my father—me life isn't me own most of the time. But maybe I can help another youngest son have the life he deserves."

Mary hesitated. Though she was practical enough to seize an opportunity when it was thrust at her, she was also practical enough to be wary. "Are you certain you're not a spy for my father? Ready to rush to him and declare you've caught Audrey in the act of betraying him? Perhaps you also want to discredit Jeremy, and his entire family?"

Malcolm looked at her in such amazement Mary realized she was completely wrong. "Ye have a wild imagination, ye do, lass. Me, work for a bloody English aristo?" He pressed his hand to his chest. "What kind of man do ye take me for?"

Mal's indignation was real. As was his hurt. He expected her to trust him implicitly, was surprised when she didn't. He certainly had plenty of arrogance.

"My apologies," Mary said. "I'm surrounded by intrigue more than anyone should be. It's made me think everyone a spy, or at least out for themselves."

"A wise way to look at the world." Mal brushed her cheek with the letter. "But that's not how I want ye to think of me. Not that my family isn't busy spying on each other, but I'll keep ye well out of that."

Hope rose in her. If Malcolm *could* help Audrey be free—and she knew from her father that the Duke of Kilmorgan's family were wealthy enough to do anything they pleased—Mary would have one worry off her mind.

She snatched the letter and shoved it into her pocket. "Thank you, Mr. . . . Lord Malcolm. This is splendid of you, but they must *not* be caught. It isn't a game. It's Audrey's life."

He flashed her another offended look. "I suppose ye can't know how expert I am at smuggling people to and fro, entirely undetected by anyone. Usually I'm smuggling meself, but take my word—I'm very good at it. I can move like a ghost, me, and anyone I move with me, is unseen as well."

According to Mary's father, all Scotsmen were duplicitous creatures who lived to outsmart the law and the excise men. The smuggling up and down the coast and even through the middle of Scotland was notorious. But perhaps duplicity was what Mary needed just now.

Mary let out a quick breath. "Once Audrey is married to Jeremy, I will certainly thank you then. Her happiness is what I long for most of all."

"What about *you*, Mary?" Mal caught her hand, trapped it. His fingers were much larger than hers, warm, and callused. He worked with these hands, the skin rough and broken. So unlike the soft, well-manicured fingers of Lord Halsey. "What will ye do after? Go tamely back to Lincolnshire? Or run away with me? I can take ye far from here, give ye anything ye want."

Mary wished he wouldn't say things like that, wouldn't stir her longing. The thought of duty today was somehow not the comfort it had been yesterday.

"Never mind about me," she said quickly. "As long as Audrey is happy, that will be enough."

Malcolm stepped closer, shaking his head. "Never let it be enough, lass. People like us, we have to snatch up our happiness as soon as we find it. And not let go."

He lifted her hand to his mouth, his breath burning the skin on the inside of her wrist as he took a tiny bite.

Mary's heart nearly stopped beating. She'd never felt anything like it, the scrape of teeth on sensitive skin, the fire that plunged straight from there to the join of her legs.

Malcolm looked at her, his mouth still at her wrist, the wickedness in his eyes stealing what was left of her breath. He took another little bite, then another. He worked his way up her arm until stopped by the lace at her elbow.

Malcolm lifted his head. He transferred his fingertips to her cheek, caressing there before he skimmed down her throat to the tops of her breasts. He stood so close now that the rise of his chest touched hers.

Just when Mary thought he would stop, finished, Malcolm leaned to take his lips along the path his fingers had—cheek, throat, breasts. Mary's head went back, her body rising to his mouth, whether she willed it or no.

"You'll ruin me," she whispered.

Malcolm studied her, his amber-colored gaze intense. "Marry me, lass, and I'll ruin ye every day."

Mary's senses came back in a dizzying rush. "What?"

"Why not? Crazed though I might be, I'll make ye a far better husband than that bastard Halsey."

Mary should want to spring to Halsey's defense, as she had last night. Even if she felt no passion for the man, she should at least have loyalty.

Yesterday, she had. She'd been proud of being useful to her father, ready to be the steadfast wife. Today, her reason had flown to the winds.

Was this who she truly was? Easily turned from her path by a man with strong hands and unusual eyes?

You've already ruined me, she wanted to say. *You're stripping away the masks I hide behind, even from myself.*

Malcolm drew the edge of his palm from her stomacher to her breasts. "Ye have such fire in ye, Mary. I want to hold it in my hands."

His warmth was intoxicating. She wanted to imbibe it and everything about him. Make memories with him to hold in the chill of the long nights to come.

She didn't resist at all when Malcolm tilted her head back, bringing her against him at the same time, and kissed her on the mouth.

Every thought in Mal's head stilled at the touch of Mary's lips. Her mouth was a place of softness, her every breath honey and spice.

She didn't know how to kiss, he realized after a heartbeat. She'd never done this before.

The thought spiked a mad ferocity through him. Malcolm was her first—Halsey hadn't gotten to her yet.

He slid his hand behind her back and eased Mary up to him, gentling his lips to show her how it was done. Her soft pressure in response sent another ache through Malcolm, one that made him harder than he had time to be right now.

He slipped his other hand behind her back, completing the embrace, and dipped his tongue between her lips.

Mary's gasp warmed his mouth. She resisted for a brief moment, then Malcolm felt her relax in his arms, and she tentatively flicked her tongue against his.

Teaching her would be the most wonderful joy of his life. Malcolm pressed her harder up into him, tasting her, opening her. Mary's hands fluttered against his arms, then her grip strengthened, pressing tight as she gave herself over to the kiss.

He opened her mouth, licked inside. His blood heated as she moved her lips in response, eager to learn. Malcolm caught her tongue between his teeth and lightly bit.

The noise in her throat as he did so completed his arousal. He was as hard as he'd ever been, but release would be a joy he'd have to put off. As much as Mal wanted to lay Mary back over the heavy desk and shove her skirts to her hips, she wasn't ready for that.

It would kill him to wait, but he had to. In the meantime, Malcolm could think of plenty of other things to do.

He released her tongue to nibble her lips, then pressed her up to him for another kiss. Mal slid his hands to her stomacher, imagining releasing her from its confines. Up to her breasts, cupping them, thumbs brushing the flesh that swelled over the lace at her neckline. Prim Mary, her chest rising, clutched his coat as she tasted what was forbidden.

She didn't want to stop. Malcolm made that decision. He knew if he kept on kissing her, he *would* lay her down on the surface of the desk and show her they didn't have to be entirely bare to take deep pleasure with each other.

Mary dragged in a long breath as the kiss eased to an end, but she wouldn't look at him. Her cheeks were red, her eyes downcast.

Mal put his hand under her chin, gently tilting her head up. "Don't feel shame, love. There's nothing shameful about kissing a man because you enjoy it."

The look in her eyes when she finally met his gaze wasn't shame. It was defiance, and fear.

But not of Mal, he understood. If he'd frightened her, Mary wouldn't shrink away—she'd gather up her skirts and kick him in the balls, then tell him what she thought of him as he doubled over in pain.

"You tempt me to what I know I cannot have," Mary said, her voice shaking. "I can't let you. You're kind to help Audrey and Jeremy. But I won't pay you like this."

"*Pay?*" The Mackenzies were famous for their swift tempers, and Mal lost his quickly. "What the devil do ye take me for, woman? Ye've been in thrall to those who use you too long if ye think *that*."

Mary looked at him in surprise. But then, hadn't Mal told himself all along that he was helping Mary's sister so Mary would smile at him, kiss him? As she was doing?

But he didn't want this. Not Mary giving him kisses because she thought it favors for favors returned.

"I'm trying to tell ye, lass." Malcolm gentled his voice. "Ye owe me nothing. If I kiss ye, it's because you're sweet in the sunshine, and I want to enjoy you. I'm following my heart. I learned at an early age it's better to do that, or I'll end up sour and rigid, like me dad."

"Following your heart." Mary's look turned wistful. "I don't think it's possible. Not in these times. Not for most."

"Now, Mary, that's a sad thing to hear ye say. And you so young. If ye don't follow your heart, what else is there?"

"Honor. Integrity. What of those?"

Mal shook his head. "Those are nothing if you have no passion. Without passion you're living only for how others see you, while inside you're dying."

Mary gave him a stricken look. She said nothing, but Malcolm knew he'd hit upon the truth. She was slowly growing numb inside, thinking honor and duty would prop her up. Mal was giving her a glimpse of something else, another choice, and it was frightening her to death.

Malcolm closed both hands around hers and pulled her to him. "Ye hold on to me, Mary, and you'll be all right. I'll never let ye fall."

Mary's eyes shone with sudden tears. And hope.

Malcolm loved how she could flash from mood to mood, much like he could. If she ever seemed cool, it was because she'd built a wall between herself and the world, so that the world could not hurt her. Malcolm was putting his hand to that wall and doggedly tearing down the bricks.

Mary rose on her tiptoes and closed her eyes over tears as she kissed him.

Warm, desperate woman filled Mal's arms, a woman hungry for the small taste of passion he offered her in this room.

A wretched shame that Jeremy had to choose that moment to fling open the door and charge inside.

"They've come," he said as Mary sprang away from Mal. "Mary, your aunt is going mad looking for you. I can't put her off any longer."

"Slow down, lad," Malcolm said. "Who's come?"

"The Jacobites, you slow-top," Jeremy answered, agitation and excitement in his every move. "Charles Stuart and his followers. They marched straight past Stirling and have come to take Edinburgh."

Chapter 8

"There you are, Mary," Aunt Danae said in relief when Mary hurried down the stairs. "We must be off." Aunt Danae was in the Bancrofts' lofty lower hall, her skirts dancing as she swung from the maid with her wrap to a passing footman. "Is our carriage here yet, man? Well, hurry and fetch it, then!"

"Off?" Mary's heart thumped as she stepped from the last stair and took her cloak from the worried maid. "To Lincolnshire?"

This was a disaster. Malcolm's last words to Mary, before he'd ushered her out the door with Jeremy, were to wait for his instructions. He'd assess what was going on and when they could proceed with their plans for the elopement. Several hundred Highlanders and Charles Stuart making camp in the King's Park might put a damper on things, Mal said, but he promised it would be only temporary.

Mary was torn between thinking him mad and agreeing they shouldn't panic. She was determined not to let a mere uprising come between her and her sister's happiness.

"Not Lincolnshire," Aunt Danae answered. "Your father has no intention of leaving now, not when he can be in the thick of things. He wants us back at the house in Edinburgh. I told him I should take you and Audrey to England, but he's adamant. They can only win if we all flee, he said."

At any other time, Mary would rush to her father, imploring him to let them spirit Audrey to safety. Today, however, she held her tongue. If Malcolm could get Audrey and Jeremy away to France, Audrey would be safer there.

Mary wasn't afraid for herself—they'd taken a large house in Edinburgh and the earl kept plenty of guards around his family. Wilfort was prideful but not reckless.

Home then. To Edinburgh. For now.

Malcolm stepped off the road into the thick grasses on the side of it as a column of Highlanders wrapped in plaids—swords, dirks, and muskets in place—came marching along. Not a lot of them—this was not the bulk of the army, which had already set up outside the walls.

Malcolm was surprised they'd gotten this far. Johnny Cope was to have taken care of the rebellion before Charles and his followers ever reached Perth, but he'd been caught napping.

That was the English for you, Mal thought. Having to take orders and get money from afar, Cope had waited too long. He'd finally marched north to intercept the Jacobites, but hadn't wanted to engage where the sons of Scotland would have all the advantage. Cope's army had skimmed past the Jacobites to Inverness, and they were who knew where now.

So Will, who had his finger on the pulse of both sides of the affair, had told Mal last night. Malcolm was following the conflict as well—though Will was an artist at it—but Mal couldn't take that deep an interest in it. The succession question had been decided long ago, and a few Campbells and Macdonalds whipped into a frenzy in the last weeks wasn't going to change things.

Malcolm personally wanted nothing more than to perfect his recipe for the best Scots *uisge* ever made, build himself a house, and find a woman to warm his nights.

He was a simple man. Sad that he didn't live in simple times.

Some of the officers were on horseback, and Mal recognized a few of them. He'd met them on his travels or on business, or at university. When they saw Malcolm, they broke discipline to give him a grin and a wave. Cocksure, they were.

One Highlander Mal knew very well indeed. The man rode with confidence on a fine bay horse, wrapped in a thick plaid that covered him from shoulders to knees. His boots were muddy but supple, made of finest leather. His basket-hilted sword hung prominently from the strap across his chest, and he had a pistol tucked into a holster at his side. The Scottish bonnet set at an angle on his head held a white silk rose, the symbol of Charles Edward Stuart.

"Bloody hell," Malcolm said.

The man turned his head and saw him. Malcolm expected him to call out, as he'd done Malcolm's whole life, *Do something useful or get out of the way, runt!*

But Duncan never spoke. He met Mal's gaze with a scornful one, berating Malcolm silently for not marching with him.

Their gazes locked for a long time, unspoken admonitions passing between them.

Then Daniel Duncannon Mackenzie, oldest son of the Duke of Kilmorgan, and Jacobite to his very marrow, turned and rode on with his men. Off to meet his prince, and plot the takeover of Britain.

"Don't be afraid, Mary." Halsey patted his nose with his handkerchief, returned it to his pocket, and picked up his heavy fork to resume his meal. "Cope has landed with his men south of here, and these rebels will be thrown out in a few days' time. All will be over, except for the hangings. I imagine those will take some while."

Mary stabbed at her quail in wine sauce and didn't answer. Across from her, Audrey flinched. She didn't like to hear about violence.

Audrey looked much like Mary—fair-haired with a touch of red in it, and blue-eyed. But while Mary's face was a bit round, holding the robustness of her father, Audrey had the more delicate features of their late mother. Her blue eyes were large in her face, her chin pointed, her mouth soft. When she smiled, she was lovely and ethereal.

"I'm still uncertain whether we should stay," Aunt Danae said.

"War is men's business. The girls and I should retire to Lincolnshire. There is much to be done there—winter is nearly upon us."

Wilfort, at the head of the table, cleared his throat and spoke in his usual steely tones. "Sending our women running will signal to the Jacobites that we believe they'll win. They won't. Even if they easily took Perth and Edinburgh, they cannot prevail in the end." Lord Wilfort had a fine-boned face and thin body, but his slight build belied a man of strength. Mary had seen men twice her father's size cower before his unwavering blue gaze. His long black frock coat was free of ornamentation, except for dark blue braid trimming its lapels, and his wig was plain with a single tail. Wilfort, like Halsey, did not believe in ostentation.

Wilfort continued. "Charles might be ensconced in Holyrood now, but he hasn't taken the castle, and he never will. Once reinforcements come from the south, they'll be done for. The entire Jacobite enterprise is badly timed and ill prepared for. It will come to naught."

Perhaps, but so far, it seemed fate favored the Jacobites. Charles had come from the west, raising an army along the way, had walked into Edinburgh with no one making much effort to stop him. Today, in the middle of the city, Charles's father, James, had been declared King of Scotland and England, with Charles his regent. The so-called Union between Scotland and England was considered null and void, and Scotland was a free country.

"Audrey should go, at the very least," Aunt Danae continued. "I shudder to think what will happen if they start breaking into houses. Mary and I are stalwart, but Audrey is only eighteen. A girl still."

"No, no," Audrey said quickly. "I'm not afraid."

The fact that Audrey had actually spoken at table betrayed her agitation. In the Lennox family, unmarried ladies were to sit in polite silence while the men talked of whatever they wished, the girls speaking only when directly asked a question.

Audrey's outburst had nothing to do with the Scots. Mary had explained to her this afternoon about the plans for her elopement.

The earl gave his youngest daughter a stern frown. Halsey appeared surprised and disapproving that Audrey had spoken. He looked across the table at Mary. "Mary, what say you? Shall Audrey stay or go?"

Mary didn't like the way Halsey pinned her with his gaze, as though his question were a test of some sort.

Mary chose her words with care. "I think Father is correct that running in fear will give the wrong impression. On the other hand, I believe we should ready ourselves in case we must leave at a moment's notice. Audrey's things should be packed at the very least."

Audrey shot Mary a grateful look before she went back to picking over her game bird. Lord Bancroft, Jeremy's father, had supplied the quail, the best his gamekeeper had bagged today.

Halsey was still watching Mary. He assessed her answer, then gave a little nod, as though she'd done well.

Why had she never noticed him doing such things before? Or perhaps she had but not paid attention. Once she'd convinced herself that marrying Halsey was the right thing to do, she'd shut her eyes to his character, his mannerisms, himself. She'd seen only his role, and not the man. With Malcolm, it was impossible to see anything but the man.

His crooked smile, his warm eyes, the rumble of his voice, the firm pressure of his lips. Mary's throat closed up, and she set down her fork.

Mal had showed her, too clearly, that there were other paths, other choices out there, an entire world of them.

But not for Mary. She was dependent on her father, his money, his whims. What would happen if she decided to run off with Malcolm, only to find that Malcolm hadn't meant to marry her after all? Had been amusing himself with her, as many a young man did with a naïve woman? Mary would be ruined, her father would be within his rights to turn his back on her, and Halsey might sue him for trying to give him damaged goods. Mary's heart burned, and her appetite fled.

No one but Audrey noticed. Halsey, her father, and Aunt Danae went on speculating about the Jacobites and how long they'd be in Edinburgh. Audrey shot Mary a puzzled look, clearly knowing something had happened.

After supper, Mary played the harpsichord in the drawing room, as halfheartedly as she always did, while Audrey pretended to embroider. Mary noticed, while she dragged her way through the piece, that Audrey was poking her needle in and out of the same hole, stitching nothing.

Mary declared herself tired after playing only one selection, and stated that Audrey was tired too. So much had happened today.

Aunt Danae clearly wanted to remain and discuss things with Wilfort and Halsey, and so Mary linked arms with Audrey, and they walked upstairs.

They'd reached a landing on an upper floor when Halsey's voice brought Mary to a startled halt. "Mary."

Halsey climbed to them while Mary and Audrey waited in trepidation. The shadows were deep here, candles in the hall above not giving much light.

Audrey's eyes widened, a mixture of terror and determination in them. She feared Halsey knew everything.

"Go on up to your room," Mary said to Audrey, patting her hand. "I'll be right behind you."

Audrey shot her a look of gratitude, gathered her skirts, and scampered on up the stairs, ankles flashing.

"You are good to her," Halsey said, reaching Mary. "A fine trait, is compassion."

Mary had no patience with Halsey tonight, but she fell back on her training and curtsied politely. "Thank you, sir."

Halsey closed his fingers over Mary's arm. "You are the perfect woman, you know. Kindness, courtesy, no foolish idea that you know better than anyone else about everything. And so very comely." He brushed one knuckle down her cheek, and Mary tried not to flinch. "And yet, not so comely as to make other men want a conquest with you."

Mary wasn't quite certain how to respond to that. *Well, thank you very much.* Halsey was master at following a compliment with a slap.

"I'll never compromise you," Halsey continued. "No one will count on their fingers and snigger when *our* first child is born. There will never be question as to the legitimacy of my sons."

Quite glad to hear it, Mary longed to say.

"But you will learn, Mary, that though I might not always show it, I am a man of needs. I'll try not to frighten you with them, but I will tell you now that I believe in making good use of the marriage bed. One reason I agreed to you is because you seem a courageous young woman. But if you have any timidity in regard to that side of marriage, I warn you to rid yourself of it now. Have a talk with your aunt if you're worried."

Blast Malcolm. Two days ago, if Halsey had said these things to her, Mary would have regarded him calmly then gone to Aunt Danae for an explanation of what he meant and would expect. If Mary couldn't have love, she could at least be held up as a paragon of wifeliness.

What a sham she was! And what a fool to think any sort of marriage with Halsey would fulfill her, in any way.

Malcolm had shown her, in two brief encounters, that there could be more to her life. Even if she never saw him again after this night, Mal had awakened something in her that she'd never put to sleep again.

Only the meticulous manners drilled into her from childhood kept her from flinging off Halsey's touch and running screaming from him. Mary made herself dip into another polite curtsy.

"You need have no qualms, sir." Because Mary intended never to go near Halsey's wedding bed. How she'd go about calling off the betrothal, which was a mesh of legal agreements, settlements, and signed documents, she didn't know yet, but she would find a way.

"Good." Halsey took her hand and squeezed it. "We understand each other. I had no doubts of it."

He lifted her hand, turned her palm upward, and kissed it. When Malcolm had done the same thing, his breath had been hot, his mouth strong. Halsey's lips were thin, his breath cool and moist. Mary want to snatch her hand away, but she swallowed and held still.

Halsey straightened. Then he deliberately reached out, put his hand over her breast, and squeezed.

Foulness rose in Mary's stomach. Halsey couldn't touch much. Her stomacher, bodice, corset, and gathered lace made certain he held mostly fabric and boning. But Mary felt the squeeze, Halsey's surety of possession.

Mal had cupped her breast as well. Halsey did it to tell her that her body belonged to him. Mal had done it to learn her, and to give her pleasure in return.

Halsey squeezed again, harder. Mary refused to let tears prick her eyes. She firmed her jaw.

Halsey didn't notice her reaction. He flicked the lace on her décolletage and gave her a shallow bow. "Good night then, Mary."

Another curtsy—Mary had perfected them. "Good night, sir."

She turned without haste and walked up the stairs with decorum. She'd never betray she was shaking all over, barely able to breathe.

Behind her, Halsey sniffled, and when she glanced back, he had his handkerchief at his nose again.

Mary reached her chamber, hurried quickly to the washbasin, and brought up the quail in sweet wine sauce into it.

When Malcolm reached home late that evening, after several hours of moving from public house to public house, he found disaster waiting for him.

He'd been out trying to shore up arrangements for Jeremy and Audrey, but the Jacobites' arrival had made things difficult. As Malcolm banged back into his house, irritated and disappointed, he found his brother Angus, Alec's twin, just coming down the stairs.

"Runt," Angus said in acknowledgment.

Malcolm stopped in amazement. Naughton shut the door behind Mal, bolting it hard, as though fearing Teàrlach would rush up the hill and press-gang them all into his army.

"What the devil are you doing here?" Malcolm demanded of Angus. "You're supposed to be looking after Kilmorgan Castle and Da. We're to join him there tomorrow." Not that Mal had planned to obey.

"I *am* looking after Dad," Angus said, a sparkle in his eyes that said he knew hell was coming. Angus looked much like Alec, of course, but there were differences—Angus's face was not as sharp, and he wore a constant smug look that came from knowing he was their father's favorite. "You're not going to Kilmorgan. Da is here instead. Wanting to see you."

He'd barely finished his words before a bellowed "*Malcolm!*" shook the entire house.

"Bloody hell," Malcolm said with vehemence, and went to face his doom.

Chapter 9

Daniel William Mackenzie, ninth Duke of Kilmorgan, was a large man of almost solid muscle. Only Will topped him in height, and only Duncan had more breadth.

Malcolm, while tall and broad of shoulder himself, had long endured being shouted at and cuffed by this giant who had no softness in him, at least none since their mother died.

Before then, though Mal had been very young before Allison Mackenzie had gone, his father had smiled, laughed, and even played with his unruly sons. The duke had been big, strong, formidable, and frightening, but at least human.

After Allison's death, their father had retreated deep within himself, growing harsher every passing year. Anything of compassion, love, and humor had dried up and vanished.

Now the duke lived to bully his neighbors and expect his sons to be brilliant men and make him even more prideful than he was. He was pleased with Angus, who could do no wrong in his eyes; William, who at least made a good spy; and Alec, who made a good spy's assistant, even if he did like to waste time drawing and painting.

The duke showed vast disappointment in his eldest son, declaring that Duncan's stubborn Jacobite sympathies would destroy the family. If Duncan were arrested and tried for treason, he would drag the rest of them down with him.

The duke also was vastly disappointed in his youngest son, Malcolm, who talked constantly of the future instead of the glories of the past. Mal spent his time thinking of ways to improve farm output, sales of whisky, and Scottish trade with England and France. Making money.

Mal was young and citified, in his father's eyes, never mind Malcolm could hunt and fish with his bare hands and thought nothing of walking miles across country, making friends wherever he went. Mal knew the Kilmorgan lands better than any of them.

But Malcolm didn't like to sit in the great hall at Kilmorgan Castle, quaffing ale and glorifying the days when the clan chiefs held all the power. Those times were gone, in Mal's opinion. Scotsmen were turning to practical matters, like building better roads, better ships, discovering the wider world, and studying it and the heavens with a new understanding. The days of cattle thieving and besting the clan in the next glen were coming to an end.

The duke sat in the dining room at the head of the table with the remains of a repast spread before him. Mal's father's idea of a reviving snack was what most people ate in a seven-course meal.

"Good evening, Father," Malcolm said before the duke could speak. He moved to the sideboard and sloshed a small measure of whisky into a glass. The only way to face his father was with strong drink in hand.

"Where have ye been, runt?" The duke sopped up the last of the sauce on his plate with a piece of bread, stuffed it in his mouth, and washed it down with a large draught of whisky. He drank the stuff like water. "Even Alec's here, though I hear Will is out whoring as usual. What have ye been doing?"

The duke's bloodshot eyes fixed on Malcolm, expecting Mal to confess he'd slipped down to Holyrood to kiss Prince Teàrlach's pale ass.

"Talking to people," Mal said without inflection. It never did to show fear in front of his father—he'd take it, twist it, and eat you alive. "Finding out what's going on."

"Your brother Duncan is here," the duke said, bitterness in his voice.

"I saw him," Malcolm said. "In passing. On a horse. He looked pleased wi' himself."

"He's a damn great bloody fool!" The duke slapped the table, making dishes and silverware dance.

Malcolm moved back to the sideboard and fetched the whisky decanter to refill his father's glass. "Is that why you've come t' Edinburgh?" he asked. "Because of Duncan?"

The duke held out the glass and raised his eyes to Malcolm. The man hadn't slept, that was apparent, probably not for some days.

As sometimes happened when the duke was overly weary, Mal saw something in his eyes that cried out to him, a desperation that the man thought no one could ease. The trouble was, whenever Mal tried to reach that desperation, he was unceremoniously shoved aside.

"We have to stop him," the duke said. "Duncan. He'll get himself killed—hanged, drawn, and quartered, the idiot. The heir of my loins, split into pieces, to my shame. Kilmorgan will be seized, and we'll be nothing. Wouldn't Macdonald love that?"

He meant Horace Macdonald, to whom Allison McNab had been promised long ago, before she'd run away to marry a Mackenzie. According to Angus, who knew the tale, Allison and the duke had met by chance, fallen madly in love, and eloped. The Macdonalds had never forgiven the Mackenzies for it. A romantic story, but anything romantic had been stamped out of this man now growling at the head of the table.

Malcolm sat down. His father didn't always like his sons sitting in his presence, but tonight the duke didn't pay much attention.

"Duncan's got a mind of his own," Malcolm said. "But dinnae worry. This uprising will come to nothing. The English will charge up here with a large army, and Teàrlach will rush to the nearest ship and sail back to France. I've seen his portrait—the prince's. He looks the sort who likes to dress up and hear men cheer him, but in the thick of things, he'll have no mettle."

"You're wrong." More steel entered the duke's voice. "He's the kind of man who does nae understand the odds against him and thinks he can win by determination alone. He counts on not only the Highlanders but the Lowlanders and the English rallying to join him. Why the hell should they? He's a dreamer, and he'll dream us all into disaster."

Malcolm said nothing, because he privately agreed.

"What d'ye expect us to do then?" Mal asked after his father had drunk a few more swallows. "Throw a blanket over Duncan and drag him home?"

"Aye!" The duke half climbed to his feet. "That's exactly what ye and your good-for-nothing brothers need to do. Go out there and find him!"

"On the moment?" It was past midnight, and Mal had hoped for a little sleep at least.

"Aye, on the moment!" The duke was all the way out of his seat. "Now, ye whelp. I want Duncan here so I can rip that cockade off his hat and throw it in the fire. Trumped up, arrogant, son of a—"

His last words slurred, then cut off. The duke glanced in sudden suspicion at his whisky, then glared at Malcolm. "Ye bloody little—"

His fall slid two plates to the floor, where they broke on the carpet with a muffled clatter. The louder noise was the sound of the duke's body hitting first the table, then the carpet.

"What the devil?" Angus rushed in, followed by Alec and Naughton. Angus gave Mal a glare worthy of the duke. "What did ye do to him?"

"I didn't have t' do much, did I?" Mal said. "He's pissing drunk."

Angus growled and demanded Naughton to help. Their father's body was limp, unresisting, as Naughton and Angus struggled to drag the man out. Alec and Mal stepped aside, happy to let Angus take over.

Getting the duke up the stairs would be impossible, so Angus took him into a side chamber they kept set up for guests who might grow too inebriated to walk home. Now the duke would grace the room.

When the door shut, Alec, so unlike Angus in personality, turned to Malcolm. "Tell me the truth, runt. What did ye do?"

Malcolm shrugged. "I dosed him with a little laudanum. He'd have gone on for hours if I hadn't, and he needs the sleep."

Alec grinned. "He'll hate you when he wakes up."

"Ah, well. Nothing new there."

Alec glanced at the door Angus had closed. They could hear both Angus and Naughton cursing as they heaved the duke into the small bed.

"He wants us to go fetch Duncan, does he?" Alec asked.

"That he does," Mal said. "I have an idea how to go about it."

Alec's eyes were as red-rimmed as the duke's had been, but he was far livelier. "How's that?"

"We get Will to do it," Malcolm said with a grin. "Then we'll have some more drink and help find me a ship out of here."

Alec laughed. "You're as mad as the rest of us," he said, but he snatched up his greatcoat and followed Mal out into the chill night.

Will was indeed with women again, as the duke had suspected. By the time they dragged him out of *that* brothel, and he threw off his drunken Highlander act, it turned out Will already knew where Duncan was. At Holyrood.

"Why?" Mal asked as the three of them strode through fog and mist down the hill toward the gates. "Is he intimate with yon prince now?"

"*Intimate* is a word that can be interpreted many ways," Will said, sounding cheerful.

"Aye, I know," Mal answered impatiently. "That's why I said it. What makes you think they'll let us in there to see him?"

"I know people," Will said.

"Of course you do," Alec said under his breath.

Mal gave Alec's shoulder a squeeze. He knew why his brother was morose, but maybe Malcolm could help him in that regard. Jeremy and Audrey would be better off with an escort to France, and Mal resolved to shove Alec off with them. Mal would miss his favorite brother, but he wanted to see the man happy. Besides, Alec's pining was getting wearying.

"So, we're to march up to the door of the palace and knock?" Mal asked Will.

"Why not?" Will quickened his pace. "Come on—don't straggle."

"Duncan probably told the soldiers to shoot us on sight," Mal said to Alec.

"Aye," Alec agreed. "Would surprise me not a whit."

Mal growled. "Ye sound like a bloody Englishman. Need to cure you o' that."

"Be quiet, runt."

Mal fell silent as they passed the jumbled houses inside the city gates. In the old days, gates like these had been made to withstand sieges. If soldiers made it through the outer gates, they still had to pass under the gate house, where holes in the ceiling could let down flaming oil, arrows, or men with large swords.

These days, gates were quaint reminders of another time, the gatehouse a place for vendors to sell flowers and souvenirs of the city to gawping tourists.

Tonight Highland soldiers lounged about, keeping watch, staying warm the usual Scots way—wrapped in kilts and passing flasks. Many were in great kilts, plaids wrapped around their shoulders and belted at the waist, cloth to keep out the chilling mists of Edinburgh. All were armed.

Will wrapped his own flapping plaid around him and walked right into the middle of them. He'd gotten most of the way through, heading across the courtyard that fronted Holyrood, before he was stopped. A lantern flashed in his face.

"Who is that?" the sentry barked.

Will drew himself up. "Lord William Mackenzie," he said in stentorian tones.

The sentry, a tough-looking man with wiry black hair and a once-broken nose, only glared at him. "What clan?" he demanded.

"Mackenzie of Kilmorgan."

"Oh, aye? What are ye doing here, then?"

"I could ask you the same," Will said easily. "We're not here to murder his highness; we're here to talk to me good-for-nothing brother. Kindly send word we're out here."

The man didn't move. A lordling asking him to kindly do something clearly had no interest for him. Other sentries had joined him, looking as implacable as the first. Another man, younger, a lieutenant or captain by the epaulets on his coat, came up behind the sentries.

"Willie Mackenzie. Well met."

The other man's hand came out, and Will clasped it. "Cameron," Will said. "Ye remember my brothers."

"I do." The large, red-haired man nodded at them. Mal recognized him as Stuart Cameron, a friend of Will's. Most people in Scotland were friends of Will's. "Come to throw in your lot with us?" Stuart asked.

"Come to have words with our brother. He in there?"

"Duncan? Oh, aye." Stuart rolled his eyes. "Are ye going to convince him to abandon us? Please say ye are."

"Meaning ye stand a better chance if he's gone?" Will paused, as though considering this. "I'll do me best. But it's really up to him, and me father."

"Lord help us." Stuart wrung Will's hand again. "We'll get drunk when this is done, eh? The ladies in Paris are anxious to have us back."

"Done." Will clapped Stuart on the shoulder.

Stuart stepped back and bellowed orders at the soldiers to let them through—and not to kill them, or rob them, or fight them. The men either glowered or laughed, and parted the way for the three brothers.

Will led them through the throng, crossing the courtyard full of fires, men, ale, and the inevitable women who would make a few pence warming a soldier's night. A small door at the side of the main gate opened for them, and Malcolm stepped inside after his brothers, into the heart of the Jacobite army.

Chapter 10

Holyrood House was built in a quadrangle around a courtyard, a bit like the house where Jeremy Drake lived, but on a much grander scale. Arched walkways surrounded the four sides, and windows marched along three floors, flanked by columns. Mal, who was interested in architecture, craned his head to take it in, consigning the columns, pediments, and symmetrical design to his compartmentlike memory.

Though those they passed were celebrating victory, Malcolm was not about to let down his guard. He knew how easily Highlanders could go from affable drinkers to killing machines in a few seconds flat. Hell, Alec could do it if you woke him too early in the morning.

For now there were called greetings, toasts to the prince, taunts to poor Johnny Cope, whose army had fled before them once, and was likely to again.

Duncan was on the far side of the courtyard, in a group of officers. Will and Alec headed to him, returning greetings to Highlanders who knew them.

Mal halted on his journey to Duncan to cut out a pair of men he knew. "Gair Murray," he said. "What the bleeding hell are *you* doing here?"

The man with a kilt so weathered Mal couldn't tell what had been its original color, sun-bleached hair, and a face as baked as his kilt gave Mal a nod.

"Looking to make coin, what else?" Gair smiled, his teeth crooked but whole. Gair was only about ten years older than Mal, but his dedication to life on the sea had aged his skin to tough leather.

The man with him, as stringy and tanned as Gair, was called Padruig, his first mate, who was never far from the man's side. Padruig, as usual, wore more weapons than Gair—two long knives, a pistol, and a musket over his shoulder. He had a patch covering one eye, giving Mal a warning stare out of his good eye, which was sea gray.

Mal hid his pleasure at finding them. He'd been looking for Gair up and down all night, but he kept his question causal. It did not pay to sound too eager or desperate with Gair. "And what are you two selling the good prince?"

Gair answered readily. "Arms, rations, ammunition, ponies, blankets, knives, swords, names of men eager to join him, transportation, message service, and souvenirs." He took from his pocket a carving of what looked to be a rose, along with a piece of tartan. "Trinkets to remind him of his glorious time leading the Scots to victory."

"In other words, anything ye can convince him and his quartermaster t' buy," Mal said.

"Aye." Gair held out the carving, which was nicely done, and the blue and green plaid. "Only two shillings, since ye're a friend."

Mal kept his hands at his sides. If you touched something Gair handed you, he considered that you'd bought it, and Padruig would finger the hilt of a knife until you paid. "Does Teàrlach know you're a thief?"

"Aye," Gair said. "Doesn't everyone?"

"As it happens, I'm glad I chanced upon ye here. I might have a commission for ye."

"What is it, lad?" The questionable souvenirs disappeared, and Gair gave Mal a solicitous smile. Like looking at a shark, it was. "What can I do for his lordship who has more money than any young lad has a right to?"

"Aye, and I bust my balls for it." Gair had all sorts of arguments for why rich men should give him their money, of their own free will, of course. "I need safe passage to France. Can ye give me it?"

"To France? Are ye mad?" Gair tried to look astonished. "With every naval frigate watching the Scottish coast, every port on the lookout for French ships coming to the prince's aid, ye want me to sail you off to France?"

"Not me," Mal said, holding on to his patience. "A young lady and her husband. Once he becomes her husband, that is. I still have to sort that."

"Ah, I see. I'm to be giving a young man and his wife a honeymoon, am I?" Gair let out his quick laughter. "What a lovely way for a couple to start out in life, running an English blockade."

"Which you do all the time," Mal said. He knew damn well Gair would do this—his arguments were to justify the exorbitant price he'd get around to demanding. "War or peace, you fly past English ships without them ever being the wiser. I'm only asking you to do what you do every day of your life."

"Ye have much faith in me. I'm getting old, ain't I, Padruig? Harder for me to man a sail, innit?"

Out of the corner of Mal's eye, he saw Duncan striding out of the darkness for Will, and Alec looking around for Mal. Mal curbed his impatience. One of his brothers would come and drag him away very soon.

"I don't have time to argue with ye," Mal said. "How much to take them away tomorrow night?"

Gair stroked his bewhiskered chin. "Well, now, I—"

"Name it. Before Duncan comes over here and throws you out on your backside."

"He can't," Gair said. "I've been recruited by the bonnie prince himself."

"Never think me brothers can't do anything they've put their mind to. Or me. How much, Gair?"

He named his price, which was three times as much as any safe passage should be, even in troubled waters. Mal rolled his eyes, said "Done," and turned around to meet Alec.

"Godspeed," Gair said, his grating chuckle trailing behind Mal.

"Duncan's as foaming at the mouth as Da," Alec said as Mal met him halfway across the courtyard. "What were you doing with Gair Murray? Ye still have everything in your pockets? The shirt on your back?"

"I stayed outside his arm's reach and didn't let him or Padruig touch me. Is Duncan coming home quietly? Or do we have to truss him up?"

"He wants us to stay. Join him. Better still, run up north and convince all the Mackenzies back with us."

"Da would go apoplectic if he heard that," Mal said, his irritation at Duncan rising. Mal's father wasn't clan chief, however, despite his lofty title, which had been bestowed on Old Dan, the first Duke of Kilmorgan for favors received by a grateful Scottish king. If the current Mackenzie chief wanted to spill all the Mackenzies out of their lands, the duke couldn't stop them.

"Not our dilemma," Alec said. "We're being taken to meet the prince."

"What for?" Mal asked, frowning. "So we can build our own gallows and be done?"

Alec shrugged, not liking it any better. They reached Duncan and followed him from the quadrangle through a column-flanked door into the bowels of the palace, a place Mal had never been.

Unlike the castle at the other end of town, Holyrood was a royal residence. Charles's grandfather, James, had lived here when he'd been Prince of Wales, but he'd gone to London to be king. These days, aristocrats with connection to the English government lived in apartments upstairs, though Charles had now commandeered the rooms and ousted their inhabitants.

If Charles and his father, James, managed to take over, though, they wouldn't stay here and rule a free and independent Scotland, Mal was certain. Charles would go to London, boot out the Hanoverian king, and bring his father in from Rome to live in St. James's Palace. They'd strut around London, cultivating connections there, and the Scots would be left out in the cold again. The fact that the men in plaids, some barefoot, lounged in the courtyard, and men in well-tailored breeches and English coats wandered about inside, in the heart of the palace, only bolstered Mal's cynicism.

Prince Teàrlach mhic Seamas received them in a large room full of people. Servants and retainers ran about attending all the different masters in the chamber. Duncan walked among the Highland leaders as though Camerons and Macdonalds were his oldest and dearest friends.

"Your Highness," Duncan said, when Charles finally found the time to receive them. "My brothers, Will, Alec, and Malcolm Mackenzie."

Charles was a disappointment for Mal. Gossip in taverns and coffeehouses had built him up to be a man of vast charm and energy, the great hope who would lead Scotland to greatness.

What Mal saw was a man his exact age, twenty-five, with a receding chin and a high, sloping forehead. He wore a fair-haired wig that had bunched curls over each ear and a tail in the back. His dress was standard for an English gentleman—frock coat and knee breeches, waistcoat, neckcloth, fine stockings and shoes.

The Mackenzie brothers were all taller than Charles, who'd rectified that fact as they approached by backing up onto a stone step that separated one part of the room from another.

The prince's eyes sparkled with energy, that was true, and also with confidence that bordered on arrogance. But he had far less charm and the verve to lead than Will Mackenzie, who could make people do anything he wanted—much of the time without those in question even realizing it.

Charles's gaze lit on Mal, as though sensing his assessment. The gaze was interested but haughty—*Yes, we are of an age, but I was born a prince, chosen by God to rule.*

Mal noticed how the other men in the room looked at Charles, and it was not entirely with respect and tenderness. Lord George Murray, who commanded the army, and his ilk were experienced at fighting and tactics—plenty of men here had fought in British regiments in the wars on the Continent.

The clan chiefs who'd thrown in their lot with Charles were wily. They knew that if they won through, their stars would rise—a grateful king would bestow on them more titles and power, and perhaps give them the coveted lands of their neighbors who'd chosen to side with the English.

And some, like Duncan, truly believed they had a duty to fight for their rightful prince, whoever he might be. That line of succession had been disrupted—little matter that it had been done more than fifty years ago—and should be restored.

These men were risking everything they had and

everything they were, but the confidence in this room was palpable. Charles's army had walked right into Edinburgh without opposition. Forced the gates open in the wee hours of the morning, bowled over the sentries, and declared the city theirs. The triumph of that sparked in the air.

The prince began speaking to Duncan and his brothers in French. Mal knew plenty of French, as did Alec, the pair of them having spent much time learning about life in the streets of Paris. Duncan, who never left the Highlands and spoke only English and the Scots language, looked annoyed.

"We need the Mackenzies," Charles was saying. "Strong, brave men, like yourselves. They could turn the tide. If the Duke of Kilmorgan joins me, we cannot lose."

Have ye met any Mackenzies? Mal wanted to say, but kept his mouth shut.

Charles went on in this way for a time, and Alec, feeling Duncan's glare, finally translated for him.

Duncan bowed when Charles finished. "I have said so all along," Duncan answered in English. "Malcolm will be returning to Kilmorgan to speak to our father. If anyone can persuade the duke to take up the cause, it's the runt."

Charles looked puzzled at the last word, until Alec explained the nickname in French. Charles flashed Mal an amused look. "You call him *runt* when he is extremely large."

"Not when I was a wee lad," Mal answered. "Now only Will can top me."

Charles again pretended to smile as he turned to Will. "You will join us, tall William?"

"Leave it to Malcolm," Duncan said. The look he bent on Malcolm told him Mal had better do as he said or have the thrashing of his life. While this had terrified Mal when he'd been a boy, these days he had more than an even chance at besting his brother in a straight fight.

"He won't have to go all the way to Kilmorgan," Alec said brightly. "Father has come to Edinburgh. With Angus."

As Duncan's face changed slowly from weathered red to angry purple, the prince's eyes sparkled. "Ah, then you can go to him now. All of you, including you, Lord Duncan. Bring back all the Mackenzies to swell my ranks. Go. *Now.*"

Duncan scowled, but erased the glower to bow to Charles.

"Of course, Your Highness. At once. I can't promise to be successful. My father is devilish stubborn."

"You will persuade him," Charles said. He waved his fingers in a dismissive gesture, and turned back to the tables across the room where his generals were planning whatever they were planning.

Alec flashed a grin at his older brother. "That seems to be that. Come on, Duncan. Let's not keep Da waiting."

Malcolm did not return home with his brothers. He slipped away and spent the rest of the night making plans.

By the time he returned home, it was daylight, and he was ready for sleep. He'd hoped Duncan would have gone again, but he heard the shouting before he reached the house. His father must have woken from his laudanum-induced sleep and found Duncan there. The duke's rage coupled with a hangover spilled out into the street.

Malcolm tried to continue walking past the house, but Will popped out the door and cut him off. "No you don't," Will said. "Get in here, runt. It's going to take us all to keep them from killing each other."

The duke and his firstborn son faced each other in the dining room, from which Naughton had cleared last night's mess. The table had been set for breakfast, holding candelabras and a silver coffeepot, as well as porcelain cups. Too many weapons for Mal's taste.

Alec and Angus stood on either side of the table, buffers between Duncan and their father. The twins didn't always see eye to eye, but this morning they'd found common cause.

". . . because you're too bloody young!" The duke was shouting at Duncan as Will and Mal entered. "Ye don't remember the last uprising, do ye? Well, I do. I was there." He banged both fists on the table, rattling the porcelain. "I was there when it all went wrong. It broke my father, and he died of grief. That's when I knew—if God wanted a Catholic on the throne, one would be there!"

"Ye believe in God only when it's convenient to ye," Duncan yelled back. Mal noticed he'd left his bonnet downstairs. Wise. If the duke had seen the white rose emblem on it, he'd have thrown it into the fire, and maybe tried to push Duncan there too. "And it's nothing to do with Catholics. It's to do with the right of the succession. *That* can't be dismissed when it's convenient."

"Ye don't give a donkey's arsehole about the right of succession!" The duke waved his arms, his loose shirt fluttering. "Ye want to strut around and be right-hand man to a prince who will hang on your every word and tell ye how splendid ye are."

"Maybe if *you'd* had any use for me, I wouldn't have to pledge my loyalty to someone else!"

The duke went scarlet from forehead to throat. A vein pulsed at this temple, and Angus stepped forward in concern.

"Any use for ye? You're my oldest son!" The duke held on to the lip of the table as his breath came fast. "You're to be duke after me, take over me lands. Why wouldn't I have use for ye?"

"Aye, and become a copy of you." Duncan said, leaning his fists on the table. "A sanctimonious, hardened, dried-up pig of a man. Ye've let the rest of us know it's *Angus* ye love, and none other. Surprised you remember ye *have* more sons."

Will's mouth compressed. "Mal."

"Aye." Malcolm signaled to Alec, and the two of them went to either side of Duncan.

Duncan didn't notice. "Ye hated me before our mum died, because I took her attention away from you. Ye hated us all after for reminding ye of her. When are ye going to notice that your offspring hate ye back as much?"

The duke reached for the nearest candelabra, spraying wax across the table as he lifted it. The man was breathing rapidly, almost choking, spittle on his lips, but he had enough strength to throw the heavy silver piece across the table at Duncan.

Alec and Mal had already yanked Duncan out of the way. The candelabra sailed across the room and clattered into the mahogany paneling, the candles guttering and falling to the carpet in a smash of soft wax.

Mal took a firmer hold of Duncan's arm, and Alec the other, as Duncan readied to launch himself at his father. Duncan fought his two youngest brothers as they dragged and shoved him out onto the landing and down the stairs.

Duncan broke away and was walking swiftly toward the front door on his own by the time they reached the ground floor. "To hell with him," he snapped. "I'll get the Mackenzies behind us another way." He snatched up his green bonnet with its white badge and turned to Mal and Alec, who stood shoulder to shoulder, blocking the way back up the stairs. "Join me, Mal. Alec," Duncan said, his voice hard. "You saw him. Why should you want to stay loyal to him?"

"Because he's our da," Malcolm said as the frightened footman opened the door wide for Duncan. "And *you're* a wee bit too full of yourself."

Duncan went red again, but he only snarled, swirled his coat and plaids around him, and was gone.

"Alec Mackenzie?" A man had come up while Duncan made his dramatic exit, waiting until Duncan had gone a little way up the street. Now said gentleman stood respectfully on the doorstep.

Alec went out to the newcomer. "Aye, I'm he. Wait, are ye going to shoot me or skewer me? In that case—never heard of the man."

"I have a letter for you."

The accent was English, but a quick look told Mal that the messenger was not a soldier. He didn't have the stance or countenance of a man who made a living marching, shooting, and fighting for his life. He was soft-faced, like Jeremy Drake, but older.

"You couldn't have sent it by post?" Alec asked with little patience. He usually wasn't this impolite to a stranger, but a row between their father and Duncan put everyone in the family out of joint.

"This was too important to trust to the post," the gentleman said. "This letter came from my sister in France, who is dear friends to Genevieve . . . to your wife."

Alec's face changed in an instant from irritation to abject fear. He snatched the letter the man removed from his coat pocket, ripped open the seal, and scanned the first lines.

A strangled cry came from Alec's throat. He quietly fell back against the stones of the house behind him, the paper dropping from his nerveless fingers.

Mal caught the letter before it reached the ground, turned it around, and read:

Genevieve went quietly to God after a day of terrible illness, but now she is out of pain. Your daughter, whom she brought to bed the night before her death, thrives. One life is gone, but another has come . . .

Chapter 11

The day after Charles Stuart's entrance into Edinburgh, Mary's father received an invitation for his entire family to attend a grand ball at Holyrood.

Aunt Danae studied the letter dubiously when Wilfort called them all into his library to tell them about it. "He means to hold court, it appears," Aunt Danae said.

"Ought we to go?" Audrey asked, curious but uncertain. "Won't the ballroom be overrun by Scottish soldiers?" She broke into a nervous smile. "Can you imagine them trying to do a minuet with all their plaids flying?"

"Of course we ought to go," Aunt Danae said. "I imagine most of my acquaintance has received such an invitation. If *they* knew what went on at one of his dos, and I didn't, I'd never live it down."

"We will go," Wilfort said. "What better way to see what the serpent intends but to go into his lair? However, Audrey, I think, should stay home."

"Oh, Papa." Audrey, who never defied her father, now shot him a pleading look. "I will face the same as Aunt Danae if I do not go. How awful to be the only lady in Edinburgh who cannot say she was there!"

"I can look after her," Mary said. It stood to reason Jeremy would have an invitation as well. "Aunt Danae and I both can. If Lord Halsey and you accompany us, we will have the best protection there is."

Wilfort gave Mary a wry look. "You flatter to cajole, daughter. But very well. I know that if I do not concede, I will hear much moaning in future. Audrey, you and Mary will stay with your aunt, and not wander off to explore the palace. This is not the home of a friend. I can imagine the delight one of these Highland warriors would have at discovering a young English lady alone. Your virtue would be a great prize to them."

Mary's face heated. She'd already been found alone by a Highland warrior, her mouth kissed, her bosom licked.

Aunt Danae mistook Mary's flush for modesty. "Really, James. To say such things."

Wilfort frowned. "I'll not shelter my daughters until they are ruined from ignorance. Forewarned is forearmed. We will go, and stay together. That is my final word."

Her father wasn't wrong, Mary thought as they dispersed. They were going into the home of the enemy, and who knew what might happen there?

Debate was hot in the bedchambers as to what to wear. Should they go in their best, or dress more plainly to show Charles that he was not due the deference of a monarch? On the other hand, he *was* a prince, descended from an old royal family. Other ladies might be at their most fashionable—should they risk not shining as well as they might?

While Audrey and Aunt Danae argued, Mary's maid, Whitman, took Mary aside and spoke in a low voice. "My lady, there is a . . . person . . . at the kitchen door asking to see you."

Malcolm?

No, Malcolm would never try to slip in to find Mary by way of the kitchen. If he wanted to see her, he'd boldly march to the front door and demand to be admitted.

But then, this might be something about their plans for Audrey and Jeremy. Mary nodded her thanks, made an excuse to Aunt Danae, and followed Whitman back down the stairs.

All the servants of the earl's house in Edinburgh were Scots, except for lady's maids such as Whitman, and the earl's manservant. The Scottish servants spoke in broad accents, with the language called Erse thrown in from time to time. Mary didn't always understand them, but they were kind to her and her family, not surly, as her other English friends claimed their Scottish servants to be.

The kitchen staff—cook, her assistants, housekeeper, butler, and footmen—all sprang to their feet when Whitman came down with Mary and took her through the servants' hall to the scullery door.

Whitman hadn't wanted Mary following her below stairs, but Mary had insisted. She feared the man would leave if she did not go to him quickly. Scots messengers sometimes did that—simply walked off in impatience if one kept them waiting too long.

She understood why Whitman had described him as a "person" when Mary stepped onto the chilly passage outside the scullery. The man had sun-weathered skin, straggling red hair going to gray, a patch over one eye, a worn kilt, and wicked-looking knives and a pistol hanging from his belt.

"This her?" he asked Whitman.

"Keep a civil tongue in your head," Whitman said with a scowl. "This is her ladyship. What is your message? Make it quick."

"It's all right, Whitman," Mary said, soothing. "How can I help you, sir?"

"Name's Padruig. Not *sir.* Have a message for ye." He glared at Whitman, clearly not wanting to repeat it in front of her.

"Please wait inside, Whitman." Mary gave her maid a reassuring nod. "I will shout if I need you."

Whitman did *not* want to leave Mary out here with this specimen, that was clear. She pinched her lips together but walked stiffly back into the house.

Once the door was shut, Padruig spoke. "Message is from himself. He says tonight, at the palace. Wait for his signal."

"By *himself* you mean Lord Malcolm Mackenzie?"

Padruig gave her a nod. "He hired us. 'Tis a fool's errand, but God favors fools, don't he?"

"I certainly hope so." Mary reached through a slit in her outer skirt to the pocket sewn beneath. "Thank you, sir . . . er, Padruig."

Padruig lifted his hands from the shilling she held out to him. "Keep your money, miss. He's already paying us well. Too well—me master's a cheating bastard. But he'll take care o' her. You don't need to worry about that."

Giving Mary another nod, Padruig turned and made his way back through the passage to the street.

Whitman nearly pounced on Mary when she went inside again. "Who was that creature? If your father kept dogs here, I'd have set them on him."

"He's no one. Someone grateful for charity is all." Mary was dismayed how easily a lie came from her lips. She had certainly changed in the short time she'd known Malcolm. "Say nothing of this to my aunt or father, I beg you. Please, Whitman. It's important."

Whitman again looked most disapproving, but she was loyal to Mary. "Very well, my lady."

All the servants seemed to have assembled in the kitchen as Mary passed through again, watching curiously. "And please tell them to say nothing as well," Mary added in a low voice.

The housekeeper, a tall woman with a soft face, heard her. "Never ye worry, m'lady," she said. "Young ladies must have their secrets. This lot will say nothing, I promise ye." The look she swept over the servants was severe.

"Thank you, Mrs. Mitchell. Thank you, all."

"Now then, my lady. You're a kindly sort. Not like *some*."

Mary said *thank you* again, and hurried upstairs. She'd already made sure Audrey had a few simple clothes packed—in case they had to flee Scotland, as Mary had suggested to her father. While they readied themselves for the ball, Mary slipped the small bundle of Audrey's things inside her voluminous cloak.

Malcolm was sandy-eyed and fatigued by the time he reached the ball held for the glory and honor of Charles Edward Stuart, supposed Prince of Wales, son of James III and VIII, King of England.

This morning, after Alec had staggered back into the house, their father had kept up a harangue against Duncan, until Angus and Mal managed to get the hungover duke back to bed, with a soothing preparation Naughton had mixed. Alec, without speaking, had gone straight upstairs and locked himself into his bedchamber.

When the house had settled down again, Malcolm softly knocked on Alec's door.

"Alec. Ye all right?"

Alec hadn't answered. Mal could hear nothing inside, not swearing or weeping. Mal had crept quietly away and returned in a few minutes to pick open the lock.

He'd found Alec sitting on an ornate settee before the fire, staring at nothing. Alec's loose kilt, open shirt, and unshaved face contrasted sharply with the room's gilded and carved French furniture, brought from Paris.

Mal sat down next to his brother. He said nothing, only let his shoulder touch Alec's so Alec would know he wasn't alone.

Mal had read the entire letter several times. Genevieve, whom Alec had married during their last visit to Paris, had perished in childbed. The daughter she'd borne—Alec's—was healthy and robust, now being looked after by a wet nurse.

The woman who'd written the letter was Genevieve's oldest friend, and she now had care of the child. She'd sent the letter to her brother in London instead of straight to Alec, fearing the missive would be intercepted by the English ships prowling the sea between France and Scotland. The letter was dated four weeks ago.

Mal had known Genevieve, a dancer with an opera company, had been present for her turbulent courtship with Alec, and Alec's subsequent wedding to her. Knowing it would take time to ease her into the Mackenzie family, Alec had left Genevieve in Paris, promising to send for her after he'd broken the news to his father.

When Charles had landed in Scotland, Alec wrote to Genevieve to tell her to stay put, where she'd be safer, until the child was born. He'd planned to bring her to Scotland once the uprising question was settled, and he had a grandchild to present to the duke. Only Mal had known about Genevieve, the marriage, and Genevieve's pregnancy, and Mal hadn't told a soul.

"I have a ship at the ready," Mal said after a time. "It will take you to France tonight."

Alec turned his head, regarding his brother with dead eyes.

He didn't ask how Mal had happened to procure a ship, or why; he simply said, "Thank you."

Malcolm poured whisky for them both, making Alec drink it. When Alec finally drooped, Mal got him into bed, laying him on his side and pulling blankets over his cold body.

Mal then assigned the most trusted servants of the household—the ones who'd sit on Alec and not let him do anything foolish—to watch him, while he went out and put things in motion.

Now, at the ball, he spied Mary strolling in at her aunt's side, and the ache in his heart eased.

Mary saw him, caught his gaze. Then with deft skill she kept her eyes moving, so no one in the room would guess she even noticed him.

Mal knew then and there that Mary was the woman for him, in all ways. She was clever and brave, beautiful and enchanting. He'd do everything in his power to bring her to his side and keep her there for the rest of his life.

Mary noted immediately that Malcolm lacked his usual exuberance. Something had happened to quell his fire, though she knew not what.

She longed to go to him, to ask what was wrong. She wanted to lay her hand on his shoulder, tell him she'd help, whatever it was. Mal was compelling that way.

Mary knew he was easing his way into her affections, into her heart, where it would be difficult to root him out again. She knew he did it on purpose, whatever his reasons, good or ill. This rebellion, no matter its outcome, would eventually send her back to England, and she'd likely never see Malcolm again. But she would never be able to forget him.

Mal moved from her line of sight, and she dared not turn her head to follow him. Her entire body was aware of him, however, giving her a flush of heat, a quickening of breath.

Mary, Aunt Danae, and Audrey were soon swallowed by the knot of Englishwomen who'd made their home in Edinburgh. "Have you seen the prince yet?" Aunt Danae asked Lady Bancroft, who was arm in arm with a countess, the countess's daughter at her side.

"Not yet," the countess said. "He will make his entrance soon." She lifted her fan and lowered her voice. "He is so young, and unmarried. They say he will doubtless be taking an English wife, to seal relations between England and Scotland."

Mary had heard nothing of the sort. If Charles were eager to take a wife from the aristocrats living in Edinburgh, her father or Lord Halsey would have learned of it, and discussed it in front of her. They'd said nothing about it.

But to most young ladies of Mary's acquaintance the words *handsome*, *young*, and *prince* were only a short step from the word *marriage*. Their mothers might scorn Charles in front of their husbands and call him the Young Pretender, but an alliance between their family and an ancient royal house was nothing to dismiss.

Mary could see the ambitious thoughts churning in the minds of the matrons, romantic ones in the minds of their daughters. An exiled prince, returning with nothing but a banner and a few loyal retainers to retake the land of his ancestors was the stuff of legend.

While the matrons chattered, Audrey and Mary were drawn into the circle of their younger friends. "A pity you're betrothed, Mary," the countess's daughter said. "You' d be the perfect wife for the prince. You'd have fair-haired children, and be queen of England."

"Alas, alas," Mary said, trying to pretend she wasn't looking for Malcolm with her whole being. "I am already betrothed, and will have to concede my position as queen to another."

"Then Audrey, perhaps," another young lady suggested. "She's young and pretty—I imagine the prince will be unable to keep his eyes off her."

"Nonsense," Audrey said. "He'll never see me past you ladies."

"Go on," the countess's daughter said, pleased at Audrey's generosity. "You flatter me. I wager it will be Audrey he begs to dance with first."

Audrey laughed in genuine amusement. "My father would fall over of apoplexy if he did. And again if I accepted such a request. I believe I will remain a wallflower tonight, and spare my father's constitution."

"You do disappoint me," the countess's daughter said, a mock frown replacing her vapid smile. "If he approaches you, you *must* dance with him. And then tell us *everything*."

"I heard that he'll not dance at all," Mary broke in. "That he'll wait until what he calls 'the greater dance' is done before he indulges in it with young ladies."

The ladies gaped at her, then melted. "How wonderful," one said, fanning herself rapidly.

"We will have to persuade him to favor at least *one* of us with a wee dance," the countess's daughter said, trying out a Scottish accent and failing miserably. "Audrey, *do* charm him."

More of this went on until a fanfare announced the arrival of the prince himself.

Mary and Audrey were perhaps the only ladies there who watched in mere curiosity, rather than avid delight. Audrey's thoughts were reserved for Jeremy—a prince could not compare.

Mary was aware only of Malcolm, who'd swung away from his brothers. His body went rigid, as though poised to spring like a predator, as Charles and his small entourage entered the room.

Chapter 12

Fans fluttered and breaths quickened as Charles made his grand entrance. Ladies curtsied in a ripple of skirts, and the gentlemen bowed. The depth of the bows indicated the feelings of each man—those with Jacobite tendencies extended a leg and bent low, while the bows of those loyal to George of England were cursory and soon over.

Mary, conscious of Malcolm standing not five yards from her, could not help contrasting the prince with him. Charles was five-and-twenty, the same as Malcolm. The prince wore a modest but well-styled wig with a tail tied with a black ribbon. The wig sat well back on his forehead, as was the fashion—he likely shaved his own hair off to accommodate.

Malcolm's red-brown hair was nowhere near as sleek. It was combed but already unkempt, the ribbon tying it limp and loose.

Charles wore a suit of fine watered silk, as elegant as anything Mary's father owned. The long coat with many buttons flowed over breeches that hugged every curve of his thighs. Silk stockings outlined his muscular legs, and many a lady's gaze slid to rest there. Charles's concession to Scottish dress was a swath of plaid pinned to one shoulder.

Mal wore the short jacket of a Scots gentleman, plaids wrapping his waist, thick socks, and leather shoes. As always, he lounged easily in them, as though he could come to the palace or go marching through the heather—it was all the same to him.

Charles seemed pleased with everyone, though he must know that half of Edinburgh didn't want him there. He moved from group to group, informally, while fiddlers began their lively music.

Malcolm drifted unobtrusively out of Charles's path, Mary noticed. Wherever the prince turned, Malcolm contrived not to be there.

One of Malcolm's brothers was here, she saw, though not the one who'd been with Mal the first evening at Lady Bancroft's soiree. He was much like Malcolm and yet different at the same time, very tall, ready with a smile. Mary saw that whenever he or Malcolm joined a conversation, people pulled their attention to them, leaning to catch every word.

Masters of getting others to do their bidding, Mary thought. The taller Mackenzie was actually engaging Lord Halsey, speaking to him in an animated way. Halsey took the bait and entered the discussion, drawing Mary's father in as well.

At the same moment, Malcolm vanished out a door.

Aunt Danae's attention, and that of every woman present, was on the prince. Mary faded back from them then moved through the crowd, sidestepping to keep her wide skirts from brushing those she passed. Heart beating rapidly, she quietly slipped through the door Malcolm had exited.

She found herself in a long stone corridor, empty and barren of decoration. A passage for servants, she concluded. But where was Malcolm?

As soon as the thought formed in her head, a firm, gloved hand landed on her arm. Mary was turned around, her back pressed against the hard stone, and found herself facing Malcolm Mackenzie, who smiled at her. Already she was familiar with his touch and the scent of wild outdoors that clung to him.

"Here you are, then," Mal said.

His smile was as wicked as ever, but there was something new in his eyes, the sadness she'd noted in the ballroom. He was hiding it from her, pushing it aside. That was worrying. Mary wanted to reach out to him, to know . . .

Malcolm leaned into her, one lock of his hair falling to graze his cheek. "Mary, lass, I'm hungry for ye."

He slid his thumb across the line of her hair.

Mary subsided against the wall, her hands locking around the lapels of his coat. She managed a nod, her voice a strangled rasp. "I thought you were going home to Kilmorgan. That your father had summoned you."

"Mm, change of plan there. My father decided t' come here and plague us instead. But that does nae need to worry ye. We go forward as I said."

Mary studied his face, still searching for what had upset him. "It will be tonight, then?"

"Aye. I have made safe passage for the pair, and a minister ready to do the service before they go. He's a Calvinist, but the wedding will be Protestant enough for ye. Your father might never come 'round if they're married in France by a Catholic priest, will he?"

Malcolm had been wise enough to think of that. Mary nodded again, her legs weak, though at the same time she felt strong with excitement. "Yes. Thank you."

"My brother Alec will be going t' Paris with them. Alec has . . . business . . . there. He'll look after them, as will old Padruig. Padruig looks like a cutthroat pirate, but I'd trust him with me life." Mal looked thoughtful. "*Have* trusted him with me life. I'd have died but for him and his rock-solid arm."

Mary made herself open her fingers and release Malcolm's coat. "They really will be all right? I want Audrey to be happy, but . . ."

"Dinnae worry, Mary," Mal said. "She'll be with her husband, who will have plenty of money, a house to stay in, and me brother to look in on them."

Mary's eyes stung, her gratitude for him swelling. "Thank you, Mal."

The sad light left Malcolm's face, his roguish twinkle returning. "Now, then, love. No need to cry. We'll seal the bargain." He cupped her face, fingers hot, hand strong, as he bent and kissed her lips.

The taste of his mouth was like raw spice and the night. The touch of him opened everything inside Mary that had been locked tight, places she'd shut away. She wanted to lean into his strength and let him banish every fear, every sleepless night she'd ever had.

"So hungry for ye," Mal whispered. He drew one knuckle down her cheek. When Halsey had touched her thus, Mary had been repulsed. Mal's touch was a line of fire—he touched her in wonder, not possession.

Well, maybe a *little* possession. His slow smile told her that if they hadn't been in this back hall, which a servant could rush into at any time, he would be doing more than giving her kisses. Sinful, fiery, forbidden kisses.

Mary dragged in a breath. She was pinned against him, and she did not want, for the life of her, to pull away. "That was hardly a kiss for sealing a bargain," she managed to say.

Malcolm's smile turned wickeder still. "Oh, aye?"

"No." Mary tried to sound firm. "Much too intimate."

"Ah. How are these kisses supposed to go, then? Why don't ye show me, lass?"

Mary had no strength, but she rose on tiptoe, balancing herself against him. The wool of his coat was warm beneath her fingers, the weave smooth, buttons cool. "The best kiss of thanks between friends is perfunctory but sincere." Feeling hot, bold, sinful, Mary pressed a kiss to his cheek, his sandpaper whiskers under her lips.

"I see." Mal's amber eyes twinkled. "And if ye are lovers?"

Mary's face warmed. "That one I do not know." She heard the regret in her voice. "But I do know how to kiss good-bye." She pressed another kiss to his cheek then stood flat on the floor again.

"I know how that one goes." Malcolm drew closer again, his breath on her mouth. "But we won't say good-bye, Mary. You and I will never be apart for long. I promise ye this."

"We can't know what will happen," Mary said. Even now events were turning, changing with the wind. The cold stones of this deserted passage sent a chill into her bones.

"Aye, but we can," Mal said. "I'm staying in Edinburgh as long as you are. Whenever ye leave the city, I leave it. To wherever you go."

He made it sound so simple. "Is that wise?" Mary asked, her heart beating too fast.

"To hell with wise, love. It's you and me now. That is all. Do ye understand?"

"Not really," Mary said softly. A man like Malcolm was new to her, an experience that both stirred her longing and terrified her of her own feelings.

Malcolm let out a breath. "Well, ye will in time. Go gather up your sister. Take her out through the passage to the abbey in one hour—if I'm not there, trust the man who comes to guide ye. There'll be so much going on with all the dancing and everyone watching his princliness that no one will notice ye slipping away."

It was madness, but Mary would do it. This was Audrey's chance, and Mary would not destroy it because she was too timid at the last.

She tried a laugh. "I did not notice *you* dancing in there," she remarked for something to say. "Do you not care for it?"

Malcolm lost his dark look. "Can ye see me capering about in a minuet?" He spun away from Mary, spread his arms, pointed his toe, and hopped in mimicry of the stately dance.

Mary didn't smile—watching his leg tightening as his kilt bared his thigh was a treat she could not look away from.

Malcolm stopped, made a bow—the same graceful sweep he'd done in Lady Bancroft's drawing room—and held out his hand. When Mary put hers in his, he swung her in a quick circle, closing his arms around her from behind. Mal enfolded her in his warmth, shielding her from all the bad things.

"Is this Scottish dancing?" Mary asked, knowing it couldn't be. "I've never seen any."

Malcolm's body shook agreeably with his laugh. "And you living in Scotland? Ought to be ashamed. No, this is me careening about." Mal moved her to stand beside him, one arm around her waist, his other hand holding hers across their bodies. "*This* is Scottish dancing—ye can hear the fiddle and the drum, aye? All right, then here we go."

Malcolm pulled Mary sideways, nearly off her feet, rapidly around a large, imaginary circle. Then he linked arms with her and spun first one way with her, then the other, until she was dizzy.

Mary didn't worry that she didn't know the steps. Malcolm's feet were sure, his strong touch guiding her wherever she needed to go. All the while he smiled at her as though she were the most beautiful woman he'd ever seen.

The world rushed away from her in a wash of pure joy, the dance obliterating all else. In this space and time, nothing mattered but herself and Malcolm—not the uprising and its dangers, not her father and his wishes, not Lord Halsey and her betrothal, not the worry of spiriting Audrey away with the man she loved.

Only Mary and Malcolm existed, the two of them in this dance. It was as though they stood motionlessly in a place where nothing could touch them, while the stone passage whirled around and around them. For one rapturous moment, Mary let herself be happy.

Outside, in the ballroom, the fiddler wound down to the end of the piece, the drummer striking one last beat. Malcolm slowed, pulling Mary close as the dance finished.

He said nothing. Mary expected him to continue the flirtation, to kiss her, to tease and smile. Malcolm only looked at her, something flickering in his eyes she didn't understand. His body against hers hummed with the dance, Mal's vibrancy going on even when he'd stopped moving.

Mal raised her hand to his lips, his breath scalding, even though her gloves. "At the side door," he said. "In one hour." He pressed another kiss to her fingers then carefully released her and stepped back. "*À bientôt*, my love." His voice was grave, his look quiet.

Mary's breath poured back into her. "*À bientôt*," she said shakily, and made herself turn away to the door she'd come through.

She paused inside the passage until she heard the fiddles begin again, then she pulled open the door. Dancers in plaids and in English dress swung by her, catching the beat of the drums.

Mary glanced back before she slipped into the ballroom, but the passage behind her was empty. Malcolm was gone, as though he'd never been there at all.

"They won't come," Jeremy said glumly.

He'd declared this about twenty times already, and Malcolm growled under his breath. "Have a little faith, lad. This is the lady you're going t' marry."

"Her father will never let it happen," Jeremy continued. His young face was morose. "He's locked her in the cellar, I'll wager."

"No, lad. She's at the ball with Mary. I saw her there."

The declaration had Mal thinking through every moment of Mary at the ball, every second burned into his brain. Mary walking with her aunt, head erect, her swift glance that deliberately did not acknowledge him. Her indifferent assessment of the prince, while all the ladies around her were eager to catch Charles's eye. The calm way Mary had slipped from the ballroom to meet him, the laughter in her eyes when Mal had pulled her into a spontaneous dance.

Mary was a woman with a capacity for exultation, but Mal realized she'd buried that part of her deep. But no matter. He would reach inside her and yank it out.

Jeremy softened for a moment, then he balled his fists, hunched his shoulders, and paced. "It will never work."

Mal let out an exasperated breath. "Dear God, man. I'm about to knock ye across the head and carry ye to the minister over my shoulder. Lady Audrey loves you. She'll come."

"But her father is a martinet. If he's caught wind of this . . ."

"No one knows but me and Mary," Mal said. He considered. "And the men I've hired. And my brother, and our footman. None of whom are going to blab to a bloody Englishman. Trust me on— Ah, there they are."

Chapter 13

Two women in hooded cloaks over wide skirts came out of the darkness near the arches of the abbey, the original part of Holyrood. They were led by a footman of the Mackenzie household that Malcolm trusted.

Jeremy moved quickly toward Audrey, but Malcolm knew the besotted fool would want to snatch her up and hold her tight, asking questions, reassuring her. Wasting precious seconds. They needed to move now.

Mal stepped between Jeremy and the ladies, opening his arms to usher the young women through. "Come on, then."

He saw Mary flash him a look of gratitude. Audrey clung tightly to her sister as both ladies hurried to the gate Malcolm led them to. A carriage waited on the other side.

The Scottish sentries guarding the small gate pretended to not even notice them. Mal had already bribed them lavishly with coin and whisky. Naughton had the door of the carriage open, rugs and flasks of hot coffee inside to fortify them.

"There you go, young Audrey," Malcolm said, handing her into the coach. "Settle yourself in. Now, then, Mary."

Mary put her hand in Malcolm's, her fingers warm through gloves. Malcolm added his grip to her elbow, savoring her brush of scent as he helped her up into the carriage. He felt her tremble, but the look she flashed him told him it was from exuberance, not fear. She was embracing the adventure.

Mal stepped back so Jeremy could leap inside. The ladies had taken the seat facing forward, and Jeremy landed on the rear-facing seat with a rush of breath. Malcolm climbed in and sat down next to Jeremy, opposite Mary.

Naughton slammed the door, and the carriage listed as he and the footman climbed to their perches. Then they were off.

Mary's eyes were sparkling, her face flushed. She'd never done anything like this, Malcolm would wager, nothing remotely forbidden. Mal was so used to looking for the most amount of trouble he could find that he barely noticed the thrill of it anymore. He simply did what he wanted, devil take those who didn't like it.

Mary, on the other hand, had been an obedient daughter her entire life. She was very conscious of this breach of obligation.

No turning back now, lass. Once you've the taste of wickedness, ye want it always.

The four of them said nothing as they clopped through the quiet streets of the city. The backstreet taverns were rollicking, but the main streets were nearly empty, everyone who was anyone at Holyrood tonight.

The minister lived in a little house in a quiet lane. He was waiting for them, and in his drawing room, with his wife and servants to witness, Audrey and Jeremy were married. Malcolm stood behind Jeremy, and Mary behind her sister, Mary's eyes welling with tears as Audrey made her vows in a clear voice.

Jeremy looked suddenly less youthful as he turned Audrey's face to him and kissed her lightly on the lips. He'd just gone from youngest son, kicking around waiting for his life to begin, to a man responsible for a wife.

Mary caught Malcolm's eye, and flushed a berry red. Whatever her thoughts were, Malcolm was certain he'd like them.

Malcolm didn't let the happy couple linger, for which Mary was grateful. Mary shared his urgency, wanting Audrey gone before their father discovered what was happening. Any moment now,

Aunt Danae would realize that Mary and Audrey weren't coming back from the withdrawing room, and the hunt would begin.

Malcolm chivvied them to the carriage, pushing Mary into it with his hand on her backside. When she turned to him in outrage—no one would dare ever touch her thus—he only gave her an unabashed wink.

"Cheek," Mary said decidedly as she settled on the seat next to Audrey.

"Aye, and a fine one it is." Malcolm yanked the carriage door closed, bracing himself as the vehicle rocked forward and away. He half fell to the seat facing her, his face creased with mirth.

Mary knew she should be most offended that Malcolm had touched her in an inappropriate place and then made a pun about it. But she wasn't. She wanted to laugh and laugh. She was breaking rules she'd upheld all her life, and enjoying it. Tomorrow she'd become obedient Mary again, but tonight she would revel in her madness.

The carriage rolled through streets that were still quiet. Charles's grand ball would blaze on for hours longer.

They moved to another city gate and easily out this one too. The Scotsmen on guard glanced inside, saw Malcolm, and stepped out of the way. Did he have every sentry in Edinburgh in his pocket? At the moment, Mary couldn't be too unnerved by that. She was only thankful he did.

The carriage rattled down lanes that led to the docks and the shipping yards, then past those and into emptiness beyond. At the end of a tiny fishing wharf, well past the main dockyards, a small ship rocked in the darkness and rising mist.

Mary couldn't see much of the vessel in the shadows, just that it was masted but small, though plenty of figures moved on its decks.

"We're going to France in *that*?" Jeremy asked in alarm.

"*That* is probably the most seaworthy craft on the waters," Malcolm answered as he threw open the carriage's door. "It will take ye there safer than any frigate."

Jeremy looked doubtful, but Malcolm didn't give him time to argue. They piled out of the carriage, Audrey clinging to Jeremy's hand.

A tall man in a kilt, the plaid thrown around his shoulders, climbed the short plank from ship's deck to the wharf. His stance, his walk, was Malcolm's, and as they neared him, Mary realized he was Malcolm's brother Alec, whom she'd seen on the night of Lady Bancroft's ball, when she'd first encountered Malcolm.

"There you all are," Alec said. He looked different tonight, haggard and pale, his eyes lacking the sparkle she'd spied in them when he'd stood so arrogantly at Malcolm's side. "Gair's about to go without you."

"The devil he is." Malcolm's scowl flashed, then he put his hand on Jeremy's shoulder. "On you go, children. Make your good-byes quick."

Audrey turned in a flurry of skirts and flung her arms around Mary. "My dearest Mary," she said in a choked voice. "Oh, but I'm going to miss you." She quickly kissed Mary's cheek with lips cold from the wind, then she seized her hands. "Don't go home," she said desperately. "Come with us."

Mary's heart lurched, the temptation of doing just that having swirled through her all day. She made herself shake her head. "Don't be silly. Someone has to break the news to Father and Aunt Danae. They will be frantic until they know you're safe." And Mary, no matter what she would sacrifice to bring Audrey's happiness, could not with good conscience let her father lose two daughters in one night.

"But they will be so angry," Audrey said, worry in her eyes. "Oh, I should not go. We'll go home, own up. When they see how happy I am with Jeremy—"

"Absolute nonsense, and you know it," Mary said crisply. "Papa would try to have the marriage annulled, and I did not go through all this to have you married and *un*married in one evening." She held back her tears with effort as she kissed Audrey's cheek. "I will smooth things over here, you write me when you're settled, and I'll persuade Papa and Aunt Danae to go to Paris for a visit. Papa will be used to the idea by then, and much more forgiving."

Mary spoke with conviction she did not feel. Her father could become so very angry, and it was difficult to predict what he'd do in his fury. He might storm across the channel and drag Audrey home, never mind that Jeremy's authority, as

Audrey's husband, would now supersede his. That technicality of law was all they had at the moment to hang their hopes on.

The bellow of the ship's captain cut through the air. "Get yerselves on board! I'm casting off *now.*"

Malcolm ran down the gangplank to the ship's deck as Jeremy gently pried Audrey from Mary's arms. Audrey was weeping. Jeremy, taking charge of her, led her down the gangplank, and Audrey sank against him, already transferring her trust to him.

Malcolm made his way to the captain, who stood in the stern, plaid like a flag in the wind. The same sharp wind brought Malcolm's words to Mary. "You'll take care of them, won't ye, Gair?" Mal put his face close to the hard-eyed captain's. "If any harm comes to them—any at all—I'll cut your balls off. You'd look funny without your bits, wouldn't ye?"

The threat, given with cheerfully voiced menace, made Gair flinch. "Ye paid me, Mackenzie," he said, sounding hurt. "Ye know I'm your man."

Mal put a hand on Gair's shoulder. "Ye better be. You know I'll find ye, no matter where ye roam."

"Mal." Alec, his plaids making him a lump of blue in the swirling mists, reached his brother. "Thank you."

Mal said nothing, but a moment later, the two were clasping each other in a tight hug.

Mary watched them with a full heart. Mal would miss Alec the same gripping way Mary would miss her sister.

She pulled out of her musings when she noticed that Mal and Alec were somehow growing smaller, disappearing into the mists. The ship's men had slipped the moorings. The slap of oars Mary couldn't see came to her, as the ship slowly made its way toward open sea.

Mary cupped her hands around her mouth. "*Malcolm!*"

Malcolm's head came up, then his voice cut through the fog. "Gair! Ye rat-tailed bastard!"

Next came a heavy splash, followed by Gair's rumbling laughter. Then Alec: "Mal, are ye daft?" and Audrey's half-muffled cry.

A dark form was bobbing through the water. The mists thickened as the wind died, and through them Mary could just see Mal swimming strongly for the wharf.

"Help him!" Mary cried.

The very thin, red-haired retainer called Naughton jumped from the carriage and headed her way, as did the footman who'd been waiting for them in the shadows of the abbey. A couple of fishermen, who'd been readying their boats for the next day, also thumped down the wharf to help. The fisherman and coachman splashed into the water to grab Malcolm and haul him, dripping and coughing, to shore.

"Malcolm!" Alec's voice boomed across the water, full of worry.

"He's here," Mary shouted at him. "*Go!*"

She heard Alec curse, then the bulk of the ship grew even smaller, until it vanished into swirling darkness.

Naughton and the others pulled Malcolm up to the wharf. He gained his feet but shivered heavily, his lips already blue.

Mary pulled off her velvet cloak and draped it around his wet body. Cold radiated from him, like death waiting to wrap its fingers around him.

"Are you mad?" Mary demanded as she tried to settle the too-small cloak around him. "Why didn't you stay on the ship?"

"And leave ye behind?" Malcolm gave her an incredulous look and shook his head, teeth chattering. "Not bloody likely. I'm going nowhere without ye, love. Not ever again." He shuddered, pulling the cloak and then a dry plaid Naughton brought about his shoulders. "Get us home, Naughton," he ordered. "That water was *bloody* cold."

It never occurred to Mary, when the carriage pulled up in front of Malcolm's tall Edinburgh house, to demand Mal return her cloak, now sopping wet, and have his coachman deliver her to her front door. Malcolm had coughed and shivered—and cursed—all the way home, and Mary now descended with him, following his entourage into the house. He'd gone to a lot of trouble for her and Audrey, and she needed to make certain he was all right.

No one but servants appeared to be home. Half a dozen of these hurried to light a fire or do other things to assist their master, but Malcolm held tightly to Mary as she supported him up the stairs of the narrow, many-storied house.

Mal started throwing off cloak, plaids, and clothes as soon

as the door closed on his chamber. Mary knew she should turn and leave, wait in the hall or in a drawing room below, but she couldn't move. The more of Malcolm's body came into view, the more fixed in place she became.

Mary had never in her life seen a man without any sort of clothing. Her father never left his bedchamber unclad. Even if he rose from bed in the deepest night, Lord Wilfort donned a thick dressing gown that covered him from neck to ankles, with a cap on his shaved head.

Malcolm's naked flesh was not what Mary expected. Instead of the softness she'd felt whenever she walked next to Halsey, she saw only firm strength in Malcolm.

Aunt Danae kept a collection of small bronze statuettes of male nudes that she hid in her room and forbade Mary or Audrey to look at. The sisters had, of course, sneaked in to see them. They'd marveled at the form of the male body, speculating on whether the bronzes were true to life.

Mal could have posed for them. His taut skin fit closely over an armature of muscle. Malcolm's chest, as well sculpted as the artist's bronzes, was dusted with dark red hair, which was repeated on his arms and strong legs.

Only the plaid around his middle kept Mary from seeing all. She was dismayed at her twinge of disappointment when Naughton came to Mal's side with a thick blanket.

Malcolm noticed Mary's interested gaze, and his return look made her flush.

"Get that blanket around me," Mal growled to Naughton. "Before I pull off this tartan. The water was *icy*, if ye ken what I mean."

Naughton, who heretofore had been lugubrious, snorted a laugh. Malcolm snatched the blanket and wrapped it tightly around his body. The very wet plaid fell from beneath it, and Mal shoved it away with his well-formed bare foot.

"Fetch Mary some coffee and make sure she's warm," Mal commanded as he turned from Naughton. "Why isn't that fire roaring yet?"

"I'm all right," Mary said. She followed him, not liking how stark his face was. "*You* need to get warm. Come here."

She took Malcolm by the blanket-clad arm and steered him to a settee that was pulled before the fire.

As with the other furnishings in this room, the couch was gilded, had finely embroidered upholstery, and looked as though it had come straight out of Louis's palace at Versailles. The rest of the room went with the furnishings—painted and gilded paneled walls, high ceilings decorated with ornate moldings, paintings of landscapes or portraits that could have been done by Flemish artists of the last century. Definitely *not* what Mary had pictured the inside of a savage Highlander's home to be.

Malcolm let out a sigh as he sank down to the cushions. As Mary turned to see whether the coffee or hot water was on its way, Mal grasped her hand and pulled her down onto the settee next to him.

"I'll be all right," he said. "So will Audrey."

Mary swallowed the lump in her throat. "If I hadn't thought she would be, I'd never have let her go."

"I know." A droplet from Mal's hair trickled across his cheek like a tear. "Ye did a fine thing, Mary, trusting me. I'll never let harm come to her, and neither will Alec. Not as long as we live."

Mal's slicked-back hair, dark now with water, revealed all of his face. This close, with growing firelight touching him, Mary could see that under his tan, light freckles brushed his high cheekbones and feathered up onto his forehead.

She touched one.

Mal's solicitous expression vanished. His eyes went warm as he brushed back her hair with a heavy hand, and pulled her against his damp, blanket-clad body.

Chapter 14

Mal smelled of salt and his mad plunge into the sea. He ought to be dead, diving into cold water like that, but no. He'd made for shore, confident that there would be hands to pull him out, and he hadn't been wrong.

His absolute self-assurance came to Mary in the vibrations of his body, and the strength of his kiss as he leaned to her and took her mouth. He parted her lips, Mal stroking her cheek with his thumb, opening her to him. The sweep of his tongue was hot, also tasting of salt. Mary wanted to clasp this feeling to herself and never let it go.

But when Mal drew away, licking across her lower lip before he pulled back entirely, she saw a flash of vulnerability in his eyes. This man ached deep inside, despite his devil-may-care arrogance.

Malcolm touched Mary's lower lip, his brows drawing together as he studied where he touched. His fingertips were amazingly gentle.

Mal started to bend to her again, but a thin, pale hand holding a steaming cup came down to them, and Naughton cleared his throat.

"Your coffee, sir," the man said. "And for my lady. And some bannocks to sustain ye."

Malcolm straightened up without embarrassment, one tightly muscled arm uncovered. "Thank ye, Naughton."

He seized a flat cake from a pile on a plate, stuffed half of it in his mouth, and poured coffee down after it. A far cry from the fastidiousness of Halsey, who took minute bites, dabbing his lips with a handkerchief after every mouthful.

Mary had heard of bannocks, of course, but never tasted them. Their Scottish cook was instructed to prepare only English food, or French.

She broke off a corner of one, popped it into her mouth, and chewed. Oats, the warm taste of fat that held it together, and the tang of something she couldn't identify met her tongue. She swallowed, licked her lips, and reached for more.

"Like it, do ye?" Malcolm asked her, eyes twinkling.

"Indeed," Mary said, surprised at herself. "It is quite tasty."

"Our chef is one for a hearty bannock. Gifted, he is."

She glanced at him as she chewed another chunk of bannock. "You keep a chef?" she asked after she swallowed. "Not a cook?"

Mal briefly studied the ceiling in exasperation. "My father is a bloody duke. Nothing will do but he has fine chefs hauled over from France and forced to make heaven out of Scottish recipes. Me dad will have nothing but the best. Though Will brings most of the furniture. Will likes his comfort, though I'm guessing the king gives it to him in exchange for him going away."

So perhaps this settee beneath her *was* straight from Versailles. Mary regarded it with more respect.

Malcolm lifted his cup and took another long swallow of coffee. Then he held it out to Naughton, who was flitting about shaking out Malcolm's sodden clothes.

"This is plain," he said.

Mary had no idea what Malcolm meant, but Naughton appeared to.

"Yes, sir. Until ye feel better."

"I do feel better. I'd be even hotter inside if you added a drop."

Naughton gave him a look of disapproval but fetched a

decanter of amber liquid from a marble-topped demi-lune table. A warm odor leeched from the decanter when Naughton removed the crystal stopper and dolloped some of the liquid into Malcolm's cup.

"Lady Mary's too," Malcolm said.

Naughton smothered a sigh and added a dribble to Mary's cup.

"What is it?" Mary asked.

"Whisky," Malcolm said. "Finest Mackenzie malt. The Scots call it *uisge beatha*. Water of life."

Mary sipped her coffee as hesitantly as she'd tried the bannock. A warm tingle rolled over her tongue, followed by a wash of heat as she swallowed.

"Is it like gin?" She'd sneaked a taste of gin once out of curiosity and found it sharp and eye-watering. This was more subtle, like very fine but strong wine.

"Nothing at all the same as gin," Malcolm said, sounding indignant. "This is Scottish art at its finest. It sits in oak for years to mature—some of what we have in our cellars is older than me."

Naughton, without being asked, brought over two crystal glasses with nothing but the whisky in them, and handed one to Malcolm and one to Mary. Malcolm clicked his glass against Mary's, and sipped.

Mary took a very small taste. Once the immediate burn on her tongue receded, the liquid warmed her mouth, spreading down her throat before she'd realized she'd swallowed.

"Take another," Mal said. "And close your eyes."

Mary obeyed. Malcolm's breath was warm as he leaned to her. "It rests in its cask in the heart of the Highlands, overlooking the sea. Ye can taste the sea winds, can't ye? The crisp air, the openness of the world."

Mary wasn't certain she could taste all that in this drop, but she tasted *something*. Mellow, strong, like Malcolm would be when he aged.

She opened her eyes. "It will make me tipsy."

"Aye, if ye drink enough of it." Malcolm looked amused. "But whisky is to be savored, not drowned in. Ale is for getting drunk with, whisky for pure bliss."

Mary took another tentative sip. While she didn't hold with spirits, having seen the evils of drink in her charity work with Aunt Danae, she had to agree this *uisge beatha* was compelling.

Malcolm drank his slowly, like a man savoring his last drop. Mary followed suit, liking the heat that permeated her body. Her skin felt flushed, her corset too tight. She longed to pull her clothes open and exhale in relief.

Naughton took away the tray after they'd enjoyed the hearty bannocks. Malcolm swallowed a final sip of whisky and set his glass on the floor.

"Now, then, Mary."

His voice was low, rough from his impromptu swim in the sea.

"Now, then?" Mary asked nervously.

"I have you alone, in my bedchamber. Hadn't planned this tonight, but I'll seize any opportunity thrust in front of me."

She should be more worried, Mary thought. Afraid and offended at the same time, but neither fear nor indignation came. She wished she could have the correct reaction to Malcolm, but she never had yet.

"I am betrothed to another," Mary said, the words lacking conviction.

"For now."

Malcolm sounded so certain she'd walk away from Halsey without looking back. He'd advised as much from the beginning.

"Breaking an engagement is more than jilting the other party, you know," Mary said. "There are settlements—my father and Halsey spent months hammering them out with solicitors. If I reject Lord Halsey's suit now, he can sue for breach of contract."

"Aye, I know all about settlements." Mal nodded wisely. "The Mackenzies also have solicitors—extremely practical and tight-fisted Scotsmen, the lot of them. They can squeeze blood from a turnip."

"They would have to do a lot of squeezing with Halsey," Mary said dryly.

Malcolm chuckled. "We'll see. You are a marvel, ye are. Ye can sit so close to me and talk calmly about solicitors and settlements, while all I'm thinking is how much like silk your skin is."

The skin in question tightened. Malcolm traced Mary's cheekbone and down across her lips, his fingertips lingering on her chin.

He didn't demand with this caress. It was gentle, giving. Mary raised her hand, her fingers shaking, and touched his cheek in return.

She felt the burn of whiskers, the twitch of muscle. Mal watched her, his golden eyes giving nothing away.

Mary let her fingers wander down his jaw, brushed with red-gold bristles, to his neck and the sinews there. Daringly, she drew her touch to the hollow of his throat, then across his exposed collarbone to his broad shoulder.

If she'd never seen a man unclothed—other than the very small statues—she'd certainly never touched one. Mal's skin was warm, despite his swim in the ocean, and smoother than she'd thought a man's would be. The skin was also tight, covering the steel of muscle.

"Ye can nae do this, Mary," he said softly.

Mary froze, but she couldn't lift her fingers. "Why not?"

"Because here I am, bare for ye to touch all ye want. But I can nae do it in return."

"I know," she said. "'Twould be improper."

"As improper as sitting against me while I'm in nothing but a blanket? Ye have strange notions, lass."

Mary felt giddy. "If you are going to ask me to sit with you in nothing but a blanket, I must refuse."

Malcolm's gaze sharpened. "And ye should nae say things like *that*. My imagination, 'tis an inventive one."

Mary swallowed. Her imagination was good too, and thinking about being naked in a blanket, the fabric touching her intimately, with Malcolm beside her, scalded her from the inside out. Her breasts felt tight, holding a strange ache.

"Turn around," Malcolm said.

"What?"

"Just here, on the sofa. Turn your back to me."

"Why?" Mary asked, her body stiff.

Mal gave her a crooked grin. "I love that ye don't obey without question. Save me from a meek woman who always does what she's told." The smile vanished. "Turn around, because I want to touch ye, that's why."

The proper Mary would refuse, offering a rebuke. After all, he was a Highland barbarian and she was a lady.

The proper Mary had been banished to the deepest dungeon tonight. Mary gathered her skirts and moved herself on the small couch so her back was to Malcolm. Her panniers pinched her, but she ignored the discomfort.

Malcolm lifted her hair from her neck with a steady hand. Whitman had dressed Mary's hair in a modish style tonight, much of it drawn up in pins to the top of her head, with a few curling locks falling to her neck. More strands had come loose from the wind and their adventure, and were now damp from mist and Malcolm.

Mary stilled as Malcolm drew his fingers slowly down her neck to the bare scoop of back her satin gown revealed.

"You're soft here, Mary, do ye know that?" he asked quietly. "Don't think I've ever seen a lovelier back."

"You look at many, do you?" Mary's words were breathy, hardly the teasing admonishment she'd meant them to be.

A laugh, hot against her skin. "When ye grow up in a Scottish castle with five men and a crowd of servants, ye see a lot more backs than ye care to."

Mal's laughter drifted away, and Mary felt his lips at the base of her neck. "I still have the lock of hair ye gave me, ye know," he said. "I put it in the box where I keep my most precious things."

Mary was melting. His touch sent heat down her spine to the base of it.

This was a man, a stranger, touching her with bare, broad hands, kissing where he had no right to. She was violating every propriety, breaking every rule.

And yet she could not imagine doing anything else. It felt right to let Mal touch her thus, forging a bond between them that was different from any connection she had to any other person.

Mary let her head drop to the side, her eyes closing as Malcolm's lips moved from her neck to her spine. He slid his hands around her waist, gliding them up her stomacher to her breasts.

"One night this will all come away," he said. "I'll be able to touch the whole of ye."

And on that night, Mary would burn up and die.

Malcolm's arms came all the way around her, drawing her against him, as he continued to feather kisses across her skin. His mouth spread fire through every limb, Mary's body growing pliant and accepting.

Mal continued to explore what her gown bared with his lips, then his tongue, then he pulled her back to him as he lay against the end of the couch. Mary turned her head to see his eyelids drooping, exhaustion finally claiming him.

Mal's arms grew heavy around her as he relaxed, locking Mary into his embrace. He hooked one blanket-clad leg around hers while his breathing slowed. In a few moments, his hold went slack but didn't entirely loosen.

Mary studied his face, so near hers. Malcolm's tightness had melted, his body relaxed in a way she'd never seen it. His cares eased from his face, as well as his arrogance, sleep erasing any sternness and rendering him the young man Mal truly was. After a moment or two, he began to softly snore.

The room was quiet, Naughton and the other servants leaving them alone. The only noise was the pop of the fire and Malcolm's breathing.

Mary was warm, comfortable lying back against Malcolm, the whisky chasing all fear from her. She felt her eyes growing heavy, but she was determined not to fall asleep. Now that Malcolm was settled, she ought to rise, go home, tell her father and Aunt Danae what had transpired this night.

But she could not move. Malcolm's chest rose and fell against her, his even breathing, with the hint of snore, more soothing than a soporific.

Mary's eyes closed, and she slept.

When she woke, the window was gray with dawn. She was still lying back against Malcolm, her head on his shoulder, his arms securely around her.

The very tall Mackenzie with dark red hair she'd seen at the prince's ball, his eyes even more wicked than Malcolm's, was bcnding down to look Mary in thc facc.

"Who might you be?" he asked. "And why is my little brother snuggled up to ye so cozy?"

Chapter 15

Malcolm felt Mary start. He woke to find Will curving over both of them, studying Mary with rapt interest.

"Good morning, runt," Will said with good humor. "Why are ye sleeping with a fully clothed woman on a couch, and where's Alec?"

"Hell." The blanket had slipped down Mal's chest, but he hadn't noticed, because Mary had been on him, cutting the cold. Damn and blast Will for the interfering bastard he was.

Malcolm carefully released Mary and levered himself to sit upright. "Alec is on a ship to France to find his daughter. His wife passed in childbed, poor lass. This is Lady Mary Lennox. Mary, m' brother, Will."

Will kept his gaze on Mary, but he straightened up, blinking. "Did you just say Alec's *wife*? And *daughter*?"

Mal gave him a nod. "Aye. He married her last year, when we were in Paris. A pretty little lass, called Genevieve. A dancer with the opera. They wed, and she soon became quick with child. No surprise, really, the way they were at it, day and night."

"Alec." Will spoke slowly and deliberately. "*Married.*"

"Aye, that's what I'm tellin' ye."

Will stood all the way up to his full height, his face awash with confusion. "And *I* didn't know?"

"We kept it a deep, dark secret between us," Mal said. "Don't blame yourself. It's Dad we were keeping it quiet from. An opera dancer, from Paris? He'd go apoplectic. We were going to break it to him gently, after the wee one came along."

"But I know *everything*," Will said. "Whether you want me to or not."

"You had other things on your mind." Mal resisted the urge to pat his brother's giant clenched fist in comfort. "The Jacobite uprising, Duncan running off . . ." He shrugged, not adding *the movements of the English troops, the state of politics in France and Ireland.*

"But she *died*?" Will went on, trying to take in the full story. He ran a hand through his unruly hair. "Ah, poor Alec. Poor, poor Alec. No wonder he's been so unhappy of late. She had the child, you say? It is well?"

"That's what Alec's gone to find out," Mal said. "He had a letter, I had a ship standing ready, and off he went."

Will blinked again. "You had a . . . Mal, *why* did you have a ship standing ready? What ship?"

"Gair's. I had other cargo to send out. Sent Alec with it."

Will made another pass of his hand through his hair, the thick strands of it standing straight up. "Let that be a lesson to me. I cast my gaze to the wider world, and miss everything at home." He shot his gaze back to Mary. "Lady Mary *Lennox*?" When Mary nodded, Will looked accusingly at Malcolm. "She's the Earl of Halsey's betrothed. She can't be here."

Mary stood up, shaking out her skirts. "You are quite right, Lord William. I must be at home before full light, or the scandal will be all over town." She gave Mal a stately nod. "Thank you, Lord Malcolm, for all your help."

As Mal and Will watched, nonplussed, Mary moved to a gilt-framed mirror to briefly smooth her hair, then headed for the door. So caught up was Mal by her feminine movements that she was gone from the room before he realized.

He was up, snatching a shirt and a plaid as the door clicked shut behind her. He yanked it open and rushed out, throwing the clothes onto his body as he went. Will, understanding his alarm, came after him.

Downstairs already, Mary was taking her cloak from Naughton, expressing her thanks at finding it cleaned and dried. Mal charged down the stairs, but too late.

The bearlike figure of his father came out of a chamber into the lower hall. He saw Mary and headed straight for her.

"Who the devil are *you*?" he shouted. The man was hungover again, his bloodshot eyes glistening in the light from the open front door. His shirt was unlaced, his coat barely shrugged on, his plaids in disarrayed folds.

Mary gave him a calm curtsy then went back to fastening her cloak. "Good morning, Your Grace. I am Lady Mary Lennox. Very sorry to have disturbed you, sir, but my errand is finished, and I am just going."

"Lennox?" The roar in the duke's voice died a little as he puzzled this out. "You're Wilfort's daughter."

"Yes," Mary said, sliding on the gloves Naughton handed her. "Lord Wilfort is my father. Again, I am so sorry to have disturbed you. Good day, Your Grace."

"Wilfort," the duke repeated, then he swung his head around and looked up the stairs. "What the *hell* is the daughter of that bloody Sassenach doing in this house? Will! Damn ye, what have ye—"

Malcolm made it the rest of the way to the ground floor and pushed himself in front of the duke.

"Lady Mary is a guest," he said. "A *guest*, if ye please. Keep a civil tongue, Dad."

The double surprise of finding Mary in his stairwell and Malcolm telling him to be quiet actually silenced the duke for a second or two. By the time he opened his mouth to shout again, Mary had walked out into the morning.

A carriage waited there, summoned by the ever-efficient Naughton. Mal gave an exasperated growl and rushed out after Mary.

He caught her hand before a footman could help her into the coach. Malcolm squeezed her fingers. "Good-bye for now, lass. But not for long. I'll settle Dad, and then I'll come for ye. All right? After that, we won't ever be apart."

Mary started to speak, but Mal shook his head, glancing back at the house. Mary seemed to understand. She gripped Malcolm's hand serenely as he assisted her into the coach.

"Good-bye, Mal," Mary said as he withdrew. "And thank you."

Mal only gave her a nod, then signaled the coachman to drive on. Malcolm knew he'd stopped her speaking, not for fear of his father, but because he'd not wanted to hear Mary say *No.*

The duke staggered out of the house. He was in a bad way, his face red, his breathing uneven. "What the devil was she doing here? Is she your doxy now? Are ye mad, runt?"

Will had also emerged, and together he and Mal got the duke back into the safety of the house. Naughton shut the door before curious passersby could look in.

"I asked ye to keep a civil tongue," Mal said in a hard voice. "Lady Mary is no doxy. She's a respectable lady, and the woman I intend t' marry."

The duke stared at Malcolm for a second or two, then his fist swung out. "Over my dead body will ye marry the daughter of a bloody English earl!"

Mal, adroit by now in dodging his father's blows, caught his fist and turned it aside. "I'm of age, and can marry whatever woman I damn well please. Go ahead and disown me, if ye have a mind. I have plenty of money, and ye have four other sons to inherit your title before me. God knows I don't ever want to be duke."

Mal's father was unused to being defied. His sons had learned a long time ago how to let him bellow and then do what they wanted on the quiet. Except for Duncan, they rarely told him plainly what they thought.

The duke's momentary shock let Mal push past him and climb the stairs to his chamber. Not until Mal had shut his bedchamber door did the duke begin shouting again.

Mal stood for a time in the middle of the room, unmoving. His shirt and plaid hung askew, but he made no move to right them and make himself ready for the day.

The chamber was forlorn and empty without the vibrancy of Mary in it. Her scent lingered, as did the remembered sensation of the warm weight of her body against his in the night. Waking up with Mary in his arms had been the best moment of Malcolm's life.

Mal needed many more moments like that. He'd do anything necessary to bring Mary permanently into his life, notwithstanding his father and hers, and the enmity of two nations. None of that mattered. Only waking to breathe the fragrance of Mary's hair, seeing her flushed and disheveled and brushed by morning light, had any importance to Malcolm. Which, to his mind, was as things should be.

Mary's cloak had been dried, brushed, and mended, and now was cleaner than her own maids had ever rendered it. She took a small comfort in the cloak's warmth, which she fancied carried a hint of Malcolm's spice, as she descended at the front door of her father's house.

The carriage stopped so close to the front door that Mary had to take only a few steps to be inside. The coach shielded her from view of the rest of the street. More gratitude for the Mackenzie servants, though she supposed they'd become very good at discretion on behalf of their masters.

Whitman came hurrying from the direction of the back stairs as Mary entered. "Oh, my lady." She seized Mary's arm with both hands, squeezing as though reassuring herself that Mary was real. "My lady, I was so worried for you. I thought for certain the mad Scotsmen had taken you."

The Scots footman, who'd shut the front door behind Mary, looked as concerned as Whitman. "The streets ain't safe, me lady," he said, bolting the door to emphasize his point.

"I am well." Mary took Whitman's hand, remorse touching her at the sight of the woman's tears. "Truly, I am. I'd like to retire now, though. I am quite weary."

Falling asleep propped against Malcolm after a cold flight to the wharves and then drinking the strange *uisge* was taking its toll. Mary's limbs were stiff, her head aching.

"Of course, my lady," Whitman said, solicitous. "Go on, lad. Make certain her ladyship has hot water and a good fire."

Whitman put her arm around Mary's shoulders and guided her up the dark stairway. In Whitman's fear for Mary, she'd not asked after Audrey, but any moment, she would realize . . .

Aunt Danae's chamber door flew open as they reached the landing two floors up. Aunt Danae, in a wrapper, her hair tucked under a large white cap, rushed out, her eyes wide and red-rimmed. Without a word, she took Mary's arm and hurried with her and Whitman into Mary's chamber.

As soon as the door closed, Aunt Danae crushed Mary in a breath-stealing hug. "Oh, my sweet gel, I thought for certain you were dead and gone. What on earth happened to you?"

"Auntie, I am so sorry." Mary broke from the hug and rubbed her aunt's arms. "I never meant to be gone this long. Is Papa very upset?"

"No, because I did not tell him I'd lost you." Aunt Danae took Mary's hands, her grip crushing. "I put it about that you were staying with friends, you and Audrey. I hoped that was what you had done. If you didn't return today, I knew I would have to . . . would have to . . ." Aunt Danae shook her head, fighting down a sob. "But here you are, safe and whole. I will scold you soundly later, but for now, I am only happy you are home." She looked suddenly uncertain, and peered behind Mary. "Where is your sister? Whitman, Audrey came in with Mary, did she not?"

Whitman turned from the bed. "No, my lady." The brick with which she'd been warming Mary's nightclothes froze in her grip, the cloth around it dangling. "I never saw Lady Audrey."

"Then where is she?" Aunt Danae hastened to the window and looked down at the street as though she'd see Audrey below, running for the house. "Where is she, Mary?"

"She is safe." Mary's heart beat faster, knowing she could put off the news no longer. "Come here, Auntie. Sit with me." She plumped herself on a sofa and patted the cushion next to her. Aunt Danae eyed her warily, but sat, the tapes on her cap trembling.

"Audrey is safe and happy," Mary said, trying to keep her voice gentle. "She is with Jeremy Drake. They are married."

Aunt Danae was silent for a full ten seconds, then she gave a strangled cry. "Married? What the devil do you mean? She can't be married!"

"She is," Mary said. She strove to remain soothing, but her head pounded and her voice rasped. "She's very happy, and on her way to France."

Aunt Danae stared for a few more moments, then she fell back against the sofa's cushions. "Good gracious. Dear God, help me."

"The marriage is a legal one," Mary said quickly. "Done by clergy, registered and witnessed. Jeremy is a good man, Auntie. He'll take care of her."

"I have never thought otherwise. But, my dear . . ." Aunt Danae looked at her limply. "How are we ever going to tell your father? You should have fetched me last night, and we'd all have fled to France together. It is the only way any of us will escape his wrath."

Chapter 16

As it happened, it was quite late before Mary was able to speak to her father. That very morning, word came that General Cope had landed south of Edinburgh and was making his way toward the city to intercept Charles's army.

The Earls of Wilfort and Halsey shut themselves up in Lord Wilfort's study that day, sending out messages and receiving visits from other Englishmen in and around Edinburgh, including Jeremy's father, Lord Bancroft. Mary feared that Lord Bancroft would spill the news of the elopement before Mary could, but her father said not a word about it.

Mary's chamber was placed such that her window let in conversations from her father's study below, provided both windows were open. Today had been fine, so she'd been able to hear everything that went on in the chamber beneath hers. No matter how hard Mary listened, she never once heard Jeremy's name mentioned. It was as though the lad's own father hadn't realized he'd gone, and that might be true.

Mary spent the day with Aunt Danae, but her mind was not on their usual tasks of sewing, letter writing, or reading aloud. Mary was distracted, as indeed, Aunt Danae was, wondering how Audrey fared, whether the ship would reach port without mishap, if they'd be safe on the road to Paris. Mary had faith that Alec and Jeremy would look after her sister, but she'd feel much better when she received Audrey's first letter.

Mary also tried not to think about Malcolm, but there, she failed. She could not look down at her stitching without seeing him peeling his wet clothes from his body, laughing at his predicament even as he shivered with deadly cold.

She remembered the warm bulk of him beneath her, the gentle snore that told her he slept. The memories of his mouth on her back and then of lying in his arms were so vivid that for moments at a time, Mary was *there*, with him, instead of sitting demurely on Aunt Danae's couch, sewing a seam on her father's shirt.

I'll come for ye. All right? After that, we won't ever be apart.

Mary had no idea what he meant to do, which alarmed her a bit, but remembering his voice quietly saying the words made her warm. This was a man capable of anything, from arranging an elopement, to sending his brother to his baby daughter, to making certain the entire Jacobite army didn't hamper him.

A dangerous man, and yet, at the same time, compassionate and understanding. Everything Mal had done tonight had been for others. Even if his actions had benefited him indirectly—getting Mary alone in his house, where he could kiss her—Malcolm could have taken what he wanted, to the devil with everyone else. He'd asked Mary to trust him, and so far, he hadn't betrayed that trust.

No one went out that night—any invitations were refused. Aunt Danae advised Mary they should wait until after their late supper to spring the news about Audrey on her father. They could be more private then, and perhaps plenty of food and drink would have put him into a mellower state.

Halsey, unfortunately, stayed for the meal. Though Audrey's place at the table remained empty, Lord Wilfort never once asked about her during that interminable supper. Likely he assumed Audrey in her chamber, sleeping or ill, or too nervous about the possible battle to come down.

Mary gathered her courage as they rose from the table and Wilfort asked Halsey to join him for brandy in his library.

"Papa, I need a word."

"Not now," Wilfort said without looking at her. "Halsey, I had another message from—"

Mary stepped in front of her father as he tried to turn away. "Papa, you really ought to hear me."

Wilfort pulled his attention from Halsey with effort. His blue eyes were as strong as they'd been when Mary was a girl, though they'd become harder since the day her mother died. "Yes, Mary, what is it?" he asked impatiently.

Mary glanced at Halsey, who waited not three paces away. "Perhaps we can be private?"

Wilfort followed her gaze, and frowned. "Anything you must speak about, Mary, you can in front of Lord Halsey. He will be your husband."

Mary growled silently to herself, but there was nothing for it. The longer she waited the worse it would be. She clenched her fists. "Papa," she began, then she launched into her tale.

Mary told it briefly, in bold strokes. As she explained that Audrey was now married, legally, to Jeremy Drake, Wilfort's expression moved from irritated to bewildered to enraged. Wilfort reached out and seized Mary by the arm, twisting it as he yanked her to him.

"She has defied me?" Wilfort's body was slender but whippet strong. He kept his voice low but vicious, unlike the beam-rattling shouts of Malcolm's father. "And you *helped* her?"

"Papa, Jeremy is a fine man from a good family." Mary was close enough to smell the wine on her father's breath, to look into steely eyes in his sharp face. "Audrey loves him—"

"*Love?*" Wilfort's grip tightened, and he shook her once. "You know nothing about love. Marrying for love is a fool's trap. You know this—you're sensible, Mary—at least I thought you were."

He was hurting her arm very much, but Mary made herself not flinch. "You loved Mama."

Something flickered in Wilfort's eyes. "We came to be very fond of each other, yes, but we married at the will of our parents, which was our duty, as it is yours and Audrey's. Love grows after a solid marriage is made. *That* is how the world works."

"James," Aunt Danae said, her voice weak. "It wasn't Mary's fault."

"You are wrong, Danae. It was entirely her fault, and yours. I will speak with you later. Audrey could not have gone without Mary's help, and that is a fact." Wilfort focused his cold blue eyes on Mary again. "And *you* could not have done this without help of your own. Who assisted you?"

"No one," Mary said swiftly. "Jeremy—"

"Jeremy Drake is a simpleton and couldn't arrange a midnight feast in his own house. Who helped you? I'll have whoever it is arrested for his part in this, then I'll go to France and fetch Audrey home."

"You can't—"

Wilfort clamped down on Mary's wrist, his face going scarlet. "Who are you to say I can't? Who helped you, Mary? What is his name? Who arranged for the ship?"

Mary shook her head, fighting tears of anger and pain. "I did."

Wilfort made a noise of derision. "With two thousand Jacobites camped around Edinburgh? You did this all by yourself? I never thought you'd lie to me, daughter. You shame me. Who is the man who helped you?"

If Mary named Malcolm, what would happen? Wilfort's power had been lessened by the presence of Charles, and Mal was a duke's son. Her father couldn't do much to Mal, could he? But he might try to call Malcolm out, or simply find him and shoot him. Mary thought of Mal's slow smile, the heat of his touch, his uncompromising belief in everything he did. She could not let him face the ice-cold wrath of her father. Mary closed her mouth and kept silent.

Wilfort hit her. Mary's head rocked from the backhanded blow. The earl's signet ring cut open her cheek, stinging it.

"James, no!" Aunt Danae cried.

Wilfort shook Mary until her hair tumbled over her face. "You ungrateful, deceitful girl. You will be locked in your room until you give me the name of the man who helped you take Audrey away from me."

Wilfort shoved her from him. Mary's high-heeled slippers caught on the carpet, tripping her, and she had to seize the back of a chair to keep from falling. Aunt Danae started for her, but her father's glare sent Danae scuttling back.

Halsey did nothing. Throughout the diatribe, he'd only

watched, listened, observed. His expression was one of strange satisfaction, the glint in his eyes unnerving.

Wilfort straightened his coat and gave Halsey a short bow. "I apologize, Halsey, that you had to witness this scene."

Halsey sniffed. "No apology necessary, sir. Women ought to be obedient, and we need to teach them so. A good cuffing or caning works wonders."

"Mary has never needed much discipline." Wilfort smoothed his cuffs and moved back to the table, reaching a shaking hand for brandy. "Rarely disobedient—this is a surprise to me. But the Lennox women are headstrong. You should be aware of that. Danae, take Mary to her chamber and lock her in, then bring me the key."

Aunt Danae came to Mary as the men turned away. Mary declined her help as Aunt Danae took her from the room, Wilfort and Halsey already deep into their discussion of the situation outside these walls. Wilfort never looked at Mary as she retreated from the room, but Halsey's parting glance held an odd interest that made Mary shiver.

They were keeping her prisoner.

Malcolm heard this the next morning from Naughton, who'd had it from a footman from Mary's house. Malcolm was in his own chamber, cleaning his pistol with brisk movements, as Naughton told all he knew.

Mal growled when Naughton was done. "Her dad's a bloody martinet. Reminds me of mine."

The duke had locked Malcolm into rooms plenty of times in his life, though Mal had never let himself stay confined for long. Neither would Mary, if Mal had anything to do with it.

"Find me a way inside that house," he ordered.

Naughton calmly went on folding Malcolm's linen. "Do you plan to rescue her, sir?"

"Of course I do."

"The prince's army is marching out to meet General Cope before he makes Edinburgh. Lord Duncan marches with them. You asked to be kept informed, sir."

Malcolm already knew this, having gone back and forth between home and camp all day yesterday, trying to persuade

Duncan away. He and Will were also trying to persuade their father and Angus to return to Kilmorgan. Both efforts had been fruitless.

"Have a message taken to Lady Mary," Mal said as he drew the rod with its cleaning rag from the pistol's barrel. "Tell her to stay put while I go out and make sure Duncan doesn't get himself killed. Then we'll take care of Lady Mary's predicament."

Naughton coughed. "Pardon me for asking, sir, but I need to be prepared for any contingency. Is Lady Mary with child?"

Mal looked up in amazement. "No, damn ye." He made himself cool. "'Tis a fair question, though. But no." Malcolm returned the pistol to its holster and checked his supply of powder and pistol balls. He lifted the strap that held holster and ammunition pouch over his shoulder and settled it across his coat. "Don't wait up for me, Naughton. If I can drag Duncan home, I will. If not . . ." He shrugged. "Make sure Lady Mary receives my message."

"Yes, sir," Naughton said. "I'll see to it personally."

Mary fumed for a time, locked in her bedchamber, before her hot anger cooled, determination taking its place.

Whitman was allowed in to tend to her and bring her small meals, but Mary was to have contact with no one else, not even Aunt Danae. Wilfort sent Mary a message, via Whitman, that he intended to keep Mary under lock and key until her marriage to Halsey, which had been planned for the next month.

But Mary knew that she could never marry Halsey. The light in his eyes when her father had hit her last night, coupled with his look when he'd waylaid her in the stairwell a few nights ago and squeezed her breast, had awakened a loathing she'd never be able to banish. Halsey had been loathsome all the time of their engagement, but Mary had not allowed herself to see it. Her pride in her duty had made her blind, foolishly so.

The fight to free herself from Halsey was yet to come. Mary used the time of her confinement to decide how to do just that, as well as to catch up on her mending and her correspondence, both of which she'd been neglecting.

Mary sat at her writing table late the first night of her imprisonment, trying to describe Charles's entrance to the ballroom at Holyrood for a London friend's entertainment, but she laid down her pen and passed her hand over her eyes. Despite all that had happened, what remained most vivid was the warm touch of Mal's lips, his strength as he held her, asleep on the sofa. The pain of the cut her father had given her could not prevail against it.

"M'lady?"

Mary snapped alert, raising her head. The whisper hadn't come from the door. It had come from the fireplace.

A fire was blazing in it. Mary stared at the flames a few moments before the muffled voice came again, along with a tapping on the wall.

Chapter 17

"M'lady!"

Mary recognized the voice—it belonged to one of the Scottish lads who ran errands for them. "Is that you, Ewan?" she called. "Where on earth are you?"

"Here."

She at last saw him in the shadows where the firelight didn't reach. Ewan had removed one rectangle of paneling in the wainscoting and was crouched inside the hole.

Ewan couldn't be more than twelve years old and was usually covered with dirt, but he was a quick thinker and remembered things. He could be trusted to send messages and fetch goods from shops without making mistakes.

Mary sank down to her hands and knees next to the opening. "How did you get in there?" she asked. The hole appeared to be Ewan-sized, no room for anyone else.

"It's meant for servant boys," Ewan said. "In the old days, they could crawl through and stir up the fires without disturbing anyone."

"Very thoughtful," Mary said, disapproving. For ladies and gentlemen who couldn't be bothered about the comfort of those who waited on them, he meant. "Where do the passages lead?"

"All through the house," Ewan said. "So when they needed to send someone, they thought of me."

Mary was getting lost. "Who needed to send someone? Where?"

"Mr. Naughton did. He's me gran's brother-in-law. He said, *Send someone to Lady Mary and tell her his lordship says he'll be there soon after his errand, and she's not to move.* When Cook—me gran—heard that, she said, *I'll send Ewan up through the passages, and no one will be the wiser.*"

Mary had a glimmer of understanding. "By *his lordship,* I take it you mean Lord Malcolm?"

"Aye, m'lady. You're to stay and wait for him. He's running off after the Scots army, but he'll be done soon, he says."

"The entire army?" Mary's heart beat faster. "Is he going to fight against the Jacobites? Or *with* them?"

"Mr. Naughton says neither one. Lord Malcolm's off to throw a net over his brother and drag him home."

Blast the man. Mal's intentions might be nothing more than Ewan said, but if Mal drew sword against the English army, he'd be labeled a traitor for the rest of his life, which might be short.

"He can't go," she said, clenching her hands. "He'll be caught up in the mess, captured, or killed. You must tell him not to go."

Ewan only stared at her. "He's already gone, m'lady. Mr. Naughton says that when Lord Malcolm takes it into his head to do something, Jesus himself couldn't change his mind. That's what Gran and Mr. Naughton say anyway."

Oh, dear heavens. Today, Mary had heard everything her father and Lord Halsey discussed below her in the study about how the English army was dealing with the uprising. She knew that men were even now being recalled from Flanders, that the king had returned from Hanover and was taking steps to crush this rebellion with firm determination.

Mary couldn't banish the image of Malcolm, in his plaids, claymore in his hand, charging straight into artillery fire. Smoke would descend on the fields, and when it cleared, Mal would be lying on the grass, bloody and dead.

Her breath caught. "No."

If Malcolm died, Mary would never be able to bear it. To

Mary, Malcolm was life itself. He'd given her a glimpse of a world she had never known, one of intense emotion, boldness, hope.

That life couldn't be extinguished. Not now, when it was young, strong, and full of endless possibilities.

When he'd told her the other day that he'd been called home, she'd mourned, feeling bittersweet sorrow at a path not trodden. She'd walked a good way down that path since then, and realized there was no turning back. Malcolm's death would grieve her more than she was prepared for it to.

"Don't worry, m'lady," Ewan said confidently. "Lord Malcolm's been in battles before and always walked away from them."

Mary made herself climb to her feet. She couldn't crumple and fall at the news—she must act instead.

"Thank you, Ewan," Mary said. She could be very strong when she needed to be, and she'd have to be strong to weather anything to do with Malcolm Mackenzie. "Please discover all you can about what is happening and come back here to tell me." She plunged her hand into her pocket and pulled out a few coins. "You'll be my sergeant, and I your captain. You're to report to me and only to me, and not get caught. Understood?"

"Aye." Ewan snapped off a practiced salute, grabbed the coins from her palm, and made them disappear somewhere in his dirty clothes. "Right away, Captain, *sir*."

Mary kept a straight face. "Off you go, then. And not a word to anyone."

"Aye, *sir*." Ewan gave her another salute, quickly replaced the panel in the wall, and was gone. Mary heard a few scrabbling noises behind the wainscoting, then nothing.

She was left alone with her troubled thoughts, her unfinished correspondence, and her fear for Malcolm.

In the small hours of the morning, Malcolm marched in silence next to his brother, the mercilessly stubborn Lord Duncan Mackenzie, toward the village of Preston, to meet Johnny Cope and teach him a lesson.

At least, that's what Duncan intended. A local lad had told Lord George Murray about a solid path across the marshes, which the Jacobite army now used to circle Cope and his men. At dawn, they'd turn and attack the English from this new angle.

Malcolm and Duncan walked near the rear of the line. They were odd men out here, having no clansmen or retainers behind them.

Mal was there to make sure that Duncan made it back alive. Though Duncan and their father went at it with words and fists often enough, Malcolm knew his father would be devastated if Duncan died.

Malcolm had told Duncan as much when he'd arrived at the camp last night, but Duncan, of course, hadn't believed him.

"The old bastard would be happy to be shot of me," Duncan had said. "He's hated me from the day I was old enough to tell him what I thought of him."

"Ye don't ken as much as ye think," Mal had answered. "You're as blindly stubborn as Da. If you die, *I* have t' live with his grief, and that I do not want to do. Besides, Will refuses to be duke."

Duncan snorted a laugh. "Will is a duplicitous snake. Ye'd do well to remember that, runt."

Mal couldn't argue. Nor could he convince Duncan to stay out of the battle and wait back in Edinburgh. His attempt to take Duncan by force hadn't worked either. Malcolm was strong and fast, but Duncan had great power, especially in his fists, which had laid Mal out cold.

When Malcolm had come to, the Highlanders had been marching. Mal had rinsed the blood from his face, swept up his arms, and hurried to catch up.

He'd pull Duncan's balls out of the fire, deliver the man home to their father, then go to Mary and take her away with him. A good plan, one Malcolm didn't intend to let fail.

Mists clogged the air, clinging to Malcolm's clothes, dampening his gunpowder as he loaded and primed his pistol. While he had no intention of joining the rebels, he'd be damned if he'd stand there and let Cope's men shoot him.

The Highlanders charged before Mal was aware they'd started. He heard one volley of artillery fire, then the English guns went eerily silent. That silence was broken by musket fire, and then the screams of two thousand Highlanders rushing the lines of Johnny Cope's troops.

Duncan sprinted forward, and Malcolm ran with him. Mal's pistol would be useless at long range, but he kept it ready.

The mists began to burn away, the sun sharpening the landscape. Malcolm ran into the morass with the others, the battle cry of his ancestors leaving his throat before he could stop it.

After a moment or two, Mal dodged out of the way of the Jacobite Highlanders who swarmed past him, muskets discarded and swords out. Everywhere, English infantry in their scarlet coats were boiling apart, dragoons wheeling horses, hooves pounding, men running.

Mud churned as horses scrambled out of the way of the charging Highlanders. The English artillery, on the other hand, a small contingent of cannon shining in the morning light, lay empty and unmanned. *Interesting.* Mal swung around and made for the guns. Duncan, seeing him go, followed.

The two brothers approached the cannons, acrid smoke and powder hanging in the air. The guns had been fired once and then abandoned. Mortars and gunpowder lay in a heap next to them, the wagons and horses to move them all waiting patiently beyond.

"Well, look what we've found," Stuart Cameron, Will's friend, said as he and a few others joined Duncan and Mal. "Sitting here nice and sweet, like wallflowers wanting a dance partner."

Mal laid a hand on a cannon's cold barrel. "What will ye do with them, then?" he asked. "Steal them for Teàrlach?"

"A feather for Duncan," Stuart said. "Capturing the entire line of artillery like that."

"Falling over them, ye mean," another Jacobite said, and laughed. "Good find, Duncan."

Mal had found them, not Duncan, but he didn't quibble. Mal had no interest in accolades from Prince Teàrlach.

He opened his mouth to explain this, but at that moment, a lone English dragoon rode out of the tatters of mist, sword drawn, face set in determination. The dragoon charged in deathly silence, his sword going right for Duncan's neck.

Duncan tried to dive out of the way, but Malcolm saw that he wouldn't be quick enough. Mal spun from the cannon and came up beside the horse, his claymore flashing as it rang against the dragoon's sword.

Malcolm twisted his blade, running it down the dragoon's,

using the horse's momentum to assist him. Mal's sword tip contacted with the hilt of the dragoon's sword, jerking the thing out of the man's hand.

The dragoon let the sword go. He wheeled his horse, sending it at Malcolm, at the same time drawing his pistol and firing.

Malcolm leapt aside and grabbed the horse's neck as the beast came past. The horse's speed swept him up, and Mal hung on with a mad grip, hauling himself onto the horse's withers in front of the dragoon. The Englishman glared in disbelief, and a growl of fury sounded as he reached gloved hands for Malcolm's throat.

Malcolm knocked the man off the horse. The dragoon landed hard but rolled and gained his feet almost instantly. The next moment, Duncan and his men were on the dragoon, dragging him down to the grass.

Mal swung up and into the saddle, finding the stirrups and guiding the horse in a tight circle. The beast, knowing an expert rider when he felt one, calmed.

Duncan's friends were beating the dragoon to a pulp.

"Leave off and take him prisoner," Malcolm shouted at them. "He's a brave man, attacking five of us by himself."

Duncan abruptly pulled a soldier off the dragoon. "Stop." He glared down at the Englishman. "Surrender to me, sir, and you'll live."

The Englishman gave him a sullen stare. "Do I have any other bloody choice?"

"Die like a man?" Stuart Cameron suggested.

"My men are cowards," the dragoon snapped. "What honor is it to die for them? Fine—I surrender. I don't care what you do to me, just keep my horse well."

Malcolm patted the horse's sweating neck. "Aye, he's a fine beast."

The dragoon folded his arms. "This will be a short war, in any case, if your only strategy is to throw aside your muskets and run at us screaming like banshees."

"Worked, didn't it?" Mal asked him cheerfully.

Around them, Cope's troops were fleeing, or dropping guns and surrendering to the Highlanders. No one came for the artillery—its wagons and horses waited, empty, the drivers having fled.

Duncan said to Malcolm, "Your prisoner, runt. What do you want done with him?"

Mal started. "*My* prisoner? I'm not part of this. Yours, brother."

Duncan's face, streaked with sweat and dirt, split with his grin. "You unhorsed and disarmed him. Your capture. What should we do? Run him through? Tie him up and take him away?"

"Bloody hell." Malcolm looked at the cluster of men around him, their stained plaids, crooked bonnets, and cocksure smiles. He growled. "Tie him up. Take him off. Prove to him we're civilized. At least that *I* am."

Duncan barked a laugh. A few of the others looked disappointed they couldn't kill the dragoon then and there, but all were awash with joy at their easy victory.

The fight was already over. Charles's army had won the day. Word came through by another Highlander on horseback that Duncan was to secure the cannon and ready them to be hauled back to camp.

It hadn't been a battle, Malcolm reflected, so much as a clash and a rout. But the British army now knew what the Highlanders could do.

Malcolm Mackenzie left the field of the Battle of Prestonpans with a captured horse, the dragoon's sword and pistol, and a prisoner all his own.

Mary knew the outcome of the battle before Ewan returned, first from the frenzy in the streets. Her windows overlooked the garden in the rear, but she could hear the running of men and horses beyond, the shouting, the cheering.

She raised one of her windows in time to hear her father's voice floating from the open window of the study below.

"Cope's only gone and run away," Wilfort was saying in disgust. "He's lost all his large guns, and, I hear, coin totaling near to three thousand pounds. Idiot. He couldn't stand against two thousand barbarians in skirts?"

"He was unprepared," Halsey said soothingly. "Wade won't be. Or Cumberland, if he's called."

"It's embarrassing," Wilfort growled. "What about what

we're amassing in Glasgow? I assume you came today with word of that."

"Yes, I . . ."

Halsey's voice faded as they moved from the window, and renewed shouting on the streets drowned him out.

Whitman entered after that to tell Mary excitedly that the prince's army had won the day, and he was heading back to Edinburgh, ready for a triumphal entry. Whitman had no love for Jacobites, but it was something to see, wasn't it?

The rest of the day was full of noise and restlessness outside. Mary's father closed his study window, so she had no more information from that quarter.

No news of Malcolm made Mary restless, worried, aching. If the Jacobites had prevailed, there was a good chance Mal had walked away unscathed, but men had died, she'd heard before her father had shut the window. Though the casualties had been few—negligible, Halsey had said—for those few and their families, the deaths were far more important than the matter of who'd been victorious.

Mary heard nothing until after Whitman readied her for bed that night and left her. Not long after Whitman had closed the door, Mary heard a soft tapping on the panel near the fireplace.

She quickly rose, snatched up her dressing gown, and hurried to kneel by the wainscoting. "Ewan?"

The panel moved, and Ewan's dirty face looked out at her. "'Tis me, m'lady." He saluted. "Captain."

"I can see that." Her heart was pounding, her mouth dry. "What news, Sergeant?"

"Lord Malcolm is well and the battle's won. By the Scotsmen, I mean."

For a moment or two, Mary couldn't see, or hear, or speak. Tears clouded her eyes, and a tightness gripped her. "Mal wasn't hurt?"

Ewan shook his head. "Not a scratch. But Lord Mal does have a new horse and an English prisoner."

Mary rapidly wiped away her tears. "He has a what?"

"Captured a cavalryman. An officer. His lordship says he has to take care of things, but will come for ye soon."

"Oh, will he?" Mary let out a breath, relief making her

want to collapse into weeping. She balled her fists where they rested on the floorboards. "Newts and tadpoles, I wish I knew what the man was thinking. And that I could get out of here. How big is this blasted passage?" She stuck her head around the corner but couldn't see much.

"'Tis a bit tight, Captain. Ye'd have to crawl, and ye'd get dirty, like me."

Ewan was filthy, that was certain, and cobwebs clung to his squashed cap. "I couldn't exactly wear skirts and panniers, could I?" she asked.

"Ye could do what Scottish lasses do," Ewan said. "Wear leather breeches under and a plain skirt on top. Keeps ye covered, but lets ye move easier."

"A brilliant idea, Sergeant, but I'm afraid I have no such clothes."

"I'll bring ye some," Ewan declared, and he was setting the panel back in place even as he spoke.

Mary rose and dusted off her hands. A fanciful idea, dressing up in breeches to crawl out of the house and escape her captivity. Heroines did it all the time in plays and books, but how practical was such a thing, really? But she truly did want to speak to Malcolm.

See him, touch him, reassure herself he was alive and well. Scold him for rushing off to battle in a war he didn't believe in.

Hold him, kiss him, have Malcolm look at her in that way when he'd said, in his chamber, *Now, then, Mary.*

Mary lay down on her bed, her heart beating in sweet relief, and was still wide awake in the small hours when the soldiers of Prince Charles's army came pounding on her father's front door.

Chapter 18

Mary's door was still locked. She rattled the handle, calling through the keyhole for Whitman, but there was no answer.

Male voices filled the stairwell. Her father's answered—Halsey was also there. Then came the shrill tones of Aunt Danae, begging to know what was happening.

"Captain, sir!"

The small voice came from behind Mary. Ewan had the panel open, a bundle in his arms, and eyes full of fear.

Mary rushed to him, going down on her knees. "Ewan, who are those men? What do they want?"

"Soldiers, sir," Ewan said. "Me gran said they've come to arrest your da for spying. Everyone's running off, even Gran." He shoved the bundle, a large plaid wrapped around something, into the room. "Come with me, Captain. I'll see ye right."

Mary pulled open the cloth, finding inside a worn woolen skirt, a small pair of buckskin breeches, a bodice of coarse brown material, and a short, stiff corset. This was the garb for women working menial labor, and Mary knew she didn't have much choice but to wear it. She couldn't crawl through a dirty passage in her silk and lace, or even her thick dressing gown.

"Hurry, sir," Ewan said.

Mary rose and ducked behind the petit point screen that stood near her dressing table. It usually took Whitman and one other maid to assist Mary into her gowns, but these garments went on rather easily. The corset laced in the back, though—she'd have to have Ewan do it up for her.

A key rattled in the door, and the lock clicked. Mary froze. Soldiers coming? She remained hidden behind the screen, and Ewan, wise lad, had closed the hole again.

The door swung opened. "Mary?" Aunt Danae whispered, then she gave a cry of alarm. "Mary, where are you? What on earth . . ."

Mary rushed out from behind the screen, and Aunt Danae put her hand to her heart. "Oh, my dear, there you are. I thought . . . But what is this? Ewan? Whatever are you doing?"

Ewan had pulled the panel off again, and was sitting on his heels in the opening, hands on his knees.

"Ewan has a way out," Mary said, holding the corset closed behind her and making for Aunt Danae. "Can you lace me?"

Without argument, Aunt Danae had Mary turned around and began to thread the laces through the little linen-and-bone corset. "What way out?" she asked as she worked.

"Passage outside, m'lady." Ewan ducked through the opening and stood up, crumpling his cap in his hands.

Aunt Danae gave him a startled look, then another one at Mary, who pulled the brown bodice over the corset. Then Danae eyed the hole in the wainscoting again. "Clever lad. Do go with him, Mary. Make for the Bancrofts. They'll look after you."

Mary fastened the bodice with its ill-made hooks. "What about you, Auntie? Are they arresting Papa? Will they take you too?"

"They say your father is passing information about the Jacobites to the English army. I don't know why they're bothering to arrest him—I imagine dozens of people are passing flurries of messages to London. They're taking him and Lord Halsey to Holyrood. Me as well, I suppose. But I want you gone. At once. You'll be safe with the Bancrofts. *Please.*"

Mary tugged on her stoutest pair of boots, snatched up a pair of leather gloves, and tucked a purse full of coins into her corset. "Auntie, I can't leave you to face them."

"My dear, I'll never fit through that hole. I'm twice your girth. I've weathered worse storms than this, but you're too young and vulnerable, and I don't want to see—" She broke off and pointed a finger at Ewan "You take care of her, lad, you understand me?"

Ewan snapped off another salute. "Aye, sir."

Aunt Danae looked startled, then nodded. "Very good. Now *go* before they storm up the stairs."

Mary threw her arms around Aunt Danae and kissed her firm cheek. "I will see you soon," she promised.

She turned to follow Ewan, her heart heavy. There was no telling what the victorious, celebrating Jacobites would do to her father and aunt, how long they'd be kept. Surely Malcolm would be able to find out, be able to do something about it. Mary remembered how the Scottish soldiers had turned away, pretending to ignore Malcolm's party as they'd ridden through the streets and out the gates to the wharves. Mal would know, wouldn't he, how to keep the worst from happening to Mary's family?

Fear and uncertainty made her stomach roil. Mary gave Aunt Danae one last look, then ducked into the passage after Ewan. Ewan closed the panel behind them, and the darkness was complete.

Ewan's passage was full of grime, old nails, and other things Mary did not want to think about. They moved carefully on hands and knees, but the way was narrow, smelly, and damp. The ceiling was low enough to scrape Mary's back if she didn't bend all the way down and go at a lizard's crouch.

The passage led to somewhere in the middle of the house, ending in a stairwell of rickety steps. Once upon a time, these must have been servants' stairs, but walled off when inhabitants had modernized the house. The fact that servants had scrambled up and down this precarious wooden staircase, carrying fuel for fires and buckets of water, gave Mary new pity for them.

The stairs creaked alarmingly as she descended, following Ewan. Mary clung to the walls, happy she'd thought to grab her gloves.

They made it to the bottom without mishap. Ewan opened a small door into a tiny passage that ran alongside the kitchen garden. He led Mary through this passage, which turned sharply behind another house, and finally emptied into the next street.

The darkness helped them slip unnoticed through lanes and emerge once again onto the street where Mary's father's house lay. The house was surrounded now by both Highland soldiers and curious neighbors. A plain carriage sat before the front door, and as Mary watched, her father was bundled into it, his hands behind his back.

Halsey was pushed in after him. The first carriage rolled away, and another took its place as Aunt Danae was led out. The soldiers looked as though they were being polite as they handed her in, her hands unbound, but they were not letting her go. Mary's eyes stung with tears as the carriage rolled away into the darkness.

Ewan tugged her hand. "This way, sir!"

Mary made herself turn from the house she'd lived in all these months and follow him into the streets.

Soldiers were everywhere, laughing, shouting, drinking, celebrating their victory at Prestonpans. Ewan led Mary through streets crowded with horses, carriages, Highlanders, and inhabitants of the city.

Ewan disappeared suddenly into a side lane for a heart-stopping moment, then reappeared with an empty basket, which he put on Mary's arm. Mary nodded her approval, though she didn't like the idea of him stealing it. But with the basket, Mary looked like any other woman of the town, going about her early morning errands.

In this way, Mary slipped through the city, blindly following Ewan, who promised he was taking her to Malcolm. All was well until they passed a tavern, which spilled men onto the street. One of the Highland soldiers there broke away from the swelling mob, saw Mary, and moved toward her.

"Come and celebrate w' me, lass," he said, his broad face red with drink. "Bring the lad too. I dinnae mind."

His friends laughed loudly. Ewan seized Mary's sleeve, trying to pull her along.

The man's heavy hand landed on Mary's shoulder, hot

through her thin shirt. "Don't run away, love. I'll make it worth your while. More coin to bring your man tonight, eh?"

He spoke a broad Scots, from the far west, but Mary understood him well enough. She knew, though, that if she responded in any way, he'd know she was English as soon as she opened her mouth. With her fair hair touched with red and rough clothes, she might pass for a Scotswoman, but she'd never be able to speak like one.

Mary tried to shrug the man off and follow Ewan, but the soldier tightened his grip. "Come on, then, woman."

Mary swung around, using the momentum to send her heavy wicker basket straight into the Highlander's stomach—*whump*. The Scotsman lost his hold on her, cursing as he doubled over.

His friends laughed uproariously. Mary spun to run after Ewan, but another pair of hands landed on her shoulders.

She was pulled around to face another Highlander, this one very tall, with dark red hair and a face flushed with rage. He looked her up and down, then gripped her face and turned it to the light, studying the bruise and cut her father had left.

Malcolm let go of her, grabbed hold of the Scotsman who'd first accosted her, and punched him full in the face.

"She's me wife, ye daft cob."

That brought astonishment and more laughter to the others. "*Wife?* Aye, is that what you're calling her, Mackenzie?"

"Bloody drunken . . ." Mal swung back to Mary, seized her by the arm, and Ewan by the neck. "I'm agog to hear *this* story. I'll lay into ye, boy, if ye've had a hand in procuring her."

"Malcolm," Mary managed to splutter.

"*Later.*" Malcolm marched them down the lane into the fog and dim glow of sunrise. "After I get ye off the street, ye ken?"

Malcolm didn't trust himself to speak as he pulled Mary along. Nor did he want to hear her explanations while they twisted and turned through the crowds. Those rising to begin the day mingled with those ending their nights, and the streets were teeming.

Mary could be out here for no good reason. He'd told

Naughton to make certain she stayed put inside her house, where she'd be safe. The bruise on her face, as well—that hadn't been put there by the drunken soldiers. The wound was at least a day or two old.

Something had happened while he'd been busy keeping Duncan out of trouble. Malcolm needed to get her indoors and shake out of her what.

Mary scuttled along beside him, her head down, asking no questions. She looked exactly like a servant being dragged away to be chastised by her master, and beneath his anger, Mal wanted to laugh. She was good.

They reached the Mackenzie house. Malcolm pulled Mary through the front door, nearly running into Naughton, who'd opened it for them.

Naughton sent Ewan a glare from his thin height. "Lad, you're filthy. Ye shouldn't be coming in by the front door."

"My fault," Mal said impatiently. "These two aren't taking another step until Mary tells me why she's roaming the streets dressed like a farm worker."

Naughton, Ewan, and Mary all started speaking at once. Mal heard Naughton's calmer tones saying something about Ewan and messages, Ewan going on about soldiers, and then Mary, frantic and angry at the same time.

"Stop!" Malcolm shouted. When he wanted to, he could roar as forcefully as the duke. The word vibrated through their shrill voices, and all three fell into a startled silence. "Mary—tell me."

Instead of calmly spilling out the story, Mary glared at him in fiery anger. "Did *you* do this? You have said again and again you'd do anything to make me come to you—did you force the arrests so I'd have no choice?"

Mary's anger made her beautiful, her blue eyes full of sparks. Her words troubled Mal, however.

"Who did I force to be arrested?" he demanded. "I told Ewan to make ye stay put. Not roam the streets dressed like a French peasant, with all the full-of-themselves Jacobites wandering about. What did ye think they'd do?"

Did she look chastised? Not a bit of it. Mary gripped the basket as though she would ram it into *his* stomach, like she had the drunken lout at the tavern.

"My father and aunt have been taken by the Pretender's men. Lord Halsey as well. Likely they'd have arrested me too, if I hadn't fled. My aunt can't be held prisoner. She'll be unable to bear it, and she's done nothing wrong!"

Malcolm stared at her. "And ye think *I* did this?"

"Is this how you plan to rid me of Halsey?" Mary snapped. "By confining my family? If so, you can get out of my way. I'll take myself to prison with them. I'd rather."

"Dinnae talk such shite, woman. *I* would never send your da and aunt to be locked up, no matter the reason." Mal stopped, grim rage replacing his agitation. "But I know some-one who might."

He stepped around Mary, ignored Naughton, and leapt up the stairs, two at a time, heading for his father's chamber.

Chapter 19

Mary heard Naughton speaking. "My lady, if you will wait here, I will bring refreshment and ready a chamber for you." She ignored him to lift her woolen skirts and rush up the stairs after Malcolm.

Houses were tall in Edinburgh, the city building upward when it could expand no more into the marshes. Mary climbed three flights before she heard Mal in a room at the end of the landing, his voice raised in fury.

At any other time, she'd never dream of hurrying to personal chambers and interfering in a family quarrel. But rules had been overturned in the last days, and her father and aunt had been dragged off to prison. Customary manners had fled.

Mary pushed open the door that was ajar to find the duke, fully dressed despite the early hour, his graying red hair hanging loose.

Mary had faced him in the stairwell the other day, when shadows had made him a looming bulk. Today, in the sunlight burning through the mist, she saw him more clearly.

Malcolm looked much like him, as did his brother Will. They had the same hard faces and eyes in some shade of amber, though the duke's forehead was wider and more prominent than his sons'. The older man's hair was as thick as the younger's, his brows drawn together as firmly, his mouth set in a stubborn line.

He and Mal had given up on English, and were shouting in Erse, the Scots language that Mary didn't know. She heard many consonants run together and fluid vowels, all of it window-rattlingly loud.

Naughton came breathlessly behind her, distressed, but Mary paid no attention. Ewan also joined them, watching and listening, mouth agape.

"The duke is saying he got your da arrested," Ewan said, explaining, "because he thinks they're English spies. Lord Malcolm is very angry at him."

So Mary gathered. The duke, seeing Mary, switched to English. "Wilfort and Halsey are two of the most dangerous men in Edinburgh," he said fiercely. "Wilfort wouldn't stop at throwing *you* in prison, runt, if he knew ye had your hands on his daughter."

"So ye threw him in first?" Mal shouted. "Are ye mad? I'm going t' *marry* this woman, whether ye bless me for it or not. I'd rather not have me father-in-law-to-be angry at me for landing him in prison!"

"He's a bloody spy, lad," the duke returned. "He and his boot-licking toady, Halsey, are stirring up the Lowlanders to murder us in our beds. To join the English in cutting down the Highland clans. Lowlanders have always sided with the English, the bleeding traitors."

A polite cough turned attention to the doorway, where Will Mackenzie leaned, clad in a shirt, kilt, and woolen socks, his arms folded. His rumpled hair indicated he'd just crawled from his bed, as did his puffy, bloodshot eyes.

"Afraid he isn't wrong, Mal," Will said. "Lord Wilfort has agents in Glasgow, and a network throughout the Lowlands. He came to Edinburgh when there was a fairly clear danger Charles would sail from France, sent here to stir up the Scots against the Scots." Will looked mildly embarrassed. "Sorry, Lady Mary."

Mary wished she could be shocked and outraged at the accusation, but she was not. She knew her father always had *some* schemes in the works, and she'd heard the words he'd exchanged with Halsey in his study.

"The fool," she said in resignation. Wilfort was a hard man, possessing intelligence with a razor-sharp edge, but he was still her father. Mary blinked back tears. "What will happen to him?"

"They'll hang him," the duke grunted.

Malcolm launched himself at his father. Will moved faster than a man who'd been lounging with a hangover ought to be able to, got himself between them, and pried them apart.

"Your Grace." Mary put force into her words. The duke turned his head and looked her over, taking in her shabby garments, his disgust plain. "He is my *father*," Mary said. "If you made certain he was arrested, then you can get him free again."

The duke's look turned incredulous. "Why would I do that? Ye heard Will. I wasn't wrong about Wilfort being a spy. I have no love for the Jacobites, but nor do I want gobshite Englishmen mucking up my life."

"Send him to London, then," Mary said. "From that distance, it will be more difficult for him to communicate with this network, and I wager he'll lose interest. My father has plenty of plots against his fellow Englishmen to pursue."

Will snorted a laugh. The duke only looked belligerent, and so did Malcolm.

"'Tis out of my hands, in any case," the duke said. "They are spies, and they've been caught. It's up to the child prince to decide what to do with them."

"Then *I'll* go," Mal said. "Will, look after Mary—make sure Dad leaves her be. Naughton, give her the finest chamber we have and offer her a meal. I want her settled and in comfort by the time I get back."

Mary had learned about Mal even in this short time that once he decided to act, his deeds followed swiftly upon his words. He swung around and was out the door, making for the stairs before she could open her mouth.

She ran after him. "I do not need to stay *here*," she called down as Malcolm made his descent. "Your coachman can take me to the Bancrofts'. I'll be safe with them."

Malcolm gave her an upward look of amazement. "No, ye won't. Stay put, lass. Ignore my father and have Naughton bring ye anything ye need."

Will joined Mary at the head of the stairs. Behind him, in

his chamber, the duke was now raging at the hapless Naughton. Ewan, who'd followed Mary out, lingered by her side.

"Ye can't go on your own," Will said to his brother. "Let me come and smooth the way for ye. I know people."

"So do I." Mal balled his fists. "God's balls, I need ye here with Mary. I can't take care of *all* of ye at the same time—"

He cut off his speech abruptly, and plummeted on down the stairs.

Mary watched him all the way down, her arguments fading. When Mal had let out his last burst of temper, there had been something in his eyes, a distress that ran deep.

I can't take care of all *of ye . . .*

Mary sensed that the words hadn't been idle ones, but had come straight from something that struck him to the heart.

Mary didn't know what to make of this distress—or of Malcolm himself—but she then and there intended to find out.

The prisoners Mal sought were not being held with the captured soldiers in the camps. Lords Wilfort and Halsey had been taken to Holyrood, locked into rooms in the lower cellars.

Lady Dutton—Mary's Aunt Danae—Duncan informed Malcolm when he arrived, had been taken to Lord Bancroft's home. Bancroft and his family were under house arrest, so Aunt Danae would sit there until she was either charged with something or sent back to England.

No one Mal spoke to at Holyrood, including Duncan, mentioned Lady Mary. Either they did not remember that Wilfort had daughters or didn't realize that at least one of them remained in Scotland.

Wilfort and Halsey were being kept in separate rooms—so they wouldn't plot, Duncan explained. Mal went to see Wilfort first.

Lord Wilfort looked up blankly when Mal entered the tiny room. The Englishman was seated at a small wooden table in the middle, and Mal sat down on the stool opposite him, studying him across the boards.

Wilfort had a thin, rather sharp face, but a regularity of features that told Mal he'd been handsome as a lad. Mary had the same clarity of face, the cheekbones that spoke of a Nordic ancestor long ago. They'd not let Wilfort don a wig, and his shaved head bore a uniform dusting of gray hair. He looked more formidable without the wig, in Mal's opinion, the man's hard face and eyes prominent.

Wilfort's frown deepened as Mal continued to gaze at him. "Are you here to interrogate me?" Wilfort asked in a voice filled with ennui. "Get on with it, if you please. I'm promised the filth you call food in a few minutes."

"Is the cut on Mary's face *your* work?" Mal asked. "Or Halsey's?"

Wilfort started, then his expression cleared. "Ah, you must be the conspirator she refused to name." A scowl settled on his fine-boned face. "I should have you arrested for abduction, sir. If anything happens to Audrey, I will have your balls on a platter."

Mal rested his arms on the table, pretending to relax. "I said the same thing to the captain who sailed the boat to France. Your daughter should be there by now, in the house of a friend of mine. My brother is there to see they want for nothing."

Wilfort's nostrils pinched. "And I should take the word of a Jacobite and a traitor?"

"I am neither of those, and you should take *my* word," Mal said. "I want to marry your daughter, I'll have ye know. Your other daughter, I mean. Mary."

The earl's brows quirked, but he masked his surprise well. "You can't. She is spoken for—not that I would let you marry her if she were not."

"Mary is betrothed to a man who will break her spirit. I promise ye, I'll never do that to her. Tear up the agreement with Halsey, and make one with me."

Wilfort contrived to look amused. "Is that why I am here? Arrested so the first ruffian in a plaid can marry my eldest daughter? I don't even know who you are, sir."

"Malcolm Mackenzie. My father is Duke of Kilmorgan."

"Ah." The earl's gaze sharpened. "Yes, I know *him*. But I have never heard of *you*, which means you're a younger son and inconsequential."

Malcolm shrugged. "I've been called worse. I am the youngest of six—five, I mean. At one time we were six." He never could seem to remember that Magnus was no longer with them.

"Then you are nothing." Wilfort made a dismissing gesture with his fingers. Mal heard a rattle as he did so—they'd chained him to his chair.

"I'd be nothing if I were English," Malcolm pointed out. "I'm Scots, I inherited a large sum from me mum, and I have a good share of the Mackenzie money too. That means Mary will be well provided for, respected, and wealthy."

Wilfort sent him a withering glance. "Living in a hovel in the bleak Highlands, grubbing for food. Go away, bonny wee Scotsman."

Mal shoved himself from the table and to his feet, barely keeping his anger in check. "I'll marry her, with your blessing or without it. At least, with me, she'll be well out of range of your fists. A cut like that will never come from *my* hand. For Mary's sake, I'll see ye sent back to England with your head intact—with your blessing or without it. Tell Halsey he's out of luck where Mary is concerned." Mal paused at the door. "No, wait, I'll do it meself. Good day to ye, father-in-law."

Wilfort half rose, but the chains dragged him back to the chair. "Be damned to you!" he shouted, the ring of it fading as Malcolm slammed the cell door.

Halsey was more inclined than the earl to bargain. He faced Mal across a similar table, dabbing his nose with the handkerchief he'd been granted, as he sullenly listened to Malcolm explain that the man should step aside and give him Mary.

Halsey too had a sharp face, but it was more like that of a weasel, his eyes alight and looking for a way to gain the most for himself.

"What will allying yourself with Wilfort and his family win you?" Halsey asked when Mal finished. "You're Scots, and you're a rebel. If you believe making Wilfort your father-in-law will keep you from being executed as a traitor, you're wrong."

"I'm not interested in Wilfort. I'm interested in his daughter." Malcolm studied the man across from him, his symmetrical face, the dark buzz of hair on his shaved head, his compact form. Mal contrasted his own large body, which had hung on him awkwardly in his youth, his hard face that could not be called handsome by the standards of the day, his nose which had been broken more than once.

Halsey might be considered attractive to Englishwomen,

despite his current disheveled appearance and unshaven chin, which must be hell for a man who liked to be fastidious. Halsey was young enough to be handsome, old enough to understand how to handle himself.

And he was cruel. Mal found nothing in the man's blue eyes but self-interest. Even his present situation didn't seem to bother him much. Likely he had many schemes already in the works that could get him free.

Mal rested one large, scarred hand on the table. "You don't understand what ye have in her, do ye?"

"Lady Mary?" Halsey sniffed and wiped his nose. "I understand that she brings a substantial dowry with her. More than you'll ever find working in the mud on your farm, Highlander. No wonder you seek to bring her home."

"Oh, is that what I am? The proud Highlander dressed in rags, eking out a living, stealing from his neighbors, uncaring about the world outside his clan's lands. A neat picture, painted by an Englishman."

"A picture that is more or less true," Halsey said.

"Mebbe in me grandfather's time. Things are changing now, even on the remotest hills. But this is how you English choose a bride? How much she's worth in pounds and shillings? I'm surprised the lot of ye have survived."

"You're young," Halsey said coolly. "A man who marries for passion is a fool. Even in your world, you pick a bride from the best families, the one with the most cattle, say."

He wasn't entirely wrong, which was irritating. Mal's fingers curled on the table. "I'd say Mary is worth more than a few shaggy black coos."

Halsey curled his lip. "That you speak of her by her given name tells me she's already ruined for me. Which means you have cheated me out of ten thousand pounds." Halsey took a breath, deliberately calming himself. "However, I am not an unreasonable man. I'll keep Lady Mary on for the sake of her dowry, even if you've rutted her. And if the first child comes too early, I'll send it up to you in your tumbledown castle."

Chapter 20

Mal slammed himself over the table and hauled the man up by his coat. Like Wilfort, Halsey was chained to his chair. He hung awkwardly in Mal's grip.

"Ye watch what ye say about Lady Mary, or I'll break your neck," Mal said with low-voiced menace. "I'd break it now if Geordie Murray weren't so keen to keep ye alive. When he's done squeezing ye for information, maybe I'll come back and finish ye off."

Halsey masked his flash of fear with another sneer. "No need for violence, Highlander. I'll step aside for you with Mary, *if* you make it worth my while."

Mal jerked him closer, and Halsey grunted in pain. "Why the devil should I make it worth your while?"

"To keep yourself from being jailed for cheating me." Halsey's voice was scratchy, his light blue eyes as cold as a winter lake. "Give me the ten thousand I was promised, and marry the chit if you want. Or make her your whore once you pay for her. I scarcely care."

Mal shook him. "I remember telling ye to be careful what ye say, Halsey. Ye'd sell her to me, then? Maybe I'll lend her a dirk, and she can rid herself of ye that way. That's what Highland lassies do to husbands they hate."

Halsey put on a tired smile. "You'd do well to remember that. Ten thousand pounds, paid to my man of business in London. Mr. Sheridan, at twenty-three High Holborn. He'll nullify the contracts."

The man was disgusting. Mal slammed Halsey back into his chair, finished with him. "Ye don't worry that ye won't be going home to collect the money?"

"No." Halsey lifted the handkerchief that had fluttered to the table. "This rebellion is doomed to failure. Your chiefs can't agree on who to support, and even the ones who've already joined can't agree with one another. The popular view is that all Highlanders are Catholic and behind the Stuarts, when you and I both know that neither fact is strictly true. Your own father is a staunch Protestant, and thinks all Catholics are the devil. He must chafe that his son and heir has joined the side of Beelzebub."

"My father has no love for anything English either," Mal said. "Good day to ye, Halsey. I might be back later to kill ye."

Halsey only touched the handkerchief to his drippy nose. Mal closed the door behind him, his anger and revulsion leaving a foul taste in his mouth.

Wilfort at least had showed that he cared for his daughters, despite the bruise on Mary's face, even if he could not come straight out and say it. Lord Halsey, on the other hand, cared for nothing but himself.

Mal walked upstairs, lost in thought. He spoke to Duncan, even gained a brief audience with Lord George Murray, and then left Holyrood. The streets of Edinburgh embraced Mal as he made his way to the close where his house lay.

When he arrived, he sought out Will and asked him to compose a letter in his elegant way to Mr. Sheridan, man of business, at twenty-three High Holborn, London.

Mary heard Malcolm return, and watched over the banisters as he disappeared into a room below and didn't come out.

The duke, fortunately, had quit the house soon after Malcolm, and a modicum of peace had come over the place. Mary had spent the time breakfasting and settling herself into the chamber Naughton had said was hers.

Mary had not had much appetite, but she'd made a show of serenely eating the bannocks Naughton brought her and drinking her tea. No giving way. She was a Lennox, from a line of proud people.

Naughton then produced Mary's own trunk full of her clothes. Somehow, he and other servants had sneaked inside her father's house and packed up her things.

Mary studied Naughton, a rail-thin man with red hair going to gray, as he announced, in his quiet voice, what he'd done. Unlike Mary's friends' conception of the oversized, ill-mannered, unruly Scot, Naughton was quietly efficient. And kind. Mary nearly lost her pride to tears as she thanked him.

"Not at all, m'lady. Anything ye wish to make your stay more comfortable, ye have but to summon me."

Naughton had departed, letting Mary compose herself and finish her breakfast. A maid called Jinty was sent up to help her wash and dress. Jinty was a beautiful girl—dark-haired and blue-eyed in contrast to the fair or red-haired servants Mary had seen in this house so far.

"I come from the islands, m'lady," Jinty said in a musically soft voice. "Iona, in the Hebrides. At least, me mum did. Then she married a Scot from the Highlands. I was born at Castle Kilmorgan. Was so excited when I first came to the city."

Jinty had not been trained as a lady's maid, so Mary had to instruct her on what to do. Jinty helped her brush out her hair and unpack her things. The girl was well mannered and eager to learn.

But after Mary settled in, dressed now in her own clothes, she paced, nervous, waiting for Malcolm and what news he might bring. Now, as she watched over the stair railings, he shut himself into the room downstairs, for whatever reason, and didn't seek her.

Mary could stand it no longer. She gathered her skirts and hurried down the stairs, barely able to make herself pause and knock politely instead of barreling inside to find Malcolm.

Malcolm himself wrenched open the door. Will was behind him, saying, "I hope to God ye ken what you're doing," before Mal came out into the hall.

Mary started to speak, but Mal gave her a silencing look, pushed her to the next door on the landing, and guided her inside.

This was another sitting room, one that faced the rear of the house and was quiet. The chamber was small, but the furnishings here were as rich and elegant as those she'd seen elsewhere. If French kings and aristocrats gave Will furniture to make him go away, he must make a nuisance of himself often.

"My aunt—" Mary began worriedly.

Malcolm touched his finger to her lips. "Is fine and well. With Lady Bancroft in that huge house with plenty of people to look after her, including your formidable maid."

Mary's hand went to her heart as it throbbed in relief. "And my father?"

The question was more fearful, and Malcolm's expression did nothing to reassure her. "He's imprisoned but in a room with a table and a bed, not a dank dungeon. I've fixed it so he will be freed soon."

Mary's knees started to buckle. Only Malcolm's quick arm around her waist stopped her from falling. She'd kept herself from speculating all this time about what would happen to her father, to her aunt. Families could be broken and destroyed so easily in these times, arrests made, executions swift. "Thank you, Malcolm," she said fervently. "Thank you."

"Don't thank me yet, love. We've a long way to go."

Mary curled her fingers against his chest. "Everything is splintering, falling away beneath my feet." She gave a little laugh. "Much of it because of you."

She expected Malcolm to respond with a smile, but the look in his eyes was bleak. "I never knew my father would go so far to thwart me. I'm sorry, lass. Truly, I am. But all will be well, I promise ye."

He again wore the haunted look he had before he'd left the house, when he'd shouted at his father and then at Will. The weight of the world seemed to press on Malcolm's young shoulders. Mary touched one of those shoulders, feeling steel strength beneath his coat.

"What did you mean?" she asked him. "As you were leaving, you said, 'I can't take care of all of you at the same time.' You looked odd when you said it."

Malcolm went still, his tawny eyes seeking hers. For a moment, Mary thought he wouldn't answer, then he shrugged.

"It's me lot in life, isn't it? To be the one to pick up the pieces? Duncan is fixed on the Jacobites. Will is interested in information—the gathering, the keeping, the using of it—no matter where it comes from and what it's for. Angus looks after Dad and can't be bothered with the rest of us. Alec falls so deeply in love, it's like he drowns. Magnus was the dreamer, lost in his own world, and he never was well." Malcolm let out a breath. "I look after them all—ye see? Even Dad. I have to. They need me. No one else to do it, is there?"

Chapter 21

The tug in his voice pierced Mary's heart. "I heard what happened to Magnus," she said. "Naughton told me while you were out. I'm sorry."

Malcolm's arms tightened around her, but his gaze went remote, looking at something far away. "I found him that day. Lying in a heap all cold. I couldn't wake him, couldn't make him alive again."

The simple statement said more than all the anguished wails he could have uttered. Mal's directness and unwavering stubbornness made a little more sense to her now that she knew the tale. Naughton had told her about it after Jinty had let slip that the brothers had lost another, long ago. Naughton had wanted to make certain Mary heard the correct story, he'd said.

Magnus's death had hurt Mal terribly, Mary could see. If Mal blamed himself for it, thinking he'd failed to look after his brother properly, small wonder he strove to make sure such a thing didn't happen again. This explained him following Duncan to battle and sending Alec to France to find his daughter.

Mary slid her arms around Malcolm's waist and ran soothing hands up his back.

"Nay, Mary," he whispered. "Don't do this."

Mary barely noticed his words. She was warm, comforted for the first time that day. She rested her cheek on his chest, hearing his heart banging away beneath his shirt. "Don't do what?"

"Feel sorry for me." Malcolm put his fingers under her chin and tilted her face to his. "I don't walk about morose over the terrible things that have happened to me family. Most of it, except for Magnus, and poor Alec's wife, is their own damned fault. I only come behind and pick up the pieces."

Mary gave him a little smile. "I'm a compassionate woman. I can't help myself."

"And when ye smile at me like *that*, I'm a man lost."

He stroked her lower lip with his thumb, then dipped his head and kissed her.

Mary tasted his need in the kiss, but also that he held back. His large hand came up between them to rest flat against her breasts, as though wanting to both hold her and push her away.

Mal didn't move, his fingertips touching the bare skin above her bodice. "Ye smell fine. Warm, clean woman. Ye had a bath, then?"

Mary nodded. She'd been filthy from crawling through the tunnels, then fleeing through streets full of mud, men, animals, and horse droppings. A sponge and a basin hadn't been enough. Nothing less than full immersion had been able to make her feel better.

"An excellent idea," Malcolm said.

He kissed her lips once more, traced her cheek, then went to the door and shouted for Naughton.

Duncan Mackenzie left his interview with Lord Halsey lost in thought. He had been invited by George Murray to help interrogate the man, since Malcolm had advised Murray to make the most of the opportunity.

It had been interesting. Halsey had smiled at them, then readily made a bargain to give them all the details on the British army landing from Flanders, exactly who in the Lowlands was prepared to thwart them, and how they might take Carlisle if they were to march south to England.

In return, Halsey asked for his life, immunity, and a little money, enough to compensate him for having to forgo the marriage to Lady Mary Lennox.

The man was in no way brokenhearted at the abrupt changes in his destiny. He simply bargained.

Duncan left the cell feeling not a little unclean. He didn't trust Halsey—motives of all turncoats were suspect—but he and Murray would use the information and milk him for more.

Their visit with Lord Wilfort was different. Wilfort was angry, had no idea Halsey had decided to turn, and would give up nothing. He only demanded that Duncan make sure Lady Mary wasn't used and cast aside by Duncan's upstart younger brother.

"My daughters are as precious to me as my honor," Wilfort said stiffly. "If Mary is hurt, betrayed, or made miserable, I will hunt down your brother and run him through." Wilfort met Duncan's gaze without fear. "And then you."

"Malcolm is no rake," Duncan growled. "If he wants this woman, he will take care of her."

"Her *name* is Lady Mary Lennox," Wilfort said in a hard voice. "Not *this woman*. Bloody barbarians."

Murray, who wore clothes as well tailored as Wilfort's, which possibly came from the same London shop, raised his brows but said nothing.

Duncan lingered after Murray departed, the guards waiting to close the door. "My barbarian brother is asking that ye be spared, for your daughter's sake," Duncan said. "I think I've found a way to save ye."

He had the satisfaction of seeing Wilfort look startled. Duncan hid a grin as he left the room. Mal wouldn't like what was planned either, but his wee brother would have to live with it.

Duncan had never been close to Malcolm, didn't really understand him. Mal frightened Duncan a little sometimes, with his unwavering determination. When Mal Mackenzie chose to do a thing, he'd not let God and all his angels stop him.

But if Mal wanted to tie himself to an Englishwoman—the Lord knew why—then Duncan would help him do it. Let the little runt be happy if he could.

When Naughton and two lads answered Malcolm's summons to his bedchamber, and came lugging a bath and cans of steaming water, Mary excused herself.

She knew that if she didn't, she'd stand with her mouth open and watch Malcolm remove every stitch of clothing before plunging into the bath. She tried to follow Naughton and the footmen out, but Malcolm caught her hand and stopped her.

"But you're bathing," Mary spluttered as Naughton closed the door, shutting her in with Malcolm.

"Aye, that I am. I'd like the company. If ye're modest, ye can turn your back."

Before she could answer, Mal released her and stripped off his coat, then his fine linen shirt. He peeled off the leather shoes he'd tramped through the city in, as well as the woolen socks that hugged his legs. Finally he started unwinding the plaid.

Mary should look away now—turn her back, sit down in a chair facing the wall, and let him get on with it.

She couldn't move. Mal said nothing as he pulled the plaid all the way off and dropped it to the floor.

Since Mary had met him, she'd moved from innocence to curiosity to circumstances that were downright scandalous. Now, standing in this room while Mal let his tartan fall, Mary knew she was utterly ruined.

She stood very still while she let her gaze drift over Malcolm's body, from his tousled hair, to his tight shoulders, to his chest with its sharp, flat planes. Down his torso, while he spread his arms, unashamed and inviting her to look.

A dusting of bronze-colored hair, slightly darker than that on his chest, gathered at the base of his phallus. He certainly didn't look like the nude statuary in this regard, because the sculpted men had either had their most intimate part hidden by the pose, or their part was so small as to be nonexistent.

Malcolm's would never be nonexistent. He hung thick and long, and was already lifting under her gaze.

"Ah, Mary, you'll embarrass me."

Mary glanced up to find his cheekbones red, his smile almost shy. She looked back down at the fascinating thing between his legs, wondering how heavy it was, what it felt like. She found her teeth at her lower lip, her hands twining together.

Malcolm growled. "Ye have no way of knowing what ye do to me, lass."

He swung away from her to the tub—and that view was fine as well. His backside was pale compared to his tanned lower legs and torso, the one part of him that never saw the sun.

Malcolm climbed into the bathtub and sat down with a splash. Mary was hot inside, the sensations chasing through her new and bewildering.

Whenever Malcolm kissed her, Mary flushed with shaky warmth, but this was different. She hungered to touch him, to feel the firmness of his flesh, to nuzzle him, then lick where she touched. The sudden and burning need made her walk to the side of the tub before she realized.

Mal flicked her a glance and a half smile. "Come to wash me back?"

Mary took all of him in, her hands clenching, her nails pressing her palms. Her heart beat thick and hard. Mal met her gaze, his face flushed from the hot water. Mary read challenge in his eyes, and also hope, and a touch of fear.

She drew a breath and turned away, but only to pull a padded stool from the end of the bed to the side of the tub. She seated herself and reached for the large cloth he'd dunked into the water.

Malcolm watched her, his amber eyes taking in her every move. "Did ye know that there's a whole book on the health of bathing?" he asked as Mary squeezed out the cloth, soapy water running over her hands. "Though its author is fond of cold water. I prefer hot."

Mary drew the cloth over Malcolm's arm that rested on the side of the tub. His skin was slick with water, his muscles moving under her touch.

"The Romans liked their baths both hot and cold," Malcolm went on, his voice going softer. "One after the other. They had whole buildings devoted to bathing. I've seen the ruins. Mosaics so exquisite ye scarce believe a human being made them, and that two thousand years ago."

"There are old Roman baths in England too," Mary said,

her voice breathy. "It's said the waters in Bath are good for the health, but they look murky to me."

"Aye, well, I prefer what Naughton's boiled up for me from the pump. Or to dive headfirst into the clear springs near Kilmorgan. Hot ones *and* ice-cold ones."

"You could build your own Roman baths." Mary drew the dripping cloth along his shoulders. Mal obligingly leaned forward, and Mary rubbed the cloth all the way across his back, her bodice growing damp where she leaned against his arm.

"I could." Mal glanced back at her, his amber eyes warm. "I'm going to build a grand, fine house, where all my family and everyone I know can stay and never have to worry about the cold winters again. I'll have a bathhouse, with water piped from the hot springs. Then they'll never leave." He gave a mock-aggrieved sigh.

"You don't want them to," Mary said. "You want everyone around you, where you can watch over them, don't you? That's why you brought me here."

Mal drew his bare knees to his chest, wrapping his strong arms around them. "I've wanted ye here since the moment I first saw ye. But it's true. I wasn't going to let ye go to Holyrood or to Lord Bancroft's to be guarded by randy Highland soldiers a long way from home. I'd have t'kill every last man of them."

Mary put her hand on his water-streaked knee. Mal's body fascinated her, from the freckles on his cheekbones to the wiry hair on his chest, to the large strength of his arms and legs. Mal watched her, chin resting on his arm, as she ran her hand from his knee down his thigh.

More wiry hair curled there, dissipating as she reached his hip. Mal's eyes half closed as she explored, his chest rising with his breath.

"What are ye doing t' me, Mary?" he asked in a near-whisper.

"I don't know." Mary explored the crease between his leg and torso. "I can't seem to stop."

"Well, *I'm* not going to stop ye."

The newfound hunger in her was intense. Mary wanted to put her mouth to his skin and lick.

This chamber high above the street and the quiet house

beneath them seemed to be outside of the world. Perhaps Mal had lured her to an enchanted place, like in the fairy lands of *A Midsummer Night's Dream* or the faraway countries in tales by Mr. Swift or Mr. Defoe.

What Mary did here had no connection to the real world, the thought took hold in her mind. Or perhaps she was befuddled by lack of proper sleep. Whatever the cause, Mary let her hand slide between Mal's legs at the same time she bit the round of his shoulder.

Mal jumped, water sloshing, then a smile spread across his face. "Sweet Mary, ye know how to welcome a man home."

Mary licked where she'd bitten, at the same time she moved her fingertips to the shaft between his legs. Malcolm opened his knees, one arm coming to rest on the side of the tub, forehead on his hand. Mal's breathing sped, his rising and falling chest making little ripples in the water.

Mal's phallus was wider than Mary thought it would be, her fingers just able to close around it. Why she wanted to hold it, she didn't know, but in this other-land, she could do what she pleased.

Mary squeezed, finding him firm and giving at the same time. Malcolm let out a groan, and Mary froze.

"Am I hurting you?" she asked, worried.

Malcolm raised his head, his face more relaxed that she'd ever seen it, even in sleep. "I'm fine, lass." He closed his large hand around her small one where she gripped him. "You keep doing that. Doesn't bother me at all."

The fact that he reacted to what Mary did pleased her. A warm throb began between Mary's legs, beating in exact time with her heart.

She squeezed him again, liking his smooth, taut skin.

She'd have gone on simply gripping him, but he moved her hand gently with his, showing her how to draw it to the tip and then back down to the base. Another soft groan escaped Mal's lips, and then he pulled his hand away, letting her play with him on her own.

Mary licked Mal's shoulder again as she copied the movements he'd showed her, taking her hand to the blunt tip and then back down the shaft. Her fingertips brushed tight ball-like projections, and Mary explored those too.

Malcolm went back to supporting his forehead with his hand, his hips moving a little as Mary touched him.

The warm quiet rendered what Mary did even more exhilarating. Malcolm made little noise, except the occasional soft moan, punctuated by ripples of water.

Mary nibbled his shoulder, enjoying his salty taste. Her nibbles turned to little bites, which made him make a raw noise in his throat.

Mary lifted her head, observed the small red mark she'd left on his skin, then closed her mouth over it and sucked.

Malcolm rose out of the tub like a whale coming to the surface, water sloshing everywhere.

Mary found herself being rolled backward, but Malcolm caught her in his strong arms. Mary's laughter grew muffled as he kissed her, then they landed on the floor on the soft and now soggy oriental carpet.

Mal's hair dripped water to her face like tears, which he wiped away. "Mary." He nuzzled her then kissed where he'd nuzzled. "Ye don't understand how passionate ye are, do you?"

"Is this passion?" Mary asked, her mind happily hazy in this not-world. "I believe I like it."

Malcolm's laughter was low. "Ye warm me heart, lass. I'll never tire of it."

Mary lay back under the satisfying weight of him, her bodice soaked through, and she did not care. "What am I to do with you, Malcolm Mackenzie?"

"And ye shouldn't let my imagination run with questions like *that.*" Mal's smile was breathtaking. "One day, I won't stop ye. Me brothers won't be below—it will be just you and me, and we'll love each other the rest of the day and on into the night."

Mary smiled shyly. "Yes, please."

"Ye sore tempt me." Malcolm traced the edge of her bodice. "I'll have this off ye, one night soon. I'll open ye like parting petals on a rose, to find the woman inside."

Mary moved her hips, liking the feel of Mal pressed against her skirts. He was naked, wet, his backside smooth when she ran her fingertips over it.

He caught her wrist and carefully moved her hand from him, then kept hold of it as he pressed her wrist into the carpet. The wool prickled her skin.

"If we start now, lass, I'll never want to stop. But soon." Mal gently kissed her lips. "What we're going to do is get your da and auntie free, and then we'll go t' France. Paris. You'll reunite with Audrey, and I w' Alec. Would you like that?"

To see Audrey again, make certain she was well? "Yes." Mary touched Malcolm's face with her free hand. "Yes, I would like that—very much."

Mal was offering this gift to her as though nothing could be simpler. Her heart squeezed.

"Then we'll go." Malcolm kissed her lips again. "I'll take care of ye, Mary. In all ways. Ye never need worry about that."

For the moment, Mary was too stunned by the events of the day, too far from anything familiar, to ask more questions. For now, it was enough to have this braw Highlander embracing her, lending her his strength.

She'd heard the maids use that term—*braw*—meaning good or brave, Jinty had explained. But much more than that, Mary sensed, was expressed in the one syllable. It meant all that was best in a man—his strength, fineness of limb, how he carried himself. Malcolm was certainly *braw*.

And in the middle of all this madness, Mary was falling in love with him.

Mal's intense golden gaze softened. He stroked her hair with a damp hand, his touch so tender Mary wanted to cry.

"Ye are for me, Mary," he said in a quiet voice. "And I for you. And this always will be."

In the breath of the moment, there was no other truth.

The moment broke when a roar came up the stairs. Not the duke—this shout held rough good humor and the timbre was different.

"Hell, it's Duncan." Malcolm climbed off Mary, giving her a satisfying view of his entire damp body as he took his time reaching for a clean plaid and wrapping it around him. "What's he so cheery about?"

"Runt!" Duncan was bellowing. "Come out here, Mal."

Malcolm helped Mary to her feet, then signaled her to stay put as he opened the door. "What d'ye want?" Mal yelled back, his voice no less wall-shaking. "I'm bathing."

"Hurry up and finish," Duncan said. There was a heavy tread on the stairs, followed by a quicker one—Will possibly.

Malcolm stepped out into the hall, blocking his brothers from reaching the bedchamber door.

"Why?" Malcolm growled.

"Because I've got Murray to agree to let Lord Wilfort go."

Mary gave a cry of relief and started for the door, but Malcolm again motioned her to stay put.

"And this has you smiling?" Mal asked Duncan. "'Tis not like you t' be glad an English lord gets to go home unscathed."

Duncan's rumbling laugh filled the staircase. Through it, Will said, in a warning tone, "Wait until ye hear the rest."

"Well?" Mal asked impatiently.

Duncan answered, sounding gleeful. "He's being released into *your* custody, Mal. You're to have the keeping of him. You're to take him and your captured English dragoon to Kilmorgan, until their ultimate fate is decided."

Chapter 22

Malcolm's fury could match his father's, and rage bubbled high inside him. He told Duncan what he thought of orders from a prince he didn't recognize, and Duncan, in better spirits than Mal had seen him in an age, only laughed again.

"Ye could leave Wilfort for the chop if ye want. Or ye can look out for him while they decide whether to ransom him or hang him," Duncan said. "Your dragoon captain too. He's proving dangerous, and they want him out of the way. A long way out of the way. Most wanted to kill him, but I saved him for ye, runt. He's yours, and *ye* say what to do with him."

Duncan loved the old ways of justice and war, where the fate of captured prisoners was up to the clan. He was enjoying dispensing this news, and also Mal's irritation.

"And if I choose t' send the pair of them back to England?" Mal asked. "Washing me hands of them?"

Duncan shrugged. "If they're caught going, they'll be killed. Better keep them at Kilmorgan, Mal, if you're so keen to save the father of the woman whose skirts ye want to lift."

"What about her poor old auntie?" Mal asked, restraining himself pummeling Duncan with his fists. "Is she in me custody too?"

Will answered before Duncan could. "No, she'll be going back to England with Lady Bancroft. Best thing for her."

At least the woman would be safe, which would relieve Mary. The situation wasn't ideal, and Mal didn't like the thought of Wilfort as a houseguest, but if he could save the man for Mary's sake, he would.

"Wait," Mal said, a thought striking him. "What about Halsey? Ye didn't mention him."

"Huh," Duncan grunted. "That's because he does nae want to go home. Halsey's turned his coat inside out, is giving Charles and Murray every scrap of information he has about anyone against the Jacobites. He's talking, talking, talking, spewing forth all his secrets. And he has many."

"Crockery and cobwebs!" The furious exclamation exploded from within Mal's chamber, followed by Mary in her water-splotched gown. "That absolutely traitorous, slimy, two-faced . . . Oh, I can't think of a word bad enough to call him."

Will's eyes widened, and Duncan looked shocked. Duncan had always been a bit of a prude about the proper behavior of women—respectable women, that is, not the ladies in brothels he was happy to tumble.

"Duplicitous bastard?" Will suggested.

Mary gave him a nod. "Yes, I think that will do very nicely."

Will burst out laughing, while Duncan continued to look stern.

Will, Mal could see, approved. "I like her, Mal," Will said. "I see ye didn't waste any time with her either. Good lad. I'm going to enjoy this."

Mary wasn't even able to say good-bye to Aunt Danae, but small Ewan was recruited so Mary could at least send a farewell message. So far, the Jacobite contingent remained unaware or uncaring of Mary's existence, and Mal said he wanted to keep it that way. Mary understood, but it was a wrench to not take leave of the woman who'd been the same as a mother to her for many years.

But someday this would be over. Mary and her aunt would be reunited, and all would be well.

Mary firmly suppressed the fear she'd never see her aunt

and sister again as she made ready to leave Edinburgh for parts unknown. She would have to take things as they came and not succumb to worry. That way lay madness.

Her father would not be brought to them until they were on their way out apparently. That night, while Charles Stuart hosted another grand ball in his ongoing celebration, Mary packed.

The Mackenzie house was in chaos. All of them were leaving for the Highlands, including the duke. The servants swarmed to answer the duke's shouts, ignoring the irritated curses of Will, Mal, and Angus. Even Duncan was coming with them, though why, Mary was not sure. He was the only true Jacobite among them, and she wondered why he wasn't remaining with the armies.

In the morning, very early, Mary climbed into a carriage pulled by four strong horses. Naughton had just shut the door for her when Ewan began to wail. He'd been told he had to stay behind and help the staff in the Edinburgh house.

His sobbed words were in the Scots language, but at one point he said in English, "I mu' go w' me captain. I can nae stay without me captain!"

"What the devil is he on about?" Duncan growled.

Mary lowered the coach's window, shivering in the late fall air. "He means me. Let him come—he can ride with me."

More snarling from Duncan, some of his sounds simply wordless mutters.

The carriage door was yanked open, and Mal boosted Ewan inside. The lad's face was streaked with tears, but he adjusted his woolen cap and climbed onto the seat opposite Mary, sniffling. Mary took a handkerchief from her sleeve and leaned forward to wipe his face.

Malcolm swung up behind Ewan and dropped to the seat next to the lad. He let out a shrill whistle, and the door slammed and the carriage jerked forward.

"All right, Mary?" Mal asked her, the same wicked gleam in his eyes he'd had that first afternoon in the upstairs gallery at Lord Bancroft's.

"I thought you'd go on horseback with your brothers," Mary said. The other Mackenzies surrounded them, horses moving smoothly alongside the coach.

"Once it gets rough, we all will. But until then, I'd rather look after ye myself."

Mary couldn't argue, feeling better with Mal's presence. Ewan seemed to think the arrangement was a perfect one and forgot about his tears, eager to go.

They rolled through the city's gate, Mal's brothers and father riding close to the coach. The duke rode well and looked as lively as his sons once on horseback, his plaids covering him to his well-worn boots.

At Holyrood, they went around the back while the prisoners were marched out and put into the carriage. Mal abandoned his place as Mary's father took the seat opposite her.

Mary knew her father was not the sort of man who liked his daughters embracing him in joy, but Mary sat forward, took Wilfort's bound hands, and squeezed them.

"I am pleased to see you well, sir."

"I can say the same about you, Daughter." Wilfort's grip tightened briefly, which Mary knew expressed his relief. "You seem none the worse for wear."

Mary gave him a nod. "Indeed, the duke and his family have looked after me well."

The earl grunted. "Hmm. There are many things for us to discuss, but at a later time."

The carriage door on the other side opened and another man was thrust in. The newcomer wore shackles on his wrists and ankles, and he fixed Mary with a piercing gaze. "No one told me I'd be riding with civilians."

Mal climbed back in, sitting next to Mary this time, and pulling Ewan to the seat between them. "Lady Mary, may I introduce my prisoner, Captain Robert Ellis of the Thirteenth Dragoons. Captain, the Earl of Wilfort and his daughter, Lady Mary."

Captain Ellis bowed the best he could. "I am pleased to meet you. Forgive me for not shaking hands."

"Not at all," Mary answered, giving him a gracious nod. "The circumstances are unusual."

Wilfort only snorted, gave the captain a polite greeting, and turned his head to look out the window.

Duncan slammed the door, and they began moving.

The hundred and fifty–odd miles from Edinburgh to Kilmorgan Castle north of Inverness took a week and more of rough travel.

Mary looked about with interest as they went, her curiosity sharp in spite of the chill weather, the constant lurching of the carriage, and the knowledge that she was moving farther and farther from everything she knew.

Her father didn't like it. Wilfort shuddered whenever he looked out at the rolling lands of the lower Highlands, and even more when the road began climbing sharp hills. "Bleak," he'd say. "No idea why it's worth fighting over."

"A man's homeland engenders his loyalty," Captain Ellis offered as explanation. "I've seen it in the most primitive natives in the Caribbean islands and in the dreariest parts of Ireland and India. Scotland isn't hot, at least. Makes a pleasant change."

They followed the roads forged into the heart of Scotland in the last twenty years by Field Marshal Wade and his band of soldiers and engineers. Besides the carriage and Mal's family, a cart carried baggage along with the few servants who'd accompanied them, including Jinty to look after Mary.

North of Perth they picked up one of the narrow Wade roads paved with tamped-down stones. Knifelike hills rose to heights of three thousand feet and more around them.

"Twenty years building roads so the British army could stamp out Highland insurrection," Captain Ellis said to Mary one rainy morning as they slowly bumped along. "And now the Highlanders themselves have used them to sweep down from the hills and take over Edinburgh. A lesson in irony."

Malcolm, who'd been apparently dozing in the corner, began murmuring in song:

Lord, grant that Marshal Wade,
May by thy mighty aid,
Victory bring.
May he sedition hush, and like a torrent rush,
Rebellious Scots to crush,
God save the king.

Captain Ellis watched him without smiling. "Does it not worry you that your loyalties are so fluid, Lord Malcolm? You fought valiantly against us at Prestonpans, yet you save me and Lord Wilfort from hanging, and argue with your brother about his Jacobitism. Everywhere we stop, Lord Duncan is out trying to recruit for his side, and your father is arguing just as loudly that all the men in kilts should go back home."

Malcolm shrugged. His look was sleepy, but Mary saw the alert gleam of his eyes. "That's Highland clans for ye. No matter how loudly we argue or how fiercely we fight, in the end, it's only the survival of our clan that matters. Duncan's an idealist. Dad only wants to make sure his clansmen and families eat through the winter."

"And you, Lord Malcolm?" Captain Ellis asked. "Where do you fit? Loyal to your clansmen? Or the Stuart kings?"

"Me family will always come first," Mal said. "What I do with my time left after that . . . I'll wait and see."

Mary's father made a skeptical sound but did not speak.

Sometimes when the roads grew too steep, those in the carriage had to descend and walk. Mary was always given a small but rugged horse to ride at these times, while the men tramped along beside or behind the carriage.

Lord Wilfort and Captain Ellis were at all times surrounded by Malcolm's brothers, but that didn't stop Captain Ellis from trying to escape. During the journey, he attempted it no less than fifteen times.

"Save your strength, sir," Wilfort snapped at him after one incident. When they'd halted for a rest, Captain Ellis had run as fast as his bound hands and feet had let him down a hill toward a stream. Duncan, Will, and Malcolm, all on horseback, had loped almost leisurely after him, caught him, and brought him back. "If you keep on," the earl added, "they'll simply shoot you to be rid of the bother of you."

Captain Ellis sat down in the middle of the road, breathing heavily. "It's a soldier's duty to escape the enemy."

Malcolm dismounted and handed Ellis a water skin. "We're the best friends ye have out here, man. Ye never know if the next knot of soldiers ye run into are for Charles or for George. And if ye keep covering yerself in grime, those for George won't recognize ye as English."

Captain Ellis shrugged as he sipped the offered water. "I do my duty as I see fit."

Malcolm took the water skin back and tamped in its stopper. "Aye, well, I respect a man with strong principles."

One night, when they rode late through a tiny village along a deserted stretch of the road, they found it full of soldiers, British ones. The duke led the way through them, telling the captain in charge clearly who he was and that he was no Jacobite. Angus and Will kept Duncan out of the way, and Duncan, who'd proved to be no fool, even if passionate about his beliefs, kept his mouth shut.

Mary held her breath as the English soldiers surrounded them. Now would be the perfect time for Captain Ellis to roll from the carriage, declare loudly that he'd been captured by the Mackenzies, and claim his freedom.

Captain Ellis volunteered nothing. He sat quietly, a rug hiding his manacled hands. When the soldiers looked inside the carriage, they saw a middle-aged English aristocrat, his respectable daughter, a captain in the British army, and a young lad who appeared to be a servant. None of them seemed fearful or the worse for wear.

The soldiers waved them through, even saluting Captain Ellis, who only nodded tiredly in return.

Once they were well away from the cluster of houses, the earl said, "Damn it, Ellis, there was your chance. Why did you not take it?"

Captain Ellis gave him a neutral look. "If I'd tried to escape into that mob with muskets, Lady Mary might have been hurt."

The earl stared at him a moment, then gave him a nod. "Ah. Then I thank you, sir, for your discretion."

Wilfort turned his gaze on Mary, with a look in his eyes she didn't like.

But, of course—Captain Ellis was English, a gentleman, a cavalry officer, who were usually wealthier than their infantry compatriots, and he'd just showed that he valued Mary's safety over his freedom.

Malcolm was Scots, by all evidence an idler, and too mercurial to pin down his loyalties. And again—he was Scots. Mary was certain her father would make that point twice.

Mary said nothing, only closed her eyes and pretended to sleep, but she remained uneasy.

When the terrain finally became too rough for wheeled vehicles, Malcolm and his brothers loaded the baggage onto stout Highland ponies they bought from a local man and sent the carriage, coachman, cart, and driver back to Edinburgh.

Mary had noted that Malcolm and Will always negotiated with the Scots they met along the way for food or lodging, while the remaining Mackenzies hung back and let them. Considering that Mary always had a soft place to sleep each night and at least one cooked meal each day, she came to believe that Mal and Will between them could charm the skin off a snake, and the rest of the family knew it.

A pony now carried Mary, who again wore the leather breeches and peasant skirt Ewan had given her. She'd worried that the small horse wouldn't carry her weight, but the little mare proved surprisingly strong, comfortable, and tireless.

"Men fight battles on these ponies," Malcolm said as he settled her. "They're sturdy beasts, from the far north. A funny sight t' see the men on them, but the beasts never miss a step."

The pony carried Mary over the mountains, which in early October were filled with brisk, sharp winds and strong sunshine. Duncan led the pack, his father beside him. Though the two blustered at each other constantly during the light of day, once night fell, they became, by tacit agreement, quiet and careful.

One evening after sunset, Duncan came riding back to where Mary, her father, Ellis, and Malcolm rode alongside the baggage horses.

"Someone's out there," Duncan said. "A whole pack of them, we think—we heard several horses. They've stopped and are waiting, either for us to pass or to attack us, we don't know. It's too steep and dangerous here to get around."

"Then Will and I need to go out and meet them," Mal said. "And discover what they want." Mal suited action to word, as he always did, already nudging his horse forward.

"No, I should," Duncan said, hand on his pistol. "They might be soldiers."

Malcolm didn't wait. "Then it should be me. The situation needs diplomacy and discretion. You don't have any." He rode out of their little circle into the darkness before anyone could stop him.

Chapter 23

Mal felt them lurking in the night, hidden in shadows even moonlight couldn't penetrate. The road itself glowed eerily, stretching in a thin pale line until it bent around a corner and vanished.

The waiting men were far too silent to be British soldiers. Anyone this stealthy had to be Highlanders, ones who knew this road. Mal doubted Jacobites would try to hide from a small party of civilians. That left only one possibility in his opinion.

He glanced at Will, who, by the look on his face, had already drawn the same conclusion. "It's all right," Mal called out in Erse. "We aren't excise men. We're Highlanders going home."

Silence. A horse snorted in the darkness and shook its head.

After a tense moment or two, a lone man stepped out. He wore a great kilt that covered him to mid-thigh, and worn boots.

"You've got a solider with ye," he said, pointing a thick finger past Malcolm.

Malcolm knew the man couldn't see Ellis from there—he must have sent scouts to find out exactly who their group contained. "He's a prisoner," Mal said. "Captured by me. I'm taking him home, to Kilmorgan."

A risk telling the man where they were from. If his clan was historically enemies with Malcolm's, there could be a bloody fight.

The man stepped forward and peered up at Malcolm. "You a Mackenzie?"

"Aye," Mal answered. "I'm Malcolm—this is me brother Will."

"Lord Malcolm Mackenzie," the man repeated, and his voice grew warmer, full of enthusiasm. "You're legend, you are, me lord. I'd be honored, sir, if ye'd try a drop."

It amused Malcolm, looking back on the incident, how quickly the train of ponies had materialized after that. They were small, wiry horses, each laden with two or three casks. Moonlight revealed a line of about twenty, which meant a great deal of contraband moving south.

The man, who said they could call him Rabbie, but cannily didn't mention his surname, brought forth one of the casks and broached it. He called for a cup and handed it to Malcolm, who dipped it inside.

Mal brought the acrid-smelling brew to his lips and sipped. A burning sensation filled his mouth then spread rapidly down his body. He coughed.

"That good, eh?" Will asked. He dismounted, took up Mal's cup, and had his own sip. He coughed too, then laughed. "My God, man. That will cure all illness."

Rabbie's eyes twinkled. "They'll water it down a bit, I wager. What d'ye think, sir?" he asked Malcolm.

"It's robust," Mal said when he could speak. "Grabs a man by his short hairs and doesn't let go, does it? But you're nearly there. A touch more malt, barley only, and longer in the oak, and ye'll command any price."

"Mmm," Rabbie said. "But malt is taxed enough to ruin a man."

"Well . . . ye can be a bit vague about how much ye have."

Rabbie chuckled. "I tell them nothing as it is. But if I keep it too long in the cask, me family starves while we wait for it to age."

"Vary your batches, then. Keep one longer, call it your

reserve, and start overlapping your producing times. Pretty soon, you'll have something t' sell and something held back, something maturing all the time until it's right. Trust me, then ye'll have plenty t' eat in the winter, and your women will have all the pretty frocks they want."

"I'll consider it, lad. But it's different for us."

"Aye, I know." Mal had been able, with his mother's inheritance, to buy a license to produce and sell his whisky legally, which gave him more leisure time to produce a decent brew. Poor men like Rabbie had to make their whisky in secret and trundle it down the Wade roads under cover of darkness.

The two exchanged more pleasantries, mostly about the conditions of the roads, and Mal told Rabbie where they'd run into the British army patrols. They parted with mutual good wishes and firm handshakes, then Rabbie's party stood aside and let Malcolm's pass without impediment.

Malcolm noticed, though, that Rabbie had been the only one who spoke. The other hard-eyed men leading or riding the ponies kept to the shadows and watched in suspicious silence. One or two gave them nods, but most only waited for Malcolm and family to go by. Malcolm also noticed that every single one of them was armed in some way.

"Smugglers," Captain Ellis observed when Mal rejoined them. "Since we're not at sea, I take it they're carrying whisky?"

"Aye. Either that or musket cleaner—it was a trifle difficult to tell by the taste."

Ellis rumbled a laugh. "Thank you for throwing yourself into the line of fire."

Mary regarded Mal curiously. "You told me the Mackenzies produce whisky. Why aren't you smuggling it over the mountains on ponies?"

"Because the Mackenzies have an approved distillery, and we can afford to make it," Malcolm explained. "Men like Rabbie—they barely survive through the winter. Not much grows in the remote Highlands, but anyone can build a still."

"So you approve of smuggling," Lord Wilfort said coldly. "The natural characteristic of the Scot."

"No, I *understand* it," Mal said. "If laws are so tight they prevent a man from eating, he's going to find ways around them. If it's a choice between following ridiculous regulations or watching your family starve t' death, risking excise men on a mountain road is but a small price to pay."

Wilfort only gave him a cool look, but didn't argue. That boded well, Malcolm thought. The man was softening to him.

"I'll say nothing about Rabbie and his band of smugglers when I get free," Captain Ellis said. "*If* you show me this whisky of yours when we reached Kilmorgan. If I reach there," he amended quickly. "I will continue to try to escape."

"Done," Malcolm said.

Mary only smiled, but she included Captain Ellis in the smile, which Malcolm did not like at all.

"There it is," Mal said several days later. "Behold your new home, lass. A bit terrifying, isn't it?"

They'd ridden down from a hill into a long valley, a wall of mountains rising to the west. In a flat, open area, about fifty yards from a thick stand of trees, lay a pile of stones—not a ruin, but quarried stone laid out, ready to be used for building. Trenches had been dug in the earth, and here and there Mary spied a stake pounded into the ground, but no work was being done.

Beyond this, up on a cliff, rose a proper castle, with a square keep topping the hill. Castle Kilmorgan.

Inverness was a half-day's ride behind them, the town and fort still held by Lord Loudon and Highlanders loyal to King George. Mary again expected Captain Ellis to desert them there, fleeing to the protection of the fort or Culloden House, but he remained with the party, hiding the fact that he was Malcolm's prisoner.

North of Inverness, with the sea on their right, the coast became cliffs, while inland was a rolling plain. Black cattle, shaggier than Mary had ever seen in her life, wandered about the grassy valleys, and even among the cluster of houses Mal told her was the village of Kilmorgan.

The cattle were unworried by their presence, peering at Mary through hair that hung over their eyes. She found the cows interesting, but the calves that trotted along after their mothers were adorable. The cows seemed curious about her, as were the people who stepped out of houses and sheds to see them go by, some to follow.

At last they reached the base of the hill, with the castle on the top. The view from it would be breathtaking, the road to it precipitous and rough going.

"The home of our ancestors," Mal said with a sweep of his arm. "The first duke built this in thirteen hundred something. It's been rebuilt six times since then, the last renovation about thirty years ago. But we need a real house. Drafty castles are bloody uncomfortable in the winter."

Will heard him. "If ye are trying to reassure your lady, Mal, I don't think ye're going about it the right way."

"She should know the truth of it," Mal said. "I'll not lie to her."

Will only gave him a deprecating look and rode off to join Duncan and Angus.

Mary was glad of her sturdy pony as they went up the twisting road to the top. The way was narrow, the drop frightening, but the beast never missed her footing.

The local lads swarmed up the hill beside them, and when the train reached the courtyard, the lads started unstrapping the luggage from the ponies and carrying it inside.

Mary was so exhausted she didn't have much wherewithal to take in all she saw. The castle doors opened to a square hall with a wooden staircase twisting up through it to galleries, doors lining all four of the walls.

Jinty and one of the castle's maids led Mary up two flights of the wooden stairs and into a large bedchamber. The room was drafty, as Mal had indicated, but a fire blazed high on the hearth, and from the small window Mary could see a long way across the tumbling country to the mountains.

"It's beautiful," she said.

"Happy ye like it." Malcolm had entered the room behind her. "Tomorrow I'll show you the house I'm going to build. But I'm a kind man—I'll let ye rest a bit before I take ye all over Kilmorgan and wear ye out with it."

Mary turned from the window. Malcolm stood in the middle of the chamber, ignored by the maids, who continued unpacking, and by the servants and Mal's brothers, who shouted to one another up and down the galleries.

Malcolm looked different somehow, Mary thought as she

watched him, and not because of lines of tiredness under his eyes or several days' growth of beard.

He looked stronger, more formidable, less the charming young man of the city. When Mary had first seen him, she'd thought him a wild Highlander in the midst of sophisticated Englishmen. She'd learned since then that he was educated, gallant, loyal to his family, resourceful, beguiling, and could talk his way into or out of anything.

This, however, was his homeland. Mal had power here. Put a claymore in his hand, and every English soldier would run away from him, as Duncan had boasted they'd done at Prestonpans.

"You love it here," Mary said.

Malcolm shrugged, his sinful smile returning. "*Love* might be overstating it. But it's part of me, ye ken? In my blood."

And in your heart, Mary wanted to add. *Maybe deeper than I ever can be.*

Malcolm came to her, took her hands, and kissed her palms. The kisses were slow and sensual, the heat of his breath burning.

"I'll leave ye t' rest." He lowered her hands but didn't let go. "Tomorrow I'll show you my world. For tonight, if ye need anything at all, ye just ask Jinty or the majordomo. Even if it's a bath." He winked at her, and Mary went hot. "I know ye like those. Good night, then."

"Good night," Mary said faintly as he released her.

Mal gave her another smile, broadened the smile to include the maids, who didn't hide their curiosity, and drifted out the door.

The duke's voice rang in the hall below. "*Mal!* Where the devil are ye?"

"Aye, all right, I'm coming," Mal shouted back in an irritated rumble, and was gone.

Malcolm was an astonishing man, with so many facets. Later, as she lay snug in bed under many quilts near the substantial fire, Mary's thoughts drifted, as Mal had known they would, to her drawing the dripping sponge across his back and then what she'd done next. She buried her face in her pillow as she remembered every detail of his slick body under her fingers, and later him pinning her to the carpet, the exact weight and feel of him.

A wind sang in the eaves—a strong Scottish wind that let nothing stand in its way. *Just like Malcolm*, was her last thought before she drifted off.

Duncan left in the morning after another loud row with their father. He'd come north with them, Malcolm knew, mainly to recruit other Mackenzies to follow him to Charles's aid. Duncan had made no secret of that.

The duke shouted over the gallery as Duncan stormed down the stairs and out the door. "Dinnae come back! I never want t' see ye again, Duncan Mackenzie, unless it's on your funeral pyre!"

"Bloody hell," Will muttered. He and Malcolm had come out of the breakfast room to witness the last of the argument. Cold wind blew through the wide front door, which had banged open again after Duncan had slammed it.

Mal caught the door and, together with Will and one of the castle's robust footman, swung it closed and bolted it.

"Sorry t' disturb ye," Mal said, reentering the breakfast room. At the table, enjoying sausages, eggs, and bannocks were Mary, Lord Wilfort, Angus, and Captain Ellis. Will rejoined them, after heaping more sausages on his plate.

Captain Ellis was no longer shackled. He'd given his word that he would not try to escape or harm anyone within the castle walls or in a circumference of several hundred feet—several hundred feet because he might want a walk to clear his head from time to time.

Ellis had declared this as though he expected them to take his word as binding. Malcolm did. Ellis was that sort of man.

Mal was far more worried about Mary's da, Wilfort. Though not as slippery as Lord Halsey, Wilfort was a crafty old devil. No doubt he was even now scheming how to overthrow the duke and capture this castle for the English.

"I'm taking Mary to show her the new house," Mal announced abruptly. "And some of the lands. She'll come to no harm by it. I give you *my* word."

Mary had dressed in her breeches and loose skirt again, Malcolm saw, when she met him in the courtyard, clothes good for riding in the wilds. She'd donned a mannish coat with many buttons over the costume, and wore a hat that pulled down over her ears. She showed no self-consciousness about the way she looked, only tugged on gloves and let Malcolm boost her onto the pony's saddle.

She was practical, sensible, and beautiful, all rolled into one. No wilting flower, Mary had already survived a trek across the Highlands, with his father and three of his brothers no less, had told Mal sincerely that the country was beautiful, and even liked the coos that wandered the valleys. By the freshness of her face and lightness of step, she'd slept soundly all night, even while a gale had blown about the castle.

She was the woman for him. Malcolm's heart warmed as he led her down the hill to show her his pride and joy.

"There will be a front wing," he said as they walked the horses along the trench he'd had cleared out before he'd journeyed to Edinburgh. "It will run the length of the whole house, with galleries and plenty of windows, so we can enjoy the view. Then wings flowing back from the main one, one wing for each brother, so our families can all live here in comfort."

"It will be enormous," Mary said, eyeing the expanse of the trench. "My father's home in Lincolnshire is nowhere near as grand, and it is not small."

"Of course it will be big," Mal said. "It's made to house Mackenzies. We need a lot of room." He swept his arm to indicate the wide-open space beyond the trench. "And behind, a garden, where beautiful ladies can walk. Alec is designing it. He's got an artistic touch."

Mary scanned the grounds, rocky and bleak, that ran to a sheer, tree-lined rise beyond. "Is it fair to build on such a scale? When I saw so many tiny cottages, so many barely eking out a living?"

"Not on Kilmorgan lands, ye didn't see such things. Anyway, I'll employ all the local lads when they're not needed on their farms, and pay a decent wage. Many of them work for me already, in my distillery. I'm not a cruel squire from a moral play."

"You're a reformist, then?"

"Mary, love, Englishmen like nothing more than t' sit in drawing rooms discussing what should be done with the world. I don't. I live me life, and cross bridges when I come to them."

Mary's face softened. "Good."

Malcolm didn't trust himself when she looked at him like that, as though she admired him. "Come on," he said. "I'll show you the best place in all of Kilmorgan."

The best place was up a steep track that became overgrown with trees as they neared the top. Malcolm descended from his horse and led both his and Mary's to the outcropping that had been his refuge as a child, a place of peace in his adult life.

Here, a flat shelf of land poked out from the trees, the cliff it perched on overlooking the rolling hills beneath, all the way to the sea. Malcolm lifted Mary from her pony, unsaddled and unbridled both horses, and let them stray—they were used to this land and knew how to graze it.

Mary clung to Malcolm's arm as he took her to the black rock. He stood Mary in front of him and enclosed her from behind, breathing in her fragrance.

"Everything ye see is ours," he said. "What do ye think?"

Mary's eyes shone. "I've never seen anything so beautiful." Her cheeks were pink from the wind, her lips red. "Or cold."

"Aye, well, that's Kilmorgan for ye. Will enchant ye and try to kill ye at the same time."

"Aren't most Scotsmen like that?"

Mal shrugged. "'Tis a good point. But I'd never hurt ye, Mary. Ye know that by now." He leaned down to her, unable to resist kissing her upturned lips. She was so trusting in his arms, believing in him and in this world from which he'd sprung. "But I want ye, do you understand?" Mal said into her ear. "Have from the moment I saw ye. I don't know how t' love without passion. If ye don't want that, tell me now."

Mary turned to face him. The wind whipped at her skirt and at the hair that escaped under her closely fitting hat. She was pressed against the length of him, and he could feel her heart beating as swiftly as his. "I think . . . passion is not so bad a thing," she said.

Mal traced her cheek with his gloved thumb. "Mary, love, I think, that in this place, I could bind myself to ye. Can ye to me?"

Mary looked at him wonderingly. But not afraid. She didn't fear the cliff, the wind, the land, or Malcolm, the crazed Highlander, who'd stolen her away. Malcolm could have sent her home with her aunt, or to any of her friends in London. She could be gone from here, out of harm's way, out of his life.

Instead, Mal had wanted her with him, no matter what. He'd brought her to this empty and forbidding land instead of allowing her to return to her father's estate, where no doubt everything was groomed and well tended, nature tamed.

Kilmorgan was nature without restraint, and Malcolm was part of it. But Mary looked at him without fear, without resentment. She wanted to be here. Malcolm sensed that she would have raged had she been sent home, and perhaps tried to follow her father anyway.

Mary had not come with him because she'd simply allowed herself to be dragged from place to place—if she'd have preferred to return to England, Mal had no doubt she'd have made her wishes plain, and perhaps already be in Lincolnshire.

She gazed up at him in perplexity at his last statement. "Bind to me?" she asked.

"We're not in a chapel, and there's no minister. And I know there'll be a hell of a fight between our dads about which sort of church we're married in—Scottish or English. But right now, between the two of us, I say we marry. Here and now."

Chapter 24

Mary's heart thumped in confusion. "But how can we . . ."

Malcolm touched his fingers to her lips. "This is a sacred place—can ye not tell? Or at any rate, a beautiful one. A fitting chapel."

He was playing with her again. Although . . . a look into his eyes showed her a stillness, a waiting.

Mary gave him a nod. "Yes. It is." She caught his hand and twined her fingers through his. "All right."

The lines around Mal's eyes tightened, then released. He squeezed her hand. "Tell me your second name, love. And any others if ye have them."

Mary cleared her throat. Malcolm was mad, but the madness was reaching out and tangling her. "Mary Elizabeth Sophia," she said in a clear voice.

"Oh, that's lovely, that is. So many names there for our daughters." Mal turned her to face him. The wind pushed at them, her skirts fluttering and his kilt meeting them, but they were fixed in this place, a part of the land, a part of each other.

Malcolm looked straight into her eyes. "I, Malcolm Daniel Mackenzie, take thee, Mary Elizabeth Sophia Lennox, as my wife. To have and to hold, from this day forward . . . And thereto I plight thee my troth."

Mary had heard the marriage service many times in the last few years, as her childhood friends, one after the other, married. Mal had skipped over a good chunk of it, but she'd never heard a groom speak the words so sincerely as he did now.

"I . . ." Mary's voice clogged, and she cleared her throat. "I, Mary Elizabeth Sophia, take thee, Malcolm Daniel Mackenzie, as my husband. To have and to hold from this day forward . . . and thereto I plight *thee* my troth."

Malcolm, with that same waiting look in his eyes, tugged her closer. He peeled the glove from her left hand, his fingers warm despite the wind. He slid a gold ring from his broad finger and placed it on her slender one.

"With this ring, I thee wed," Mal said, his voice quiet. "With my body, I thee worship. With all my worldly goods, I thee endow."

The ring was cool and heavy on Mary's finger. Malcolm held her hand tightly, his gaze hard upon hers, as though he expected any moment for her to laugh, say it was a silly game, walk away from him.

Mary pressed her lips to the ring, then to his rough, windburned hand. "Amen," she whispered.

Malcolm gathered her closer. "Well, then, Mary."

Mary felt the length of his body, the warm wool of his kilt as the wind wrapped a fold of it around her. "Well, then," she said back.

He tilted her chin up, sealing their bargain with a kiss that burned. Mal's great kilt had come loose from his shoulders, and he drew it around her, enclosing them in a snug cocoon.

"'Tis a bit warmer under the trees," he said.

He wouldn't ask. He wouldn't demand. Mal's eyes held the gleam of the hunger she'd seen in him, the one he'd awakened in her. But he wouldn't coerce. This had to be Mary's decision, her choice to plight him her troth.

"Yes," Mary said.

Malcolm led her from the rock. He helped her down the tiny stone path that led to it, and back under the stand of thick firs that lined the hillside. The ponies, grazing, watched them without much interest, then went back to cropping whatever grass they could find.

Mal had been right about the trees. They cut the wind, and here, under their shelter, the early October air was soft.

Malcolm unpinned and unwrapped the folds of his kilt, emerging, unashamed, in only his shirt and boots. He spread the kilt upon the ground, then made short work of the rest of his clothes, standing naked, as the natives of this land must have eons ago.

He didn't wait. Malcolm came to her, and with deft hands unbuttoned and pulled off her bodice, then her small corset, and unfastened her skirt. He caught her breasts in his hands as they came free, and paused to press a long kiss to her mouth. The roughness of his palms against Mary's bare flesh had her melting into his kiss, rising on tiptoes to seek more.

Mal eased back after a time, his breath hot on her lips. "Mary, ye taste so sweet."

Mary licked the hollow of his throat. "So do you."

"Wicked lass." Mal's smile was slow. He leaned to kiss the hollow of *her* throat, the rough silk of his hair brushing her chin.

Malcolm lowered himself to his knees on the plaid, and now he was kissing her abdomen, hands warm on her waist. He glanced up at her, amber eyes glinting in the half light, then licked the undersides of her breasts.

Heat whipped through her. "Mal."

"Not long now," he said. "And all this fire inside ye can come out." Mal slid the edge of his hand up between her breasts, just as he had the day in Lady Brancroft's sitting room when he'd said he saw her fire.

She was burning with it. Mal kissed her abdomen again, then popped open the buttons of her breeches.

The leather came away easily, slipping from her legs. Here she was, bare, outdoors, while this untamed Highlander knelt before her.

When his lips brushed between her thighs, Mary let out a cry and took an instinctive step backward. Mal caught her with strong arms and tugged her to him again.

"Fire," he said, his own eyes full of it. "Now you'll see."

He swept his tongue over the most intimate part of her, the

one Mary didn't even know the name for, not the proper one anyway.

It knew what to do even if she didn't. Mary's feet slid apart, opening her for him. Mal made a satisfied noise in his throat, pressed himself closer, and licked her again.

He did magic with his tongue. Mal rubbed her opening with it, the friction of that white hot. He encouraged her legs to part even more, then put his mouth over the hottest place of her and suckled.

The world spun away. Mary floated alone in darkness, nothing real but Mal's mouth on her, his arms a band of strength across her hips. She was aware only of the spark igniting beneath his mouth, the incredible power that shot through her body.

She cried out with it. The trees echoed the sound, and then the wind swept it away.

"Malcolm!"

Mary had no idea what was happening to her. Her skin burned, but from the inside, her heart skipped and pounded. She couldn't see, or hear—only feel, as though she'd lost all sensations but one.

Her cries grew frantic, wordless, mad, and then Malcolm lifted his mouth away.

The world came splintering back, and it hurt. Mary bit back a sob.

Mal came up to her, arms going around her. He laid her down on the ground, his plaid their bed, then he was on top of her, his warm, bare weight comforting.

One strong hand parted her legs, and the next new sensation was Malcolm sliding into her, the full length of him that she'd seen and touched in the bath in Edinburgh.

Mary tightened in panic. She couldn't do this. Every warning her aunt had given her, every terrible story about how brutish men could be in bed, flitted through her head.

But she wasn't with a brutish man. She was with Malcolm.

Her body wrested control from her, and Mary's fears vanished, along with every sensible, practical thought. All she wanted was now, *this*—her existence stripped to nothing but the hardness of Malcolm inside her, his body on hers.

This wasn't duty, or penance, or breeding. It was basic . . . and splendid.

Mal groaned softly as he thrust. He brushed a lock of hair from Mary's face and smiled into her eyes. "Ah, Mary, you're the most beautiful lass I ever did see."

Mary tried to answer, but no words came. She was nothing . . . and everything. The two of them were one, and the wind, the sky, the trees, the ground.

They twined together as Malcolm thrust, each movement sending him deeper. He raised himself on his fists, the round of his backside moving, brushed by sunlight that reached through the thick boughs. Mary's hips rose to meet his, the coming together more wonderful with every stroke.

"Love," Malcolm breathed. "What have ye done t' me?"

Mary could only touch him, finding no words for answering.

"Ye took me, and turned everything around. And now there's no relieving it but *this.*" Malcolm thrust again, harder. "Inside my hot, sweet Mary. There's only you for me now. Nothing but you."

His voice broke off, harsh sound taking the place of words. Mary's body rocked beneath his, his kilt, the symbol of him, cradling her, warming her, keeping her safe.

"Aw, *damnation.*" Mal's face twisted into a sudden, furious scowl. At the same time, his thrusts built, and built, until he slammed once more into her, and she felt sudden, liquid heat.

Malcolm's seed, carried inside her by their hunger for each other. Mary tightened her body, drawing it in and holding it gladly.

Malcolm gave one last, long thrust, and then collapsed, as though all the strength had gone from him. A lassitude stole over them, the woods quieting, as Mary stroked his hair.

"Blast and damn," Malcolm murmured. He pressed an open-mouthed kiss to her lips. "I wanted to go on the rest of th' day."

"So did I," Mary said, smoothing his whisker-roughened jaw. He'd shaved since last night, but his beard grew quickly. "Cats and crumpets, I did."

Malcolm's body shook with quiet laughter. He lifted his head, and she saw, for the first time in his eyes, peace.

"Why d'ye say things like that? *Bolts and bodkins. Crockery and cobwebs.* Ye make me laugh, ye do."

Mary shrugged. "Ladies aren't allowed to swear. But I have

to express my feelings somehow, don't I? So I make up my own phrases."

"So, when ye feel something strongly, out it comes?"

"Yes. I never quite know what it will be each time."

"I will think on that." Mal's smile deepened. "What ye mean now is that you really *do* want to go on like this all day."

Mary laced her arms around Mal's neck. She felt clean, free, more profoundly *herself* than she ever had in her life.

"Oh, yes," she said.

"Well." Malcolm slid his hand between her legs, his palm pressed right where she wanted it most. "I think we can manage it."

Mal and Mary did not reach the castle again until darkness was falling. Mary worried that their long absence would be met with disapproval, but no one appeared to notice. Duncan had returned, declaring he had found more Mackenzies ready to rise and follow Charles than his father supposed. Lord Forbes, from Inverness, had been preaching as loudly on the side of King George, and Duncan and the men he'd recruited had already had a tussle with them, Duncan receiving a deep sword cut in his arm.

Despite the duke's declaration he never wanted to see Duncan home again, he had the household scrambling to help him. Swearing loudly at his son the whole time, of course.

The shouting and carrying on over Duncan and his wound eclipsed Mary riding in with Malcolm, both of them flushed and tousled, as darkness fell.

Mary believed so, that is, until Captain Ellis steered her aside when she came downstairs again after washing and changing into an afternoon gown. Ellis towed her into a small chamber—leaving the door open, like the gentleman he was—and spoke to her in a low voice.

"Now that Lord Malcolm has gotten what he wanted," Captain Ellis said, his words clipped, "what do you suppose he'll do?"

"Do?" Mary sought refuge in hauteur. "Explain what you mean, sir."

"Do not become the disdainful aristocrat, my lady. I know

when a woman's been with a man—you have a look, and so does he. Lord Malcolm took you out today to have you. Has he mentioned marriage? Settlements? A betrothal?"

No, he hadn't. But they had married—in their hearts. Mary thought of the ceremony they'd shared on the cliff overlooking the sea. That had been real, far more real than any of the weddings she'd witnessed at St. George's, Hanover Square. In the eyes of the Church of England and English law, of course, it meant nothing.

"No," she had to admit. "He hasn't."

"If he does not soon, I shall shoot him." Captain Ellis had dark blue eyes, and those eyes held deep anger as well as concern for Mary. "These Highlanders are not like us, Lady Mary. They're a law unto themselves. Lord Malcolm could keep you here, calling you his 'wife' and giving you little recourse to dispute it. What the laird or the clan chief declares is law, is."

"I've never seen that kind of harshness in Malcolm," Mary said. She'd watched him treat his servants with benevolence, and people like Rabbie and the smuggler called Gair with generosity and trust.

"Not yet you haven't," Captain Ellis said. "You've only just arrived here, in his world, which is different from the streets of Edinburgh. If it becomes necessary, I would be honored to have you as my wife."

"Oh." Mary came out of her thoughts of Malcolm with a thump. "That's very kind of you, but—"

"Not kind." Captain Ellis reached a hand toward her, but at the last moment, pulled it back. "I do it to preserve your honor. In this world, a woman has very little that is purely hers, but her honor is hers alone. Let me help you keep it."

He was sincere. He was offering her a rock to rest on, a support against the world. Her choice was to take Captain Ellis's offer of safety, or to trust in Malcolm.

"I thank you," Mary said. "Truly. You are a noble man. But I have decided I want more out of any marriage than duty and honor."

Captain Ellis's eyes flickered, anger and disappointment flaring for a brief instant. He felt this deeply, she realized.

Then he slid his polite mask into place and gave her a bow.

"The offer stands, in case you need it. But if he makes things so you do need it, Lady Mary, I promise you, I will shoot him."

Mary believed him. She returned Captain Ellis's bow with a polite curtsy, and he walked out of the room, his tread even.

October was always glorious at Kilmorgan, and this one was tinted rosy red. Malcolm spent every waking minute he could with Mary, inside the castle and out of it. He took her to their bower on the hill in good weather, and there they learned each other, amid laughter, touching, loving.

Malcolm had every intention of marrying her once he could talk around both his father and hers. Not for Mary a scandalous elopement. He wanted to have the banns read, to have the world watch her stand up with him at an altar and show them she'd made her choice.

In his romantic moments, he did consider them already married, in the eyes of nature and God. Mary was the only woman for him, for whom he'd forsake all others.

First, though, he needed to stop this bloody uprising interfering with his plans. Forbes and his men came from Inverness a few times, looking for Duncan, who was busy stirring up trouble. Duncan, it seemed, had gone so far as to lead raid-and-run attacks against British military forts.

The duke, while he snarled that his son was no friend to him anymore, would never tell Forbes where Duncan had gone. Malcolm knew his father probably knew very well where Duncan was, but the duke wasn't about to give up his son to Hanoverian loyalists.

Lord Wilfort remarked on this when Forbes was sent away empty-handed yet again.

The two fathers had moved from cold hostility to grudging respect. The duke discovered that Lord Wilfort had a mutual interest in the game of chess, and started inviting him to play.

The play reflected the personalities of each man, Malcolm decided—the duke, ruthless and aggressive; the earl, quietly cunning.

"You soundly rail against the Jacobites," Wilfort observed in his dry way as he captured one of the duke's bishops. "Yet you send away the soldiers who would put them down."

"I've no love for German George either," the duke returned. "The sooner all soldiers, on either side, are out of my glens, the better. Highlanders are ruled by their chiefs, not kings so foreign they can't even speak the native tongue. We rule ourselves."

"That's not the way of the world anymore," Wilfort said.

"Untrue," the duke growled. "You stand up in English Parliament, stealing more and more power from your king and putting it in the hands of people like yourself. It's the same damn thing."

Wilfort looked thoughtful. "You could have a point. But I don't have the power of life and death over my family."

"Neither do I, if ye've noticed," the duke said. "You see my sons terrified of me? No, they defy me, like the devil's get they are. And you're a magistrate, aren't you, in your little corner of the world? You dispense local justice, because it's too far to drag everyone off to London for every transgression."

Wilfort conceded. "Another point. But while you've argued, I've captured your queen."

"Worth the sacrifice," the duke said, and shoved his rook across the board. "Checkmate."

Not long later, Alec came home.

Malcolm, from the castle's hill, saw his brother riding in. He'd taken Mary to the sunny side of the craggy castle to warm themselves and hold hands, when she shaded her eyes and peered down to the road.

"Who is that?" she asked, pointing. "Another soldier looking for Duncan?"

Mal followed her gaze, and his heart leapt with gladness. He'd recognize that casual slouch on horseback anywhere.

"It's Alec!" he shouted, and was running down the narrow path before the words died away.

Chapter 25

Mary picked her way down the hill after Malcolm, as excited as he was. Alec would have news of Audrey.

The wind and Malcolm's running lifted his kilt and fluttered it over his back like a flag of his clan. His firm buttocks moved in the sunshine as he leapt from rock to rock.

Alec swung off his horse as Mal reached the bottom of the path. Mal swept his brother up in a bear hug, lifting him from his feet. By the time Mary reached them, they were both talking at once, each drowning out the other.

Alec broke off when he saw Mary, his tawny eyes widening. There were lines about those eyes, of fatigue, grief, dirt in the creases, but his expression was one of good humor. "Good Lord, you *did* steal her."

"She came willingly," Mal said. "Well, willingly enough."

"Lord Alec." Mary moved to him, catching the odor of wet plaid, sweat, and horse. "I will be impolite and not ask you how your journey was—what news of my sister, Audrey?"

"Well, now." Alec made a show of patting the thick kilt that wrapped his shoulders. "I had a letter about me person somewhere. I meant to take it on to Edinburgh when I went, but you are here, and so I'll deliver it to ye now."

Mary nearly leapt on the tall man, wanting to burrow into the folds of his plaid and find the precious missive herself. Alec, eyes twinkling, yanked a fat fold of paper from under the fabric and laid it into her outstretched hands. "There ye are. Lady Audrey is well and happy, eating bonbons in a fine *appartement* in Paris with Jeremy Drake worshiping at her feet."

Mary had already ripped open the letter's seal and hastily unfolded the sheets. "She's well," she said after she'd read a few lines. "She's loving being married, and they are hoping for a child."

"Aye," Alec said. "From the idiotically pleased looks they give each other, I'd say they were trying for one day and night."

Mary's eyes were wet as she folded the letter and pressed it to her chest. "Thank you. You've made me so happy—I thought I could never feel this happy again."

Alec shot Mal a look of mock alarm. "Then ye can't be pleasing her right, Mal. What's the matter with ye?"

"Aye." Mal gave his brother a solemn nod. "Trust a woman to put a man in his place."

Alec roared with laughter. Mary flushed, realizing what she'd implied, and Alec, seeing her blush, laughed harder.

"What about you?" Mary asked quickly. "Is your daughter . . ."

"My daughter is a bonny wee lass, the most beautiful thing ye ever did see." Pride rang in the deep rumble of Alec's voice. His face under his tangle of hair lit up, the fatigue instantly erased.

Mal made a show of looking around him. "Where is she, then? Did ye leave her strapped to the horse?"

"In Paris, runt. Ye didn't think I was going to bring a child as tiny as Jenny across the sea in Gair's leaky tub? With English gunners prowling? Then across the Highlands? She's settled with Genevieve's sister, and Audrey is looking in on her from time to time. I'll be going back for her, but I need t' settle some things first."

Mal slung his arm across Alec's shoulders. "No matter—'tis a fine thing to have you home. Duncan's out fighting the Hanoverians single-handedly, but the rest of us are home. And Mary's dad. And an Englishman I captured."

To Alec's startled look, Mal grinned widely. Alec caught

his pack-laden horse, who'd started to wander off, and pulled him up the hill after Malcolm and Mary.

The Duke of Kilmorgan glanced up from his afternoon meal as Mal led his brother into the dining room. Mary was some steps behind them, Mal saw, absorbed again in Audrey's letter. Of Wilfort, Ellis, and Mal's brothers, there was no sign.

"Oh, it's you," the duke growled as Alec began unwinding his plaid. "The good-for-nothing twin. What are you doing back here? Where's Angus? I haven't seen him this morning."

"Thank you very much, Father." Alec approached the table, undaunted by the duke's sarcasm. The stricken light had left his eyes, Mal noted, though an underlying sadness remained. The shock had gone, though, and Alec could laugh again.

Alec took a paper out of his sporran and unfolded it with broad fingers. "I've come to tell you about your granddaughter." He laid the paper on the polished oak table, in front of the duke.

Mal looked over Alec's shoulder. The paper bore a pen drawing of a tiny baby wrapped in cloths and wearing a lacy cap. The only features of the child were its tight fists, chubby face, and closed eyes. Mal knew Alec had drawn the picture. It was his style—a few simple lines to tell a beautiful story.

Under the picture was written *Genevieve Allison Mary Mackenzie*.

The duke stilled. He stared at the picture for a long moment, then touched the paper with one blunt fingertip. "My granddaughter?" he repeated, his words almost a whisper.

"I call her Jenny," Alec said. "I married her mother, Genevieve Millar, a few months ago. Malcolm was a witness."

Another few seconds went by before the words penetrated the duke's senses. "Married?" He came to his feet, rage in his eyes. "What the devil do you mean, *married*? Where is this woman? *Who* is she?"

Alec's mirth dampened. "She did not survive the birth."

The duke's gaze met Alec's. He'd opened his mouth to shout again, and his lips remained parted, no sound issuing from them. For the first time in years, Mal saw his father at a loss for what to say.

The duke cleared his throat. "Alec, I'm sorry."

"I loved her," Alec said, a scratch in his voice. "I loved her very much."

The duke looked down at the picture again, his throat moving. Then he closed the distance between himself and Alec and wrapped his arms around his son.

Mal felt Mary's hand slide into his, her eyes shining with tears as she looked up at him. She understood what had happened in this room—a connection, family forgiving, and family continuing.

Mal leaned down and kissed her then led her out.

Mary never wanted this time of her life to end. She'd found happiness. As the weeks passed, her feelings for Malcolm deepened, blossoming into something she barely comprehended.

She came to realize Captain Ellis was wrong—Malcolm *did* mean to marry her. He was waiting for the right moment, for everything to be perfect. Malcolm was a planner, wanting every contingency taken care of before he executed his scheme. He worked by talking to people, charming them, slipping them coin, anything needed.

His thoughts went so lightning-fast that it sometimes seemed he acted impulsively, but Mary soon saw that he worked out every scenario to its end before he leapt upon the best one.

Mal was taking more time over Mary, because he didn't want to make a mistake. He feared that any misstep would destroy what he'd won. And so he was silent, testing his way as he might put his feet down on an uncertain path.

Mary knew Mal would never, ever admit this, of course. He behaved as though they had all the time in the world—they were young, together, and falling in love. That Mal believed he and Mary would be with each other forever, there was no question.

Nights grew shorter as October progressed, and the wind took on more chill. At Kilmorgan, the castle was never quiet—not only filled with the shouts of Malcolm and his brothers and father, but also the horde of retainers who lived there to keep the place. These retainers had families on the farms around, and came and went as they raced to harvest their grains before winter set in.

Kilmorgan was lucky in that it had more arable land than most of the area. An inland cut of sea and high banks around it trapped moist air that kept things a touch warmer in the glen and the soil rich. Even so, the farmers labored hard for even the smallest crops, and the Mackenzies went out to help them.

Lairds took care of their people, Mary soon realized. Mal and his brothers made certain that the crofters' houses were sound for the winter, roofs didn't leak, and that their tenants would have food to last the long cold season. The Mackenzies rode the bounds and worked the lands alongside the farmers, bending their backs to menial labor a London gentleman would scorn.

Wilfort had told Mary that some lairds felt that the women among their tenants were theirs to do with as they pleased, but Mary saw no fear or worry about that with the duke or his sons. The duke was deferential to the wives and daughters and respectful of the men. His people liked him.

Mal relayed that the duke had been devoted to their mum, Allison McNab, whose portrait hung prominently in the downstairs sitting room. The picture showed a regal-looking woman with a longish nose and black eyes full of fire as she gazed down upon her family. The portrait had been painted by Allan Ramsay, depicting the duchess at a three-quarter profile, her head turned to the viewer. The blue and white silks of her gown shimmered in soft light, finished by a piece of blue and green plaid wrapped over one shoulder and pinned with a brooch of dull silver. The picture was so breathtakingly real, Mary thought that at any moment, Allison might open her lips and speak.

Mal had the look of his mother about the cheekbones and chin, though in most respects he strongly resembled the duke. Alec, Angus, and Duncan bore more of her features, including the sparkle of her eyes, the firm set of mouth, and long, straight nose. Will, on the other hand, Mary observed, was pure Mackenzie.

Mal explained that the duke had completely changed when their mother died. He'd become bitter, angry, and hadn't wanted anything to do with his sons. No reminders of Allison.

For some reason, he'd only been able to abide Angus. None of them knew why, not even Angus.

Eventually, the duke had come out of his terrible grief, but even now, he was rarely pleased with his sons. The duke's swift acceptance of Alec's marriage and baby had been a surprise.

"You're softening him," Mal said to Mary. "He likes having you about—I can see it in him."

Mary was skeptical about her hand in changing him. She'd already discerned that the duke cared more for his family than he let people understand.

Though the castle was remote, they were not entirely cut off from the wider world either. They had deliveries most days of the week, of letters and newspapers, books and parcels. Mary's father could even have the papers and journals he preferred from London. The duke grumbled that most letters arrived open and gone through, both by the English government and the Highlanders.

Plenty of goods came from the north also, from the secret coves and inlets that ran close to Kilmorgan. French brandy and other luxuries landed often on the Mackenzies' dining room table—Mal's friend Gair was hard at work.

Mackenzies had a wide network through which they were able to keep an eye on what was happening with Charles and his army. Charles had spent the month in Edinburgh, they learned, while many small skirmishes took place between the Jacobites and the Highlanders who remained on the British side.

"Do not call them *loyal*," the duke had snapped, when Wilfort referred to Scots who supported King George as *loyalists*. "They simply want to be on the winning side. If Charles starts to prevail, ye can be assured many of them will turn around and start shooting the other way."

Wilfort had only shrugged in his bland way, unoffended.

Mary sometimes felt as though they were riding out a storm that raged around them, while Kilmorgan bobbed in a bubble of calm.

The calm didn't last. Near the end of October, the Jacobites tried to attack one of the military forts near Inverness—Duncan was one of that attack's leaders—but they were repulsed. Not many days later came the news that Charles had ridden out of Edinburgh, taking his army south toward England.

Duncan was riding with him, leading three hundred men behind him to join the cause. Angus, to everyone's amazement, announced that he was going with them.

To say that Malcolm's father was furious with Angus would be to understate it. As the duke's voice rose to fever pitch, Mal decided it was time to take Mary and discreetly depart the house.

In the end, Angus simply had to run for it. He came charging out of the castle and down the hill. The duke tried to pursue him, but Angus dashed down the path on swift, youthful feet, leaving his father raging and panting halfway up the hill. Angus had a pack slung over his back, and he'd wisely hidden his weapons under the trees at the edge of the grounds before he'd made the announcement.

"Why?" Alec asked, even as he helped Angus gather his things. "Why are ye doing this, Angus? Ye've no love for the old kings."

Angus mounted his horse, then gazed down at Mal and Alec, who stood together as ever. "Because I need to look after Duncan," Angus said without heat. "If Dad loses him, it will kill him."

"No, lad," Malcolm said. He put his hand on Angus's booted leg. "It will kill him if he loses *you*. He loves ye best of us all."

Angus shook his head. "No, he doesn't. He likes me taking care of him, but it's not the same thing. He wants Duncan to be duke when he's gone—he's always wanted that."

Mal didn't agree. "It's ye he loves, Angus. None of the rest of us can understand why." He patted Angus's leg as he said the last, his throat aching. He'd always known he couldn't keep Duncan safe, but Angus did not have the same mettle as their oldest brother. Mal closed his hand around the leather of Angus's boot, as though that would keep him tethered to Kilmorgan.

"When Mum died, he nearly went mad w' it," Angus was saying. "I made sure he lived. Now he thinks he can't do without me, but he needs to learn he can."

"Don't be daft," Mal said, his breathing tight. "Will or me

can go along and save Duncan's head. We're good at keeping ourselves in one piece. *You* don't even like t' fight."

"Ye might be surprised about that," Angus said with dark humor. "Will's a spy, not a fighter, Alec's got a wee one to think about now, and you've got Mary. So it has to be me."

"Damn and blast ye," Mal said, feeling desperate. "If ye go, we'll have t' lock Da in the cellar until he calms down. Which might be a few years from now."

"Have Mary talk to him," Angus said, giving Mal a wry look. "He likes her. Ye've done well there, runt. Don't let her get away."

Angus nudged his horse into a walk, but Alec stepped forward and caught the horse's bridle. He'd said nothing as Mal and Angus had argued, but his look was as distressed as Mal's. "Ye look after *yourself*, ye hear me?" Alec growled up at him. "I'm your twin. If something happens t'ye, it will happen t'me. Don't you forget that."

Angus gave him the ghost of a grin. "Never bothered ye before, Alec. It's always been you and Mal. I want ye to go on having each other. Now turn me loose before Dad charges down here and shoots me to stop me from leaving him."

Alec released the horse but pressed his big hands together, as though ready to pray. "God go with ye, Angus."

"You too, Alec. Mal."

Angus gave them both a nod, turned the horse, and urged it into a trot. All too soon, he was lost under the trees. Shadows gathered after him, his plaids fading last thing.

Mal didn't like the shiver the sight gave him. Alec came to stand beside him, the warmth of his shoulder bolstering as they watched their brother be swallowed by darkness.

Soon after that, Will disappeared. Since Will often left in the night without a word, Mal didn't worry unduly. Will knew how to survive as he slipped through the Highlands, and Mal made himself believe he was well.

Mal and Alec, the only brothers left, continued to work the land. Cold came, and with it, earlier darkness. Mal no longer felt it safe to take Mary to their secret bower in the woods, so they found places to be together inside the house.

As Castle Kilmorgan was large and not all of it used, there were hideaways aplenty. Mal converted a room at the top of the keep into a cozy nest, with blankets and a featherbed for the floor, paper to stop up the cracks in the windows, and the fireplace unblocked so it could be lit.

He knew the servants were all aware that he brought Mary up there and why, but they said nothing, bless them. Mary loved the subterfuge. She'd retreated a long way from her everything-must-be-proper self, smiling up at him from a sea of blankets, raising herself on her elbow to listen to Mal's stories as the night passed around them.

She'd always been this woman, Mal realized. She'd been waiting for him when he'd seen her in the vast room at the Bancrofts', waiting for the world to drive them together.

They'd have a grand wedding when the time was right. Mal had sent his letters off to Lord Halsey's man of business before they'd left Edinburgh, telling him to free Mary from the contract her father had signed with Halsey. He wanted no legal way for Halsey to make Mary's life—or even Wilfort's—miserable.

Once Mal received word that the contract was clear, and Prince Charles either went home or sat uncontested on the throne, he and Mary would wed.

Mal was daydreaming of his life with Mary as he rode home one day in late November. She'd grace his behemoth new house and its gardens, and more importantly, their bedchamber.

A plume of smoke rose from the hills ahead of him. For a moment, Mal didn't understand what he was seeing, until a blacker smoke billowed from the trees, and he heard distant shouting. His body chilled while his heart pumped, and he moved his horse faster, then faster.

He reached the bottom of the hill to Kilmorgan and found what he'd dreaded—fire and smoke pouring from the castle. Mal leapt to the ground and sprinted up the path, his breath labored, as though his chest were being crushed to one, hard point.

Ewan burst from the castle's door, straight into Malcolm. "Everyone's gone!" he yelled, his voice cracking. "They took 'em. Except your da. He's inside, and I can't bring him out!"

Ewan collapsed in a fit of coughing, and Malcolm, his world spinning into madness, ran inside.

Chapter 26

Stone didn't burn, but the wooden paneling and floorboards of the rooms did. The massive old staircase twisting through the heart of the keep was alive with flames. Smoke blanketed everything—thick, black, and nasty.

"Dad!" Malcolm bellowed. "Where th' devil are ye?"

No answer, but from a room above, Mal heard a tinkle of glass. The lower stairs hadn't caught yet, and Mal charged up them.

At the same time, the duke came out of a room on the first landing, dragging a bundle that clanked. He saw Mal and bellowed, "Get up here and help me, runt! Hurry!"

The duke dove back into the room. Mal took the stairs two at a time, nearly tripping over the bundle, which he saw was a rug wrapped around silver and gold objects.

Fire was coming down the upper stairs and bursting out of the back of the keep below. They'd never lug this all and get away at the same time.

Mal lifted the bundle and threw it over the stair railing, watching it land with a clatter on the floor below. Ewan started dragging it away with his small hands.

"Dad!" Mal charged into the sitting room to see the duke

tugging the large portrait of his mother from the wall. The frame was heavy and gilded, but Mal knew the picture inside was worth everything in this house to his father.

"I have to save her!" the duke said frantically.

Smoke poured in through the door, stealing the air. Mal's father dropped the picture, coughing. "Help me."

Mal slid his dirk from its sheath, turned the painting over, and cut it out of the frame. He hastily rolled the canvas, stuffed it into his plaid, and grabbed his father's big hand.

"Out!" he commanded. "Now!"

The smoke had thickened so fast Mal could no longer see the door. He pulled a fold of plaid over his nose and mouth and dragged the duke, both of them stumbling, to where the door ought to be.

Mal smacked straight into a wall. Breathing shallowly, he groped his way along it, bumping into furniture, tripping over whatever the hell things were that he swore had never been there before. The duke clung to Mal, the two linked in the thick mass of smoke.

Mal's hand finally contacted open air. He pulled the duke through the door to the stairwell, which was burning fully now. With a crackle and hiss, the railed gallery on the other side of hall leaned forward and pitched into the hall below. More fire raced toward them at high speed.

"We have t' jump!" Mal shouted.

His words were muffled by the plaid, but his father heard. Together they sprung up on the railing, then dropped, down, down, their kilts rippling around them.

Mal landed hard, rolled, came to a stop, his hand around the painting under his plaid. His father thumped into a heap beside him, grunting in pain.

Mal grabbed the duke's arm, hauled him to his feet, and pulled him outside. The duke limped, but Mal, his father's arm around his shoulders, ran them both out into clean, sweet air.

Behind them, inside the house, the rest of the gallery fell, and the keep became an inferno.

Malcolm dragged his father along the narrow path around the west side of the castle, where the thick walls would contain smoke and fire. They sank to the rocks and yellow tufts of grass, gasping for breath, as the last of the day's light touched them.

Ewan came running, towing the carpet that held what his father hand managed to save. The duke didn't look at any of it.

"The painting?" he demanded, his voice a faint croak. "Did ye get it?"

Malcolm unfolded his kilt from around it and put the canvas in his father's hands. The duke quickly unrolled it and stared down at Allison McNab's handsome face and defiant eyes. She looked back at him with the same serenity she'd always had, a hint of a smile on her face.

The duke began to weep, tears streaming from his amber-colored eyes. He clutched the picture to his chest, holding to his heart the wife he'd lost so long ago.

"Ewan, ye have t' tell me what happened, lad."

Malcolm had his hand on the boy's shoulders, trying to keep the terrified Ewan calm, but it was difficult when Mal was shaking with rage and absolute fear. The duke still sat with his back to the castle wall, his head bowed, unable to speak.

Ewan's eyes were huge in his small face, but he nodded. "They came—soldiers. From Inverness. English ones."

Malcolm restrained himself from letting his fingers bite down on Ewan's shoulders. "And what? Go on."

"They came into the keep and started tearing things apart. Captain Ellis, he tried to stop them, and so did your da and Lord Alec, but there were too many. They said we were a secret Jacobite stronghold and had to be super . . . supper . . . *suppressed*. All the servants but me ran away, and the soldiers started burning things. They took Lady Mary and her da and Captain Ellis. And Lord Alec. They tried to take your da, but he had pistols and blasted away at them."

Mal had no word for the feeling rising inside him, the mixture of desperation, fear, and over it all, incredible rage. "*Took* them? *Where* did they take them?"

"I don't know. They had Lord Alec in shackles, but Lady Mary's da and the captain, they walked away with them."

"And Lady Mary?" Malcolm was amazed at how calm his voice was, as his emotions churned and danced inside him.

"She was fighting them—and swearing something hard.

Very bad words, sir. I never heard an English lady say such bad things. But then, she's a soldier."

Mal rose to his feet. Inside he was raging and shouting all the words he imagined Mary had said and many she didn't know. Outside he was steely, a cold, cold shell descending over him. Every feeling within him dissolved into a strange sense of purpose.

"Ye need to stay with him," he told Ewan, gesturing to the duke. "Help him carry the stuff down the hill—take him into the hollows, set up camp in the distillery, if they've left it alone. If they destroyed it, go to the crofters. They'll have t' take ye in. Find someone to look after him. All right?"

Ewan nodded, scared. "Are ye going after them?"

"Aye, lad, that I am." He remembered the game Mary played with Ewan to keep the boy calm. "Those are your orders, Sergeant. Carry on."

Ewan's salute was shaky, but he looked less pale. "Yes, sir."

Malcolm settled his kilt around him again, adjusted his dirk, and checked his pistol. He'd carried the weapons as he'd ridden the lands, and he had a pouch full of bullets and powder as well.

Mal caught his horse, mounted, and rode off in the direction Ewan had pointed—the small company of soldiers had left a broad trail, in any case. He faded into the mists, as silent as the smoke that poured from his ancestral home, and went to fight his enemy and rescue the wife of his heart.

~

The man who greeted Mary and her father as they were shown into the commander's tent was not who she'd expected.

George Markham, the Earl of Halsey, Mary's former fiancé, rose from a camp chair and smiled gently at them.

"I can tell by your faces that you are shocked," Halsey said. He wore a clean and elegant frock coat, leather breeches, and boots, the very picture of an English country gentleman. "It is good to see you again, my friends. I am pleased we are in much happier circumstances."

Halsey reached for Wilfort's hand and shook it. Wilfort stared at Halsey in disbelief, then jerked from the man's grip. "I'll not shake hands with a traitor," he growled.

Mary stood rigidly, transferring her terrible fear for Malcolm to anger at the man before them. "Nor I," she said clearly. "You saved your own neck, while my father bravely resisted interrogation and was kept a prisoner. What secrets are you now selling these men?"

Halsey lifted his hands. "My dear Mary, you do have a sharp tongue. I remember our discussion, Wilfort, about clouting her every once in a while to keep her tame. I think you have grown lax in that regard." He gave Mary a patient look. "Did you truly think I gave up the positions of the British army and the resistance in the Lowlands to the Jacobites? I fed them what they wished to hear, nothing more. Prince Charlie's men might find a few scattered squads to skirmish with on their way south, but they'll have to discover more important intelligence from another quarter."

He looked very pleased with himself. On the one hand, if Halsey was telling the truth and hadn't, in fact, betrayed his own people, he'd be admired for it. On the other, he'd done nothing at all to save Mary's father from being a Jacobite prisoner.

"Did you send troops to Kilmorgan?" Mary asked. "They set fire to the place. Was that necessary? That lovely, lovely castle, with . . ." She broke off, the jumble of horrors cutting away her words.

She again heard her maid Jinty screaming as the soldiers broke down the doors, the confusion of the servants being herded by Alec to the cellars, which opened to tunnels leading out to the glen. The splintering of wood, the shouting of the duke, the orders of the commander to burn the place, his men grimly doing just that.

All the time, Mary feared Malcolm would return, try to fight, and be shot by the soldiers ready with their muskets. Or he might already have been taken when he was out seeing to the crofters. He'd ridden off alone, saying it was too cold for Mary to come with him, bidding her to remain warm and comfortable at home.

Home. Mary had begun to think of Kilmorgan as such, not her father's house in Lincolnshire. And now Kilmorgan was gone, burned from the inside out.

"I did not have to," Halsey said in answer to Mary's question. "The commander here has long wanted Kilmorgan brought to heel. I traveled north from Edinburgh as soon as Charles rode out of the city. I knew you'd been taken to Kilmorgan's stronghold, and I hoped to find you. Edinburgh Castle is still held by the British and so is Stirling. The Scots prince will find it a bit more difficult holding Scotland than he imagines."

The politics of it didn't interest Mary. "What about the duke? Is he all right? And Lord Alec?"

Halsey looked surprised. "I have no idea. You were wrested from the Mackenzies' clutches, Mary—why should you be concerned?"

"The duke is a good man," Wilfort said, frowning. "Hospitable."

"And Captain Ellis," Mary said.

Halsey looked blank. "Who?"

Wilfort answered, "A fellow prisoner, who became a friend."

"Oh, him." Halsey waved a hand. "He's off somewhere being questioned about his capture, I imagine."

"And Lord Alec?" Mary repeated, wanting to launch herself at Halsey and shake him. "Is he well?" *And alive?* The soldiers who'd captured him had beaten him again and again.

"You mean the mad Highlander who fought like the devil? I believe they brought *him* in and chained him up somewhere. Serves him right. He came to my cell in Edinburgh and offered to pay me the price of your dowry if I released you from our betrothal, cheeky devil."

Mary's lips went numb. "That could not have been Alec . . ."

"No—his name was . . . Ah, I have it. Malcolm Mackenzie. So difficult to tell these barbarians apart."

Mary wanted to sit down, but no chair was handy. She kept to her feet, her knees shaking.

Even the syllables of Malcolm's name made Mary's heart squeeze. Was he still alive? Well? Lying bloody and dying?

She had to escape this place, find him. Once she knew he was alive, could touch him, *then* she could shout at him for offering to pay the price of her dowry. *If* Halsey told the truth—he had proved himself to be a vile liar.

"Wilfort, may I speak to Mary alone?" Halsey was asking. "I have been quite dreadfully concerned for her. I would like to express my sentiments in private."

"No," Wilfort answered coolly and without hesitation. "I'm

not certain about your actions, Halsey. We will have to discuss the question of the betrothal at length, when we are home and safe."

Halsey's smile turned sour. "An agreement is an agreement, Wilfort. I haven't broken my side of it. Has Mary?"

Wilfort stiffened. "Mary has been in my care during this entire ordeal."

"But barbarians, with such a pristine lady in their midst . . . I cannot expect they respected her as they should. Perhaps you let them do as they wished, in order that your captivity was not as dire as it could be."

Wilfort's face went dark red. "Now, see here, Halsey—keep your disgusting thoughts to yourself in front of my daughter . . ."

"*Yes*," Mary broke in. Her fear and rage whirled together. Images of the burning castle and soldiers battering the furniture with their muskets spun together with Malcolm making love to her in their aerie above the castle, where she'd be wrapped in his plaids and warmed by the fire.

"I am Malcolm Mackenzie's lover," Mary said fiercely to Halsey. "I am not ashamed of it. I love him, and if he's been hurt, I will find a way to kill you."

Halsey's eyes widened during this speech. Then they narrowed in fury and he struck out. Mary ducked the blow, having expected it, and Halsey found his fist caught in the steely grip of Captain Ellis.

"Please do not attempt to strike this lady again, my lord," Ellis said, his voice chilly. "Lady Mary and her father are under my protection, and I might take offense."

Halsey tried to jerk away but Captain Ellis held him fast. "Let go of me, sir. Do you know who I am?"

"You are the man about to apologize to Lady Mary," Ellis said, his gaze unwavering.

"No, I am the man who can make your life very difficult. I can have your commission taken and you facing court-martial in a moment's thought."

"If it's done after you apologize, then very well."

Halsey jerked again, and Captain Ellis deliberately opened his hand, letting him go. Halsey straightened his coat and glared at Mary. "I do not apologize to whores."

Captain Ellis didn't blink. "I see."

In the next moment, his fist struck Halsey's jaw, and the man went down.

Shouting outside the tent pulled Mary away from the delightful sight. Captain Ellis calmly turned and exited the tent, and Mary ducked out after him.

The night beyond the camp's fires was dark. The commander had halted them here, a bit north of Inverness, wanting to wait for light to travel the final fifteen miles to the town. With the loyalties of the Highlanders in this area in question, it was safer to camp and set guards than be spread thin on the trail in the dark.

Mary hurried as quickly as she dared after Captain Ellis, her father behind her. She stopped not far from the tent but close enough to the commander to hear him shouting at his men. The commander was from Yorkshire, and his northern English accent cut through the night.

"*Gone?* What d'ye mean, he's gone? Ye shackled him proper, didn't ye?"

"Locked him in the stocks, sir," a young English lieutenant, face smeared with mud, answered. "Locks were picked, chains empty."

"Bloody hell, Lieutenant. Then take some men and go after him!"

The lieutenant hesitated and exchanged a glance with the sergeant of a Highland company next to him. The commander noted the look.

"Well? Speak up, Sergeant," he said to the Highlander. "It's clear you have sommat t' say."

The sergeant stood to attention. "Begging your pardon, sir, but Lord Alec didn't set himself free. His brother must have done it."

"His brother, eh?" The commander looked thoughtful, then returned to full bellow. "Well, then get after them both! You should have brought the pair of 'em in in the first place."

"Sir," the Highland soldier said. "With respect, sir, you're speaking of *Malcolm Mackenzie*. There's no one knows this part of the Highlands better than him. You'll never find them. Mal Mackenzie will creep up behind your men in the dark and slit their throats before they even know they're dead."

The commander, a rather squat man with a round, red face under a simple, one-tailed wig, considered the sergeant's words with ill-concealed impatience. "Take ten men," he told the lieutenant. "Including you, Sergeant, since ye know this Mackenzie so well. *Find* these brothers, and then bring 'em to me. Do ye understand?"

Both sergeant and lieutenant looked resigned, but barked a brisk, "Yes, sir," and turned to their men, the sergeant bellowing orders.

The commander's gaze fell on Captain Ellis. "Go with them, eh, Ellis? Be off and capture your captor."

Ellis came to attention. "Sir. Please make sure Lady Mary is well looked after. She has been through much."

The commander gave him a dry glance. "Lady Mary and Lord Wilfort are personal guests, Captain. They will lack for nothin'."

Ellis looked straight at the commander for a moment, seemed to be satisfied with the answer, saluted him, and jogged off after the small knot of men fading into the darkness. Firelight brushed his red coat, then he was gone.

The commander watched him go then turned to Wilfort and Mary. "It's me pleasure to host you, my lord," he said. "We'll repair to me tent, if you don't mind, and dine. But don't worry about having to eat army rations, my lady. Me chef cooks a fair bit of grub."

Chapter 27

Malcolm slipped into the crack in the rock above the river and hauled Alec up beside him. The brothers braced their boots on the slippery gray stones, hands on the rock wall.

They hadn't exchanged a word since Mal had crept in through the edge of the camp and knelt behind the stocks where Alec sat, his hands and feet locked into wooden clamps, one of Alec's hands chained to a metal pole. Mal had picked open the locks, silently unscrewed the chain and manacle, and led the bruised and bloody Alec off into the night.

"Dad?" Was Alec's first gasped question, nearly drowned out by the water rushing below them.

"He'll do," Mal answered in brief syllables. "Castle is burned."

"Damn it t' hell."

"Mary?" Mal asked, voice tight. "I saw her—what are they going to do with her?"

Alec folded one arm across his chest, hurting and striving to hide it. "As much as I could hear, she and her dad are guests of the commander. Commander's taking them to Inverness—from there they'll be sent back to England. No one touched her. I made sure of that. So did Wilfort and Ellis."

Mal nodded. He'd been curiously cold and precise ever since he'd gotten his father out of the burning castle and heard that Mary had been taken away. He'd felt the same cold precision as he'd crawled on his belly into camp, right past the sentries, to set his brother free. He and Alec had waited until the guards were distracted by the bullets Mal had set at the end of a slow fuse, and then they'd run together into the darkness.

"How many men in the camp?" Mal asked.

"Sixty, under one commander, a Colonel Wheeler. They're roaming about, looking for those keen to follow Charles to England, trying to convince clans who might join the Jacobites to think again."

Mal didn't question Alec's numbers. He'd have observed what he could and filed it away in his sharp brain. Alec thought in pictures—he could never memorize a column of figures or words in a book, but he'd remember every single object in a room, every placement of every person there, long after the event.

"How are they dispersed?" Mal asked him.

"Men from several companies, sort of a delegation. Mostly Foot, a few cavalry, and Highland guards. Like this." Alec put his hand on Mal's chest in the darkness and traced the outline of the camp. "Infantry patrolling here and here. One or two cavalry soldiers circle in and out here. Commander's area *here*. That's where Mary will be."

Mal followed the lines his brother was impressing and merged them with what he'd observed himself. He knew he could fetch Mary away from these soldiers, but he'd have to do it before they reached Inverness. At Inverness, Mary would be taken to some house in the town, or worse, into one of the army forts along the loch to the south. Only a dozen or so English soldiers inside the fort at Ruthven had held off Charles's advance, and Charles had had hundreds of angry Highlanders on his side.

Mal took Alec's hand, squeezed it. He'd already given his injured brother his gloves, as Alec had been taken without any. The November wind was icy, slicing down this cut in the rock.

"Dad's at the distillery," Mal said. "Can ye get there?"

"Aye. But what about you? You're not going to try to snatch her on your own, are ye?"

"I can get in and out quicker alone. You're hurt, and ye

have a wee one to think of now. You find Dad, and then head north and look for Gair."

Alec did not want to leave Mal, that was apparent, but Alec was no fool. He'd understand that he'd slow Mal down at a time when speed and absolute stealth were necessary.

"So that's your plan, is it?" Alec asked over the water's noise.

"It's *one* plan. I'll have others. Go on, now, before they catch you again."

"They won't." Alec clasped Mal's forearm. "They only grabbed me because I was trying to fight them off Dad and Mary."

Mal pulled his brother close, the two of them balancing while trying to hug each other. It might be a long, long time before they saw each other again.

"God go with ye, runt," Alec said, releasing him.

"And you," Mal said, his voice rough. "Godspeed."

Alec squeezed his hands one last time, then climbed back up the cut, waited a few moments, watching at the top, and was gone.

Mal felt emptier when Alec was gone, but Mal had been right. He'd be able to do this much better alone. One day, though, this would be over. They'd all be together, his brothers, their families, *his* family. *I swear this*, he vowed silently.

Mal waited nearly two hours. He needed to give Alec time to disappear, to evade his hunters and find a trail north. Also Mal wanted the soldiers to have time to settle down and give up the search. The camp was going nowhere—they'd be there all night.

Finally Mal emerged, keeping to deep shadow in the cut of the stream. A small amount of mud from the stream's bank blackened his face, and he hid his weapons well inside his plaid so they wouldn't gleam. Then he left the relative shelter, becoming another shadow himself in the rising mists.

He headed south, toward the camp. Mary was there, and the pull to her overrode all else.

Mal's mind became cool and precise once more, his thoughts filled with nothing except finding Mary and taking her from her captors. Nothing else existed; nothing else mattered.

Mal had a purpose, and he would pursue it until he succeeded or died.

Mary picked at the fish in sauce that was tasty but dry as dust in her mouth. The commander—Colonel Wheeler—had a fine cook he took with him wherever he went, who fixed him meals fit for an aristocrat. The colonel also provided them with sweet white wine he'd brought back from a campaign in the southern German states, light enough for ladies, he said, but fine enough for a gentleman.

Colonel Wheeler was a gracious host and deferential to Mary, her father, and Lord Halsey. However, an undercurrent of tension flowed beneath the conversation, making Mary's fingers cold and her food tasteless.

They'd go to a house in Inverness, where they'd be safe, Colonel Wheeler assured them, and then Mary, Wilfort, and Halsey would be escorted the long way back to Lincolnshire. Charles Stuart had taken his army south through Carlisle, and now held that city, so Mary and her father would take the eastern roads.

Mary's fingers clenched around her fork as she strove to keep herself still. She wanted to leap from the table and flee the tent and camp to go in search of Malcolm, who she knew was out there somewhere. He'd be waiting, watching. Wheeler was a fool if he believed the reports that his soldiers had lost both Alec and Mal, that they must be long gone, fleeing back to Kilmorgan. Mary's feet twitched, longing to run after him, and she curled her toes in her boots.

Her common sense told her that such a flight would be imprudent. First, she'd be caught and brought back before she went ten steps. Second, even if Mary did manage to break through the camp's perimeter, she did not know her way around in the darkness of the Highlands. She'd likely plunge into a stream or fall over a cliff—or some such foolish thing—or possibly be shot by a nervous sentry.

The likelihood she could find Malcolm out there by herself was small. She wasn't even certain which direction Kilmorgan lay from here. North, yes, but which way was north?

The practical side of her told her to sit still until she reached Lincolnshire and home. Then she could gather money and provisions and make her way back up through Scotland to Kilmorgan. If Kilmorgan proved to be entirely destroyed and the Mackenzies gone, she'd go to France and stay with Audrey. Alec's friends were there, possibly some of Mal's too. They could help her find Malcolm and contact him, if he was alive to be found.

Everything would be fine, as long as Mary kept her head and did nothing stupidly rash.

She calmly ate her fish and sipped her wine without being able to appreciate any of it. Outwardly, her movements were steady and mechanical, like a clockwork automaton's.

Inside, Mary was a roiling mess of emotions—terror, uncertainty, rage. These men had burned Mal's home, cheerfully destroying all he and his family had, in the suspicion that Mal and his father might—*might*—be a danger. They were brutes, no matter how talented Colonel Wheeler's chef was, or how sweet was his Bavarian wine. They'd pillaged the castle with glee, smashing things, stealing them, laughing as Alec and the duke fought—two against five dozen.

Fury spun around Mary's heart, twining with her fear. She'd believed all her life that the English were good and just people, rational in matters of learning and good government. But give a man a weapon, tell him another man was a *possible* threat to him, and he became a ravaging boor, destroying all in his path. And then the commander of these brutes had brought his captives to his tent to try to impress them with a fine supper. She exchanged glances with her father and saw, to her surprise, that he appeared to agree with her. The thought warmed her.

Colonel Wheeler, oblivious to Mary's condemnation, brought out brandy for his male guests. He'd enjoyed his meal, and now settled his wig on his round head, preparing to enjoy more of his luxuries. He poured the brandy into tiny glasses that were nearly lost in his thick fingers, and asked Mary if she would like coffee.

Mary opened her stiff mouth to reply coldly in the negative when a piercing scream sounded outside, followed by confused shouting.

Wheeler heaved a sigh, his wide-sleeved blue coat brushing the tablecloth as he down set the brandy decanter. "Ah, now what?"

He pushed back from the table, came to his feet, threw his napkin onto his chair, and strode out. Halsey lifted the brandy Wheeler had served and sipped it, undisturbed, but Wilfort left his seat and went out after the colonel.

Mary rose, her skirt nearly knocking the chair over in her agitation. Halsey put out a hand and steadied it.

"Let the colonel take care of whatever ails his soldiers," Halsey said languidly. "Sit down and behave yourself."

Mary shot him a venomous look and ducked out of the tent into the firelight and noise.

Soldiers were shouting, other men were trying to calm them down and demand to know what was going on. "What the devil is this?" Wheeler bellowed into the mix, his deep voice carrying over the others'.

"Poxy corporal saw a ghost," a sergeant snapped.

"Not a ghost," one of the young soldiers cried. "Dead men. They're strung up in the trees. *Our* men, sir."

"I saw them too," another soldier, just as young and fearful, said. "All white, covered in blood."

"Where?" Wheeler snapped. "Show me."

Wheeler strode after his men as they went out from the edge of camp and down a hill. Wilfort gave Mary a *stay here* look as he followed, but Mary was having none of it. She gathered the plaid she'd been wearing as a shawl around her shoulders and hurried after her father.

At the bottom of the rise was a rushing stream lined with a string of trees. White fluttered from the black branches of the trees, long, pale forms caught by moonlight and mists. When one of the things turned, Mary saw gashes of black. Blood?

Wheeler halted, his back stiff, round face scarlet. After a long moment, he barked, "Lieutenant—have 'em cut down."

A lieutenant, sergeant, and a few soldiers moved forward, joined by others. The younger lads did not want to go, but they were cowed by harsh words from their sergeant. Captain Ellis, who'd emerged from another tent when the shouting began, walked after them.

Mary waited, her hands balled at her sides, the wind cutting through the plaid. Her father stood close beside her, the ends of his coat moving in the sharp breeze.

The soldiers went closer, Wheeler directly behind them. The

lieutenant stopped when he was beneath the first of the hanging figures. "Damnation!" he shouted and swung on the younger soldiers. "Is this a joke, lads?"

Captain Ellis came back to Mary and Wilfort, grim humor in his eyes. "Sheets stained with paint, hanging in the wind like efreets."

Mary let out a breath. Not soldiers with their throats slit. Bed sheets to frighten the susceptible in the dark. *Malcolm.*

"Why—?" She heard Wheeler begin, then the colonel wheeled around and charged up the hill. "Back! Everyone back to camp! *Now!*"

His last word was drowned by a *boom!* Men were shouting, and a cloud of black smoke drifted up through the mists.

The camp was chaos. Another officer came rushing past Mary. "He got to the armory, sir," he said, his eyes so wide Mary saw the whites of them in the dark. "Every bit of spare ammunition and powder was in there."

"Son of a poxy whoring bitch," Wheeler spat. "Every man who should have been guarding it gets a flogging!"

The officer swallowed. "Yes, sir."

Spittle flecked the edges of Colonel Wheeler's mouth. "Ghosts and dead men," he said in disgust. "I never heard owt so daft. Burn those bed sheets and put double guards out for the rest of the night."

"Yes, sir."

Two more tents went up in flames. Mary let out a cry at the surprise of it, and Wheeler stopped cursing and simply stared.

Mary's father put his arm around her. Mary shook, torn between fear and elation. Malcolm was taking his revenge. But he alone against so many—he was sure to be caught by the angry Wheeler, who would no doubt put him to death.

Wheeler saw Captain Ellis. "Take the woman inside," he said. His jaw hardened as he turned back to his men. "I want that bastard found and brought to me. *Understand?*"

"Yes, sir," the lieutenant said, and faded into the smoke and gloom away from his commander's glare.

The soldiers searched but never found Malcolm. Not a trace of him. Another tent had been robbed while Wheeler and his soldiers stood at the bottom of the hill—the one that housed the colonel's private food stores—but no one had seen anyone go in or out of it. What foodstuffs hadn't been stolen had been trampled and ruined, and Wheeler's beloved bottles of wine were smashed, the wine soaking into the ground.

A few of the men who'd gone out after Malcolm returned while Mary and her father stood with the colonel outside his commissary tent. The soldiers looked about nervously, their leader, a Scots sergeant with a hard face and beefy arms, white about the mouth.

They'd so far found no sign of Malcolm. However, horses had spooked, noises and lights had drawn them off the paths, but they'd found nothing when they investigated. Thin ropes stretched across the ground had tripped horses, and one officer had been pulled completely off his mount, his pistol stolen by ghost hands.

The sergeant had had enough. "He's no' a man; he's a *brollachan,*" he snarled, then stamped away to begin cleaning up the mess.

"A what?" Halsey, who'd finally emerged from the colonel's private tent, asked. "What sort of word is that? It sounds like a throat full of phlegm."

"A *brollachan*," Mary repeated. Mal had told her stories while they'd lain together, tales of old Scotland and its legends. "A formless creature with red eyes who can possess a man's body and do terrible things in the dark."

"Ah," Halsey said, trying to sound wise. "Superstition. The Highlands are full of it."

"Superstition can teach us much," Captain Ellis said, the look in his dark eyes a mixture of amusement and wariness. "Lady Mary, I agree with the colonel. You need to be inside."

He watched her expectantly. So did her father, Halsey, and the colonel. They wanted her out of sight, where she wouldn't be a bother—at least, the colonel and Halsey did. "Yes, all right," Mary said woodenly.

She took Captain Ellis's arm and allowed him to escort her to the small tent that had been prepared for her. As they went, Mary scanned the darkness around her.

Malcolm was out there. She could sense him. Somewhere

in the mist he waited, biding his time, leading the soldiers a merry dance.

When he was ready, he'd do what he'd come to do. Mary had no doubt about that.

By morning, Malcolm had not shown himself. As the sun rose, and the mists faded, the soldiers discovered that all but two of their horses had been cut free and were gone. The only beasts remaining were those that Mary and her father had ridden.

Wheeler, who Mary had gathered was on most days an even-tempered man, had reached the end of his tether.

"I want every man in this camp out there hunting him! Not a one of us leaves until he's found."

Mary stepped in front of Colonel Wheeler as he turned to shout more orders. "I beg your pardon, sir."

Wheeler stopped, his round face reddening as he looked down at her. His wig was soiled with the night's search—his batman, whose task would be to keep it clean, was no doubt out searching with the others.

Mary watched the colonel rein in his temper with effort. "Don't worry, lass," he said, his voice scratchy from shouting. "I'll keep ye safe. Now that it's light, we'll find this so-called *brollachan* or chase him off."

He spoke impatiently, wanting her to be gone. Mary stood her ground. "You don't understand, Colonel. He wants *me*. Let him have me, and he'll leave the rest of you alone."

Wheeler pulled his attention from the camp and his harried men to regard her sharply. The blue eyes that looked into Mary's were shrewd, those of a man who'd risen through the ranks by his abilities, not his money or family. A man who knew exactly where he stood in life, and what he'd do to advance still further.

"You're a brave young lady," Wheeler said after a time. "T' come out here and face me alone and make that sort of offer. I have a daughter about your age, and I'd like t' think she'd be as brave as you, were she in your circumstances. But because of that daughter, I'll not turn ye over to a dangerous man like that. Highlanders think it's a fine thing t' steal women, but I'll have nowt of it." Wheeler gave her a nod, regarding her with more respect. "It's good of you, lass, but ye mun not worry.

We'll be in Inverness by tonight, and you'll be safe from this monster. I give ye me promise."

Mary swallowed, her throat sore from smoke, cold, and fear. Wheeler did not understand what Malcolm was capable of, and Mary was coming to realize she hadn't understood him either. She remembered the night she'd first seen Mal, when she'd thought of him as a wolf among sheep. A dangerous man, no matter that he wore civilized clothes.

Wheeler was not going to budge. He'd protect Mary from the Highlander she loved, no matter what she wished. Mary could only return to her tent, her heart beating faster, the rain thoroughly chilling her.

The men packed up the camp and set off along the road, everyone on foot now except Mary and her father. The baggage horses were gone, so supplies had to be abandoned, the soldiers carrying what they could.

Because of the slower pace; the steadily falling, freezing rain, which turned to ice upon the ground; and Wheeler expecting his troops to bring him Malcolm at every turn, they were nowhere near Inverness by nightfall.

Chapter 28

Colonel Wheeler's men came upon a cluster of crofters' cottages, most abandoned, set back from the road, as darkness settled over the empty glen. Colonel Wheeler took over the cottages, and housed his soldiers there for the night.

Mary found herself alone in a tiny, one-roomed house made of crookedly piled stone with wide cracks where mortar should be, shivering in the borrowed Mackenzie plaid and the blankets the colonel's batman had brought her. She made herself eat the food she'd been given, cooked by Wheeler's chef from the meager supplies they'd managed to salvage. The meal made Mary feel a bit guilty, because she knew most of the men were getting by on nothing but soldiers' rations.

She also knew she needed to eat and keep up her strength. If Malcolm managed to slip in and take her away, Mary being hungry or ill would slow their escape.

She finished the small meal and settled down for the night on a hard cot that took up most of the room.

Mary didn't sleep. Malcolm was out there, and it was only a matter of time before he struck.

As the night wore on, all was quiet. Mary heard the tramp of the men as they circled the cottages, alert and on the lookout. One soldier stood guard at her door—she could see his red coat through the gaps in the boards, shifting as the man grew bored and tired.

It was well after midnight by her reckoning, when a rustle in the corner of the tiny room made Mary sit up. She'd already seen a rat scuttling away when her father walked her to this cottage and bade her good night—rats and other small animals loved to nest in houses, abandoned or otherwise.

The rustle came again. Mary peered hard into the corner . . .

. . . And saw a *brollachan.* It rose from the stones on the floor, a shapeless being, its red eyes piercing the gloom.

Mary didn't believe in ghosts, but she was up off the bed, grabbing the plaid as she raced for the door.

The *brollachan* caught her. A hard arm closed around her body, and a rough hand clamped over her mouth as Mary was dragged unceremoniously back from the door, her feet catching on the stone floor as she tried to scramble away.

The ground seemed to open out from under her, and Mary plunged downward, unable to shout, even to breathe.

She landed on top of the *brollachan*, which grunted a very Scottish-sounding *oof!*

"Malcolm!" Mary cried in a fierce whisper.

She could see nothing in the dark but the gleam of his eyes, but she could smell him. Peat, mud, muck, and blood.

Mary let out a sob of relief and collapsed onto Malcolm, flinging her arms around his neck. He held her in the gloom, his embrace strong, his body cradling her.

They stayed like this for a time, then Malcolm gently pushed Mary to her feet and scrambled up beside her. "You all right, lass? That was quite a fall."

"Blast it all, Malcolm," Mary said as Malcolm brushed himself off. He was whole and real, warm and solid in the dark. "You scared the *wits* out of me!"

"Aye, I'm prone t' do that." Mal's teeth gleamed in the darkness with his lopsided smile. He took her hand. "Time t' go, love."

"Go where?" Mary clung to his hand, her boots slipping on the damp ground. "What is this place?"

"'Tis where the whisky is made, of course." Mal's breath

was warm as he leaned close. "Ye don't think the crofters do it where the excise men can find it, do ye? This way."

He tugged her with him along the stony floor. Mary was grateful she'd worn her gown and even her boots to bed as she stumbled along behind him, not daring to let go of Mal's steadying hand.

The tunnel was warmer than the house above it, no wind blowing through cracks under the earth. After a time, Mary heard rushing water, a sound that grew louder with every step. Finally, after what seemed a long time of walking, Malcolm guided her up a rickety set of wooden stairs and through a door that led outside into the cold.

Mary found herself on the bank of a hurrying stream. Hills rose on either side of the stream, and no cottage was in sight, not even lights of any in the distance. Mist gathered above the water in thick patches, and wind pushed the stream's spray at her. Mary shivered, the cold strong.

"Not long now, love," Mal said over the water's rush. "I'll have ye warm soon."

He turned and led her by the hand along the stream, into the chill of the mist. Mary couldn't see him, though he was but a step ahead of her. Mal had become the *brollachan* again, a shapeless bulk against the shadows.

Mary stumbled along, her feet numb, Malcolm's hand a lifeline. There was no sound of pursuit—no sound at all except the stream clattering over rocks below.

"How did you know I'd be in that cottage?" she asked when she had the breath. "And that there was a tunnel underneath it?"

"The tunnels are under all the cottages," Mal answered readily. "I knew which you were in because it was the only one with a guard at the door. I knew the Yorkshireman colonel would stop ye at those cottages, because it was as far as ye could go in one day without the horses."

Which was why he'd rid the colonel of his beasts. "You herded them there?" Mary asked in surprise.

"That I did. Best place to steal ye, before ye were locked into a house or an army fort at Inverness."

Mary thought about this as she picked her way along behind him, balancing on the slippery bank. Mal had used his knowledge of the land against those who'd invaded it. Here was the ruthless barbarian she'd always known him to be, in spite of his university education, furniture and art from Paris, and interest in fine food and drink. Mal was the sort of Highlander the English feared, one who'd throw off civilization, rise up, and come plunging down upon them.

"Malcolm," Mary said after a time. "What did you do with the horses?"

"Hmm?" Mal halted, sending Mary into him, his body warm and hard in the cold. "I cut them free. Don't worry, lass. Horses know their way home. I wager the colonel and his men will return to barracks to find them already in the stables. Well, those that don't get stolen along the way."

"What I mean is, did you save one for yourself?"

"No."

Mary squeezed his hand, her feet aching. "I see. Whyever not?"

Mal squeezed her hand in return. "Because the moment a soldier sees a grubby Highlander riding along on a British warhorse, I'll be shot as a Jacobite. We'll find a ride soon enough."

With that last statement, Malcolm pulled her along. He eased his speed a little, but he didn't stop, tramping on over the Highlands, heading who knew where. Mary hung on to his hand, far more contented to be in the icy cold with Mal than in Colonel Wheeler's comfortable tent, and let Malcolm take her into the night.

Malcolm was cold, exhausted, and furiously angry, but at the same time, he rejoiced. He had Mary, she was free, and she was safe.

As safe, that is, as she could be rushing about the Highlands in the middle of the night, while British soldiers roamed the glens. Mal needed to get her indoors, warm, out of the clinging mists that seeped under cloth to wet their skin.

He led Mary at the quickest pace he could down the hidden trails that followed the twists and turns of the stream. He'd been walking these paths since he'd been a child, at first with his brothers, then on his own. Highlanders knew the safe ways—had known for generations. The roads forced upon them by the English hadn't changed that.

After an hour or so of steady trudging, Malcolm turned away from the stream and made his way down into a hollow between hills. A line of cottages nestled here, hidden from all roads and even from the sight of anyone on the hilltop above. If a man didn't know the houses were here, he'd pass them altogether, oblivious.

A light gleamed once then went out. Mal led Mary to where the light had been, a door in a dark wall opened, and they ducked inside, out of the wind.

The house was a one-roomed rectangle, much like the croft in which Mal had found Mary, but the walls were solid, the cracks well plastered with mud and mortar. A fire smoldered on the hearth, not emitting much light, but filling the tiny house with fragrant warmth.

"All right, Rabbie?" Malcolm asked.

Rabbie, the whisky smuggler they'd met on the road to Kilmorgan, nodded. "All right, me lord. This here is me missus."

A woman bundled in a thick dress and plaid nodded to them as she came out of the darkness near the fireplace. She said nothing at all, but passed two steaming mugs to Rabbie, who thrust them both at Malcolm.

"This is *my* missus," Mal said as he handed one mug to Mary. He wasn't sure what beverage Rabbie's wife had given them, but it was hot—all that mattered.

Mary, who'd been looking around in wonder, gave Rabbie and his wife a gracious nod, as though they were the aristo friends who'd invited her to their drawing room. "Thank you for your hospitality," she said.

Her voice shook with fear and weariness, but she sounded as gracious as a queen. More so, Mal reflected. He'd met a few who were sneering harpies.

Mary lifted the cup Mal had given her and sipped. She made a face but sipped again.

Mal drank from his mug, finding coffee that tasted as though it had been boiled with the same grounds for three or four days.

Rabbie peered nervously behind Mal, though the door was

shut and now bolted. "Soldiers ain't going to pour down here on us, are they?"

"Not tonight," Mal said. "Tomorrow we'll be gone, I promise ye. My lass just needs to rest for a time. She can't walk all night."

Rabbie didn't respond, which meant he was reassured. Men like Rabbie didn't waste breath on small pleasantries.

Rabbie waited until they finished the coffee, then took the mugs from them and passed them back to his wife. He snatched up a dark lantern, lit the candle inside, adjusted the metal sides that would blot out the light from watchers, and motioned them to the door.

He led them back out into the cold. Rabbie's wife had not said one word the entire time they'd been in the house, and she said nothing now, not even a good-night.

Rabbie took Mal and Mary along a narrow path that ran behind the house and down a short hill to an even tinier house. This cottage too had one room and was built of the same dark stone as Rabbie's, its roof thatched.

A fire smoldered on a raised stone hearth in the middle of the room, the smoke rising to cracks in the roof. The sharp smell of peat fire coated the room but wasn't unpleasant—the cracks drew the smoke as well as any enclosed chimney. Blankets and plaids had been piled on one side of the little room as a makeshift bed. Nothing else was inside.

"Abandoned," Rabbie said, by way of explaining why it was empty and available. "Half of 'em are—folk have gone off to the cities or joined up with the Jacobite army. Me son nipped down here and built a fire while we nattered. He'll be moving in here with his wife once you're gone."

"Ye've been kind, Rabbie," Malcolm said sincerely. He shook Rabbie's hand, pressing a coin into it at the same time.

"Thank ye, sir. Good night."

Rabbie made a quick retreat, closing the door behind him. He'd left the lantern, which cast an eerie glow over the dark stones where Rabbie had set it down. Mal slid the wooden bolt across the door, fitting it into the curved wooden strap that would bar any intruders.

He turned around again, and Mary's warm body slammed into him.

Mal staggered, but steadied himself by dragging Mary tightly against him as her arms came around him. They held each other hard, and Malcolm buried his face in the curve of her neck. She was alive, well, and with him.

"Malcolm." She was crying, his brave Mary.

"Hush, sweet. I've come to take care of ye."

Mary touched his face. "I was so afraid for you. I thought they'd find you—the colonel gave his men orders to shoot you on sight."

"They never had a chance, love." Malcolm brushed a kiss to her lips, then another. "The English soldiers stumble around in the dark, while I flit away like a will-o'-the-wisp. They walked right past me several times. Close enough for me to smell."

Mary gave him her best severe look. "They had Highlanders with them as well, who presumably *could* track a will-o'-the-wisp. You took a great risk."

Mal shook his head. "No one knows the land as I do, my Mary. And I'd risk anything for you."

He bent to her lips again, the softness of her easing him. He'd been so long in the dark and cold. Mary was warmth and light.

When they eased apart, Mary rested her head on his chest. "I am very angry at you," she said. "However, for the moment, I do not remember why."

"Something besides me risking me neck to drive King Geordie's soldiers mad?"

Mary nodded against him. "It will come to me. Though not, I think, right now."

"Well, that's a mercy." Mal drew her closer. His knees were shaking now that two days of no sleep were catching up to him, but he didn't want to admit it. He had other things on his mind.

Mary raised her head. "Gracious, you're swaying like a sapling in wind. Come and lie down."

Malcolm *fell* down. He landed on the blankets—which took up one half of the small room—and pulled Mary with him. She landed on him with a crush of feminine body.

"You shouldn't have come after me," Mary was saying. "I'd have been all right. You had no need to single-handedly fight an entire army camp to get to me. I planned to go home with my father then make arrangements to return to Scotland and find you."

Malcolm wrapped himself around her and rolled over with her until he lay on top of Mary, she a warm cushion beneath him. Mary's cheeks were pink from her scolding, her eyes sparkling in the dim light. Mal brushed a loose lock of golden hair from her face.

"Then I would have followed you home, lass. I'd have climbed in your window and spirited you away. I couldn't have taken the chance that your father would lock you up or force you to marry someone else. I'm not waiting forever for you."

"Frogs and toadstools, Malcolm." Mary glared at him, though her voice was weak with tiredness. "You did it because you enjoyed tormenting the soldiers. But you sealed your fate. They have you down as a traitor now."

A slice of anger broke through Malcolm's immediate happiness. "No, *they* sealed it when they burned out Kilmorgan Castle and nearly killed my father. They sealed it when they took you away from me. They forged into *my* lands, stole *my* lass, and tried to break us. I'll not meekly submit to a bloody lot of British soldiers and let them get away with taking everything we have. If that makes me a traitor, then I am. Prince Charlie is a fool, but the English are tyrannical bastards sent to make our life a misery. They went too far with me, Mary. And so—I'll be their *brollachan.* Aye, I heard what they called me. They need to fear what lies in the dark."

Mary blinked back tears as the rage surged through him. She stared at him in shock, but when she touched his cheek, her fingertips were gentle. "Mal, I'm so sorry."

Malcolm growled low in his throat. The tenderness of her touch broke through the anger flaring through him like a bright flame, bringing him once more to the present. He had Mary with him, away from the soldiers, back in his arms. His heart beat hard with his need, his love.

Mary was in the simple clothes she'd liked to wear at the castle, the plaid she'd been wrapped in now part of their bed covers. Malcolm unfastened her bodice one hook at a time, spreading the cloth. He licked her breasts where they swelled over the corset, and slid his fingers beneath her to unlace it.

Mary brought her hands up, but her push against him lacked strength. "You need to sleep, Mal. You're half-dead."

"Doesn't matter." Malcolm nuzzled her as he tugged the corset's laces free. "I can't keep away from ye. I crave ye, lass, and I'll never sleep until I have ye."

The corset came away. Mary made an intoxicating little sound as Malcolm licked between her breasts, then closed his mouth over her. Another sound as he began to suckle, her body moving as though he were already inside her.

Mary started to laugh. "Mal, you're filthy. Covered in mud."

"I know." More kissing, licking. "And ye taste so sweet. After we're done, ye can bathe me. Ye already ken how."

Mary's laughter shook her agreeably. "I love you, Malcolm Mackenzie."

Malcolm stopped. He carefully lifted his head and stared down at her, stunned. Mary lay under him, her eyes heavy with need and exhaustion, her little smile piercing his heart.

Mal had never thought himself lovable. He'd been told over and over, all his life, that he was anything but that. Charming, yes—people liked to say he was charming. He was well liked by some, he knew, but no one had ever said the words *love* and *Malcolm* in the same breath.

That *this* woman, the beauty Mal had coveted from the moment he'd seen her, spoke the words, penetrated his senses and splintered him.

He wasn't quite certain after that how he got both of them unclothed, but before the warmth of her words died away, he gathered Mary into his arms and slid himself inside her.

Chapter 29

Home. I've found home.

Malcolm groaned as Mary closed around him. In the darkness, there was only her. Firelight outlined her face, her body held his, and her warmth surrounded him.

She tasted of salt and fire, and everything Mal needed. He kissed her lips, gently suckling each one, licking inside her mouth. Mal held her wrists to the makeshift bed, the heat of her making him wild. Mary lifted to meet him, her cries breaking the darkness.

The fact that controlled, ever-practical Mary forgot to be quiet and sedate in his arms made Malcolm's excitement spike. He came down to her, hot skin to hot skin. Her breasts were tight against his chest, her nails on his back a dark bite amid a wash of pleasure.

Inside this room, the true Malcolm emerged. Not the charmer, or the man with the burning need to make sure everyone in his life was safe. The selfish being that was Malcolm took over. He wanted this woman, wanted her with mindless passion, would do anything, fight anyone to make sure she was his.

"You're fire, Mary," he murmured. "Burning so bright, I

can barely see." His words drifted to incoherence, but his thoughts went on.

Ye complete me. I'll never be whole again if ye aren't beside me, my brave, beautiful Mary.

Mary dropped away from his kiss to let out another loud cry as her sweet heat flowed over him. *Ye pretend to be so cool, but with me, you're my passionate, beautiful lass.*

A few seconds later, and Malcolm came apart, but he kept thrusting, the two of them needing to hold each other, hands clutching as though they'd never let go. Mary was sobbing by the time Malcolm came down on her, dark lassitude picking him up and whirling him away.

He said, "Shh, don't cry, my Mary," and tried to brush away a tear.

The words were a mumble, his hand didn't work, and he crashed onto her. Mary caressed his hair, her lips featherlight on his face.

"It's all right, Malcolm. Sleep. I've got you."

Malcolm fell into oblivion.

Mary was finishing the bowl of porridge Rabbie's wife had brought her when Malcolm finally awoke. She found it odd to eat the porridge plain without fruit or anything else to sweeten it, but she knew this was all Rabbie had.

Malcolm blinked in the small amount of light that came through the oil-paper window next to the door. He'd used plaids to cover them both, and now they slid from his torso, one hip emerging from the folds. His amber eyes peered at her through the dirt on his face.

When he saw her demurely eating porridge, his slow smile blossomed. "Ye're real. Not a dream."

"No, indeed." Mary licked the last of the oats from her spoon. As strange as the meal was, it filled her belly and was quite satisfying. "I have remembered now why I was angry with you."

The smile dimmed. "Aye? Why's that?"

Mary carefully set her bowl on the floor and rose to her feet. She clenched her fists but faced him calmly, head high. "I have heard that you *paid* Lord Halsey to not marry me. Is this so?"

Malcolm sat up, crossing his legs, the plaid stretching over his thighs. "I sent his man of business a letter telling him t' tear up the contracts, and that my man of business would forward the sum of your dowry to him. I did it t' keep that bastard Halsey from hounding ye the rest of your life, and from hounding your father. It's a small price to pay to make Halsey stay the hell away from you and your family." His scowl had returned, the affable Mal gone.

"Halsey ought to honor my choice," Mary said crisply, "and sever the agreements without penalty." She knew, though, even as she spoke, that Halsey would never do so. His pride would put Mary in thrall to him for the rest of her life.

Mal gave her an incredulous look. "You're a dreamer, you are. Halsey's no gentleman—I don't care that he's a peer. He understands money and power, nothing else. I'd rather give him nothing, and to hell with him, but I'm realistic. He'd never stop unless he saw the price of ye. This way, he'd have to work hard to make a case if he tried to bring your da to court."

"It hardly matters now." Mary stretched her fingers. "You've sabotaged an army camp and kidnapped an earl's daughter. I'm certain Halsey will laugh as they drag you off to prison, and even harder when you're on the gallows."

Mary's words brought the image to her strongly. Mal in a linen shirt and dark breeches—they'd never let him wear his plaids, a symbol of pride—as he was hoisted aloft from the wooden floor of the gallows, his face covered with a hood, his hands bound behind him. His strong legs would kick as the air left him, the rope crushing his throat. He'd kick and dance until he dropped, breathless and limp, his body swaying gently. Dead. The affable, slant-smiled Malcolm gone, never to give her his hot, sideways glance again.

Mary's strength gave out, and she collapsed. She landed on the pile of bedding with him, and he steadied her with an arm around her. He was alive for now, and here.

"What are we going to do, Malcolm?" Mary asked in a rush.

Mal rubbed his chin, as calm as though discussing what amusement to take in that afternoon. "Not sure yet. We have several choices that I can see."

"Do we?" Mary asked, giving him a skeptical look. "What are those?"

Mal touched each finger as he listed them, continuing to be maddeningly calm. "We return to Kilmorgan and make certain my da's all right, then we go north and I put you on a ship bound for France. Or, we find Will and help him make sure the English don't chase Prince Charlie back to Scotland to plague us. Or, we stay here with Rabbie, help him make whisky and sneak it south. I like the first one best, personally."

"I don't." Mary sat cross-legged, as he did, settling her skirts on her knees. She hadn't done so since she was a girl. "We ought to see that your father is all right, then *both* go to France. We take your father with us and keep him safe."

Malcolm studied a pinched fold of his plaid. "Dad will never leave Kilmorgan. I can't abandon him there on his own to the mercy of English soldiers. But you can be out of this, away from Halsey, away from Yorkshire commanders who drag ye off where ye don't want to go. Ye wait in Paris for me t' come when the Jacobite cause is either won or lost. Ye'll be with your sister, and all."

His tone was so reasonable that Mary glared at him. "Sit by myself worrying to death whether you're alive or dead, or whether you've done some bloody fool thing to get yourself arrested or killed? What do you expect me to do all day while I'm fretting—embroider?"

"Mary, these are dangerous times." Mal looked up at her, a sternness in his eyes she'd never seen before. "They'd be dangerous for you even in Lincolnshire, even in London. The Lord only knows where Charles will take his army and what he'll do to those in his way. The English won't rise and join him—they've no wish t' go starry-eyed after ancient princes. King Geordie will send a powerful force to chase him and crush all his Highlanders. I don't want you caught in the middle of that."

Mary jammed her arms across her chest, cold but angry. "Well, we should have thought of that before we decided to be illicit lovers and run away together. You should never have followed me upstairs in Lord Bancroft's house. I'd still be in Edinburgh, whiling away my time until the uprising was over." *Not hidden away in a crumbling stone cottage, loving you and breaking my heart.*

"Aye, and ye'd have married that bastard, Halsey." Mal's golden eyes glittered. "Your sister would be pining for love of

Jeremy Drake, who couldn't wake up and carry her away until someone kicked him in his backside. Your father would have shoved Audrey at another man for his political schemes, married her off whether she liked it or not. You really wanted that life for her? For yourself?" He let out a derisive breath. "You're damn lucky I came along to save ye from all that."

"And I know *you* can twist anything to your own purposes, my dear Malcolm."

"True enough, but if ye think ye'd be safer in Edinburgh now, ye'd be wrong. There will be fighting, and it will be bloody. Who knows when the Jacobites will decide to cut the throats of English aristos who've been sneering at them all these years? Your father has a nice bit of land in Lincolnshire, doesn't he? Why shouldn't a Scotsman have it for his sons, turning your family out into the cold?"

Mary went quiet. "Are Highlanders so ruthless?"

Malcolm gave the ceiling a brief glance. "Oh, they are that. I've lived with them all me life. I ought to know."

"*You're* a Highlander," Mary reminded him.

"Why d'ye think I know so much about it? Let me put you out of harm's away, Mary, love."

Mary firmed her jaw. "No, indeed. If you are off to Kilmorgan, I am going with you. We can send word to my father and Aunt Danae that I am well and not to come for me. If you are staying at Kilmorgan, then so am I." She stopped, a qualm stealing over her. "In any case, don't you think Colonel Wheeler will have sent men to Kilmorgan, waiting for you to return? He is very angry at you. We may already be too late."

Mal dismissed this with a wave of his hand. "I won't be marching t' the front gates brandishing me claymore, will I? I planned to use stealth, sweet Mary. Wheeler will tire of looking for me soon—he can't spare the men to chase one annoying Highlander around the glens."

"Very well, then." Mary's chin came up. "I will sneak to Kilmorgan with you."

Malcolm closed his eyes and pinched the bridge of his nose. "Ye aren't going t' be an obedient and unquestioning wife, I'm thinking, are ye?"

"Certainly not. Englishwomen are resilient creatures. I do not know why people assume we are sweet and docile, innocent and weak." Mary unfolded her arms and rested her hands primly in her lap. "Look at Boadicea, who led forces against the Roman army for a long, long time. Queen Elizabeth, who often had to remark she was 'only a woman' to spare the feelings of gentlemen she could outthink. Even Aunt Danae has survived three husbands and is entertaining thoughts of a fourth, on her own terms. You have no need to worry about *me*."

A slow smile had spread across Malcolm's face as he listened to her speech. When she finished, his eyes were alight, the depths of gold warm.

"Ye see? I knew ye had fire inside you, lass. An inferno of it. You and me—we're going to burn up the world." Mal reached for her and took her hand. "But I was wrong about one thing."

Mary's throat hurt, dry from her adamant speech. She closed her hand around his and held on, his strength bolstering her own. "What is that?"

"You're not yet my wife." Mal's smile turned wicked. "But we'll be fixing that today."

Malcolm purchased a sturdy pony from Rabbie for Mary to ride. He also gave the man money for extra tartans to wrap around her and keep her warm.

They waited for dusk to fall before they left. Mary was happy with that, mostly because Malcolm needed to sleep. He might enjoy acting the part of *brollachan*, but he was only human, and days without rest could be deadly.

Also, Mary still feared Malcolm being found by the soldiers. The colonel and Mary's father might have ordered the men to scour the land for them. If Mal took her wandering in daylight, would they be seen, two figures bent into the wind, hurrying deeper into the Highlands? Would the soldiers instantly shoot Mal dead, even if Mary begged for his life? She thought about the exasperated anger of Colonel Wheeler and decided that, yes, they probably would.

They left the cluster of cottages once it was dark, Mal pressing on Rabbie more coin and warm thanks. Rabbie's wife nodded her good-byes, but for their entire visit, she'd never spoken a word. Mary wondered if perhaps she was unable to.

No other crofters had appeared all day, though Mary had

seen the smoke drifting in thin wafts from their houses. *Wise of them*, she thought. These people had too much to lose to risk anyone discovering how many of them lived in this hollow.

She mentioned as much to Mal as they made their way uphill after sundown, Malcolm leading her pony.

"Aye, they're a careful lot," Mal replied. "But Rabbie seems to have a kindness in him, and the others do what he says. If not, they'd have tried to rob us while we slept."

Mary stared at him. "Good heavens—I thought you trusted them completely. Such thoughts certainly didn't keep you awake today." Mal had snored all afternoon long, and when he'd woken, he'd loved her again.

"I wouldn't have let them touch us," he said, his voice a comfort in the darkness. "Now cease your chatter. We've a tricky bit to go through."

The "tricky bit" was a flat open plain. Clouds parted to reveal a bright moon, which spilled a path across the land. Mal kept the moon at his right shoulder, leading her and the pony quickly across the open ground.

Mary had no idea where they were. When Colonel Wheeler had taken them toward Inverness, they'd been making straight south for the ferry at Kessock—at least, so she'd been told. Malcolm had sneaked her across country when he'd rescued her from the crofters' village, following no road. Mary hadn't stepped outside Rabbie's cottage all that day, and when they'd finally emerged, the sun had been gone, setting quickly this time of year. She'd seen only a high ridge of hill above a stream, and then this wide stretch of moor.

The drawback about Mal sleeping all day, Mary thought, was that now he was at his full energy. He charged ahead like a mad bull, setting a quick pace through the ice-cold night.

The open heath ended in a thick woods, which Mal plunged into without hesitation. He seemed to know his way through, though to Mary it was dark as pitch, except where mist glowed ghostly white. Branches reached out to tug at her, and she lowered herself to the sure-footed pony's neck.

Lights flickered at the edges of her vision. At first she thought she imagined them, but Mary once turned her head in time to see a very clear glow that immediately winked out.

"Malcolm!" she called in an urgent whisper.

"They're will-o'-the-wisps," Mal said without turning around. "Pay them no heed. If you don't follow them, they can't hurt you."

Another light flickered. Mary turned swiftly, but it had winked out before she could pinpoint it. She gave a nervous laugh. "So, you do believe in ghosts, after all?"

Mal made that scoffing noise she liked. "The light is caused by gases rising in marshy ground. Don't know how it works, but that's what happens. If ye chased it, and fell into a bog and drowned, well, the effect would be the same as if it really were a ghost, wouldn't it?"

He had a point. Mary kept an eye out for the lights, but they came fewer and farther between as they pushed through the woods, and finally stopped altogether.

Mal led them out of the trees not long after that. Moonlight shone on a long stretch of water that smelled of brine, and Mary heard the whisper of waves lapping gently at the shore.

"Gracious, where are we?" she asked. This couldn't be the sea—she'd had the idea that they were steadfastly moving away from it. But they couldn't have reached the other side of Scotland, surely.

"Firth of Cromarty," Mal answered. "The west bank of it. I circled us well away from Inverness and any place we'd have to take a boat or ferry. Couldn't risk that ferrymen aren't loyalists who'd give me up for a shilling. There's a village I know here with no love for the English, and a church with a minister."

Mary's heart constricted, his last words more alarming than his first. "A minister? You mean to do this, then?"

Malcolm finally turned to face her. He patted the pony's neck then laid his hand on her plaid-covered knee, his eyes dark in the gloom. "It's not what I wanted for ye. I wanted it all t' be beautiful, perfect, a wedding ye could be proud of for many a long year."

Mary answered softly, "That's not so important to me anymore."

When she'd been resigned to marrying Halsey, she and Aunt Danae had begun planning a wedding that would be the envy of every lady in England—a glittering pageant in St. George's, Hanover Square, a wedding breakfast and celebration at Lord Wilfort's London mansion that would be discussed in every newspaper from Dover to Carlisle. But she had realized after meeting Malcolm that it was not the wedding that was important—it was the marriage itself.

Mal thumped his fist on his chest. "It's important t' *me*. I seduced ye, coerced ye, and now am leading ye around the country as though we're a pair of beggars. The least I could do is give ye a decent wedding."

"You did," Mary said, trying to smile. "Up on the cliffs above Kilmorgan. It was a marvelous ceremony."

Mal abruptly began to adjust the pony's bridle, turning his face from the betraying moonlight. "Aye, well. That was a bit of theatre."

"No. It was lovely."

Malcolm gazed across the firth. "Even if I can't give ye the wedding ye deserve, I will marry ye this day. Giving you my name will restore your reputation now that I've tarnished it and see ye right if the English succeed in ridding themselves of me. Ye will have all my worldly goods, never ye worry. I have a lot of them, and not simply those stashed under the floorboards of Kilmorgan. I have accounts in London, and in France, and other bits of land here and there. I don't want us t' live in exile, but if we have to, we'll do well."

Malcolm at the moment was nothing but a shapeless lump of plaid—as Mary was—his hair unwashed and flyaway. Anyone would mistake him for an impoverished vagrant, instead of the son of a duke with wealth stashed all over the world.

Mal wasn't one simple thing, Mary had come to understand—not the rakish charmer, or the practical businessman, or the crazed warrior who blew up tents filled with ammunition and rescued his brother and Mary out from under their guards' noses. Nor was Malcolm merely a man of the land, at home on the edge of this inlet of moonlit sea, equally at home helping his tenant farmers bring in the harvest or in drawing rooms filled with furniture given to his family by a king.

He was all these things and more. Mary uncovered another layer of Malcolm Mackenzie each day, which deepened her love for him further.

"But I'm forgetting one thing," Mal said, the charmer coming through in his smile.

Mary attempted a lofty look to tease him. "Oh? What is that?"

Malcolm pulled her from the pony to her feet, then he dropped to one knee in front of her, never mind the mud. He took her hand, his bare, cold, and callused.

"Lady Mary Lennox," Mal asked in a solemn voice. "Will ye marry me?"

Mary's pulse jumped. Wind blew across the firth, dragging her hair into her face, and stinging her eyes.

She closed her other hand around Malcolm's and answered with her heart.

"Yes."

Chapter 30

In a small village at the edge of the firth, Malcolm stopped at the house of the minister just after dawn, and hammered on the door.

A severe-looking housekeeper wrenched it open, then gasped and tried to slam it again. Mal caught the door before it could close and pushed his way inside, leading Mary into a small square hall with an equally square staircase. The wind blew the door shut behind him, closing them into this warm, stuffy place. Mal's skin began to tingle, his body happy to be cut off from the wind.

The housekeeper was shouting, rousing the place. Presently, the minister came down the stairs, a tall Highlander with the prudish sneer of a follower of John Knox. "What is this?" he growled.

"I need ye to marry us," Malcolm said. "Right away, if ye please."

The man looked them up and down. Malcolm knew he saw a ragged Highland vagabond with a dirt-smeared face and his equally ragged lady, who was wrapped in several layers of plaid. The dun-colored kilts Rabbie had given them were so faded that the pattern was barely distinguishable.

"No," the minister said. "Be off with ye."

He was a big man, with large hands and tight muscles. Malcolm pulled a pistol from the folds of his kilt and pointed it at him. "Now."

The minister glanced at Mal's pistol, looked at Mary, and returned his gaze to Mal's set face. He heaved a long, resigned, Scottish sigh.

"Verra well. Go in there." He pointed at a door. "And put away that damned shooter before ye hurt someone, lad."

For the second time, Mary let Malcolm put his heavy ring on her finger and say the words . . . *With this ring, I thee wed.*

This time, the ceremony was spoken by a minister, witnessed, and recorded. The housekeeper and a solid, squat man who did the minister's heavier chores stood in the front room with them as Mary and Malcolm were joined.

If the minister was surprised he married Lord Malcolm Mackenzie, son of the Duke of Kilmorgan, to Lady Mary Lennox, daughter of the Earl of Wilfort, he made no indication. He finished, noted the marriage in his register, collected his fee, and bade them both a good day.

Malcolm led Mary outside again, his grip on her hand tight.

She was now Mary Mackenzie—or more properly, Lady Malcolm Mackenzie. Legally wed in Scotland, a place of very liberal marriage laws, so she'd come to understand. Two people could be considered "married" if they claimed, before witnesses, that they were. As simple as that. With so much isolation in the Highlands, Malcolm had said, sometimes it was the only way people could wed. *This* marriage was more proper than that, he said dryly, which should satisfy Mary's father, and his.

They rode away from the village, Mary light of heart, but they were very shy with each other the rest of the day. Malcolm would glance at her, then smile and look away. Mary would blush and study the firth as though its wind-rippled surface was the most fascinating thing she'd ever seen.

They continued north along Cromarty Firth for the rest of the day, Mal leading the pony down a narrow road that skirted the shore. They passed clusters of farm buildings and stubbled fields, brown and waiting for the first dusting of snow. Clouds lowered around them, the high hills Malcolm called the Suitors at the mouth of the firth fading into and out of sight.

Darkness fell early, sunset at half past three, but the clouds and mist made it darker more quickly still. Malcolm had told Mary they'd stay the night with trusted friends, but before they could reach the village he made for, Mal veered from the road and struck out over a barren field to woods beyond.

Mary said nothing, having heard the tramp of horses and jingle of bridles. She and Mal reached the shelter of the woods just before the riders came into view, mere smudges in the failing light.

The blue and red of uniforms were easy to discern, however. British soldiers, some mounted, others walking, a mix of cavalry and infantry as had made up the troop Colonel Wheeler commanded. This was not Wheeler's band however, Mary saw as she studied them. There were fewer, and nowhere did she see the short, rotund Yorkshireman with the loud voice.

The men were passing a deserted farm. The farmhouse, black stone like Rabbie's, had no roof, its burned beams etched against the mist. Not far from it stood a larger, square building that Mary guessed would have been a barn. A few stone sheds lay around it, most of them falling to bits.

Mary's pony seemed to know to keep quiet—no snorting or calling a greeting to the horses on the road. But then, they were English horses, and this pony was all Scots. Perhaps the mistrust spread to beasts as well.

Mary's fanciful thought died as Malcolm stiffened. Near the end of the line of men were four Scotsmen in shackles.

The four were surrounded by guards, but the Highlanders walked with heads high, arrogance in every stride. One of them said something in Erse, and the other three laughed.

Malcolm remained silent. Mary watched as one English soldier smacked the butt of his musket between the shoulder blades of the Highlander who'd spoken. The Highlander stumbled, fell, then groaned as he tried to gain his feet.

"Sir!" the soldier who'd struck the Highlander called to the nearest officer. "This one's down."

A man in a red coat came riding back. "Damn it." The commander looked up and down the trail, then whistled through his fingers. The lead riders circled around, and the line of men ground to a halt.

"Find out if anyone's in those outbuildings," the commander said, waving his hand at the barn and sheds. He was more quiet voiced than Wheeler, the flattening of his vowels putting him from somewhere in Berkshire. "We'll put up for the night here."

"What about the prisoners, sir?" the man who'd jabbed the Highlander asked.

The commander looked around again, uneasy with the growing darkness. "We'll get settled in for tonight. In the morning, stand them against a wall and shoot them. They're marauders and Jacobites, and they're slowing us down. Sergeant, give the orders."

A sergeant with a powerful voice shouted for the men to fall out and make camp, and to check the barn and sheds.

Malcolm took Mary's hand and led her soundlessly back into the woods. "I'm sorry, love," he said, his voice quiet. "I've got to stay here a bit. I can't let them execute those men."

"Well, of course not," Mary answered indignantly. "I never thought you would."

Malcolm didn't answer, head bowed in thought. When he looked up, his eyes gleamed in a chance bit of moonlight. "I'm not sending you off alone either. What do ye know about slow matches?"

Mary wet her lips. "Not much."

Malcolm opened the small bag he carried. He drew out a few narrow metal tubes with a short length of cord attached to each. More loose cord lay coiled inside the pack.

"I found these at your captors' camp. Slow matches aren't much used anymore, but they can be handy."

Mary stared at them, mystified. "I've never seen any before. What do you do with them?"

"Light it here." Malcolm pointed to the bit of cord that protruded from the metal tube. "And let it burn. The cord smolders, taking a long time. So ye can light things without worrying about sparks or a high flame. Good for setting off cannon—used to be used in muskets too. Or ye can set one down near a cask of gunpowder and be well away before the cask explodes."

"Is that what you did at Colonel Wheeler's camp?"

"Aye. That and a few other tricks. Want to learn them?"

Mary felt herself smiling. "Oh, yes."

"Good, lass." Malcolm chuckled. "I knew ye had it in ye. Come on, love. I'll show ye what we'll do."

Over the next several hours, Malcolm taught Mary enough to make her dangerous. He'd always known she was brave, but he was surprised at her resourcefulness and her willingness to bend her hand to tough labor.

The first thing Mal did was lead her to a narrow stream that cut a deep path through the woods then wended down into the field where the soldiers had made camp. He found a loose limb that was stout enough for his purpose and began digging to alter the stream's channel. Mary watched him for a time, then tucked her skirts into her waistband, waded in, and began to help.

Mal stopped digging to lift loose stones from the banks and place them into the stream's bed. "We don't want to dam it up completely," he explained. "Just to divert it so it will overflow into the field where the company is settling in for the night. The water will come up right under their tents. Be an ice-cold bed for them."

"Oh, the poor things," Mary said, but she kept piling the stones where he indicated.

Mal decided this was a good place to leave the pony and their few belongings. He loaded one pistol, though he didn't prime it, and left one empty, which he gave to Mary to carry. Strapping the pistol's holster around her torso led to some deep kisses, but Mal didn't let himself pause long in his task.

Hand in hand, Mal and Mary crept quietly to the edge of the farm, which was now shrouded in darkness. A light flashed in the camp—the men weren't worried about their lanterns being seen.

They'd set sentries, though, aware that Highlanders in this area could be hostile. Mal wondered what the Highland captives had done to earn the soldiers' wrath. Might have been anything from taunting them to trying to murder the entire troop.

Mal pressed the handle of one of his dirks into Mary's hand. "Use this t' cut the men free. Start with the biggest one, and he'll help you with the others. If ye get into trouble, if one of the English soldiers grabs ye, jab this into him, hard as ye can, and run like the devil. Don't be squeamish or hesitate, because he'll do much worse to you."

Mary nodded, her eyes grave. "I understand."

She did, the little love. Mal pretended to shiver. "Now I know why Englishmen don't let their ladies fight alongside them. The women would take over in a heartbeat."

Mary squeezed his arm in the darkness. "Don't be silly."

"'Tis true, and the English bastards know it. That's why they write laws t' keep their women tamed. And why I keep having to rescue ye."

"You mean abducting me."

Mal heaved a mock sigh. "Well, we're never going to see eye to eye on that. Are ye ready?"

Mary gave him another squeeze, then quickly kissed his cheek. "On your orders, Colonel."

Mal explained to her in detail what both of them would do, and had her repeat the plan to him. Then they crept forward at a low crouch.

Mal knew from long experience how to take advantage of a patch of mist, of the changing direction of the wind as it blew in from the sea and became caught in the firth. He and Mary circled the camp to approach from the north. Mal could hear the soldiers speaking together in tight groups, the men both tired and wary.

The Highlanders had been put into the barn, which was empty, the cattle gone. No farmers had been found anywhere—they might have abandoned the land for fear of Englishmen or the Jacobites, or had gone to the cities to look for work. So many Highlanders had begun doing so as an alternative to starving.

Before they drew too close, Malcolm turned his back to the camp, took the unloaded pistol from Mary, and used its flint to create a spark. He cupped his hands around the sparking flint until one caught a slow match.

He lit a second slow match and handed it to Mary. "Keep it out of sight, but don't set yourself on fire."

She nodded in their circle of light. Mal kissed her, and then they separated to carry out their mission.

Mary moved noiselessly toward the barn as Malcolm melted out of sight. Her heart beat swiftly, more awareness than she'd ever experienced tingling through her body. This was very dangerous, and she could die, but at the same time, she was exhilarated, filled with a sharp sense of purpose.

One guard patrolled the barn's door, a young lad. Mary wondered why only the single guard, but perhaps the commander felt his prisoners were secure.

Mary waited in the darkness beyond the barn, as Malcolm had instructed. The small building, built of local stone, was a rectangle of walls that leaned slightly together. The door, a slab of wood, looked rickety.

A sudden light flared in the field a little way from the camp. The young guard came alert.

Bang! Bang! Bang! A series of brief explosions, like fireworks, sounded in the middle of the camp. Men were shouting, running. The guard, nervously cradling his musket, started toward them.

As if on cue, the trickle of water from the diverted stream that had been quietly filling the field grew into a flood. A tent folded in on itself, and the men who ran toward it slipped and slid.

The guard at the barn hurried to see what was going on. As soon as he left the door clear, Mary moved from the shadows of the wall and slipped inside the dark building.

She could see nothing—the soldiers had not left their prisoners any light. She heard Highlanders muttering together, questioning in their own language, somewhere in the middle of the room.

Mary made her way toward them, touching her slow match to a candle. The darkness was so complete that the single candle gave her plenty of light.

The men broke off, eyes glittering as they swiveled to look at her. One barked a question to the others, keeping to Erse, but she knew he was saying something like, *Who's that?*

The men were standing with their backs together, hands bound behind them to a pole in the center of the room. One man could barely stand—the one who'd been pushed down. He favored his left knee, and his face was drawn in pain.

Mary decided to free him first. Malcolm had told her to cut the biggest man loose, but her compassion made her move to the hurt man. She jammed the candle between rocks on the floor, then pressed the dirk to the injured man's ropes.

He grinned down at her. "Ah, things are looking better," he said in English, voice scraping. "Who are ye, lassie?"

"Shh," Mary said severely.

The others chuckled, very pleased with themselves for men who'd be shot in the morning.

It took longer than Mary had guessed to cut ropes, even with the sharp dirk, but at last the man was free. She caught him as he fell, his large body taking her down with him to the stones on the floor. He smelled of sweat, blood, and fear.

"I think I've lost me heart," the man said as Mary struggled out from under him.

"Be still," she whispered. Mary went to the burliest man and sawed his ropes loose, then started to work on the remaining two. The second man she'd freed rubbed his wrists, then helped her pull the ropes from the others.

"What now, lass?" the injured man asked from the floor. "There's one door out o' this place and an entire camp on the other side of it. Not much of a plan is it?"

"Ma—*my friend* will give us a signal," Mary said. She strove to make her voice not shake. Malcolm would be as cheerful as these men, but Mary was impatient and terrified.

"She's English, and not working alone," the injured man confided to his fellows. "Verra suspicious." They agreed with various comments in Erse.

Mary blew out the candle. "And you must be *quiet*."

She heard laughter in the darkness, but at least, mercifully, they ceased talking.

Chapter 31

They waited. The injured man stifled a groan whenever he tried to move, but the rest crouched in the gloom, warriors used to lying low until the right moment.

The shouting outside escalated. With it came crashes, horses neighing, and the lowing of cows.

"Now!" Mary said.

She led the way to the door, and the men followed, the strongest propping up the hurt man. Mary peered through a crack in the door frame, and saw that outside all was chaos.

Great, shaggy Scottish cattle charged through the camp, frightened out of their wits by the banging behind them. The horses, not happy either, had broken free and bolted with the cows. Tents were falling, and the lone wagon that had carried supplies lay splintered on its side. Everywhere soldiers ran, trying to round up the cattle, to go after the horses, to keep out of the muddy water that gushed everywhere.

No one was paying attention to the barn. Mary opened the door and led the prisoners out.

They slipped around the walls to the back of the barn, preparing to run from there into the darker fields shrouded in mist. Mary was to lead them to the woods and rendezvous with Mal where they'd left the pony.

"Go!" she whispered.

They dashed from the shelter of the wall, the men moving with the silence of hunted animals. Mary struggled to keep up with them, her skirts tangling her legs. She put on a burst of speed when she heard heavy footsteps behind her, and then a large, horny hand landed on her shoulder.

The man who'd caught her was nothing but a bulky shadow in the darkness. He yanked Mary around, and she smelled sweat and rank breath, felt the buzz of whiskers against her face.

"Now, where th' devil are *you* going?" he asked in an accent of Norfolk. "Are you the one causing us all this trouble, pretty lass?"

Mary could not see or hear the Highlanders in the dark. They'd run on, perhaps thinking she was directly behind them, or perhaps they'd abandoned her, an Englishwoman, to her fate.

. . . if one of the English soldiers grabs ye, jab this into him, hard as ye can, and run like the devil. Don't be squeamish or hesitate, because he'll do much worse to you.

Malcolm's words rang in her head. Mary steadied the dirk in her hand and thrust it into the arm that held her.

The man yelped, his hold loosening. "Filthy bitch!" His fist came around, catching Mary in the face. She spun dizzily, sick, but she struck again with the blade.

This time the man grunted, hand clutching his shoulder, blood rapidly staining his clothes. "I'll kill you!"

Mary wobbled, trying to get her breath. One of the Highlanders, the burly man, had seen, had turned back, coming for her. Unfortunately, so had a few English soldiers from the camp.

A soldier bellowed, sending up the alarm. Mary staggered, found her feet, and ran.

The Highlander who'd returned for her grabbed her and pulled her along with him. At the same time, two British soldiers sprinted around the other side of the barn, muskets in arms.

And then about ten shaggy cows ran between the soldiers and Mary with her rescuer. The soldiers cursed, and the

Highlander pulled Mary after him through the open field at an astonishingly swift pace.

A man in a kilt ran out of the dark and caught Mary's other arm. Mary recognized Malcolm's touch as he sprinted along beside her, the two men more or less carrying her between them. Mary's feet scarcely touched the ground as they fled.

Mary couldn't speak, could barely breathe. They reached the cover of the woods, but Malcolm kept on, weaving through the trees, ignoring branches that reached down to slap them. They caught up to the other Highlanders, who waited, the injured man sagging between them.

"Run," Malcolm urged them. "Scatter—go where ye must."

Two nodded and disappeared into the trees. The burly man who'd pulled Mary along stayed with the injured man. "I'll get him t' safety."

"How did you become captured in the first place?" Mary asked them. "Are there battles being fought here now?"

The injured man shook his head. "We were with a convoy to carry French gold to Prince Teàrlach from the coast. We were diversion for the main body t' get through." He grinned, then grimaced. "Worked all too well. One of the bastards shot me in the leg. Only winged me, though."

"Shut it!" the larger man said in alarm.

"Nothing to worry us," the injured man said easily. "This lad's one of Kilmorgan's get. None o' them have any great love for the English."

"Too true," Mal said. "But your sacrifice is done. Now go, before all my hard work is for naught."

The injured man struggled to his feet, leaning heavily on the burly man. "Let the lass come with us. I need something nice to look at after being so long with these ugly faces."

Malcolm's dirk came out, its blade glinting in the starlight. "And I'll thank ye t' keep your hands off me wife."

The man's face fell. "Damn. Of course, ye Mackenzies always take the prettiest ones. No matter. I won't forget what ye've done, lad. Ye ever need a favor, ye call on Calan Macdonald. Good night to ye."

He sketched Mal a salute. He and the other man turned away, the larger man supporting Calan, and were soon lost in the darkness.

Malcolm boosted Mary onto the pony. "No rest for us for a time." He started to pick up the reins, then he came back to the pony, caught Mary around the waist, and kissed her hard on the lips. His mouth was hot, shaking. "Ye did well, love."

Mary knew by the haunted look in Mal's eyes that he'd seen the soldier grab her and hit her, that he'd been too far away to help, and that Mal wouldn't forgive himself for that anytime soon.

"I'm all right." She gave his hand a caress. "The cattle were a nice touch."

Mal nodded, but his look remained fierce. "Aye, well. Always game for a bit of fun, is a Scottish coo."

"Coo?" Mary tried to laugh. "Is that what you call them?"

Malcolm only turned and began leading the horse into the shadows. "Can ye credit it? Me, earning a favor from a *Macdonald*. Well, miracles sometimes happen."

The journey to Kilmorgan was both the happiest and the most frightening time in Mary's life.

They rode at night and hid during the day, Malcolm holding Mary in his arms while they slept. Mal seemed to know absolutely everyone in the lands bordering Kilmorgan's, and they were given cellars or attics to sleep in, food when they woke, water for washing. The villagers and crofters were delighted when Mal introduced Mary as his wife.

"Bairns be coming then?" One woman with very few teeth grinned at them, with a pointed look at Mary's abdomen. "Them Mackenzies go at it like rabbits. Lots of bairns, I'm thinking." She chuckled, her sagging belly shaking.

Mary blushed, but Malcolm didn't look embarrassed at all.

There were other soldiers moving up and down this part of the Highlands, trying to stamp out any support for Charles Stuart before it arose. *Too little too late*, Mary thought. She and Mal would hide, watching in silence as the soldiers marched by, often only a few yards away from their hiding place.

These small troops seemed to have the worst luck. Wagons that moved forward after a brief rest might have their axles break for no apparent reason. An entire load of supplies might tumble from a cart down a cliff toward the sea. Tents mysteriously fell in the night, ropes snapped, food disappeared or was trampled by loose cattle.

No one was ever seen, and any Highlanders in the company brought out the tales of mischievous Fair Folk and the *brollachan.*

Jacobite soldiers did not necessarily fare any better from Mal's spates of vengeance. One morning he and Mary came upon a small huddle of cottages surrounded by Highlanders attempting to recruit more men to the Jacobite cause. Mary had learned by now that if a clansman didn't respond to a call to arms, he could be beaten, his houses and crops burned, the men of his family press-ganged into marching.

Six Highlanders surrounded the inhabitants of a group of cottages in a fold of hills, one man with his claymore in hand. A woman and two little boys boiled out of their cottage as a puff of smoke billowed from the thatch.

Mal rose from the ground where he and Mary had been hiding and sprinted toward them in deathly silence. At the last minute, Mal bellowed a berserker cry and launched himself at the Highlander with the sword. The Highlander swung around, but Malcolm was on him before he could recover from his surprise. Malcolm had him disarmed swiftly, raising the claymore in a practiced hand.

The other Highlanders closed on him. Malcolm drew his pistol and pointed it at the head of the Highlander he'd disarmed.

"Put out that fire."

"What the hell are you doing, boy?" the Highlander Mal held the pistol on said. "Get on with ye, or pick up your sword and fight for your prince. We need men."

"You're on Kilmorgan land now," Mal said. "Or hadn't ye noticed?" He glared at the others. "Put out that damned fire, or I leave his brains all over the road."

Two of the men didn't wait for confirmation. They jumped to the cottage's roof and started beating out the flames.

"Ye don't ken what you're doing, Mackenzie," the Highlander said.

"I *ken* that these people are under my protection. If ye can't get them t' fight on their own, what hope have ye got?"

The Highlander turned an evil glare on Malcolm. "Oh, ye want King Geordie to slaughter us, do ye?"

"I'd rather have *him* do it than one of me own."

The fire died, having been quenched before it could grow out of control. The crofters looked terrified, the little boys huddled in frightened silence.

"May God have mercy on ye," the Highlander said, Mal's pistol still at his head. "You'll die just as easy as we will."

"Ye seem t' have little confidence that your Teàrlach will win through," Mal pointed out.

The Highlander's mouth was hard. "Ye haven't heard, have ye? He's on his way back. The help he needed didn't come, and he's turned for home. The English will chase him all the way to the Highlands, and here, we'll have to stand."

"How do ye know that?" Mal didn't move the pistol. "Ye get secret messages from the man?"

The Highlander sneered. "Ask your brother Willie."

Mal upended the pistol. "Just get off me lands." He lifted the claymore. "When ye want *this* back, come and ask me dad."

The Highlander growled, but he gave an order, and the others fell in with him, moving with a long stride up the far hill.

"Kind of ye, me lord," one of the crofters said. "But I think ye made an enemy, lad."

"Aye, I tend t' do that." Malcolm rubbed his forehead. "Best ye get back inside and be wary. More will come. If they do, get yourself down the road a few miles and hide on Kilmorgan land. They won't risk the wrath of me da."

The crofter chuckled, possessing a Highlander's stoic mettle. "Aye, that they won't."

Mal gave them a few more reassurances and returned to Mary.

"You told the soldiers we were on Kilmorgan land already," she said as they rode on. "But said to the crofters that it was a few miles away. Which is it?"

Mal shrugged in his maddening way. "We're more or less there. As the crow flies."

"How about as the pony walks?"

His grin flashed. "A bit longer. By tomorrow morning we'll see if we have a bed at home or if it's all ash and dust."

They rode west until they reached a tiny path that followed the sea. Cliffs dropped alarmingly down to the water, but the land on top was flat and rich. Snow came as they made their way south, thick fat flakes that settled on Mary's plaids and in Malcolm's hair.

At one point, Mary looked down through the windblown snow to see what looked like pillars rising from the ocean to march along the rock-strewn beach. She turned and watched the strange formations fade into the fog and snow, until they were lost to sight.

Approaching Kilmorgan from the north took them past the turnoff that led to the overlook where Mary had lain with Malcolm for the first time. She remembered the warm October sun, Malcolm's weight on her, the incredible fulfillment of becoming one with him.

So much had happened since then. And what was to come flitted like the *brollachan*, a flicker of dread at the corner of one's eye.

The dread began to take on life when they reached the foot of Kilmorgan Castle as the moon began to rise.

The place was abandoned. Stones from the walls littered the path to the top. When they reached the huge front door, they found it smashed, and the inside of the castle gutted. Fire had burned the paneling, and the rest of the house had been looted. Ash lay everywhere, wet from the rains and snow that had drifted in through the broken windows.

Mal flashed his lantern around grimly, saying nothing. He'd expected to find this, Mary realized. He'd come here to confirm that it was ruined, not in hope that all would be well.

Mal gazed up at the remains of the gallery, its stairs smashed, one railing hanging crookedly from above. Silence lay over all, broken only by the whisper of wind.

Malcolm turned his back on the mess, squared his shoulders, and strode out of the house without a word.

He was finishing with it, Mary decided as she followed. This was the Kilmorgan of the past. Malcolm Mackenzie was leaving it, never to return.

Mal led Mary back down the path from the castle, then

caught the pony and boosted her on again. He struck out across the valley, past the site of the house he so longed to build, moving neither in haste nor hesitation. Down into another dell, chased by nightfall and snow, along a path that hugged a hill, and so to a stone house built against a rock face.

For a few moments, Mary couldn't see a house at all—it blended so well with the cliffs around it. Then a light flashed in a window, and the outline came to her. Two floors, real windows, chimneys that let out thin streams of smoke.

Malcolm made straight for this house without stopping. He led the pony right up to the front door and pressed the latch.

The door was locked. Mal thumped on it, kicking with his hard boots. "Damn ye, let me in! This is my bloody house!"

After a few moments, the thick door was wrenched open and the tall form of Will Mackenzie filled the opening.

"Malcolm!" Will shouted the word, then he let out a shrill Scots cry and yanked Malcolm off his feet into a crushing hug.

Pounding footsteps sounded on flagstones, and the hall was filled with Mackenzies, including the duke, who was demanding to know what was going on. The Mackenzie retainers rushed after them, including small Ewan, who saw Mary.

"Captain! Sir!" The boy ran at her.

Alec Mackenzie was one step behind him. "Bloody hell, Will, are ye letting Mary sit out in the snow? What's the matter with ye?"

Alec lifted Mary down before she had time to say a word, and had her and Ewan inside the house. Another man slipped out to see to the pony, leading it off into the dark.

Mary's feet touched the flagstone floor when Alec put her down, and she started unwinding the plaids, glad to breathe out of the wind.

The house was unusual. Instead of a foyer or a hall with stairs leading to the upper floors, Mary found herself in a large, echoing chamber that was open to the top of the house. The walls ran a long way back, farther than she'd thought they could, until she realized the house had been built into the side of the hill.

"What is this place?" she asked.

Mal came to her, scooping her to his side. "The distillery. We'll live here on whisky and hops until the battles are done. D'ye mind too much?"

"Well . . ." Alec said.

Mal looked around sharply, taking in a sea of glum faces. "What? What does *well* mean?"

Will answered. "The Englishers have already been here. Couldn't burn the house around it, because it's all stone, but I'm afraid they did burn down one thing."

Mal stared at him, his face draining of color. Then he uttered a cry of anguish and rushed down the corridor that led straight into the hill.

When Malcolm's scream of despair reached her, Mary wrenched herself from Alec's hold and ran after him.

Chapter 32

Malcolm gazed at the ruins of the room and clutched his head, digging at his mud-streaked hair.

Everything he'd worked for, built, and accumulated over the last four years was gone. In place of the vats and pipes was a charred ruin, the walls around him black with soot.

He heard his brothers and his wife run in after him, Mary joining him to look around in perplexity.

"They blew up my still!" Malcolm shouted. "Those bloody English bastards blew up my *still*!"

Will came to stand at Mal's side, folding his arms. "The rest of us are fine, thanks very much for askin'."

"Burning down a man's house is one thing," Mal said, ignoring him. "But taking his livelihood . . ." He turned to his father. The duke looked older than he had even a week or so before, when Mal had run out of here after Mary. "What about the rest of it?" Mal asked, his heart a cold lump.

"They found the casks, and stole those," the duke said. Then his face cracked with a smile. "But not all of them."

Mal didn't relax. "How many are left?"

"About twenty." His father's amused look grew. "Ye didn't get your cunning from your mother, runt."

Mal blew out his breath. "Well, that's something. We can call them special, special reserve, and sell the bottles for a very high price to snobby Londoners."

"We might not have the chance for that," Will said.

The fact that Will was here, not off roaming the countryside, pushed Mal's immediate worries aside but brought forth others. Alec was here too, not sailing off with Gair or waiting in the smuggler's ship, as Mal had told him to do.

Mary, who stood like a warm pillar on his right, voiced the question. "What has happened, Will? Some Highlanders on the road told us the prince was on his way back."

Will looked unhappy. "Aye, that he is. And the Duke of Cumberland, King George's own son, is following him with a very large and well-experienced army."

The days and weeks that followed were filled with uncertainty, which Mal didn't like. He'd never been indecisive in his life—he'd always known what he wanted then done what he needed to do to get it.

Now he had to wait. Will kept them apprised of all events outside Kilmorgan. He was a superb gatherer of information; his primary source—women.

He'd explained to Malcolm many a time that soldiers, even commanders, spilled their secrets to women. They underestimated them. A woman couldn't possibly understand or care about what they said, they believed, and they used their power and knowledge to impress them. So had been true down the ages.

"A woman wants to know you'll listen to her," Will would say. "That ye take her seriously. Many men of power use them and discard them, and they're happy to vent their spleen and give up all the commanders' secrets."

Through Will, they knew exactly what was happening. Charles and his army had crossed back into Scotland, leaving troops in Carlisle and making for Glasgow. The Duke of Cumberland, as young as Charles and fresh from bloody battles on the Continent, marched straight to Carlisle and took it back.

Charles and his forces departed Glasgow rather quickly and made for Stirling, setting siege to it. Stirling Castle, Edinburgh

Castle, Inverness, and all the military forts were still in the hands of the English, and those would have to be taken before Charles could have a strong hold of Scotland.

Already the Highlanders were disgruntled, wanting to return home to see to their lands over the winter. They weren't professional soldiers, but farmers and landholders who worked the land and looked after their tenants. The duke was pleased at the turn of events, because his sons Duncan and Angus might come home.

Scotland was tense, and none more so than the inhabitants of the Kilmorgan distillery. Malcolm knew Mary was uneasy, though she looked surprised if Malcolm mentioned it.

She'd written a letter to her father, which Malcolm had sent via messengers he trusted, and it should have reached Lincolnshire by now. Wilfort never returned to Kilmorgan, so Mal could only assume he and Lord Halsey had been shunted back to England.

"Mary, love, if ye want to go home, ye can," Mal said to her one night as they lay together in their bed.

The upper floors of one half of the distillery held chambers they'd turned into bedrooms. The castle's servants had remained with the duke—t'look after Himself, they said—which meant a pile of people lived together in one small place. The chamber Mal had commandeered was miniscule, with room only for a wide bed, a dressing table for Mary, and a fireplace to warm them.

Mary, with determination seen only in the feminine half of the human race, had set about to make the distillery habitable. Thanks to her, they had soft blankets on the beds, makeshift curtains at the windows, and plates to set on the table at supper—plates that matched. Mary had ransacked both the distillery and the castle, had sorted and organized, and had bits of furniture hauled hither and yon, until all the Mackenzie men learned to disappear when she said, "I need someone to help me with . . ."

Mary rose on her elbow and traced a line on Mal's chest. "I *am* home," she said.

Mal caught her fingers and raised them to his lips. "Sweet of ye t' say, but I wager your father's house is more comfortable than this."

"I like Kilmorgan," Mary said stubbornly. "Besides, Scotland is crawling with armies moving every which way. Though they're too busy to come up here to annoy you, I'd never get through them to return to Lincolnshire." She looked triumphant when she said it, as though challenging him to argue with her. Mary was no docile creature.

"I can send you around in a ship," Malcolm said. "Sail you right past all the trouble, land you only a few miles from home."

Mary's brows drew together. "I'm not going, Malcolm. What happens if all those English armies do overrun Scotland and drive Charles out? How would I know what happened to you? I am staying until the end."

Malcolm kissed her fingers again and brushed her hair back from her face. "Ye think there is an end, then?"

"I mean until the fate of Charles is decided. He might win through."

"I only want ye safe," Mal said. He thought of his father, clutching the portrait of his wife to his chest and weeping. If Mal lost Mary, the grief would be endless.

Mal rolled Mary into the blankets and made love to her like a man starving.

Will Mackenzie disappeared again in frosty January, sending messages back to Malcolm through many sources—smugglers, itinerant blacksmiths, camp followers, even English soldiers whose loyalties were fickle.

They learned of the battle at Falkirk, outside Edinburgh, where the British were marginally defeated, but both armies dispersed in the heavy weather. Duncan had been there, *and you'd think he'd won the battle himself*, Mal thought when they received his letter through Will.

The Duke of Cumberland was coming, so Will said, heading to Stirling to relieve the British besieged there. Prince Charles retreated deeper into the Highlands, and reached Inverness.

After fighting there, Fort George fell, blown apart by Duncan, Angus, and his men. Will shook his head as he related this, but the duke looked proud.

As the weather began, gradually, to warm, and snow changed to rain, Duncan himself returned home, with Angus, explaining that they were pursuing the armies commanded by Lord Loudon, who'd been routed and chased west and north.

A small celebration was held at Kilmorgan, welcoming the two. It was a celebration with tension underlying it—Will reported that Cumberland was in Aberdeen, waiting for the weather to change while he amassed men and supplies for a final blow to the Highlanders.

"Oh, and, runt," Duncan said as they gathered near the warm fire in the chamber Mary had made into their drawing room. "Everywhere I go, I hear tell of the *brollachan* who makes mischief with the British soldiers on the march. Concentrates in this area of the Highlands, I'm told, and is never seen, never caught." He took a sip of whisky. "Wouldn't know anything about that, would ye?"

Malcolm, who had more than once enjoyed himself making the life of British soldiers in the area hell, shook his head. "No idea. How could I? I'm busy putting my business back together. Besides, I have a wife now. I've settled down." He sent Mary a wink.

Mary serenely took a sip of tea, which she'd asked for rather than the whisky. "Malcolm *has* been rather busy here," she said, keeping her expression deadpan. "He has been helping me go through the wallpaper samples Will brought from Edinburgh."

Duncan gave Malcolm an incredulous look, then roared with laughter. "Wallpaper samples! Malcolm the mighty warrior, a dead shot and fearsome with a claymore. *Wallpaper samples!*"

"'Tis a tricky decision," Malcolm said, rolling his whisky glass between his palms. "I'm thinking the salmon and gold fleur-de-lis, but alas, Mary favors the blue."

Duncan was off in laughter again, and Malcolm glanced over at Mary. They shared a look.

In that moment, Malcolm knew she was his. He'd pursued her, wooed her, seduced her, all the while hoping to make her fall in love with him. He'd done it because he was selfish, he knew. Mal had wanted Mary, and decided he would have her.

In the tiny joke they'd made against Duncan, without rehearsing, Malcolm realized that Mary knew his heart. She was truly his, and he hers.

Only one thing more would make his life with her complete.

Mal hoped, as February became March, and spring eased life into the ground, that she'd tell him his fond wish was coming true.

But Mary said nothing, and Mal began to fear, with a cold touch of worry, that maybe it would never happen. With some women it didn't. He and Mary had been lovers for months now, but time passed, and she never spoke.

On a blustery March day, Duncan returned from the north, his exuberance gone. He rode with his head bowed to his chest, his plaids fluttering in the wind. Across the saddle of the horse he led was the body of Angus Mackenzie, Alec's twin, dead, shot through the heart.

Chapter 33

Mary heard the keening wail of the Duke of Kilmorgan from the chamber she shared with Malcolm. Shouts and cries followed, and Mary hurried to the window, wrenched it open, and looked down into the courtyard. Below, the duke was trying to yank Angus's limp body from the horse, but Duncan had tied it fast so Angus wouldn't fall.

Duncan swung down from his mount, his knife out, ready to cut the ropes. The duke turned on him, grabbing Duncan so swiftly that the knife sliced a thin cut across the duke's face before Duncan could stop it.

The duke didn't notice. "Is this what ye've done t' me?" he roared. "Taken my best son from me and killed him?" He drew back his fist to strike Duncan a furious blow.

Battle-hardened Duncan caught his fist and twisted it away. "I tried to stop it," Duncan said. "I tried. I couldn't."

"Ye could have stopped it by keeping him from coming with ye! Ye bloody bastard, ye've killed my *son*!"

Mary left the window and hurried down the stairs. She nearly ran into Alec on the next landing, he white-faced, his eyes fixed in shock. Mary steadied Alec as he swayed, and they went down the rest of the stairs together.

"Angus." Alec's voice broke as he ran out into the courtyard. Mary was still beside him as he approached the horse to stare at the gray, still face of his twin. Alec rested his closed fists on the horse's neck, and bowed his head.

Duncan wrested himself free of the duke. "Where's Malcolm?" he demanded of Mary.

Mary shook her head, her heart squeezing with dismay and grief. "Not here. He's visiting the farms. He'll be on the west end of them by now."

Duncan pointed a blunt finger at Ewan. "Lad—run out there and send him back. We need to bury Angus right away."

The duke shouted and went after Duncan, both fists raised. While Duncan struggled with him, Alec, his amber eyes red-rimmed, managed to loosen the ropes around Angus and catch his brother in his arms.

Life these days was such that Mary had already seen death several times in her young existence. By the amount of gray in Angus's face, she knew that Duncan was right—Angus should be interred quickly.

The duke swung from Duncan and pulled Angus away from Alec. "No! Ye leave him be!" He cradled Angus in his arms, as gently as he would a baby, and strode swiftly away from them all into the house.

Duncan went after him. "Father!"

The duke swarmed up the stairs, strode into his bedchamber, and kicked the door closed. Duncan, a few steps behind him, grabbed for the handle, but the duke had already turned the key in the lock.

Duncan pounded both fists on the door. "*Father!*"

Mary reached the chamber in time to hear the duke shout through the heavy paneling. "Stay away from my boy!"

Duncan drew back, ready to kick the door in, but Mary caught his arm. "No. Give him some time. He needs to grieve."

Duncan glared down at Mary, eyes glittering. He was the brother Mary least understood. Duncan was a hard man, absolute in his convictions, ready to beat down anyone who stood in his way. He'd make a formidable enemy, but he also made a difficult friend.

Duncan's eyes didn't soften, but he gave Mary a conceding nod. He left her and strode to the stairs. Alec, coming up, turned and went down with him, and after a moment, Mary followed.

"What the devil happened?" Alec was demanding of Duncan. "What battle?"

Duncan shook his head. "No battle." He unwound his plaid from his shoulders, revealing his stained coat and linen shirt. "We were chasing Loudon's troops after they fled into the western Highlands. Bloody man kept running."

Once he reached the bottom of the stairs, Duncan lumbered into the dining room, tossed his plaids over a chair, and went to a whisky decanter, pouring himself a measure. His hands shook as he lifted the glass to his lips. The man was next to exhaustion, Mary saw, his pinched cheekbones and loose hang of his coat telling Mary he hadn't eaten or drunk much lately.

Duncan swayed, and Mary pulled a chair out a little way from the table for him. She didn't suggest he sit, but she took the armless chair next to it. Duncan set his glass on the table and dropped into the chair as though it had been his own idea.

"We were ambushed by a British patrol," Duncan told Alec, who stood at the foot of the table, arms folded. Duncan took a gulp of whisky. "We fought, evenly matched. Their backs were to the cliffs—we should have won. But we're marching on empty stomachs, and that takes the vigor out of a man." Another drink.

Alec didn't sit down. His face, a near mirror of Angus's, was flush with life; Angus's, wan with death. "So what happened?" Alec asked. "Obviously *you* got away."

"We finally started to drive them off, but we knew we had to flee into the hills," Duncan went on. "A couple of infantrymen grabbed Angus and dragged him off his horse. I turned back, tried to reach him. Angus fought like the devil, but it was close fighting, dirks and knives. One of the soldiers stuck a pistol right against Angus's chest. I couldn't reach him in time." Duncan faltered. His gaze fixed on the polished top of the table, his hand tightening around the glass until his knuckles whitened. "The man shot him dead, without mercy. Angus didn't have a chance."

Mary's eyes burned with tears, but rage followed sorrow. "Why?" she cried. "They had no need to kill him. He could have been taken prisoner. A duke's son would be worth a ransom."

Duncan's head came up. "Why? Because they're be-damned

English bastards, that's why! They're poised to kill us all. Maybe Angus struck lucky."

"Shut it, Duncan," Alec said fiercely.

"It's true. We're starving and cold—Cumberland's men are well fed, well trained, and holed up warm in Aberdeen. We're running around the Highlands scratching to survive."

"Then leave it alone," Alec snapped. "Come home. We need ye here."

"Not until it's done." Duncan tossed back the rest of the whisky and wiped his mouth. "I'll go see about the funeral. Angus'll be put in the family tomb."

He was as swift to act as all the Mackenzies. Duncan swung out of the room just as Mary heard Malcolm at the front door.

"Duncan, man," Malcolm said in a hard voice. "Stop and tell me."

Mary rushed out in time to see Duncan push past Malcolm without a word.

Mal saw Mary. "Ewan said Angus was dead," Mal growled at her.

Alec, in the dining room doorway, nodded. "Dad has him."

"For God's sake," Malcolm demanded, "one of ye tell me what the hell happened!"

Alec, his voice a monotone, repeated Duncan's story. Malcolm stilled as he listened, his eyes losing any softness they'd ever had. His youth faded from him even as Mary watched.

"Dad has him upstairs now?" Malcolm asked when Alec finished. His voice was far too calm, making Mary uneasy.

"He's locked the door," Mary said. "I wouldn't let Duncan force his way in, but I'm afraid . . . Mal, would you speak to him?"

Mal shook his head, a weary look settling on him. "I'm the last person he listens to."

"You're wrong about that." Mary's mouth was dry, her fingers cold, so cold. "Please, try."

Malcolm shot her a skeptical glance but turned away and climbed the stairs, Mary coming close behind him.

Mal reached his father's door and rapped on it. "Dad—it's Mal. Let me in."

"Please," Mary added through the door.

They heard the crash of falling glass, then the duke's voice. "Go the hell away!"

Malcolm knocked again. "I just want t' see me brother."

"*No!*" Something hard slammed against the door, which jumped on its hinges. "Ye stay away from him. Ye as good as killed him—he, who's always been better than the lot of ye."

Malcolm said sternly, "Dad, open the door."

"Get away from here or I'll flay the skin off ye!" The duke's voice choked off, horrible coughing sobs replacing the words.

"Bloody hell," Malcolm whispered.

He groped into his pockets and pulled out a few thin pieces of metal. Mary knew exactly what he did with those by now—there wasn't a lock made that Malcolm couldn't open. He'd never explained where he'd learned the skill and why, only said that it came in handy.

Mal dropped to his knees, carefully pushed the key out of the keyhole on the other side, and started scraping at the lock. He had it undone in a minute or two, then rose and reached for the door handle.

Mary stopped him. "Let me."

Malcolm gave her a long look, then he seemed to understand, and gestured her to go ahead. Mary drew a breath, opened the door, and entered the duke's bedchamber.

Malcolm closed the door behind her, remaining outside of it, shutting her in with the duke.

The Duke of Kilmorgan sprawled on the low couch Mary had caused to be brought here from the castle. She'd chosen to put it in the duke's chamber because it fit his muscled bulk. He'd grumbled he didn't need soft furniture, but the duke's valet told Mary he napped upon it all the time. Now the duke sat forlornly on the edge of the couch, his head bowed over Angus across his lap.

Father and son. The duke rested his hand on Angus's unmoving chest, his own body moving with sobs. The choked sound of the duke's weeping was terrible.

Mary drew a breath. She knew she needed to help him, and Angus as well, but she hardly knew how to approach him. Her chest was tight, limbs cold, her heart beating too quickly. She moved softly toward them.

The duke heard her step and jerked his head up, ready with a snarl and a shout. Then he said, "Oh, it's you," and bent over Angus again.

Mary laid a hesitant hand on the duke's large shoulder. She rarely touched the man, who'd made it clear he didn't like sentimentality, but now he didn't flinch from her comfort.

"Ye have keys to all our rooms, do ye?" the duke asked without looking up. "Bloody English busybody."

Mary drew a shaky breath. "We need to lay Angus to rest," she said gently. "Let him go with honor."

The duke jerked from her touch. "Ye stay away from him."

"Father-in-law . . ."

The duke glared up at Mary, his golden eyes bloodshot, his face mottled red and white. "He's my boy, don't ye understand, woman? He's the only one who ever cared whether I lived or died. I won't let them take him away from me!"

His raw grief sent a wave of both fear and compassion through her. The duke was a hard man, uncomfortable with deeper emotions. He swam in a sea of bewilderment but was too enraged to take the hand stretched out to keep him from drowning.

Mary gathered her skirts and sank to her knees beside him. Her fingertips rested on the sofa's cushion near Angus's limp body. "All your sons love you very much, sir."

The duke had bowed over Angus again, but he shot her a sideways glance. "You're a dreamer, lass. Ye can't begin t' understand the Mackenzies. My lads don't know how t' love anything but themselves."

"You're wrong." A few months ago, Mary would never have dared to say such a thing to this daunting man, but she now drew the courage to speak. "Your sons are perfectly capable of loving. They wouldn't be so gentle with me if they weren't."

"'Course they're gentle with ye." The duke's voice had calmed the slightest bit. "You're a woman."

Mary bravely rested her hand on the duke's large knee. His body tightened, but he watched her, eyes glittering behind the graying hair that straggled down his face. He wanted the lifeline, Mary realized. Wanted to cease feeling as he did. She only hoped she could give it to him.

"I'm wise enough to know men aren't necessarily kind to women," she said, keeping her voice quiet. "Quite the opposite, in fact. It is easy to be cruel to those weaker in body than you are. Your sons have compassion, and caring. Let them give it to you."

The duke shook his head. "You're wrong, lass. Only Angus ever took care of me. When I needed my sons, Angus was the only one who answered. He looked after me. Always did."

"I know." Mary made herself study Angus, lying so cold and still, his eyes closed, never to open again. "And now you need to look after him. He died fighting valiantly, Duncan said. Let him be honored for that."

The duke drew Angus close, rocking him as he must have done when Angus had been a wee babe. This man had lived through so much—the loss of a wife he'd desperately loved, sons he'd grown estranged from, and now the destruction of his home and the death of the son he'd been closest to. He'd dealt with the horrors by defying them in his belligerent way, raging when the pain inside him became unbearable.

Mary, her heart full, gently squeezed his knee through the Mackenzie plaid that covered it. The duke grunted at the gesture, but when he looked up, his lined face wet, the terrible light had gone from his eyes.

"Ye have a way with ye, Mary." He wiped his cheeks with the back of his hand. "Mal had better watch out for that." The duke drew a long breath then let it out. "Let me sit vigil with him, child. Let me say good-bye tonight. Tomorrow, we'll lay him with his ancestors."

Mary climbed to her feet, her limbs aching. She put her hand on the duke's shoulder, then leaned down and kissed the top of his head. "I'll have your man send up something warm to eat."

The duke nodded, his attention returning to Angus. Mary left him, slipping away through the door to leave them alone.

Mal waited just outside. As Mary emerged, he shut the door for her then pulled her into the circle of his arms. He held her, not speaking, his head bowed to her shoulder.

They were so fragile, Mary realized, these men. In spite of their physical strength, their bluster, the ear-splitting loudness of their voices, they were vulnerable. Broken if struck the wrong way. They needed someone to love them, to care for them, to keep them whole.

After a time, Mal led her to the staircase landing and the window there, Malcolm looking out at the rain that had begun.

"I heard what ye said to him," he said quietly. "It was good of ye."

Mary rubbed his broad shoulder. "Your father needs you. No matter how much he denies it."

"Aye, I know." Malcolm gazed out at the rain again, his hand curling at his side.

Mary recognized the gesture. He clenched his fingers in that way when he was about to go for his dirk, or his sword.

"You want to fight, don't you?" she asked him.

Malcolm's expression was bleak. "Aye." He wouldn't look at Mary. "There'll have to be a stand, Will says, when Cumberland comes out of Aberdeen. I want to stand against him, to shove him away from Scotland."

"Then he'll come back," Mary said, fear lacing her. "Even if you defeat him and send him running back to England, he'll return, likely with more soldiers."

"Then we'll push him again. This is what Highlanders do—we fight to defend our homes against all comers. I've tried to keep us out of this mess, but both sides have dragged us straight into it."

"And you want to avenge your brother."

Mal nodded. "Aye, and my father. This has broken him. I want to make someone pay."

"Then go." Mary's heart was heavy, but she understood Malcolm's anger. She'd feel the same in defense of Audrey, Aunt Danae—Malcolm himself. "Go and do your worst. I'll be here, waiting for you." She lifted his clenched fist and pressed a kiss to it. "But you come back to me."

A ghost of Mal's grin broke through. "Aye, Mary. That I will. Nothing will ever keep me from you. Not Death himself. I promise ye that."

They buried Angus in the morning, in the family's tomb that had been cut directly into a hillside. It was an old place, with centuries of Mackenzies resting here. Angus was laid next to his mother and his brother Magnus. The stone above him was blank for the moment, but Mal had sent for stone cutters to come and chisel in his name. Everyone from Kilmorgan lands came to pay respect to the Mackenzie son, taken from them too soon.

The family ate a cheerless meal back at the house, in the darkened dining room. Mal picked at his food, his stomach roiling, his usually insatiable appetite gone. Duncan was ready to leave after they finished the meal. The duke said nothing, only nodded when Duncan declared he'd go.

"I'm going to murder Cumberland." Alec's voice rang through the room. Mal jumped, and Mary's head came up. She'd been quiet all morning, standing back and letting the family grieve. "I'll shoot him dead, then go off to France," Alec said. "I lost my wife, and my brother. I'm done."

Mal's heart ached for him. Mal and Alec had always been close, but Mal had known that Alec had a special bond with Angus, no matter how much both twins had scoffed at the idea. A man couldn't be born alongside another and not share that bond.

No one contradicted Alec. The duke only looked at him. Duncan grunted his agreement. "Aye, we'll deal with Cumberland. When I catch him, I'll save him for ye."

Mal felt Mary's eyes on him. She expected him to leap to his feet, offer to join Duncan when he rode away today, heading back to Inverness, where the Jacobites had holed up, waiting to fight.

Mal had no plans to go with Duncan. He saw no reason to kick his heels in Inverness—he and Alec would wait for Will's news that Cumberland had poked his head out of Aberdeen. If Cumberland tarried too long, Mal would go to Aberdeen himself and chop that head off.

No, he needed to bide his time, to plan. Let Duncan ride off, vowing revenge. Mal approached problems in a different way.

After the meal and seeing Duncan off, Mal took Mary's hand and led her to their bedchamber. Only with her could he release his grief, only in her arms could he find his comfort.

Weeks passed. Mal continued to restore his distillery, Mary to feather the nest of the cold stone house. The duke became quieter and more taciturn, but he didn't snarl any longer when Mary suggested improvements to the rooms, including the duke's. Mal's father began to look upon her with fondness, Mal was glad to note, letting Mary gently chivvy him into going on with life, keeping up his strength.

Before Will—who'd gone off again after Alec's funeral—could send any word about Cumberland, Duncan came barreling back home in the first week of April, announcing that gold from France and extra troops had landed in the north, only to be seized by Highlanders loyal to King George.

"We need that gold," Duncan said. "Cromartie is leading the Mackenzie clan to get it. We need someone like you, Mal. Come with us. Please."

Chapter 34

Mary said nothing at all as Malcolm turned away from Duncan and led her back up the stairs. He hadn't answered his brother, but Mary knew, from the way his hand pressed into hers, that he would go. In silence Mal took her into their bedchamber and closed and locked the door.

He pulled her to face him in the middle of the room, his amber eyes dark. Mal cupped Mary's face, studying her for a time, as though memorizing her, before he slowly kissed her.

Mary tasted the burn of the whisky he'd had at dinner and the spice that was his alone. Mal drew her closer, his fingers unfastening the back of her frock, finding the laces of her corset.

The kiss deepened as Malcolm pulled her bodice away, then the thin linen garment Mary wore between herself and her stays. The corset loosened, falling to the floor, baring her to Malcolm's touch. Malcolm caught the weight of her breasts in his hands and bent to her lips again.

His shirt was already loose, and when Mary tugged at it, Malcolm slid it off and dropped it onto the pile of her clothes. He came to her, bending down to kiss between her breasts.

"You're always beautiful, my Mary," he whispered, his breath hot on her skin. "Never more beautiful than when you're bare to me. And the way ye taste." Mal licked her breast. "The gods can't know anything this good."

Mary could only make a sound of need as Mal drew her breast into his mouth, fingers cupping it. The pull of his teeth sent darkness through Mary's body, heating and awakening her.

Mal slowly slid to his knees, pressed a kiss to her abdomen, and loosened her skirt. The waistband opened, and the skirt slid down, as did the linen underskirt beneath it. Mary hadn't worn panniers since she'd come to Kilmorgan, and now there was no barrier between her and Mal's mouth.

"And here, lass," he said, his voice soft as he grasped her hips with hot hands and kissed the curls at the join of her thighs. "Ye taste best of all."

Mary laced her fingers in the silk of Mal's hair, her feet moving apart, her body knowing what was coming.

Malcolm moved his hands to the inside of her thighs, thumbs caressing the soft flesh there. His whiskers burned her as he closed his eyes, came forward, and drank.

Mary's head went back, her hunger for him leaping high. Malcolm slid his tongue into her, licking, drinking her, while Mary's toes curled against the carpet.

Malcolm played his tongue over her opening and then suckled the bud that drove her wild. Mary cradled him closer, unworried that she stood naked, in stocking feet, in the middle of her chamber, while her husband knelt before her.

She rocked to him, succumbing to the rhythm he coaxed from her, letting sounds of pleasure escape her throat. Mary had learned how to dampen the noise, with so many people in this small house, but today, she couldn't quiet herself. Her cries poured out of her, notes of joy that echoed through the chamber.

As if in answer, Mal increased his torment. Finally, when Mary was nearly screaming, Mal released her and stood up. As cold brushed Mary's legs, Mal wrapped his arms around her and lowered her to the floor.

Their chamber's rug had been rescued from the castle—Mary had found it in one of the unburned cellars. The rug had a soft, thick pile, fine on the feet. The wool prickled Mary's back now, as Malcolm stripped off his kilt and met her, body to body.

Mal touched her face, eyes fixed on her. He slid his hand between her legs, where she was wet and very sensitive now, parting her thighs.

"I need ye, sweet Mary," he said, his voice thick. "So much right now, I don't know if I can go slowly."

Mary only nodded, the urgency in her matching what she saw in his eyes. Mal gave her a look that was almost despair and, in that moment, slid inside her.

Mary had never grown used to how big he was. Mal never hurt her, always easing himself in, drawing pleasure out of her with slow tenderness.

Today, however, his gentleness fled. Mal's thrusts came right away, hard and swift. She sensed him try to slow himself, but his face was drawn, as though it hurt him to try to stop.

Mary slid her hands down his back. "It's all right, Mal," she whispered. "Come to me, love."

The despair flashed again, then Malcolm closed his eyes and bent his head. His thrusts came harder, faster, a rush of need. They burned, and at the same time opened her to a pleasure Mary had never known.

She cried his name, begged with hands and body for him. The room filled with their voices, weaving together as their bodies did. Mary lost where she was, *who* she was. She was Malcolm's, body, heart, and soul.

Malcolm shouted. He came down on her, his hips moving, Mary's back digging into the carpet.

The peak of his frenetic need matched hers. They clutched each other, rocking together, separate and one at the same time.

As a Scottish wind rose to sing through the eaves, Malcolm collapsed, his body a warm weight on top of hers. He tumbled Mary's hair, cradled her, brushed slow, open-mouthed kisses over her lips.

"Mary," he whispered. "Ye know I love ye. I love ye so very much."

"I love *you*, Mal," Mary said, her eyes full, sorrow swooping in to dissolve her joy. "Please come back to me."

"Always." Mal raised his head, his expression holding white-hot Mackenzie determination. "Ye know I'll always come for ye, Mary. Ye'll never be rid of me that easy."

Riding away from Kilmorgan took all Mal's strength of will. He refused to look back, to lift a hand to Mary or even note whether she watched from the house. The feeling of her was still around him, filling him while his heart hurt. If Mal said good-bye to her, something inside him told him, then it would be forever.

Duncan was impatient to be gone. They took leave of their father, who was both unhappy to see them go but pleased they were off to cause trouble for the English. Duncan and Mal rode into the dusk together, heading for the road that would take them to the waiting column of Mackenzie clansmen.

They met the company five miles north of Kilmorgan, falling in with Highlanders marching hurriedly along in the gloom, the April night a chilly one. But before they had gone two steps, the commander, a dour Scotsman with ropy muscles, sought out Duncan to tell them that he'd been ordered back to Inverness.

"Why, for God's sake?" Duncan demanded. "I was to lead the men on the search."

"I got word while you stopped at home," the commander said. "They want you back in case Cumberland comes a'calling. The prince himself asked for ye. It's a compliment, man. Go."

Duncan looked unhappy. "If we dinnae get these supplies and money, there will be no falling back. The food and arms at Inverness are all we have."

"Aye, and Geordie Murray says they need everyone they can to defend them."

Mal broke in, trying to soothe his brother's temper. "Sounds like they want commanders who can bully the men to stand and fight, no matter what. That would be you, Dunc. Go on. I'll find the French gold and haul it back for ye."

Duncan scowled again. But he knew he had no choice, and Duncan was ever a man to be obedient to what he perceived was his duty. Finally he nodded, clasped hands with Malcolm, and turned and rode away, his plaids fluttering in the gathering twilight.

As Malcolm watched his oldest brother, the one he'd never

understood well, go from him, he realized that Duncan was the bravest and best of them. Duncan was not afraid to hold to his convictions. He wanted Scotland free of England's yoke, and he'd use any method, even a prince who was proving to be more of a liability than he was worth, to achieve it. If backing Charles didn't work, Duncan would find another way. Nothing would stop him.

The gloom swallowed Duncan, and he was gone. Malcolm turned north, his heart heavy, and fell in with the line of Mackenzies.

The search for the French gold turned frustrating quickly. No one knew where the bloody stuff was. Malcolm and his clansmen beat the bushes all over the north, looking for the remains of the regiment who'd stolen the cargo.

They did come across plenty of men to skirmish with. Just because Lord Loudon's army had been dispersed, Loudon fleeing to the west, the remnants of that army hadn't necessarily ceased fighting. The wild Highland lads enjoyed it too much.

Most of the northern lands, too, were loyal to the English throne, for reasons Mal did not understand. As they battled, though, he began to see that these Highlanders were a bit like him—they didn't want *anyone* ruling them but their clan chiefs.

The military roads had ended far south of them at Inverness, and these remote clans had been more or less left alone for centuries. If English King George stayed in London and never ventured this far, that would be fine with them. The Stuart Prince Teàrlach was proving annoyingly demanding.

Mal fought hard at the head of the troop he led. Sometimes they were victorious, sometimes Mal knew when to call a retreat, but mostly the Highlanders chased one another around the treeless hills, neither side accomplishing much of anything.

Finally, Mal's company received the order to march back south. Cumberland wouldn't wait much longer to strike, the messages said, and Murray needed every able body in Inverness.

Mal happily abandoned the pursuit of French gold, which had become just about mythical by now. No doubt the contingent of Highlanders who'd originally seized it had taken it, divided it, tucked it away. The Jacobite troops couldn't raid every croft in every glen.

Mal's home and Mary were at the end of the road, and Malcolm happily turned his steps toward her.

At least he did until Will Mackenzie found him, just as the column was approaching Dunrobin Castle, seat of the Dukes of Sutherland.

Will came riding flat out up the road, making for the commander. "Cumberland's left Aberdeen," he said breathlessly. "He's advancing on Inverness and Teàrlach's army there. *Right now.*"

"Bloody hell." The commander spat on the road. "While we're dancing around up here? Go tell Murray we're marching as fast as we can."

Will nodded, unworried about playing messenger. Mal, however, watched him narrowly, and turned aside with him. No doubt Will knew exactly where Cumberland was, what his plans were, when the man would reach Inverness, what he'd eaten for breakfast, and the color of his underclothes.

"Ye didn't come up here just to pass on orders," Malcolm said in a low voice. "Ye'd have sent someone for that. What is it?"

Will's eyes were quiet, all mirth gone. "The news of Cumberland's advance reached Kilmorgan before I could get there. Dad and Alec have gone south, off to fight for Charles."

Tightness gripped Mal's chest. "Ah, *damn* it! What the devil did they do that for?" Kilmorgan had been raided, yes, but beating off raiders was a far cry from facing down Cumberland's mighty army.

"Dad didn't want Duncan to go alone. He's afraid for him, Mal." Will held Malcolm's gaze, all signs of his usual humor absent. "*I'm* afraid. Almost all battles up until now have been skirmishes or routs. There's been a lot of feinting, no out-and-out thrusts. This will be different. No going back. Come and help me save them, Mal."

Mal barely heard the last of his speech. He was thinking of the brother, Magnus, he'd lost long ago, of opening the door and finding him on the floor, his life gone. And then Angus, lying gray with death on his father's lap. He thought of Duncan riding off into the darkness days ago, his plaids flowing around him, the white rose on his bonnet the last thing to fade.

Something gripped Mal's heart. He was losing his family, one by one, and nothing he'd done had been able to stop it.

"Mary?" he asked, his lips barely able to form her name. "Please tell me she hasn't taken up a claymore and followed them."

"She's safe at Kilmorgan," Will said.

Mal nodded, hiding the relief that made him want to slide to the ground in a heap. He settled into his saddle, pulling his plaid closer about him. "Cromartie is leading these men south, but they'll be too slow," he said with conviction. "Think ye can keep up with me?"

Will's grin broke through. "Can *I* keep up with *you*? Who d' ye think you're talking to, runt?"

"Then we go."

Mal broke from the column and headed off down a path, Will following. No one stopped them going. They knew Mal and they knew Will, and would understand.

The two had ridden only about half a mile when they heard shouting behind them, then firing, explosions, a cacophony of sound. They turned back as one, making for the top of the hill they'd just descended.

Mal gazed down in amazement at the scene. Red-coated soldiers boiled out of hills and the flat area surrounding the castle, and more were coming up from the sea. They converged on the Mackenzie columns, hundreds swarming, shouting, roaring their triumph. Gunfire peppered the air, smoke floating into the gray sky. Men met, shot, engaged, fought.

"*Shite,*" Mal said.

Soldiers whom Mal had joked with, eaten with not an hour ago, screamed as they died, crumpling into blood and death. The entire contingent of men Mal and Will had left were surrounded, fighting for their lives. The commander leapt forward on his horse, claymore raised, and died when two shots slammed him out of his saddle.

Mal swung his horse around, ready to charge to them and help. Will, who fought by different rules, grabbed Mal's horse by the bridle.

"We need to go," Will said swiftly. "We can't do anything if we go back but die heroically. Won't help Dad or Mary."

Malcolm swallowed. He saw more Highlanders shot, fall,

Mackenzies who'd never see their lands again, their homes, their families. Bile bit his throat as he conceded that Will was right.

"Damn it," Mal growled.

Will gave him a nod. Mal saw the same conflict in his brother, the need to help his fellows warring with the need to protect his family, to live to fight another day. Will must have to face these kinds of decisions all the time.

Mal made himself turn his horse and follow Will back down the hill. Behind them, the Mackenzie clansmen died or were taken, their part in this war over.

The trouble with traveling south quickly was the firths. Between Malcolm and Inverness was Dornoch Firth, Cromarty, and Beauly, inlets of the sea that pushed across the land. The roads Mal and Mary had used on their way to Kilmorgan took travelers far inland around the firths, but this cost time.

Mal and Will skirted the shores of Dornoch, eyeing the fishing boats moored there, but none looked sturdy enough to float them across. If Mal had been able to summon Gair, he would have, but even though he'd put out word that he was looking for the smuggler, there wasn't time to wait for him.

The two brothers cut back east after they left Dornoch and reached Cromarty Firth. There, as they searched a village on the north shore for a craft that might take them across, a tall Scotsman came off a dock and strode to them.

"Malcolm Mackenzie, isn't it?" he asked, eyes crinkling in the corners. "I hear you're looking to take ship."

Mal recognized him as the injured man he and Mary had rescued from the English soldiers not many months ago. He was injured no longer, striding proudly along the dock, moving with only a slight limp.

"Calan Macdonald," Mal said, dismounting and clasping the man's hand. "Well met. Aye, m' brother and me, we're off to crush Cumberland's army. But if we don't hurry, we might miss our chance."

"That is a worry," Calan said with slow Scots deliberation. "As it happens, I have a ship. A little merchantman. It's at your service, Lord Malcolm. I told ye I owed ye a favor."

Chapter 35

Calan's ship took them out between the Suitors to the open sea, then back into Beauly Firth and so to Inverness.

Malcolm and Will landed on the sixteenth of April, to find the armies already out of Inverness, gone to meet Cumberland in a field near Culloden House.

They hastened the few miles there, covering it in less than thirty minutes. Gunfire popped in the distance, then the roar of men fighting came at them in a wave of sound, punctuated by the shrill wail of the pipes. Mal and Will halted near the edge of the field, catching their breaths and surveying the scene.

Colors swirled across the open moor—the red of English soldiers; the blue, red, and dun of plaids; the bright coats of dragoons. Flags moved forward, precious standards that flapped in the wind. The ground was littered with bodies, the black red of blood washing into the grass. Smoke drifted upward to mix with mist, lending to the confusion.

Will seized Mal's arm. "Find Dad and Alec—there are things I can do. Meet up here afterward?"

"Aye. Give 'em hell."

There were things Mal could do as well. Today he wanted to stand and fight, to find Cumberland's standard and take the man's life, but he'd become the *brollachan* again if that were the only way. The next few minutes would decide.

Will clasped Mal in a hug, Will's tall body crushing Mal's, the scent of wool and damp Mackenzie cutting the acrid stench of gunpowder. Will released Mal, then sprinted away, disappearing into mist in the way only Will could.

Malcolm loaded his pistols, straightened his weapons, and made for the battlefield and the sounds of the pipers.

I love ye, Mary, he said silently as he broke into a run. *Never forget that.*

A quarter of an hour later, Mal realized that the battle was lost. He ran through marshy ground, trying to find a solid path, his boots sinking into mud and water. Bodies lay everywhere, blood mixing with water on the damp ground. The smoke, stink, and damp hampered him, as did the pockets of soldiers that swarmed him, a lone Highlander, and tried to cut him down.

Mal fought with dirk and claymore, diving under the reach of those with pistols and muskets, spinning from bayonet thrusts to sink his dirk into the men trying to kill him. The stink of blood splashing him made him sick, but at the same time awakened the warrior that lurked beneath his surface. Mal knew how to fight and how to live. No heroic and legendary last stands for him.

He'd found no Jacobite company he recognized, no clans he knew, in spite of the pipers still calling to clansmen. Mal didn't find his own family either, until he broke away from a skirmish to make for an open area of the battlefield.

He saw them to his left, amid smoke and mists floating over the ground. There was Duncan, swinging his deadly sword at a knot of soldiers in red, bellowing as loudly as the duke had ever done. Near him was their father, also with sword and dirk, and Alec, firing a musket into the line. There was no order—they were fighting on their own, as so many were.

Malcolm ran for his father and brothers. Mists flowed up from the damp ground, obscuring his vision. He was aching and tired, his right side stinging where a redcoat had gotten in a lucky jab. His plaids were covered with blood, most of it not his own. His hair, uncovered, was wet, water and sweat dripping into his eyes and smarting.

The mists cleared before him in time for Mal to see Duncan's body jerk, a spray of red spattering outward from his back. Mal heard Alec's cry of rage as he sprang in front of Duncan, musket gone and sword raised, as Duncan fell and lay still. Smoke billowed upward, obscuring the scene, but Mal had seen.

A roar worthy of his father surged from Mal's throat. He rushed through the closing lines, swinging claymore and dirk, cutting through Cumberland's soldiers between himself and his brother. The men who'd shot Duncan converged on the family, and Mal sprinted toward them, his throat hoarse from his raw shouts.

The duke had gone down on his knees next to Duncan, reaching for his son. Alec stood over them both, sword swinging to defend them.

A musket ball whistled by Mal, missing him by an inch. Mal dove forward, rolling through the mud, and came up at his family's side. Cumberland's men, muskets spent, tried to draw sabers, but not quickly enough.

A strange, red rage rose up in Malcolm, one that took over his body and his thoughts. He felt nothing, no pain, no grief, naught but this fury. Mal cut and thrust, knocked weapons from men's hands, plunged his sword and dirk into flesh. There were five soldiers on him, then four, then three.

Alec was with him, his face set, blades working. Back-to-back the brothers fought, until the remaining men lay dead at their feet.

Malcolm's breath came back to him with a slap. The battlefield returned to focus, and with it, his family, and Duncan. His brother was dying.

Mal dropped to his knees next to Duncan. At least three musket balls had gone through him, blood soaking through his kilt in a gush of red. Mal's oldest brother, who'd driven him mad since he could remember, struggled to breathe, blood slipping from his mouth to trickle down his chin.

"Help me with him," the duke said, looking at Alec. "Angus . . ."

Mal went cold, but Alec didn't correct him. He only nodded and bent to slip his hands under Duncan.

"Don't." Duncan closed a hard hand over Mal's wrist. There was strength in the grip, though Duncan's eyes were clouding over, and he couldn't raise his head. "Don't drag me off to die in pain waiting for Cumberland's soldiers to come for me. Give me some peace."

"We'll get you to a surgeon," Alec said quickly. "We'll nurse ye back t' health, and ye can snarl at us all while we do it."

Duncan smiled, and that's when Mal knew it was too late. "I'm as full of holes as a sieve. Ye can't put me back together. I'd die of rot and fever, and ye know it. Spare me that, eh?"

The duke brushed Duncan's hair from his face, stark sorrow in his golden eyes. "I'll do it. I understand, son."

Duncan's hand tightened on Mal's wrist. "You look after him now," he said to him. "He needs you."

A hard lump blocked Mal's throat. He swallowed, and nodded. "Aye. I will."

"Thank you." Duncan kept hold of Mal, but transferred his wavering gaze to his father. "Do it."

The duke's face was streaked with tears. There were lines there Mal hadn't seen before Angus's death and more gray in the red-brown hair. His father had become an old man in a matter of weeks.

Alec lifted a pistol from his holster and passed it to his father. The duke checked it, making sure it was loaded, the pan primed. This had to be a sure shot, and not leave Duncan alive and in pain, ready to be captured by the enemy.

The duke again brushed his son's hair from his forehead, taking with it the bonnet and Charles Stuart's badge of the white rose. He tucked the bonnet under his kilt, and touched Duncan's face again.

"Good-bye, son."

Duncan's smile widened. "Thank ye, Da."

The duke firmed his mouth, placed the pistol in the center of Duncan's forehead, and fired.

Duncan's eyes, which had remained open and fixed on his father, went blank. The hand that had held Mal's wrist went slack, and dropped.

The duke remained on his knees, the pistol at Duncan's

head. His body began to heave, the sobs that he'd held back rising up to engulf him.

Shouting came at them in waves. Cumberland's men were returning.

"Dad." Mal got to his feet, grabbing his father's arm. "We have to go."

The duke shook his head. "I can't leave him."

Mal felt new strength surge through him. It was as though Duncan had passed the last of his vitality through the conduit of his hand into his brother.

"He told us to look after ye," Mal said, voice firm. "So we're looking after ye. They're coming. We have to go."

The duke stared down at Duncan, slowly moving the pistol from him. He drew another breath, and Mal saw him deliberately suppress his sobs. He handed the pistol back to Alec, closed Duncan's eyes, arranged his son's hands over his chest, and covered him with his plaid.

Alec and Mal helped their father to his feet. Around them the English army surged, determined in this last blow to crush the rebellion forever.

"Come on," Alec said. "We need t' hurry."

The duke nodded. "All right, Angus. Stop fussing."

Mal and Alec exchanged a glance, pain sharp in Alec's eyes. He said nothing, only pushed his father into the smoke, away from Duncan's body.

They didn't make it out of the field. Soldiers saw them and came for them. Mal had his sword out again, Alec his pistol and dirk. The duke let out a Highland battle scream and ran at them, all his grief in his voice.

The English soldiers fired, bayoneted, drew swords. Alec shot then threw down his pistol, attacking in a flurry of plaid and blades.

The three men fought side by side, ducking blows, raining them down in return. Around them smoke clouded the field, and the stink of shot and the screams of the dying clogging Mal's senses.

Malcolm saw his father go down, Alec dive on top of him to defend him to the last. Mal leapt for them both, but something caught him on the side of the head.

He spun around, sword and knife flashing. A bayonet came

at his chest, and he slammed it away. Another blow to the head, from the back of the musket this time, and Mal fell. His sword, made by one of the best sword masters in Scotland, tumbled from his hand and plunged into the earth, the hilt standing straight up.

This battle has slain Scotland, Malcolm thought dizzily, then something else heavy crashed on him, and everything went blank.

Mary . . .

Mary found Duncan in the middle of the battlefield. Around her, the British soldiers were rounding up the Highlanders with ruthless efficiency, marching them off or simply killing them in place. It was over.

Mary saw one man in plaid struggle to crawl away, to reach the border of the field. A red-coated British infantryman walked up to the Highlander and calmly shot him dead. Mary pulled her plaids more securely around her, turning from the sight.

She'd traveled from Kilmorgan when Ewan, who had come running home from who knew where, told her that Will had gone off to find Mal and drag him to the battle against Cumberland. Will had sent Ewan back to keep Mary informed, and also to take care of her.

Mary put together a small pack of belongings and marched off down the road toward Inverness. She'd not stay in Kilmorgan, wringing her hands and waiting. She wanted to be close as soon as the battle's outcome was known.

She knew in her heart what it would be. If Malcolm was going to die in defense of his land, she would be there to bring him home.

Mary did not want to take a child into such danger, but Ewan wouldn't leave her. He had no one but his gran in Edinburgh and Mary, whom he still stubbornly called his captain. He'd followed her from Kilmorgan, and Mary gave up leaving him, not daring to take the time to return him to safety. This afternoon, though, she made sure he stayed in Inverness, away from the fighting.

She heard rumor after rumor as she made her way from Inverness to Culloden House. Charles Stuart had fled the field, running for his life. The British soldiers were pursuing Highlanders down the road to Inverness, and to the forts the Jacobites had taken. Everywhere men were surrendering, or fighting to the last drop of blood. The soldiers had been told to give the Scots no quarter—they were to die, whether they surrendered or not.

Mary avoided any man she'd seen in a British uniform, and even those in Highland dress. Too many Scotsmen had fought for Cumberland for her to simply trust a man in plaid. She hid, putting the lessons Malcolm had taught her to use.

Malcolm. The syllables of his name drove her on. Mary refused to let herself think of his touch in the night, his amber eyes that could flash from anger to sinfulness to laughter, and back to wickedness in a heartbeat. If she existed in anything but numbness, she'd collapse and never rise.

The first Mackenzie she came upon was Duncan. He lay on his back, a plaid covering him, his hands folded over his chest as though he'd been laid out to rest. Bodies lay around Duncan, heaps of plaid unmoving, cloth fluttering in the wind. Mary's heart squeezed so hard it nearly stopped beating.

So many. Each one could be a Mackenzie, from the duke to Malcolm.

For a long time, Mary only stood and looked at the men around her. They were dead, no movement, blood long since dried. She'd have to go to them, turn them over, see who they were.

Somehow she believed that if she didn't discover Malcolm dead here, didn't look into his face and know he breathed no more, he would be all right. So would Alec, and Will, and the duke. If she never looked, they would never be gone. She could go through her life believing they'd survive, were somewhere in the world, lifting a whisky and remembering her.

A man rode across the grass toward her. He wore a surly look, and had his saber out, ready to strike.

Mary pulled the plaid back from her head and gaped at him in shock. At the last minute the cavalryman swerved, lowering his blade, but he swung his horse around and came back to her.

"Clear off, woman!" he yelled. "Or I'll arrest you as a traitor."

The man's accent put him from somewhere in Lincolnshire, the familiar vowels stirring a strange longing. Mary lifted her chin, gazing up at him with all the haughtiness of a peer's daughter.

"I am Lady Mary Lennox," she said clearly. "Am I not to be given leave to collect my dead?"

"Not if they were Charlie's men, ma'am . . . my lady. There'll be a grave for them, don't you worry."

"I am taking this man." She pointed at Duncan. "Have someone arrange for a litter for me."

"No, my lady." The cavalryman wasn't going to budge. "Now, you have to clear off. The men have orders to finish off anyone in Highlander clothes, and they might not stop themselves running you through until it's too late. I'd go."

Mary didn't move. "A litter, sir, if you please."

The man growled. "I don't care if you're the daughter of his majesty the king. Clear off." He brought his sword up and pointed the tip directly at her chest.

Hooves rumbled, and another dragoon rode straight at the first one. The cavalryman started, then wheeled his horse as the second dragoon pushed himself between him and Mary.

"Leave her be, Lieutenant," came the voice of Captain Ellis. "That's an order. *Go!*"

The cavalryman looked furious, but he turned his horse and rode away, shaking his head.

Captain Ellis swung to the ground. "Lady Mary, you can't be here."

Mary clenched her hands, fighting a shaking that threatened to overwhelm her. "I have to take them home."

Ellis glanced down at Duncan, recognized him. His jaw tightened. "I'm sorry."

"Please, let me take him away from here. The duke will want him buried properly. And I have to find the others. Malcolm . . ."

Her voice broke. She could hold her bravado with her enemies—rage saw to that. But Captain Ellis was a friend, and that she feared. If she let down her guard, with it would go her strength.

Captain Ellis came to her. "I'll see to it," he said. "I promise you. And I'll look for the others. But you have to go from here, all right?"

Mary could barely stand. Her eyes burned, the tears refusing to come. "Malcolm. I can't leave without my husband."

Ellis's eyes widened. "He married you?"

Mary tugged off her thick glove enough to show him the gleam of gold on her finger. "Properly. Witnessed and all."

Something flickered in Ellis's eyes. His face was drawn, and for a moment, Mary thought he'd turn away and abandon her. Then he gave her a nod, his polite mask coming down.

"I'll find him." He brought his horse forward and boosted Mary into its saddle, the strength of his hands a sharp contrast to her shaking body. Ellis signaled to another cavalryman, who rode quickly over.

"This is Lieutenant Carter," Captain Ellis said. "He'll look after you. Take Lady Mary back to camp, Carter, and make sure she's safe. I'll join you there."

Lieutenant Carter made her a polite bow from his saddle. He was younger than Ellis, fresh-faced despite his blood-stained uniform and smoke-grimed face. "Yes, sir. My lady?" He turned his horse in such a way that it nudged Ellis's. Ellis's horse, well trained, fell into step.

Mary looked back. The lumps of plaid lay unmoving in the middle of Culloden field, left in the care of a British cavalryman, who'd do his best by them.

Chapter 36

Will Mackenzie slipped through shadows, his eyes burning—there was so much smoke, and the wind carried it straight over him.

He'd watched, from a corner of a wall, as his father took Alec's pistol and shot his brother Duncan dead. Will had sworn he could hear the pistol's retort even through the roar of cannon and musket fire. The distinct *pop* of the black powder tore a hole through his heart.

Duncan, gone. Damn the stupid, brave, blustering, pain-in-the-ass bastard.

Now Lord Will Mackenzie was heir to the dukedom of Kilmorgan. *Damn ye, Duncan, look what ye've done t' me.*

Will hated tears. They got in the way when a man had to slip out into the night or read a message that might mean the difference between life and death.

He wiped his eyes, blinking, as he ran. He hadn't been able to see, around mists and the soldiers that surged between him and the field, what had happened to his father, Mal, and Alec. But Mal would make sure they were all right. Mal was a genius at surviving and ensuring others did too. Mal would return to

Kilmorgan, take Mary somewhere safe, and live happily ever after.

Will had a fondness for Mal that ran deep. The little runt got away with everything. He deserved the love he'd found with Mary.

A dragoon lieutenant came riding out of the smoke straight at Will. The man had his pistol drawn, which made sense, Will thought. A saber wouldn't work with the angle he'd have to approach Will, who ran along a wall at the edge of a farmer's field, but a pistol was good at close range.

Will watched the dragoon clamp his legs around his horse, turning him and urging him forward at the same time. The dragoon pointed his pistol as he thundered by, and fired.

At nothing. A pistol ball struck mortar where Will had been. Will rolled from where he'd slammed himself to the ground, came up behind the dragoon, grabbed the man by knee and thigh, and tore him out of the saddle.

As the dragoon climbed to his feet, steadying himself for a fight, Will vaulted into the saddle, turned the horse, and galloped into the mists, disappearing like a ghost before the dragoon could so much as shout.

Alec Mackenzie dragged his father to Gair Murray's small ship, which rocked in the twilight at the end of a pier. The duke was flagging, his strength gone. Alec held him upright, pulling him along, fearing he'd not get his father to safety before the man collapsed and couldn't be moved.

Alec heard shouting, gunshots, the clang of steel. A knot of British soldiers were trying to commandeer the ship, and Gair and his men were fighting hard. It spoke volumes about how much Mal had paid Gair that he was still there at all.

The duke came alert and drew his dirk, showing he was not yet ready to cease fighting. He and Alec charged down the pier, Alec's claymore raised.

The bulky form of Padruig, Gair's mate, slammed himself in front of them. He shoved Alec toward the ship at the same time he fired two pistols, one into each soldier that had been coming for Alec and the duke.

Padruig tossed the pistols behind him into the boat and pushed Alec at the gangplank. "Get aboard."

The duke was fighting madly with more soldiers who'd run down the dock. He was laughing, enjoying it. Alec grabbed his father by his plaids and hauled him around. The duke's eyes were full of fire, but he followed Alec and leapt down the gangway to the deck.

Padruig landed after them. The boat was already moving, the ropes cut, the gangplank quickly lifted.

"We need t' wait for Malcolm," the duke shouted.

Alec had his hand on his father's arm. "Mal's not coming, Dad." His chest was tight. "I saw him go down."

A soldier with a bayonet had plunged it straight toward Mal's body. No one could have survived a blow like that, not even Mal. A moment later, Alec had dodged a sword blade coming for *him*, then had gained his feet and dragged his father away. Alec had looked back, hoping he'd see Mal spring up again, shouting and cursing in his wild way, but Mal never appeared.

Alec had known that if he did not take his father to safety, the man would die a sure death. If Mal could get away, he would. Their father couldn't, not on his own. And Alec's daughter waited, across the stretch of water, for him to come. Alec had made the gut-wrenching decision and pulled his father away.

"Get them below!" Gair shouted. "Let's see if we can avoid the whole bloody British navy, damn and blast it."

Padruig sheathed his sword, ignored a pistol shot from the mooring that barely missed him, and led them to a cabin below. It was Gair's cabin, which stretched across the entire stern, its small lights showing murky darkness behind them. Padruig, without word, left them.

The duke collapsed onto the bunk, his claymore and dirk falling from his hands. Alec braced himself against the sudden roll of the ship, pulled out Gair's whisky decanter, and poured two glasses. He brought one to his father, who took it between shaky fingers.

"To Duncan," the duke said, raising the heavy cut crystal glass. Gair could put his hands on the best of everything. "And Mal. Damn the bloody English."

"Aye," Alec said. He drank, the whisky burning.

The duke thunked his empty glass to the table and heaved a sigh. "Angus," he said irritably, "where the hell are we going?"

Alec chilled, and he poured another swallow of whisky down his throat. "Paris," he said. He set his glass next to his father's. "I'm Alec, Dad. Angus is dead."

The duke put a hand over his eyes and sat thusly for a long moment. When he raised his head, his expression was weary. "Aye, I know. It comforts me t' say his name." He slowly sat up straight. "Paris, eh? Does this mean I get to meet me granddaughter?"

Alec's bleak heart warmed at the thought of his daughter, Jenny. He hadn't seen her in months, and his entire being craved her. He would take her in his arms, kiss her little face, and never leave her again.

"Aye," he said. "God help her."

The duke barked a short laugh, and then they were silent, as the waves of the open sea took the boat toward their destination.

At camp, word went around who Mary was, and she was greeted more as a released prisoner than a woman who'd run away with a Scotsman. She was taken to a large house where the commanders had set up base and given a room, food, and coffee. A few of the men in charge knew her father and promised to send him word that she was well. They were deferential to her, as such men would be to the daughter of an important peer.

Captain Ellis returned after midnight. Mary was still awake, unable to sleep, unable to do much but pace.

Ellis gave her a polite bow when he entered the sitting room she met him in, but Mary was too stiff and agitated to curtsy in response.

"Duncan's body is ready to be taken back to Kilmorgan," Captain Ellis said. "I have made sure you will not be hampered in any way as to that."

"Thank you," Mary said sincerely. "And the others?"

Ellis hesitated, but the look in his eyes told Mary all she needed to know. "I never found their bodies. I'm sorry."

Mary's heart pounded swiftly, her throat closing up. "What are you saying? That they escaped?" But she knew he didn't mean that.

Ellis let out a sigh. "Mary, there were so many. His Grace of Cumberland has ordered that the Jacobites be given no quarter. The wounded are being killed instead of tended to, those likeliest to live taken off to trial and execution. No Jacobite Highlander is going home alive from this."

Mary stared at him. "But he can't. They surrendered. The war is over, and Prince Charles is gone. They should be left in peace."

Ellis shook his head. "Not this time. The fear is that the clans will try to rise again—they did a good job of it this time, until the end. Cumberland wants to crush the rebels once and for all."

Mary couldn't answer. Ellis was saying that even if Malcolm had managed to elude death, he'd be pursued, cut down or arrested, taken to London, hanged. Her breath wouldn't come, and blackness danced before her eyes.

Captain Ellis caught her as she collapsed. She found herself seated on a couch, the captain's steadying hand on her arm. "I'm sorry, Mary. So sorry."

Still the tears would not come. "You believe they're dead, then."

Ellis slid a paper from his pocket. "Culloden's men are making lists of those dead or taken prisoner as they go through the field. I was able to get a partial one." He unfolded the paper and held it out to her.

Mary didn't want to look at it. As on the battlefield, she thought that if she didn't see, the worst would not have happened. She'd go home and believe Malcolm alive, somewhere out in the world, the *brollachan* causing trouble wherever he went.

But she had to know. Mary had told Malcolm she was resilient, stronger than he realized. She could not go through life wondering, waiting for him, always uncertain.

She took the paper from Captain Ellis. It was a list of names, a long list, so many Mackenzies. She'd heard that much of the extended clan had perished at Dunrobin Castle, but the number at Culloden looked large to her eyes.

They'd been listed in alphabetical order:

Mackenzie, Alec William
Mackenzie, Daniel Duncannon
Mackenzie, Daniel William (Duke of Kilmorgan)

Farther down the list was:

Mackenzie, Malcolm Daniel

And finally, near the bottom:

Mackenzie, William Ferdinand

Mary pressed the paper to her face, and closed her eyes.

Mary took Duncan's body back to Kilmorgan. Captain Ellis obtained leave to go with her, and she fetched Ewan from Inverness along the way. She and the Kilmorgan servants gathered to lay Duncan in the family tomb next to his mother and brothers.

Captain Ellis had never found the bodies of the others, though he'd diligently searched. They'd likely already been buried, he'd been told, in a grave with so many others.

Mary asked the stonecutter from the village, who'd come to carve Angus's name beneath *Magnus Hart Mackenzie* to add the others, in order of birth.

She waited, watching, while he carved out the name *Malcolm Daniel Mackenzie.*

Mary traced the letters, her fingers memorizing the feel of the words. She heard the whisper of his voice in the soft Highland wind—

Nothing will ever keep me from you. Not Death himself. I promise ye that.

Mary left Kilmorgan the next morning, and went home to Lincolnshire.

Malcolm slipped through the mists and the shadows, running, crawling, flattening himself against the ground.

He'd survived the battlefield by a piece of damned, bloody luck. When Mal had come to, surprised he wasn't dead, he'd been underneath an Englishman, the bayonet that had killed the man digging into the ground half an inch from Malcolm's ribs.

Rain had been falling in the darkness, mists swirling around him like ghosts. He'd heard voices, Cumberland's soldiers wandering the field, looking for survivors. Mal had heard the occasional crack of a pistol or laughter, and English voices. *That slid right into him like a knife through butter. Skewered with his own claymore. Nice blade. Will take it home to show the wife.*

Mal had lain motionless, one of the dead, until there was relative quiet around him. And then, inch by inch, he'd crawled, the dead Englishman still on top of him, out through the dark, the way slow and perilous.

He'd wormed himself along through black mud, dizzy from the blow that had knocked him cold, muck seeping into his mouth and nose. He halted when anyone neared, fearing they'd lift the English soldier off him and shoot Mal through the head just to make sure he was dead.

At the edge of the field, he'd found trees. Once under their cover, he'd quietly rolled the English soldier over, undressed him, and stolen his clothes, pistol, bullets, dagger, and few coins in his pocket. Then he'd laid the man out for his fellows to find, and slipped into the darkness.

Mal refused to let himself think. His brothers and father were gone, perhaps all dead. It was over.

Mal's only thought, the driving force in his world, was that he needed to get to Mary. She was safe at Kilmorgan, but she wouldn't be for long. Cumberland's men were spreading out, searching the Highlands, killing anything in plaid. She was in danger—as was everyone on Kilmorgan lands. He'd make his way home and run with Mary to France.

Everything Mal had tried to avoid this past year—everything he'd vowed he'd not let happen—had happened. He'd become a traitor to the crown, and his only destination, if Mal remained in Scotland, was the end of a rope.

He was already a long way from Culloden when he watched from the shelter of a copse three Highland men be surrounded by soldiers and bayoneted. They died bravely, did those lads, but they died.

Malcolm played the *brollachan* again that night, burning a wagonload of supplies, but not before stealing some food and brandy. The commander's tent went up in flames; the horses broke free and ran. One lieutenant came tearing out of the woods where he'd been helping himself to a young woman, his trousers halfway down his thighs. He gibbered about strange lights in the woods and a wild animal that had attacked him. As he spoke, more tents caught fire, and the lieutenant screamed.

You'll like this story, Mary, Mal thought, as he took the young woman to the safety of her family.

He reached Kilmorgan after many days of erratic travel, mostly at night, slowed by rain, cold, and dense darkness. Mal went a long way west, around the firths, to come at Kilmorgan from the north. The English were searching into the west and the islands, since Charles Stuart was rumored to have escaped that way. Mal wouldn't chance seeking out help from Rabbie or Calan Macdonald, knowing that he'd only endanger those men, whom Mal hoped had wisely fled.

He came to Kilmorgan on a blustery day. Mal didn't approach the house that was the distillery directly—he hid and watched to see if soldiers had come to arrest him. He saw no sign of uniforms, but carts stood in the courtyard outside the distillery, waiting to take things and people away. Good.

Mal left his shelter and made his way silently down the hill, slipping into the house without announcing himself.

Ewan saw him first. Malcolm had started up the stairs just as the lad ran out of the kitchens with a bag of something bulky.

Ewan let out a shriek. He dropped the bag, which proved to be full of oats. Malcolm caught it before it fell to the floor, then Ewan launched himself at Malcolm.

"Me lord, me lord, we thought you was dead!"

The retainers rushed out to see what Ewan was yelling about. There were shouts, cries, and hearty relief. "Lord Malcolm. Ye've come!" "Aye, I thought you were a ghost." "What happened to ye, lad? We've gone and buried ye!"

Malcolm waved them all quiet and pried Ewan's clinging arms from around him. "Where's Mary?"

Everyone talked at once until Malcolm held up his hands again. "Stop it! Ye're makin' me ears ache. Ewan—where is me wife?"

"Gone, sir." Ewan swallowed, his young face serious. "She put up a stone to ye and your dad and brothers, then she went home to England."

Wise of her. If Mary thought Malcolm dead, if she understood what was happening in the Highlands, she'd go to ground in the safest place she knew. Her father would take care of her, would not let one hair on her head be harmed.

On the other hand, it was unlike Mary to leave people in trouble. She was very loyal, and she'd come to be fond of Ewan, Jinty, and the others. So why had she left the duke's retainers here, believing no one was alive to come home for them? She might have reasoned that they'd find safety deeper in the Highlands on their own . . . or Mary had returned to England to preserve someone more than only herself.

The thought took hold of Malcolm, and would not leave him.

"You lot, clear out," Mal said to the others. "Take anything ye need from this place—it's yours. Ye've worked for it. But scatter. Burn your plaids and go anywhere far from here. They're calling him Butcher Cumberland for a reason."

Jubilation waned, faces paled, and they gave him nods. Malcolm left them to it, but took Ewan aside.

"You, lad, I have a commission for ye."

Chapter 37

When Mary rode up the drive of Stokesay Court, the ancestral home of the Earls of Wilfort, she had a feeling of unreality.

She'd left here a young lady of not much experience, in a velvet-lined carriage, cocooned against the world. She'd thought herself wise and practical, saving romance for her younger, prettier sister. Mary returned on horseback, wrapped in a man's black cloak, escorted by a dragoon captain who, ten months ago, would have been considered far beneath her station.

She'd been abducted, rescued, married, drawn into a family of obsessive and passionate men, and had fallen in love as she'd never believed she could. Mary loved Malcolm with all her heart and now she grieved with that same intensity.

Stokesay Court, a square, tall, Palladian-style house was elegant, austere, and tidy, the exact opposite of Kilmorgan. Kilmorgan had been an ancient jumble, new piled on top of old, made cozy by its inhabitants. The Earl of Wilfort's house was cold, regular, and constrained, and now Mary wondered that she had ever found it beautiful.

At the same time, her heart beat hard in relief. She was home. She'd grown up here, played here, learned here, loved her family. This house was her refuge from a world that had turned cruel, and now it was where she needed to keep herself safe.

But whether Mary would be welcome she did not know. She hadn't been able to send a letter to her father since the missive she'd written him in December, and he'd never replied.

Captain Ellis rode ahead of her. He was a strong man, kind beneath his hard exterior. Mary knew he was in love with her. At any other time, she might learn to return that love, but at the moment, with every breath a reminder of Malcolm, Mary wasn't certain she could ever love again.

The first person out the front door, which swung open as they approached, was Whitman, Mary's maid. The thin, middle-aged lady, always so severe, burst into tears when she saw Mary, and ran at her.

Captain Ellis swung down from his horse and lifted Mary from her saddle. Whitman reached Mary and flung her arms around her, weeping unashamedly.

"My lady, my lady . . . Oh, my sweet, dear girl, it is you! You've come back to me."

Mary hugged Whitman's familiar form, closing her eyes. In all this time, in her entire journey from Kilmorgan, she hadn't been able to cry. She didn't cry now. She laughed shakily at Whitman, who drew out a large handkerchief and blew her nose with a trumpeting sound.

"Come inside," Whitman said, tucking the handkerchief away. She seized Mary's hand and pulled her across the threshold. "You're father's here, and your aunt."

Captain Ellis remained behind, speaking quietly to the groom, who'd come rushing around the house to them. Every stable hand had joined him, it seemed. More of the staff filled the front hall, some openly weeping, most smiling, all of them turned out to see Lady Mary come home.

Aunt Danae, who never moved quicker than a stately walk, charged down the stairs, her shrieks ringing through the house. She ran straight to Mary, not stopping until she had Mary in her arms. "Mary, my lovely Mary."

Sobbing, Aunt Danae clung to her niece, holding her in a breathless embrace. Mary laid her head on the shoulder where she'd sought comfort since childhood.

Aunt Danae finally lifted away and seized Mary's hands,

pressing through her gloves. "My dearest girl, we feared that you perished with the rest of them. Or been taken to some prison. Your father has been asking and asking about you . . . Oh, my dear, you are so changed." Aunt Danae looked Mary up and down, taking in her stained plaid skirt, linen shirt, soft boots, and the cloak Captain Ellis had lent her.

Ellis came in behind her, and Mary turned. "Aunt Danae, this is Captain Ellis. He has been a good friend to me."

"Yes." Aunt Danae sniffled, wiped tears from her eyes, and approached the captain. "My brother told me about you—a fellow prisoner. I am so grateful to you for all you've done for him, and for Mary."

Captain Ellis made a short, uncomfortable bow. "My lady." He was a man who didn't like formality, ostentation, or too much gratitude thrown his way. "I do my duty."

What he'd done for Mary had gone far beyond duty, however, and the blasted man knew it. "Great heavens," she said in a tired voice. "You are far too modest, Captain."

Ellis didn't like Mary's gratitude either. He wanted more than that, she knew, and Mary also knew she could not give it to him.

Captain Ellis looked relieved when Aunt Danae took Mary's hands again. "Your father is upstairs. Go to him. He'll be waiting."

The earl hadn't appeared, not even to see what the noise was about. But he'd know. Wilfort always knew everything that happened in his house. He was not the sort of man, though, who'd come flying down the stairs in joy, as Aunt Danae had. Dignity always came first with Lord Wilfort.

And perhaps, Mary thought, *he will not welcome me back at all*.

That idea, which would have upset her at any other point in her life, barely penetrated the cloak of sorrow that now surrounded her.

Mary gave her aunt a thin smile. "Please do not tell me Lord Halsey is with him."

Aunt Danae looked surprised. "Halsey? No indeed. Your father and he had a great falling-out, thank heavens. I never liked the man. Halsey has married, you know—or perhaps you didn't. Olivia DeWitt. Poor creature."

Mary's mouth popped open. "Married? Gracious, he certainly didn't waste any time."

"He did not. He transferred his affections so quickly your father believes he was holding her in contingency all this while. But then, Olivia's dowry is some twenty thousand pounds, even if her father is only a viscount."

The relief to never have to worry about Lord Halsey again stretched one finger of warmth through Mary's coldness.

She left Captain Ellis in Aunt Danae's care and walked sedately up the stairs, making for her father's study.

Mary had entered through the doors at the top of the stairs many times—eagerly as a child when privileged to come here and visit with her father, in trepidation as a youth when he called her in to scold her, and with pride when she was finally accepted into the room as an adult. Now Mary wondered what reception she'd find behind the white-paneled, gilt-trimmed double doors.

She opened one and slipped inside.

Wilfort turned from the window. Mary had not seen him since the night Malcolm had taken her from the tiny Scottish village that Colonel Wheeler had commandeered. Her father looked older, his shoulders stooped, his hair holding more gray than had been there before.

Wilfort studied Mary for a long moment, as though making himself believe that she was truly standing before him. Then, everything stern and distant in Mary's father fell away. He moved swiftly to her, took her by the shoulders, and then, his eyes filling, pulled Mary into his arms.

"My daughter," he whispered into her hair. "My own Mary. Oh, my love, I thought I'd lost you forever."

Mary held him close, amazed to find her father shaking. "I'm here," she said.

"I'm sorry," her father said. "So, so sorry."

Mary wasn't certain what he apologized for, but she stroked his shoulders, her love for this man no longer confused. "I'm home now," Mary said. "I love you, Papa."

Even then, Mary could not cry. She'd become a rigid statue, going through the motions, numb inside.

Not until she was alone in her chamber, Whitman finally

convincing everyone she needed to rest, did Mary's grief break through.

She lay in bed, bathed for the first time in weeks, a hot brick to warm her. In the darkness, Mal came to her thoughts. She was transported back to their bedchamber in the distillery at Kilmorgan the day Malcolm had said good-bye. The memory of Mal lying against her on the rug was so vivid that Mary felt his weight, his bare body on hers, his warmth. Malcolm touched her face.

Ye know I'll always come for ye, Mary . . . I love you so very much . . .

The wall around Mary's heart splintered, and the tears came.

Malcolm's journey to Lincolnshire took nearly three weeks. Scotland was boiling with soldiers and Highlanders fleeing, Lowlanders either taking in their neighbors or working with the English to capture them. Malcolm made his way south and east, avoiding military outposts and forts as he could.

He witnessed soldiers putting innocent people to the sword, simply because they wouldn't reveal whether a clan leader had passed their way. Men were arrested merely because they wore a tartan. Malcolm helped the best he could, warning villagers that soldiers were coming, diverting those soldiers' attentions with his tricks, melting away before he could be caught.

He traveled at night, slept during the day, kept his hair muddy so the red of it wouldn't be a beacon to those searching for anyone looking remotely Scottish. He spoke slowly and carefully, when he spoke at all, trying to keep the betraying lilt from his voice. He'd abandoned the clothes he'd stolen from the soldier, burying them at Kilmorgan, and now wore the dark breeches and linen shirt of a farmer. No plaid anywhere about him.

Mal was exhausted and grief-stricken, but his spirit wasn't broken. Not yet. At the end of his long road was Mary—his lady, the other half of his heart, his life.

That was not to say the way was easy. He had to fight many times to stay alive, the victim of soldiers who were rounding up *anyone* they happened to see.

Malcolm had rolled away through boggy ground after one encounter, thrashing around in the marshes until he found a solid path again. Will-o'-the-wisps danced about him, enticing him to follow. Mal resolutely ignored them, trying also to ignore his gnawing hunger and burning thirst.

He made his way from the marsh to find himself in a wood of thick trees. He heard men approaching, damn them.

Nothing for it. Mal scrambled up the nearest tree. He lay on a thick branch, like a cat reposing, watching two English soldiers, red coats cutting the gloom, wander about below, looking for signs of the man they'd chased.

Mal lay still, willing his body to blend with the tree. The soldiers decided to pause under his tree and have a chat, mostly complaining about the cold and their annoyance that one of the Scottish bastards had gotten away.

"'E's in here somewhere," one soldier said, his accent putting him from the gutters of London. His coat was wrinkled, its back stained. "Not many places 'e can go."

"I say we go back and claim we shot 'im and dumped his body," the second said. "'E'll be rounded up sooner or later."

The first sniffled. "Bloody damp out 'ere. I'll be dead of the ague soon."

A light flashed deeper into the woods. Mal just stopped himself from snapping around to see what it was. The soldiers came alert.

"Wha' was that?"

"Swamp gas," the second said, but nervously.

Another flash and then a *bang!* "Not gas," the first soldier said. "Gunfire. Go!"

The two forms rushed deeper into the woods. Another flash and explosion sounded in the opposite direction. Mal watched, mystified, as the men charged toward it.

There was a low, growling moan, another explosion, gunshots, a wailing scream. Brush bent, and the sound of running and the soldiers' voices came to Mal.

"Wha' *was* that?"

"Banshee—no, don't look at it. Go!"

The soldiers fled, making much noise as they did, then silence descended. Mal waited a long time before he moved—

the soldiers could calm and decide to return. If they did, they'd be angry. Or they'd bring more men with them.

An hour passed. The moon rose, bathing the woods in a pale glow. No one came, and no more odd lights and noises occurred.

Mal slid from the branches and landed on his feet . . . and knew instantly he wasn't alone.

He wasn't sure how he sensed this, but something in him told him that a man hid in the brush on the other side of the tree. And that man was aware of *him*.

Malcolm quietly drew the dirk out of its sheath under his arm. Bracing himself on a fallen log, he abruptly launched himself into the brush.

A blade flashed at him in deadly silence. Malcolm ducked it and came up again, his dirk ready . . .

. . . To find himself facing a knife point, a bulk of a man in the darkness. The eyes glittering over the knife were ones Mal knew.

"Will!"

At the same time, the apparition shouted, "*Runt!*"

Then they were laughing, slamming together, pounding fists on backs. Will Mackenzie, alive, solid, real. Joy and relief flowed over Mal, warming him for the first time since he'd crawled from the battlefield.

"Ye damn, devious, cunning bastard," Mal cried, lifting his taller brother off his feet. "I knew they couldn't kill ye."

Will traveled with Malcolm from that point forward, the pair moving swiftly and stealthily through the English countryside. It had been Will playing the tricks on the soldiers in the mist, he told Mal, smug about his cleverness. Swamp gasses could be made to explode, lanterns hung on trees to flash in the gloom. A bulk of a fallen tree haloed by sudden light could look like a huge beast rising from the marsh. The moaning had been a bit of theatre. That was Will, the man who'd taught Malcolm all his dirty tricks.

Mal watched the big man striding next to him, chuckling over his pranks. Will had darkened his hair with mud as Mal had, and he wore nondescript breeches and a linen shirt, heavy shoes, and a bulky wool coat. He could easily be mistaken for a farm laborer from England's north, one with a spring in his step and a deep laugh.

But Will grieved, Mal knew. Will had watched Duncan die, he said, had fled for his life and gone to ground, certain he'd never see his family again. Lines had deepened about Will's eyes, etched there permanently. He'd not been able to discover what had happened to Alec and their father, and it haunted him as it haunted Mal.

Will, of course, knew exactly where lay Stokesay Court, the ancestral home of the Earls of Wilfort, in Lincolnshire. Or nearly exactly. He did get them lost once.

At last, the two men skirted the village of Stokesay in the dark, a neat collection of cottages set around a perfect square. Of course it was neat—Mary lived here.

Stokesay Court was a typical English estate house—lofty, expensive, haughty. The gardens were just as haughty, but well laid out, Mal had to admit. He'd have to take note of them.

Will's knowledge failed when it came to exactly which room in that house was Mary's, or whether Mary was even there.

They both agreed that walking up to the front door and knocking was a foolish idea. Mal had no idea where Wilfort's loyalties lay—would he embrace Malcolm as an old friend, his daughter's husband? Or call the local militia to arrest him and Will to try them with the rest of the Scottish traitors?

Mal and Will crouched near a hedgerow like thieves, peering up at the windows in the rear of the house, several of which were lighted. Lacy curtains hung against the glass, obscuring the rooms beyond.

Will touched Mal's shoulder, pointed.

One curtain had drawn back. A lady stood in the window, two floors above the flat flagstone path that skirted the garden. Her silhouette showed her in a dressing gown, her hair tumbling down. She peered out into the night, but did not seem to be looking at anything in particular.

Mal's breath left him. She was so beautiful, his Mary, one arm holding the lace curtain in a graceful arc. A picture Alec could paint.

Mal knew he should dash across the yard, wave his arms, catch her attention, bring her running down to him. He couldn't move. He remained fixed in place, barely feeling Will's exasperated nudging, until a single thing happened.

Mary absently drew her hand down her body to her abdomen. She rested her palm there, as though cradling whatever lay beneath.

Malcolm had sprinted halfway across the open ground before he realized he'd moved. He reached the house and swarmed up the almost sheer wall, finding hand- and footholds all the way. He grasped the window when he reached it, and flung it opened.

Mary gave a strangled scream. Her blue eyes widened in her colorless face, her hand falling from the curtain.

Malcolm swung his knee to the sill, then his muddy hands slipped as the curtain slapped them. Empty air behind embraced his back, enticing him to fall.

"Damn it all, woman," he snarled. "Help me."

Chapter 38

The ghost of Malcolm, the formless *brollachan* that had risen to Mary's window and peered at her with burning yellow eyes, growled at her in a very Scots voice. The hand that clung to the window frame was broad, sunbaked, rough-skinned, and Malcolm's.

Mary couldn't breathe. He couldn't be real, and yet . . .

Another snarl galvanized her. Mary lunged forward, caught Malcolm's arms, and braced herself to pull in his bulk. Mal heaved himself up and over the windowsill and fell against Mary and into the room.

He took her down to the floor with him, landing full-length on top of her. The weight of him, the familiar feel of his body on hers, convinced her.

"Mal . . ." Mary struggled to speak. "*Malcolm.*"

Mal didn't wait to say good evening, didn't let Mary gasp out questions, offered no explanations. He bore her down into the carpet, his kisses landing on her face, hair, throat. He pulled open her dressing gown and nightdress, hands and mouth on her bare skin.

Malcolm was filthy, covered with mud and grime, his hair

black, his face nearly the same color. Mary was dirty too now, dark smears across her breasts, stomach, thighs.

She didn't care. Mary impatiently helped him open his clothes—no kilt now. Malcolm shoved everything out of their way, not waiting, and slid himself straight inside her.

Everything stopped as they came together. Tragedies and triumphs, hopes and fears, vanished, no longer mattering. They were Malcolm and Mary, face-to-face, body to body, the two of them against the world.

Mary said, "Malcolm," this time in complete happiness. Mal was alive, whole, with her. What they had to face after this they could—they were together now.

Malcolm growled under his breath. He made love to her in a frenzy of passion, his body encompassing hers, Mary's cries breathless. Mal came apart with her, pounding his balled-up fist into the carpet as he hoarsely whispered her name.

"My Mary." Malcolm came down to her, his mouth warm. "Not Death himself, love. I promised ye."

Mal hadn't forgotten that Will waited outside for them, but he didn't hurry. He carried Mary to the bed and made love to her again, taking his time. He got dirt on her pristine sheets, but then, it was a fitting metaphor. Mary was all that was clean and unsoiled, and he was . . . well, he was Malcolm Mackenzie.

As they quieted, Malcolm slid his hand to her abdomen and cupped the softness there. "Did I guess right?" he asked.

Mary hesitated, then she nodded, her look warm.

Mal's heart swelled until his eyes moistened. Every hurt and sorrow he'd endured was eased in that moment. Here in this sanctuary with Mary, the wee babe under his hand, nothing mattered. Nothing in the world.

"Come away with me," Mal said. "Ye can bring the bairn, if ye want. We'll go someplace where men aren't aching to drive a sword through anything Scots."

Mary had started to smile at his joke, but worry returned to her eyes. "They're hunting *you*, Malcolm. My father says they're handing out little mercy to any who raised a hand against King George's men. You need to get away . . ."

"Not without you, love." Mal gazed down at her, tight with determination. "I'll not be apart from ye again, understand?"

"I do, but—"

She broke off abruptly, her eyes widening at something behind Malcolm. Mal felt a presence there and spun around, not a stitch on, not even a blanket between himself and the world.

He found himself facing the dragoon captain he'd once unhorsed, Captain Ellis's pistol pointed straight at Mal's nose.

Ellis's eyes flickered in surprise, and the corners of his mouth twitched down. He hadn't expected the intruder to be Malcolm, but his shock quickly faded, and the pistol did not waver.

"I *must* be tired," Mal said to him, "if I didn't hear ye."

Ellis kept the pistol trained on him. "You're alive, then."

"As ye see."

Mary was covered with a sheet at least. Ellis carefully didn't look at her, but his gaze took in the dirt-stained pillows, the wreck of the covers, the pile of clothes on the floor.

"It is my duty to arrest you," Ellis said to Mal, his voice even. "In the king's name, for bearing arms against him, for treason."

Mary had lain utterly still, her chest barely rising, but at Ellis's words, she flung up her hand, palm out. "*No.*"

Ellis's eyes flickered again. He still would not look at her, the gentleman in him pretending Mary wasn't even in the room.

He cleared his throat and directed his words at Mal. "But for Lady Mary's sake, I will tell you to go. Quickly, before I change my mind."

Malcolm rose from the bed, but slowly, not wanting to startle Ellis with any sudden moves. He didn't trust the man not to shoot if Ellis decided that would be best.

Mal leisurely took up his grubby clothes and drew them on. "Mary," he said. "Can I pack anything for ye?"

Ellis shot a quick glance at Mary as she sat up, holding the sheet to her chest. "You're going with him?" Ellis asked her in a hard voice.

Malcolm held his breath, masking his sudden fear by carefully tying the laces of his shirt.

"Yes," Mary said.

Ellis uncocked his pistol and lowered it, even as Malcolm masked his sigh of relief. Ellis gave Malcolm a resigned look, and in that glance, Mal understood exactly what letting them go was costing him.

Ellis loved Mary. The return of her crazed Highland husband had now put paid to any chance Ellis might have had of winning her.

Mal sympathized with the man, but at the same time, damned if he'd do the noble thing and step aside. Should Mal turn himself in and let himself be hanged, so that the brave English captain could be with the beautiful Englishwoman he loved?

He'd never do anything so daft. Mary was Malcolm's, and there was an end to it.

Captain Ellis conceded to step outside the room for Mary to dress. He didn't sound the alarm or rouse the house; he simply waited for them to emerge from Mary's chamber, then escorted them downstairs to a side door, unbolting it so they could walk out into the night.

Mary paused on the threshold and rested her hand on Ellis's forearm. "Thank you, Robert."

Captain Ellis nodded once, always formal. "Lady Mary."

He said nothing at all to Malcolm but sent him a severe look, then disappeared back into the house, quietly shutting the door.

"*Robert*, is it?" Malcolm said lightly as he led Mary away. "I've only been dead a few weeks."

"Captain Ellis has been very good to me," Mary said. Her melodious tones flowed over him, and Malcolm did not much care what she said, only that he could hear her voice again. "He brought me home safely. He's a good man."

"Aye, and I'm grateful t' him," Mal said. "But he didn't do it t' be *good*, ye know. He was hoping ye'd wed him to assuage your grief for your poor dead husband. And now I've risen from the grave."

Mary glared at him, her eyes lovely in the starlight. "Stop talking like that. Thunder and moonbeams, Malcolm, I thought I'd never see you again."

The tears in her voice cut Mal to the heart. He stopped near the hedge that marked the end of the gardens and took his wife into his arms.

"And I thought I'd never hear you say those maddening phrases again. Mary, love, getting back to you was the only thing that kept me alive. I *missed* ye . . ." Mal's voice broke, the emotions he'd been suppressing in order to keep going threatening to overwhelm him.

Mal showed her how much he'd missed her without further words, loving the warmth of her against him again. She was both softness and steel, his Mary, a bulwark against the gruesomeness of the world. But the world couldn't be an entirely bad place if it had created Mary.

"Ye took your time," a voice sounded through the bushes.

Mary started, then her face flooded with surprise and joy. "Will!"

"At your service, madam." Will helped her through the break in the hedge, growling in his bearlike voice. "The pair of ye could nae wait until we were safe before going at it, could ye? And me out here freezing in the damp."

"Ye look dry to me, " Mal observed as he took his brother's offered hand and scrambled through to join them. Will's coat, though dirty like Malcolm's, had dried, and Will's gloved hand was warm. "Find a place out of the night, did ye?"

Will shrugged, unabashed. "Aye, well, there was a lady in a house down the lane . . ."

Malcolm laughed out loud, not bothered for this moment about stealth. He clapped Will on the back and put his arm around Mary.

"Come on, love," he said to Mary, kissing her cheek. "Ye'll have t' put up with him, but that's the price ye pay with family."

"It's all right," Mary answered, the happiness in her voice bolstering him. "I love every one of you." She slid her arm through Will's, and sank into Mal's embrace, Mackenzies together. "Take me home, gentlemen."

"Home" for now was a tall, narrow house in Paris, reached after an arduous journey, but was it was a journey Mary undertook with gladness. They'd traveled by back lanes to the coast in Lincolnshire, where Gair came for them in his ship.

Ewan was with Gair, the lad bursting into tears when he

saw Mary. He'd been commissioned by the colonel, he told her, pointing at Malcolm, to find Gair and have him put in at Lincolnshire. Ewan had also brought a few treasures at Malcolm's command—the painting of Mal's mother, a bundle of Mary's clothes, and a small cask of whisky. The whisky was something to sell to the Frenchies, Ewan explained, in case they needed money.

The voyage to France was rough, roundabout, and heart-pounding in places. Too many English frigates, both of the navy and those of the excise men, floated through the sea. They landed in a cove of a tiny place Mary never learned the name of, and traveled in easy stages to Paris.

The house they reached—belonging to the Mackenzies, Mal said—was already inhabited. Alec Mackenzie clattered down the stairs as they entered, a wee mite with curly red hair in the crook of his arm. Alec bounded down the rest of the way when he saw them, and Mal caught him, babe and all, in an exuberant embrace.

Mary had the treat of seeing her husband break down and cry. Mal held Alec, his closest brother, in a hug that threatened to break Alec's bones and crush the baby. Mary rescued the child, bouncing little Jenny in her arms while Mal and Alec tried to occupy the same space at once.

Will rushed in from the street and joined the pile, the brothers laughing, crying, hugging, all of them jabbering at the same time.

The front doorway darkened, and the bulk of a man came inside. "What the devil is all the noise?" he shouted.

That voice broke a moment later when he saw Malcolm and Will. Mary stood aside with Alec, who was wiping his eyes, as the duke, moving in shock, went to Malcolm and gathered him close. They clung to each other, father and son, until the duke pulled back and put Malcolm's face between his hands.

"I thought ye gone forever, runt," he said. "Willie . . ."

"I'm hard t' kill, Dad," Mal said, stepping back as the duke drew Will to him. "I'm a *brollachan*, remember? I'll always find a way to come back."

The duke lifted his head and saw Mary. Alec had taken Jenny from her, and the baby looked on, fingers in her mouth, but in curiosity, not fear.

The duke took Mary's hands. "Daughter," he said. "Thank you for bringing him back t' me."

Mary dared to fold her arms around the duke's large body, her heart full. "I am so very happy to see you, Father."

"Well, now." The duke's usually brusque voice went soft.

More happiness was to be had when two visitors followed the duke inside. Audrey rushed to Mary, her extended abdomen reaching Mary first.

Mary held her sister, her tears coming as she once more felt Audrey's slender arms around her. Jeremy wove in and out of the melee, shaking hands, thumping backs, looking embarrassed at this outpouring of emotion, but no less pleased.

Mal came to Mary as soon as her sister released her. "Here we are, then," Malcolm said. "I brought the whisky. Anyone have a glass?"

Soon they stood in the drawing room, lifting tumblers full of amber liquid that matched the Mackenzie men's eyes, lemonade for the ladies, milk for Jenny. They drank to Duncan, to Angus, and to Magnus, then to the fallen Highlanders, and all they'd lost.

"T' the Mackenzies," Mal said, his voice a little slurred after all the toasting. "And what the future might bring for them."

They raised glasses again.

"To Malcolm and Mary," Alec said. He bounced Jenny, who gave them all a wide, milky smile. "May their love ever grow, and may they fill the house with many wee bairns."

"Aye," Will said. "We love the bairns." He chucked Jenny under the chin, and she gurgled, already charming.

"Ye won't have t' wait long." Mal slid his hand to Mary's abdomen. "We've already begun."

After a moment of silence, the room filled again with laughter, congratulations, Scots voices rumbling.

Sunshine warmed the room, as did Malcolm's arm around Mary. They might be far from their homes, from Mary's beginnings in Lincolnshire, and Mal's at Kilmorgan. But Mal and Mary were together, surrounded by family, surrounded by love.

And that, more than anything, meant home.

Mal and Mary lay together in bed that night, celebrating

once more in their own private way. Mary held her husband close. “I love you, Malcolm Mackenzie.”

“I love *you*, sweet Mary.” Malcolm rested his hand between her breasts, over her heart. “There it is, your fire. I always knew ye had it.”

“You set it free,” Mary said. “Thank you, Mal.”

He smiled at her, the sinful grin that had first melted her in the shadowy hall in Edinburgh, when no one in the world had known where they were. No one again knew where they lay tonight, no one but family, and that was as it should be.

“Ah, Mary, ye are so very welcome,” Mal said. “I told ye that I’d always come for ye, remember? That ye’d never be rid of me that easy.”

“I know you will,” Mary said. “My fearsome *brollachan*.”

“But ye never have to fear me, love.” Mal touched her cheek. “Not you.”

“And I don’t. I love you, Malcolm, with all my heart.”

“And I you, me wicked lass.”

They ceased speaking then, receding into the place without words, where they gave each other love, and knew nothing but that.

Epilogue

Two years later

Malcolm Mackenzie gazed over the bare ground that had once held the markings of a foundation and his pile of quarried stones. The ground had been scarred over, the stones gone. Whether Cumberland's men had scattered them or local Highlanders had taken them to shore up their own houses, Mal didn't know. Nor did he care. Let those who needed them use them.

Mary, in her practical Highland skirt and bodice, a little boy slung to her back in peasant fashion, joined him. She was breathless, her face flushed.

"That's all the baggage settled in the distillery," she said. "I think. Will didn't have to give us *quite* so much furniture."

"He has an obsession for it," Malcolm said. "He acquires it to impress ladies or soften those he's spying on, then doesn't know what to do with it."

"I daresay it will come in handy."

Mal nodded. He drew Mary to him, but kept studying the view—the empty land that rose to hills, the wall of mountains hidden in clouds.

"Bittersweet," Mary said.

"Eh?" Malcolm turned to kiss the top of his son's head. Little Angus was asleep, his amber eyes squeezed closed, his red-gold hair protected by a small cap.

Malcolm had thought his ability to love had reached its capacity until he'd beheld the wee lad in Mary's arms after a long night of worry. The little one had done something to him.

Mal's burning need to take care of all those around him had only escalated. He'd never be rid of it, he thought. *Ah, well. It is me lot.*

"Bittersweet, I said," Mary repeated. "Coming home, but finding it so changed."

"Aye, it would be, wouldn't it?"

Mal didn't like to talk about it—the emptiness of the Highlands, the large houses deserted or filled with ambitious Englishmen, smaller farmers gone, land fallow. The wearing of kilts had been banned, so had the playing of pipes and speaking Erse. The Highlanders were crushed, so many clansmen either killed by the Butcher or taken away to be hanged.

But not all, Mal knew. People like Rabbie and Gair spoke the Scots language out of earshot of anyone English, keeping it alive. The sounds of pipes could be heard sometimes, faintly, in the hills. Kilts became blankets, the looms clacking away in secret spaces.

Highlanders would never entirely be defeated.

Mal's own situation was an example. His family was believed dead, the title stripped from them. Until, that is, the Earl of Wilfort, a powerful man with the ear of the king, convinced those who made these decisions that the Kilmorgan title should be restored.

The youngest son, Malcolm, was alive and married to his daughter, Wilfort had explained, and in exile in France. Wilfort had come to know Mal Mackenzie well, and said that Malcolm had been as loyal as he could have been, under the circumstances. Mal's character had also been vouched for by a dragoon captain, Robert Ellis, and a young lordling, Jeremy Drake, son of Viscount Bancroft.

Therefore, the arrest warrant for Malcolm was lifted, and he was eventually allowed back into Scotland without harm, the title of Duke of Kilmorgan restored.

Alec, Will, and their father elected to stay in France and be considered dead back home. The old duke said he wouldn't be able to bear Scotland now—without his wife, his home, without Duncan and Angus.

Alec had already begun a life in Paris, becoming a drawing master to the offspring of the King of France. The strangeness of a wild Scotsman who could draw and paint was an oddity that fascinated Alec's new clients.

And Will . . . was Will. He told Malcolm that being dead gave him a great freedom to do anything he liked. He'd already been back to Scotland and England many times in the last two years, with the authorities none the wiser.

Malcolm, who'd never, ever in his life wanted to be duke, learned to take it without fuss. Mal had a family to look after now, and he'd carry on the name. No price was too high to maintain his father's and brothers' freedom.

Besides, Mary liked Kilmorgan.

"I suppose we start all over again," Mary said now, readjusting Angus's weight on her shoulder.

"Aye. But it's better that way, eh? Our life in France gave me many new ideas for the house, for the gardens. We can use whatever stones are whole and strong from the old castle to start building the new."

Mary looked skeptically up the hill, where the ruins of Kilmorgan Castle perched on the top. "That will take a lot of carrying."

"No matter. As I told ye a long time ago, the lads around here need work and paying. We'll have it begun in no time." Malcolm waved at the expanse before them. "It will be grand, Mary. An elegant palace beloved by generations to come."

"You're very sure of yourself," his wife said in her dry way.

"Of course I am." Mal thumped his hands to his chest. "It's *me*. Malcolm Mackenzie." He grinned and took her hand. "Ah, Mary. We're going to change the world."

Mary's smile filled up the empty spaces inside him, banishing the bitter to replace it with only the sweet. Malcolm drew her close, kissing the lips that were as soft as the English roses that grew outside her country home.

Mary kissed him back and touched his face, love in her eyes. "We'd best get started, then," she said.

Dear Reader:

I hope you enjoyed this look into the past of my favorite Scottish family! When I was writing the first books of the Mackenzies series, particularly The Duke's Perfect Wife *and* The Wicked Deeds of Daniel Mackenzie, *I became intrigued by the ancestor the Mackenzies referred to as "Old Malcolm."*

According to the tales, Malcolm was the youngest of five Mackenzie sons of the mid-eighteenth century Duke of Kilmorgan. He was a brave fighter who'd been the only one of the family to survive the battle of Culloden during the 1745 uprising (or so the nineteenth-century brothers believe). Malcolm was also responsible for building the huge Mackenzie house in the north of Scotland to replace the original castle at Kilmorgan.

The more Malcolm and his wife, Lady Mary, walked through my imagination, the more I wanted to delve into their story. Malcolm was regarded as a formidable warrior who'd had a passionate and loving marriage with Mary, his very proper English lady wife. I wondered what Old Malcolm had been like as young *Malcolm and how he and Mary came together, and I began to explore the tale of the two lovers.*

What grew was much more than I expected. I fell in love with Mal and his brothers—Alec, Angus, Will, and Duncan, and even the belligerent old duke grew on me. What the 1880s Mackenzies know about their illustrious ancestor is only the tip of a far larger story.

As I researched the historical details of the Jacobite uprising I learned much that I had not known before, and I grieved for the men who'd laid down their lives for Scotland and Charles. I placed Mal and Mary and their families into these events, watching how Mal and each of his brothers dealt with them.

The result was The Stolen Mackenzie Bride, *which can be read as a standalone, or as an introduction to the world of the Mackenzies. More about the Mackenzie families and the books in their series can be found on my website www.jenniferashley.com.*

Read on for a peek at A Mackenzie Clan Gathering, *a new story featuring Ian Mackenzie and Beth.*

Best wishes,
Jennifer Ashley

Look for *White Tiger,*
the next book in Jennifer Ashley's Shifters
Unbound paranormal romance series
Coming Spring 2016
Turn the page for a preview of

A Mackenzie
Clan Gathering

Available November 2015 from InterMix

SCOTLAND 1892

Something woke Ian Mackenzie deep in the night. He lay motionlessly, on his side, eyes open and staring at darkness.

A dozen years ago, awakening to total darkness would have sent Ian into a crazed panic, ending up with him on his feet, roaring at the top of his voice in English, Gaelic, and French. Servants would have rushed in, restoring lights some foolish footman had put out, finding Ian standing up beside his bed, swearing in rage and fear.

Now, he lay calmly, absorbing the soft quiet of the darkness.

The reason for his calm lay behind him on the bed—his Beth, curled against him in a nest of warmth.

Whatever change in the huge house had alerted Ian had been too subtle to wake Beth. She slept on, her breathing even, one hand soft against his bare back.

Ian's mind rapidly churned through every possibility of what had dragged him from his dreams. His children—Jamie, Belle, and Megan—were fast asleep in their nursery. Ian knew whenever one of them was awake, knew it in his bones. They were shut behind the door of the large nursery at the end of the hall. Safe.

He let his senses expand to every tiny sound of the night. This was Scotland in the autumn, and winds flowed down the mountains to swirl around Kilmorgan with the shrieking of a dozen banshees.

The vast house itself, built a century and a half ago, was alive with noise. Creaking of pipes Hart had installed to bring running water to the bedchambers. The crackle of Daniel's electrics experiments, the tinny sounds of the interior telephone system nephew Daniel had also created.

At the moment, all those noises, except the wind, were silenced. All except the *snick* of a window somewhere in the darkness of the house.

Ian and Beth were the only residents at Kilmorgan Castle, the vast mansion that stood twenty miles north of Inverness. Hart, the Duke of Kilmorgan and master of the house, was in Edinburgh with Eleanor and his two children. His other brothers, Mac and Cameron, were at their respective country homes with their families, not due to Kilmorgan for a day or so.

Ian knew the exact location of each house of his brothers, and how long it would take the families to travel to Kilmorgan to celebrate Hart's birthday next week. None of them could have arrived in the middle of this night without Ian knowing about it.

Kilmorgan was quite empty for now, except for Ian's family, the skeleton staff needed to run the place, and three of the dogs.

Dogs . . . They were in the stables, guarding the prize racehorses. They weren't barking or making a fuss.

But Ian knew, without understanding how he knew, that someone who shouldn't be there was inside the house.

He slid out of bed, moving smoothly enough not to wake Beth. He stood a moment at the bedside, strong toes curling on the soft carpet, cool air brushing his bare skin. His valet, Curry, had dropped a nightshirt over Ian's head when he'd headed to bed, but when Beth had joined him, the nightshirt had been quickly tossed away.

Ian moved past the shirt, a pale smudge on the carpet, to

reach for the long folds of plaid Curry had laid across a chair to warm before the fire. Ian wrapped the kilt around his large frame, tucking the excess folds in around his waist. He then moved to the chest of drawers, opened the top one, and slid out a Webley pistol.

Ian never kept loaded guns in the house. Far too dangerous with children around. All shotguns were locked into cabinets in the steward's house near the stables, and any personal handguns were kept unloaded, ammunition locked away in a separate place. Ian had made this a firm rule, and Hart agreed.

Ian moved from the bedroom to his connecting dressing room, unlocked a cubbyhole within a cabinet, and pulled bullets from a box there. He lined up six in a perfect row, returned the box and locked the cabinet, and slid the bullets into their chambers with precision.

He left the dressing room through the door that led to the corridor, paused long enough to click the pistol's barrel into place, and strode swiftly and silently down the hall toward the gallery at the end.

Clouds covered the moon tonight, but a gaslight near the staircase illuminated a long stretch of corridor lined with windows. This was the front of the house, overlooking over the drive that led to Kilmorgan. From the outside, the row of floor-to-ceiling windows was part of the grand facade created by Malcolm Mackenzie, the ancestor who'd first turned Kilmorgan from cold castle into a home.

Ian saw no one in the upper hall, no furtive movement in the shadows, nothing out of place. He crept toward the staircase, his bare feet making no noise on the carpet.

Lights on the landings were kept burning all night, so that members of the household who wandered about wouldn't fall headlong down the stairs. Tonight, no one but Ian was in sight as he went quickly down the steps.

Not until he turned along the ground-floor gallery that ran toward Hart's side of the house did Ian find anything wrong.

A flurry of movement at the far end of the gallery caught his eye. Ian took in everything he saw, assessed it quickly, then pushed the conclusions to the back of his mind as he sprinted toward the half dozen men in dark clothes trying to exit through the garden door.

Ian could move swiftly and in silence, and he was upon them before they realized. He heard muffled curses in several languages, saw the bulk of bodies and what they carried. Several of the men made it out before Ian wordlessly landed amongst them.

The man Ian caught by the back of the neck expertly broke from him, swung around, and jammed a short cudgel toward Ian's stomach. Ian, who'd learned about dirty fighting both from his brothers and on the streets of Paris, avoided the cudgel and grabbed the arm that wielded it.

He swung the man around and into a second. Ian shoved his pistol into the second man's face.

In the next moment, both men crashed themselves into Ian, fighting for the gun. One man got his hand around it, but Ian yanked hard, and the pistol fell, skittering across the floor into darkness, out of sight, out of reach.

The toughs were good, but so was Ian. They had layers of clothes hampering them, while he fought like his ancestors, in kilt and bare feet, with his fists or by stealing another man's weapons.

The first man grunted as Ian ripped the cudgel out of his hand and bashed it into his abdomen. The second man's fist came at Ian's face, which Ian caught with his big hand, then the second man punched him right in the gut.

Ian spun away, fighting pain. The man he' d cudgeled was doubled over, and Ian spun back to the second man, battling until he got him into a headlock.

The first man, holding his stomach, went for the pistol. A growl escaped Ian's mouth. He slammed the second man way from him and went after the first.

The second man dashed out the garden door, but Ian didn't care. The first man, seeming to recover at every step, ran to where the pistol had fallen and scooped it up. Instead of turning to shoot Ian, he raced along the gallery toward the main stairs.

Ian went ice cold. Beth was up there. Ian had heard the echo of their bedroom door closing as he'd fought—the galleries and staircase let sound carry in an almost magical way. He knew Beth would have made her way to the stairs and started down, as Ian had, to see what was going on.

This thug with a pistol was running directly toward her.

Ian sprinted after him, kilt flying up over his thighs as he put on a burst of speed. Ian knew this gallery and the thug didn't—where the bare spaces between carpets lay, where tables had been placed in the middle of the floor so a piece of sculpture could be viewed from all sides. Ian dodged these and leapt from rug to rug, gaining on the man before he reached the stairs.

Ian tackled him. He heard Beth give a sharp scream as the thug went down under Ian's body.

Ian felt the cold pistol touch his ribs. In the next second, he'd be dead.

He used that second to roll, grab, and twist. The pistol came away from the man's hand and went off, the bullet striking somewhere high in the ceiling.

Beth's scream came again, and her shouts for help.

Ian hauled the thug around and punched him full in the face. The thug, instead of fighting, wrenched himself out of Ian's grip, charged for the front door, yanked it open, and ran out into the darkness. Ian heard the man's boots crunching on gravel, and then nothing.

Ian dashed out after him, but the tough was gone, swallowed by night and swirling mists. Dogs were barking now, and men were coming out from the stables with lanterns.

Ian closed the door. The thugs didn't matter now. The safety of Beth and his children was all to him.

Beth ran down the stairs, her dressing gown floating behind her. "Ian, are you all right? *Ian?*"

Ian caught her as she came off the staircase, lifting her from her feet and crushing her to him.

If the man had reached Beth . . . The thug was the sort to grab a woman and use her as a shield, and then shoot her when she was no longer useful.

If Ian had been a few seconds too slow . . .

He buried his face in Beth's neck, inhaling the warm scent of her. She was beautiful, and well, and in his arms. Safe.

People brushed past him—servants coming see what was wrong. Lights flickered and grew brighter. Men came into the house through the front and garden doors, exclaiming, making sounds of disbelief and dismay.

Ian wanted them go away, to leave him with Beth alone in this bubble of peace he found in her arms, a place where the world couldn't touch him.

But it wasn't to be. His valet, Curry, once a London street villain, clattered down the stairs on swift feet. "Bleedin' 'ell!"

Beth tried to lift away. "Ian—love—I'm all right. We must see what is happening."

She was correct, of course. Ian had learned in this first decade of his marriage—ten beautiful, sparkling years—that he could not withdraw from the world. Once in a while, yes, with Beth and privacy, and maybe a lick of honey, but not always. He'd grown used to facing immediate situations without panic, without having to bolt and think it over later.

Letting out a long breath, Ian raised his head. Beth gave him a little smile and tucked his kilt, which had come awry while he' d chased the thug, more securely around his waist.

The little gesture made Ian's heart beat swiftly. To hell with facing the world. Ian would take Beth back upstairs now and let her unwrap him, enjoying whatever she found in whichever way she wanted to enjoy it.

Beth, catching the look in his eyes, let her smile grow wider, but she shook her head. *Not yet,* she meant. *But later . . .*

Ian would be sure to take her up on the unspoken promise. Resolved, Ian twined his fingers though Beth's and let her lead him the rest of the way down the stairs.

The entire gallery glowed with light. The servants had turned up every lamp in the place.

Beth gasped in shock. Ian had seen and noted everything out of place as he'd run past in the dark, but he'd pushed the vision aside so it wouldn't distract him in his pursuit of the intruders. Now he faced the gallery and what he'd seen.

Most of the tables that had held sculptures were empty, and almost every painting from the garden end of the gallery was gone. These pictures had been painted by famous artists through the centuries, plus a precious handful by Ian's brother

Mac. Only those that had been hung high, out of easy reach, remained. A few paintings lay piled on the floor, half-ripped from frames, the frames broken. Ruined.

Hart Mackenzie's priceless art collection had just been ravaged and stolen, the thieves fleeing with the loot into the night.

FROM *NEW YORK TIMES* BESTSELLING AUTHOR

JENNIFER ASHLEY

The Mackenzies Series

THE MADNESS OF LORD IAN MACKENZIE

LADY ISABELLA'S SCANDALOUS MARRIAGE

THE MANY SINS OF LORD CAMERON

THE DUKE'S PERFECT WIFE

A MACKENZIE FAMILY CHRISTMAS

(An eBook)

THE SEDUCTION OF ELLIOT MCBRIDE

THE UNTAMED MACKENZIE

(An InterMix eBook)

THE WICKED DEEDS OF DANIEL MACKENZIE

SCANDAL AND THE DUCHESS

(An InterMix eBook)

RULES FOR A PROPER GOVERNESS

THE SCANDALOUS MACKENZIES

(An anthology)

THE STOLEN MACKENZIE BRIDE

A MACKENZIE CLAN GATHERING

(An InterMix eBook)

Praise for the Mackenzies series

"The hero we all dream of."

—Sarah MacLean, *New York Times* bestselling author

"I adore this novel: it's heartrending, funny, honest, and true."

—Eloisa James, *New York Times* bestselling author

"A sexy, passion-filled romance that will keep you reading until dawn." —Julianne MacLean, *USA Today* bestselling author

FROM *NEW YORK TIMES* BESTSELLING AUTHOR

JENNIFER ASHLEY

SHIFTERS UNBOUND

PRIDE MATES

PRIMAL BONDS

BODYGUARD

WILD CAT

HARD MATED

MATE CLAIMED

LONE WOLF
(An InterMix eBook)

TIGER MAGIC

FERAL HEAT
(An InterMix eBook)

WILD WOLF

SHIFTER MATES
(An anthology)

BEAR ATTRACTION
(An InterMix eBook)

MATE BOND

"Sexually charged and imaginative . . .
Smart, skilled writing."
—*Publishers Weekly*

"Exciting, sexy, and magical."
—Yasmine Galenorn, *New York Times* bestselling author

jenniferashley.com
facebook.com/ProjectParanormalBooks
penguin.com

M1103AS071